D0343576

A SHADOW FALLS

ANDREAS PFLÜGER is a German screenwriter and author. He has written a number of episodes of the hugely popular German police procedural *Tatort*. *In the Dark*, the first book in the Jenny Aaron trilogy, is published in eight languages.

ASTRID FREULER is a German to English translator based in Gloucestershire.

ALSO BY ANDREAS PFLÜGER

In The Dark

A SHADOW FALLS

ANDREAS PFLÜGER

Translated from the German
by Astrid Freuler

First published in Germany as *Niemals* in 2017 by Suhrkamp Verlag
This English translation first published in 2018 by Head of Zeus Ltd

9 7 5 3 1 2 4 6 8

A catalogue record for this book is available from
the British Library.

ISBN (HB): 9781786690968
ISBN (XTPB): 9781786690975
ISBN (E): 9781786690951

Typeset by DivAddict Solutions

For the one

Happiness makes us blind

But pain enables us to see

A note on German police and politics

The Bundeskriminalamt, or BKA, is the German Federal Criminal Police Office, the federal investigative police agency directly subordinate to the Federal Ministry of the Interior, and based in Wiesbaden in the west of the country, with a second large base in Berlin. The agency coordinates cooperation between the federation and state police forces, and focuses on cases of international organized crime and those involving terrorism and national security.

The Landeskriminalamt, or LKA, is the State Criminal Police Office, the independent law enforcement agency in most German states, analysing police intelligence from home and abroad and investigating serious crimes such as drug trafficking and terrorist offences.

The Interior Ministers' Conference – Ständige Konferenz der Innenminister und Senatoren der Länder, also known as the Innenministerkonferenz – is a regular conference on law enforcement issues of the Interior Ministers of the various German states.

Rome

Ten years ago

S he imagined the man for whom she might have to die to be taller. As she steps out of the Grand Hyatt Berlin and into the drizzle, she sees him leaning against the James Dean Porsche, on his face a smile like a postcard from the South. She walks towards him, knows that he will kiss her. His lips are cool against her cheek. He smells of a clean shave and the kind of confidence that doesn't need cologne. The second longer that he holds her in his arms betrays his surprise at how beautiful she is. That is compliment enough for her.

Casually, as if they were just out for a spin, he drives to the airport and they talk like two people who haven't seen each other for weeks because they are both terribly busy and she lives in Rotterdam. For an Irishman, his German is impressive. And the charming way in which he fails on the umlauts makes it perfect. He calls her Sarah, as her cover story dictates; he's never heard the name Jenny Aaron.

They know that every word is being recorded.

Aaron tells him about a business lunch with a promising

Berlin sculptor, whom she would like to engage for her internet auction house. As they cross Checkpoint Charlie he passes on greetings from a friend, Benjamin, who thought it was a pity that she couldn't join them yesterday evening. She reapplies her lipstick and checks in the mirror to see if they are being followed.

BMW, 7 Series. Two men. Pretty close behind.

On the Kochstrasse, the Porsche speeds up.

'Honey, please drive a bit slower, I've got a headache.'

'Sorry, darling.'

Reassured, she sees the BMW overtake them.

With a yawn, he mentions that he didn't get to bed until one, had five hours before the alarm went off, one whisky too many, which was Benjamin's fault of course. Today it's been meeting after meeting, now he feels like a boxer in the final round. Yet his glacier-grey eyes shine as if he'd just climbed out of the pool, totally relaxed after his fifty lengths.

Aaron reckons he slept better than her.

Even though Leon Keyes has every reason to be afraid.

By the time he was in his mid-thirties, he was already a partner in Dublin's leading law firm. He wanted more. Keyes went to Singapore and learnt to print money. When he settled in Berlin with his own corporate law firm, he had already made his fortune.

He's a bachelor, jogs round the Grunewaldsee three times every morning, puts in eighty hours a week in a glass tower in the Friedrichstrasse, likes linguini with salsiccia from the best Italian on the Gendarmenmarkt, and had no idea that his phone calls were being tapped by the BKA, Germany's Federal Office of Criminal Investigation.

They'd found out that he was hiding a client's illegal funds in offshore companies on Antigua. There are two options in such cases – arrest, or what is known in BKA terms as a solid investment: wait and bank on the likelihood that a smart guy like Keyes will sooner or later enter in his diary an appointment with one of the top players.

Pay-day came at the end of June. Keyes received a call from Italy. And the name of the man who wanted to meet with him was so big that the BKA Commissioner got straight on the phone to the Federal Minister of the Interior.

Matteo Varga.

Capo dei capi of the Camorra. On the wanted list of dozens of countries.

He invited Leon Keyes to Rome for the weekend, to discuss a business opportunity.

Further details to follow.

Of course Keyes knew who he was dealing with. To his credit, he did ask for a little time to consider. Shortly after the call, BKA investigators turned up at his office and put it to him that his life as he knew it was over. The pencil Keyes was holding in his hand broke. That was the only display of emotion he permitted himself.

As they pass behind Platz der Luftbrücke and drive onto the urban motorway, Aaron checks her make-up again. The mirror tells her they aren't being followed. But that doesn't mean anything.

Keyes keeps strictly to the speed limit, and she feigns delight when he says: 'Haven't you always wanted to see the Rolling Stones live? They're playing at the Waldbühne next Friday; I've been given backstage tickets.'

This shows he's got a firm grasp on their relationship story. How they met. (A cocktail bar in Berlin, last year.) Whether he minds that she smokes. (Likes it.) What films they enjoy. (Hitchcock, Scorsese, Fincher.) Where they spent their one-week holiday. (Palm Island, The Grenadines.) Shared friends. (Three.) How close they are. (As close as two people for whom work is better than sex.) Does she like operas? (No.) Has she ever been to Rome? (Many times; she loves everything that is made of light.) What style is her Rotterdam penthouse with harbour view furnished in? (Bauhaus.) Does she sleep naked? (Pyjamas.)

A few more details; but not too much, otherwise one gets bogged down. Most of it is close to the truth. A completely fictitious cover story has no life, appears contrived.

Aaron splits her internal RAM into three parts, one that continuously scans their surroundings and analyses every car, one that chats to Keyes in a seemingly relaxed manner and one that memorizes his dossier.

The BKA had handed him the bill for his little misdemeanour in Antigua. He could either work with them or be remanded in custody awaiting trial.

Keyes decided to hang on to his Porsche for now.

In Rome, Varga met him at his town villa and said that he wanted to get into the German gas business; a joint venture with the Russian Danilowskaja Mafia, which was going to be in charge of bringing the Gazprom managers to heel. Varga needed a fixer who would establish contact with the right people. Keyes' firm secures Gazprom's German investments; he knows everyone who's important to Varga and the Danilowskaja.

He has since been to the Italian capital three times, and once to Naples. He has delivered a non-stop stream of information to the BKA. Most recently, that Varga is planning to fly to Norilsk in October to seal the deal with the head of the Danilowskaja. The BKA told their Moscow liaison officer to share this information with the Russian secret service, who in turn promptly issued an arrest warrant.

Everything was going like clockwork.

Until two weeks ago, when BKA investigators found a bugging device in Keyes' Porsche that wasn't from them.

Varga.

This could mean two things: either he liked to keep his associates on a short leash, or he suspected something. The BKA much preferred the short leash theory.

The following day, Varga invited Keyes for the fifth time. Again to Rome. For today.

Aaron had read the transcript of the phone conversation. 'A relaxed dinner among friends,' said Varga. 'Bring your wife or your girlfriend along – assuming you're not gay.'

Though there's nothing noted down in the file, Aaron knows what they were agonizing over at the BKA.

Since discovering the bug, they couldn't rule out that the Capo knew who his new associate was running back to. In which case Rome was Keyes' death sentence. But if Varga was unsuspecting, cancelling would be fatal. He would become wary and wouldn't fly to Siberia.

They had to protect Keyes in Rome. But how? The BKA couldn't go there without making an official request to the Italians. The chance of this being successful was equal to zero, and in any case, the information would be fed straight to Varga.

The BKA Commissioner was running out of options.

This is where the Department came in.

It isn't part of the BKA, it is autonomous; Germany's smallest and most secret organization. Forty men and one woman take on assignments that are too risky for everyone else. As Aaron's boss Lissek put it: 'We're the bad bank of the German police.'

BKA Commissioner Palmer took Lissek for a long walk along the river Spree. Unofficially of course – if necessary Palmer could feign innocence.

Lissek took it in his stride. Though he did record the conversation, 'just to be on the safe side,' as he later revealed.

Keyes is patted down for weapons before each meeting with the Capo, so he has to be accompanied by someone who is a weapon in themselves.

Aaron.

*

As they glide along the urban motorway, she loads Varga's dossier into her working memory. The dossier that she knows off by heart because Leon Keyes' life might depend on it.

And her own.

Varga started out as a run-around in his Camorra clan and cold-bloodedly fought his way out of Naples' Quartieri Spagnoli, all the way to the top. Like his predecessor, he initially lived off the weapons trade. Then he decided to specialize in a business that is even more profitable, and less risky too: the disposal of toxic waste. He set up shipping companies with front men and ships that operate under flags such as Liberia, Tonga or Tuvalu. Multinational corporations employ Varga to dispose of old pesticides, chemical waste, asbestos and radioactive sludge, and they don't want to know where the muck ends up. When even puppet regimes no longer wanted to accept the cargo, Varga took to sinking countless ships across the world's oceans. He rakes in the cash for the passage and the fictitious disposal, and finishes up by collecting the insurance sum. The environmental catastrophes don't bother him in the least.

Last year, Varga decided to let a freighter go down near Heligoland, polluting a body of water the size of Slovenia. Understandably, the Russians are after him too. The chemical disaster in the Bering Strait, courtesy of Varga, is just two years back.

There were several European requests for his extradition, but witnesses disappeared in mysterious ways or suffered fatal accidents. Although there is speculation that Varga has let ships from his fleet go down off the Riviera coast, the Italian government is keeping shtum. If the information were to reach the public, it would spell disaster for seaside tourism in one of the country's most idyllic regions. Varga controls two construction firms which are raising one hotel complex after the other along that stretch of coast. A former justice minister is a member of the board. The Italian prime minister has been known to have dinner with Varga.

Varga is untouchable.

They are on the slip road to the airport. Aaron can smell the dubbing on the leather seats of the immaculately restored silver 356 Speedster. She taps a Marlboro out of the case and christens the ashtray. It's sacrilege. But Leon Keyes just smiles and, with that slight rasp in the voice that she likes so much in men, he says: 'That was always missing.'

She imagines him asking for her phone number. Aaron would bet anything that he'd casually scribble it onto the lily-white sun visor.

At Schönefeld airport they get into Varga's jet. For two hours, they sit in cream-coloured seats made of goatskin leather, telling each other stories of which not a single word is true and drinking still water out of crystal glasses with ice cubes.

Keyes has cooperated with the BKA in every way. He has placed himself in the hands of a man who orders contract killings as though he was sending someone to the bakery. He is a textbook informant.

But the whole time, Aaron is thinking: *What are you concealing?*

Rome Fiumicino is a shower of blazing light. On the tarmac, she sees Varga's chauffeur leaning against a Daimler. Around a hundred kilos, she estimates, and well trained. When he goes to take Aaron's travel bag, she pretends to let it slip from her hand and he catches it five centimetres from the ground.

Along the motorway, fields lay creased like the abandoned bathing towels of giants. Grass bakes in the sun. It has been a long summer, and now, in mid September, every stone lies parched. The air conditioning of the luxury limousine cools Aaron's first wave of adrenalin. As yet it's no more than a twitch in her heart. But she already knows what lurks behind.

Some cities are there all of a sudden, jumping up in front of the windscreen, like Hong Kong or New York. Rome has villas and antique ruins dotted here and there, then social housing that sprawls out into the countryside. Finally the car glides over boulevards lined with dusky pines, Aaron's favourite trees.

She hears Pavlik's voice through the earbud. 'Hi, beautiful.'

Of course, Fricke has to put his oar in. 'Nice rags. I bet you twenty Euros that Keyes will be needing a cold shower very soon.'

'Your chauffeur is already being missed in the zoo,' comments Nowak.

A faint giggle tells her that Vesper is also online. He keeps quiet as usual. When he once put more than five words in a row, they teased him with 'blabbermouth' for days.

Together with Aaron these men form the team. In the Department, they call it a 'small set'. The others travelled here ahead of her in two cars. They couldn't take the plane because of the weapons. Pavlik is the marksman and has picked a quiet nook from where he has Varga's villa in his sights. He will have been lying in position for some time, observing the weather conditions, familiarizing himself with the wind speeds and thermals. She knows where he is and smiles involuntarily.

Three days ago, they had brooded over the high-resolution images from a Federal Intelligence Service satellite, and Pavlik had pointed to a spot. 'Hey, you're not there as a tourist,' Fricke teased.

Pavlik acted hurt. 'You're just jealous.'

It's close to three hundred metres from there to the villa. No distance for him. They had considered using a drone, to get a view of the garden. But the risk of it being discovered is too great. In any case, the meal will take place in the house. According to Keyes, Varga hates the heat and spends almost all of his time inside, where the temperature is a constant twenty degrees.

An adjacent building probably contains eight bodyguards. Perhaps ten. Varga likes his peace and makes a point of keeping the bodyguards out of view.

No reason to relax. Two or three of his best men will be in striking distance this evening.

'We'll do it old school,' Pavlik had said.

The dining room faces the road. Two windows are situated in a clear line of fire, the others are hidden by cypresses. But they can disregard that. Keyes has told them that Varga always sits at the top left end of the large table, so Pavlik will easily be able to see him. He uses special ammunition he has cast himself, with a tungsten carbide core. This will allow him to shoot through the armoured glass if necessary and eliminate Varga. Even Marcus Aurelius knew that rule: if you want to defeat an army, kill the leader.

The rest is Aaron's job.

To the left, St Peter's Basilica heaves into her view, unexpected as always, even though her eyes were searching for it. Built to intimidate people and make them feel small, nothing about the palatial hulk is playful. The dome is like something from another world, a UFO that landed five hundred years ago and might take off again at any moment.

The Via del Gianicolo hugs the old Aurelian city wall. They drive through the antique archway of the Hotel Gran Sasso Rome and arrive in an oasis, where even the bright yellow blossom of the Mahonias being misted by sprinklers smells of money.

Varga is expecting them at eight. They still have two hours before their chauffeur picks them up again. The manager personally takes them to their suite on the second floor. Aaron has him show her around all the rooms and, unnoticed, activates the radio sensor under her belt buckle. If there are hidden cameras, it will locate the transmitter signal and vibrate.

Nothing.

When the manager has left, she complains that her headache is killing her and says she is going to lie down for a while. Aaron takes the bug detector out of her travel bag. Keyes silently watches as she scans the walls and furniture.

The device registers a weak energy source under a side table in the living room.

A bug.

Damn.

Aaron checks both bedrooms and the bathrooms.

Another two bugs.

Damn, damn.

She steps out onto the enormous terrace.

Clean.

Aaron gives Keyes a nod. He joins her, quietly closing the sliding door behind him.

'That doesn't necessarily mean anything,' he says.

'Yeah right. Like a burst motorbike tyre at two hundred kilometres per hour, or a live atomic bomb.'

'He's cautious.'

'So am I,' she retorts.

'Do you want to call it off?'

'Of course.'

'Varga could have had me killed in Berlin. He doesn't need to fly me to Rome to do it.'

'Perhaps he enjoys watching.'

'That's not what he's like.'

'You don't know anything about him.'

'I have excellent insight into human nature.'

'Last words of a murdered missionary in Papua New Guinea.'

He shrugs. 'My mother always said: "Why is six afraid of seven? Because seven ate nine."'

Aaron studies Keyes. His life is at risk. She is serving him a get-out on a silver tablet. And he is prepared to take the gamble?

'Varga told me a story,' he says, 'about him and his brother. They're very close, although his brother doesn't want to have anything to do with his business activities. He's a doctor in Naples. They speak on the phone every week and see each other a lot. Varga is the godfather of both his daughters. But that hasn't stopped Varga from tapping his brother's phones for years. He said: "It doesn't hurt him if I sleep well."'

Keyes goes to the small terrace bar, opens a twenty-year-old whisky and looks at her. She shakes her head. While he pours himself a drink, her gaze wanders down to the pool, where children are shrieking and trying to splash the sun. Aaron reaches into the pocket of her dress and removes a tiny brown plaster from a plastic case. It's an artificial birthmark. She sticks the microphone under her chin and moves away a few steps, so that Keyes can't hear.

'I'm online.'

'Nobody followed you,' mumbles Pavlik. 'But that's no surprise.'

'Where's the driver?'

'Twiddling his thumbs in the underground car park,' Vesper reports.

'Blabbermouth,' says Nowak, quick as a shot.

Without moving her head, Aaron permits her eyes to wander across to a sixties apartment complex rising up behind the Aurelian wall.

The Department's logistician wanted to house the team next to the suite that Varga had reserved for his guests in the Gran Sasso. But the hotel is fully booked, so they had to make do with this solution. Only Vesper is in the building. He's down in the garage in a transporter with blacked-out windows.

'That mole is making me real horny,' says Fricke.

'Have the rooms been checked?' Pavlik wants to know.

'Yes.'

'And?'

Keyes sips on his drink and watches her. Aaron looks out across the brick-red roofs to St Peter's Basilica. The cross on the dome shimmers like a mirage.

If she tells Pavlik about the bugs, he will immediately order them to pull out. She doesn't know what's stopping her, but she has learnt to trust her instinct.

'Clean,' she says.

She feels wretched as she lies.

'Good,' she hears his deep voice, 'we'll go through with it.'

'I'm off.' She puts the microphone back in the case.

Keyes goes over to her. 'So we're going ahead?'

'Yes.'

He rotates his Oxford signet ring, brushes a black strand of hair off his forehead. For a second, Aaron thinks he's going to kiss her.

Instead, Keyes asks: 'Have you ever killed anyone?'

She is silent, thrown off course.

But not by the question.

Aaron remembers what her father said in the old quarry when she was twelve years old: 'Killing is simple.'

That's true.

She is a third Dan in karate. She can do it with her hands, with a gun, a knife, her sunglasses, a cigarette box and, should it become necessary, with the pretty scarf from Hermès that she will wear later on; the scarf that has a piano string woven into it.

Yet, what her father said next is equally true: 'But it doesn't come easy.'

'Why do you want to know?'

'Because you're so young.' Keyes hesitates. 'And because my life may possibly depend on you.'

'Not if you're right about Varga.'

'I could be wrong. Like I was on the morning I went into work and thought everything was OK in my world. Then three of your colleagues made themselves comfortable in my armchairs and informed me that I was no more than a lackey.'

'Shall I get the violins out?'

'Would you die for me?'

'I'll be in the bathroom.'

What is it you're not telling me?

Before taking a shower, she does the splits and flattens her upper body against the terracotta tiles. She stretches, takes hold of her toes, then comes back up and pushes herself into a one-armed handstand. Slowly she tips her torso until she is floating horizontally over the floor, then twists to touch a heel with her fingers. She rises back up into the vertical position and returns to standing via a backwards arch. This she repeats five times, without breaking into a sweat.

Then she stands in front of the mirror and says silently: 'If mastering your body is all you've learnt, then you've learnt nothing at all.'

She walks into the living room at quarter past seven, dressed in black leggings, a cream-coloured blouse with a low neckline, the scarf, ballerina shoes and the mole.

Keyes is sitting on the sofa, leafing through a magazine. He looks up. 'Is your headache better, darling?'

'A little.'

'Let's have a drink before we go.'

They move out onto the terrace.

'Those shoes won't work,' he says.

'Why?'

'One evening, while sharing grappa and cigars, Varga and I chatted about what we like in women. He grew up in the slaughtering yards of Naples. I aligned myself to his tastes in order to create closeness. He thinks that I like high heels, just like any healthy man would, in his opinion. Sorry, I understand that you're more mobile in flat shoes. But this evening, Varga needs to see you as the kind of woman I have the hots for.'

He disappears into his bedroom and returns. 'I took the liberty to visit the hotel boutique.'

Aaron eyes the bright red high-heeled shoes that are dangling from his index finger. Zanotti, stilettos. In her earbud, Fricke gives a quiet whistle. She discreetly gives the other side of the road the finger and puts on the shoes. Keyes has judged her size perfectly. With the additional eleven centimetres she is more than one ninety, half a head taller than him. That's not easy for a man to take.

But Keyes just grins. 'You should never wear any other shoes.'

Aaron moves her ankles, bends her torso to the left, the right, arches her back, lifts the soles, balances on the stiletto heels. That will do.

'I bet you could even sprint in those,' he mutters.

I hope I won't have to.

'Call the chauffeur,' she replies.

'We still have half an hour.'

'We'll make a little detour.'

Varga's villa is in the south-east, on the left bank of the river, but she wants them to go to the Gianicolo, the hill that rises up this side of the city. Fricke, Nowak and Vesper follow them. They maintain radio silence. There is much that Aaron values in these men, not least that they have a feeling for when she has to concentrate and mustn't be distracted.

The Passeggiata del Gianicolo winds its way up the hill in twists and bends. Aaron lowers her window and inhales the pine scent wafting down from the branches that fan out above the road.

She senses for the first time that Keyes is tense.

Because he isn't sure whether I've understood the signals.

At the top, they drive round the Garibaldi monument. Aaron's black hair swirls out of the window. A flock of white birds suddenly changes direction, like smoke in the wind. The dense green opens out onto a piazza, they are at the Fontana dell'Acqua Paola.

Aaron asks the driver to stop and gets out with Keyes. As always, she avoids looking to the left at first, and instead gazes over to the baroque marble triumphal arch. Glittering water shoots out of the eagles' heads and into the basin. The sky is an endless blue, tinted dark by the onset of evening.

She walks across the road to the stone balustrade. The city lies below her. Ochre-coloured houses tumble down towards the Tiber. Aaron seeks out the Pantheon and delights in its perfect geometry. She imagines herself standing inside it, directly below the large central opening of the oculus, bathing in the last light.

Next to her, Keyes doesn't say a word. She's thankful to him for not buggering up the moment. Aaron looks out across the seven hills as far as the Albanian mountains, where a snowy white bank of cloud is perched like meringue on a cake. She thinks of Keyes' smile. The hairs on her arms prickle.

Aaron places a hand under her chin and covers the microphone with her thumb. 'We're alone. I'm listening.'

'You're a good psychologist.'

'I have excellent insight into human nature.'

'What if I turn out to be a cannibal?' he asks.

'You'd find me a hard nut to crack.'

'Varga has a safe.'

'How exciting.'

'It contains a file with the names of all the European politicians that are on his payroll.'

The hairs on her arms prickle even more.

'How do you know that?'

'Because he waved it in front of my nose and bragged about how he can buy anyone.'

'You don't know the combination.'

'I do.'

Two words. Sound like one: jackpot.

'Where in the house?' she asks.

'Depends on what you have to offer me.'

'What do you want?'

'Immunity from prosecution. I want my life back.'

'I'm not a public prosecutor.'

'I don't know who you work for. It certainly isn't the BKA, they wouldn't have the guts for this little excursion to Rome. It must be an organization that resides even higher up. I'm important. And so are you. Otherwise they wouldn't have entrusted you with this mission. Being in the position I'm in has made me amenable. Your promise to put a word in for me is good enough.'

She hears the murmuring of the city, an aeroplane that invisibly whispers through the sky.

The blood in her temples.

'Where are you?' Pavlik asks quietly.

'They're taking in the sights,' Fricke replies.

'It's an extensive file,' Keyes adds.

Aaron looks at him. His eyes are no longer grey, they are black like a winter cloud over the Pantheon's oculus. The lowering of her head by five degrees serves as a nod. 'Where?'

'In the study, behind an antique map of Rome.'

'What does the safe look like?'

'Around sixty by forty centimetres. Beige. Numeric keypad. There's a red emblem engraved on the left.'

A Duke & Pendleton.
'And the combination?'
'One-nine-one-eight-three-zero.'
'How did you find out?'
'I was standing in the door as he entered it.'
'He wouldn't be that careless.'
'Varga had no idea that I was there. I'd been to the toilet, he didn't see me. I snuck back and loudly closed the toilet door. That's the ridiculous kind of man the BKA has turned me into.'
'May we?' Fricke asks.

They cross the Tiber on the Ponte Sublicio, head north-east along the embankment road and turn off at the Circus Maximus. A kite has torn free and is reeling over the large sandy oval. Two dogs are chasing a torn ball while beggars dressed up as gladiators count today's takings. The Daimler drives along the arena, at the same speed as the charioteers two thousand years ago. Back then it was a breathtaking spectacle, now it's a trundle behind tourist coaches. Eventually, a gate opens up on the right. The two-storey villa is built in antique Roman style. A townhouse in Mayfair would be cheaper.

The chauffeur opens Aaron's car door. Before the gate closes, she snatches a glimpse over the Circus and up to the Palatine Hill, home to the ruins of the Imperial palaces. She knows Pavlik is there. Protected by bushes, he is lying in a hollow next to the entrance to the cave in which, according to legend, the she-wolf suckled Romulus and Remus. Aaron pictures him, stretched out, motionless, the stock of the rifle pressed against his shoulder, his pulse the same rate as a sleeping man's.

Two hundred and ninety metres.

At such a distance, Pavlik normally works with his old Mauser, but the armour-piercing ammunition he is using requires the higher muzzle velocity of the Steyr HS. The standard model is a single-shot rifle, but he has modified it and integrated a box magazine. When it's empty, Pavlik can exchange it for a new one in two seconds. He has the ability to turn the villa's window into a sieve.

The other three are taking up position nearby. They can't intervene inside the property. In an emergency, Aaron will have to make it out onto the road with Leon Keyes. Fricke, Nowak and Vesper are their rescue team.

Pavlik sees her through the telescopic sight, in twenty-four-fold magnification. 'Got you,' he whispers.

Now Varga has three guests in his house.

Aaron, Keyes and Pavlik's rifle.

The chauffeur says: 'È permesso.'

He pats down Keyes. Aaron couldn't hide a weapon on her body, her clothes are too figure-hugging for that. A short skirt would have been an alternative option to the leggings, with a small pistol on the inside of her thigh. But that would make her gait uneven, so she decided against it.

She opens her handbag. Smartphone, Dupont lighter, cigarette case, make-up.

'Grazie.'

They go into the house. Aaron is surprised at how tastefully the entrance hall is furnished. Pale stone, Art Deco dresser and matching wall lamps, silk wallpaper with lily motif; good interior designer.

Varga lumbers down the stairs, a man like a roughly cut rock. Everything about him is square, even his face, on which there are pores large enough for ants to hide in. His mouth looks like it was broken out of his skull with a crowbar.

'Leon, che bello.' The words tumble out like boulders.

'Hello, Matteo.'

Varga turns to Aaron. He kisses her hand the cheap way; his fat lips are moist. 'Welcome to my humble abode.'

She was prepared for his good English. When Varga was made 'captain' of his clan, the Capo sent him off for further training in New York, where a branch of the tribe showed him how to control trade unions. Later Varga moved to Las Vegas to enter the casino business and stayed there for seven years. He married a waitress from Phoenix because his family expected a man in his forties to settle down. The woman fled from him after six months, but only made it as far as LA, where her body was found in a sewer. Varga returned to Naples and blew the old Capo's brains across the mirrors of a brothel. He married again, a Campanian beauty, but she left him and survived it because her father's clan was nearly as powerful as Varga's. The fact that he, a divorced man, receives the sacraments in the Basilica Clemente every Sunday that he's in Rome answers any questions concerning his relationship with the Vatican.

'Excuse me, may I briefly…?' asks Aaron.

'Of course.' Varga points to a door.

Aaron goes into the guest bathroom. She stands still, closes her eyes. Five rooms on the ground floor. The kitchen is to the left of the entrance hall. On the right is the hallway that leads to the dining room, where there are three double doors. These open onto the terrace, the living room and a room which Keyes hasn't been in yet. On the upper floor, there are two bathrooms, three bedrooms and another room of unknown function.

And Varga's study.

She can reach it from the dining table in thirty seconds without rushing. She'll need another ten to open the door with a hairpin, assuming it doesn't have a security lock. Fifteen for the safe. Forty until she is back at the table again.

Ninety-five seconds. It's doable.

She activates the toilet flush, lets some water run, then rejoins the others.

'Vieni qui.' Varga puts his arm around the minuscule waist of a tufty blonde woman, at least thirty years his junior, who swiftly gives Aaron the once-over. The woman glares at her: mine!

Varga doesn't introduce her, she's just a pretty table decoration. He calls the two men that join them friends, 'Sandrone' and 'Vincenzo'. Sandrone is bullish and has taken a fair few hits, judging by his cauliflower ears. Though she can tell from his hips that he isn't fit, it's clear he could end a fight with a single blow at any time. Aaron checks out the other one, Vincenzo, while they move into the dining room. His nonchalant gait shows that he knows how good he is. The open black shirt is tapered, outlined underneath is a perfect latissimus. He's wearing trainers with soft soles, a precision engineer.

She enters the room.

'Surprise,' whispers Pavlik. 'Smile.'

Two housemaids are clearing away the table settings.

'We're eating outside,' says Varga.

Aaron feels a chill. The garden and terrace are at the back, behind high walls secured with lasers. She smiles as she breathes out slowly, using her diaphragm. 'How lovely, in September.' She moves to follow the others.

'Wait, you'll like this.'

After a brief hesitation, she joins Varga at the window. It's been drilled into Keyes never to stray more than two steps away from Aaron. He follows her, they look out. The Palatine glows in the evening light as if coated in red Japanese lacquer. Aaron knows that Pavlik has her in his sight, in large scale. Even though it is infinitely difficult, she plants a look of awestruck wonder on her face.

'Take what you've got,' he murmurs into her ear.

Vincenzo and Sandrone are standing behind her by the terrace door; she can see their reflection in the glass of the window. Seven metres. They could have guns planted in various locations. What does she have? The scarf. And the fruit bowl with knife that is standing on the table.

I kick Keyes' legs out from under him, he slides under the table. Vincenzo is the more dangerous one, the knife is for his throat. I strangle Varga with the scarf and turn with him as a shield. Pavlik pierces the armoured glass with precision fire. He kills Sandrone. Are there cameras anywhere?

How fast can Varga's bodyguards be here?

'You're looking straight at Augustus's palace,' Varga says next to Aaron. 'Of all the Caesars he was the cleverest, and he had a great sense of humour. The new commander of his household guard was the spitting image of him. Augustus called out: "Hey you, was your mother a servant in my father's house?" The man replied: "No. But my father was one of your mother's slaves – until she gave him his freedom."' Varga laughs.

'How did Augustus's sense of humour manifest itself?' Keyes asks.

'He didn't have him killed – he had him sold as a slave instead.'

The oleander, mimosa and bougainvillea have wilted, but a large open greenhouse is full of tiger lilies, which flood the garden with their scent. To Aaron it is as unpleasant as a slutty perfume. She knows why Varga loves these flowers. The lily is the sign of his clan, the symbol of his power.

'Do you like lilies?' he asks.

'They remind me of funerals.'

He smiles. 'Me too.'

Vincenzo and Sandrone sit down at the left and right sides of the table, the Capo flops down opposite Aaron and Keyes. A servant pours the wine. Mid-fifties, withered, lizard's neck. Sometimes a servant is just a servant.

Varga rolls up his shirt sleeves. His forearms are as thick as drain pipes. He gropes Blondie's leg. 'What do you know about my business, Sarah?' he asks, then sucks on an olive and spits the stone onto the lawn.

'What the newspapers say.'

'And what do they say?'

'That it's best to stay away from you.'

'Don't rile him,' Pavlik warns her quietly.

'So you're scared of me?'

'I'm just scared that my new shoes are going to kill me before the evening is over. È permesso?' she slips off the high heels.

She sees the garden shears on the upturned plant tub.

Varga laughs. 'I like you.' He runs his tongue over his gold crowns. 'And do you know how Leon earns his crust?'

Aaron lights a cigarette. 'He increases other people's wealth and does quite well out of it himself.'

'Is there an art to that, Leon?' Varga asks.

'The art is to keep a sense of proportion,' Keyes replies. 'What's the benefit of being the richest man in the cemetery?'

Varga mulls that over. Then he grunts: 'That's an art I know nothing of.' He nods at Sandrone. 'How much have you got in your pocket?'

Sandrone fumbles a thick wad of notes out of his trousers.

Varga motions with his index finger; Sandrone throws the wad over to him. 'Ask me if you'll get it back.'

Sandrone just grins.

Varga pockets the notes. 'That's all anyone needs to know about my business.' He bites into a pickled artichoke; oil oozes out over his chin. 'Where did you two meet?'

'In Berlin,' she pre-empts Keyes. 'I went to a bar to drown a failed exhibition opening. Leon planted a glass of Dom Pérignon in front of me and said: "You're far too beautiful to look so sad." After he'd driven me to my hotel, he wrote my phone number on the lily-white sun visor.' She leans her head against his. 'That was the most romantic thing that any man has ever done for me.'

'That's what sun visors are for,' Keyes grins.

Blondie's pout suggests that the stock of romantic stories she could tell is limited. Varga guzzles Barolo like water. 'I'd sooner shit on my most expensive carpet than mess up a 356 Speedster with red leather seats.'

Vincenzo and Sandrone laugh. Aaron feels Keyes stiffen. She immediately knows: he hasn't mentioned his car to Varga. It was Varga who had it bugged. But he communicates exclusively with his underboss, who only talks to the captains, and they in turn talk to the soldiers. In the end, the assignment will have been passed to two freelancers, who carried it out without any fuss. The 'principle of the thousand strangers' is a fundamental rule in all Mafia organizations. It guarantees that the lower ranks can't testify against the Capo. He never gave them an order, they have never seen him.

A man like Varga doesn't want to hear any details. Details are dangerous. Details you don't know, you don't have to deny.

It's unlikely that he would know that Keyes drives a Porsche.

What model: even less likely.

The colour of the seats: impossible.

Unless he had asked to be informed of the specifics.

Aaron tenses her muscles and decides that she will ignore the blood and the pain when she tears the cactus next to her out of the pot and thrashes it into Sandrone's face, then hurls it at Vincenzo, using the split second he needs to dodge it to fly across the table and ram his wine glass into his eyes.

She doesn't underestimate Varga. He had to kill to climb the ranks in his clan. But that's a long time ago. He's piled on too many kilos, his reflexes aren't what they were. The garden shears will be embedded in his back before he makes it to the terrace door.

He changes the subject. 'This auction house that you work for – what would I have to lay down there for, let's say, a Lucas Cranach?'

Although tension throbs through Aaron's veins, she is still amused. Varga has let drop the name of an artist whose work he has most likely never seen, except perhaps in a magazine. His bedroom is probably adorned with the Blue Grotto of Capri. It doesn't worry her that he is asking about the auction house. Keyes casually mentioned it in his last telephone conversation with him, it's what they'd arranged. The auction house really exists; the Department has an agreement with the management and occasionally uses it for a cover story.

'I'm afraid that's not our market segment,' she says. 'We only represent young living artists. For us, Jeff Koons would already be an old master.'

'They only produce filth, those modern painters,' Varga grumbles. Then his face lights up. 'Well, at last, I'm starving!'

The starter is served.

The meal would be a delight if Aaron didn't have to continually consider her options, which vary with each of the four courses. The garden shears, the cactus, the Hermès scarf and her body are the constants, the other weapons change. With the antipasto, goose liver on brioche, the knives are rounded off, therefore useless. That leaves the plate, to be used as a discus, and a broken glass as a thrust weapon. Plate and glass are also her choice during the primo piatto, clear tomato soup. However, the secondo piatto, veal entrecôte with herbs and fennel gratin, rewards her with a sharp steak knife.

But they finish their dessert, semifreddo with lime jelly, without her receiving any further signals.

Time for the safe.

Aaron is just reaching for her wine glass, when Varga wipes his mouth. 'I have something that might interest you.'

*

They follow him to the room that Keyes hasn't been in yet. Aaron's collarbone scar gives a twinge even before Varga opens the sliding door. She slows her step, so that Keyes, who immediately understands, passes her and she can position herself close behind him.

The curtains are closed. Varga switches the light on and she is so surprised that, for seconds, she forgets everything around her. Aaron is looking at the painting *The Temptation of St Anthony* by Lucas Cranach the Elder. It's a perfect copy. She knows the original from the Vatican Museums.

The ragged Anthony is kneeling in the desert, in front of the devil, who is extending a flat hand. On it stands a woman, close to Anthony's eyes, her hand on a crib with a child. Her gaze is longingly directed at the horizon, from where a figure is approaching. It is Anthony.

Varga, who had seemed as intellectually impotent as he was financially potent, now teaches her a lesson. 'Anthony had abjured from everything, never loved a woman, never held a child in his arms. All his life, he knew nothing but bare stone and prayers. And how does the devil tempt him? By showing him what he could have had, and by promising it to him as a reward if he turns away from God. I haven't had this painting for long. It's my second most valuable possession. The most important thing is my family, my friends.' He turns to Aaron. 'Could David Hockney create such an artwork? Damien Hirst, Georg Baselitz?'

She is too stunned to answer.

'Leon, what have you told her about me? That I'm shrewd, but have the sophistication of a Neanderthal?'

Keyes calmly returns Varga's gaze. 'Pretty much. And that you crack walnuts with your teeth.'

Sandrone juts out his jaw, Vincenzo shifts his weight onto his dominant leg. They're just waiting for a sign from Varga. But he lays his arm around Keyes' shoulder. 'I've got plenty of arse-kissers, heaven knows. Underestimating a man isn't as bad as lying to him.'

Aaron steps closer to the painting. She sees the delicate cracks in the varnish, the patina of five hundred years.

'This is the original,' she says blankly.

'But of course,' Varga replies. 'I occasionally assist the Vatican, they couldn't refuse me my request. The reproduction that hangs in the museum cost more than a Gerhard Richter. I've never parted with money so gladly.'

Keyes steps next to her, admires the painting.

'It hides a secret which only revealed itself when I had it X-rayed,' Varga continues. 'Underneath, there's another work which was painted over: Jesus and Judas. How ingenious. Anthony resisted every temptation, while Judas was weak. It must have greatly amused Cranach that nobody except him was aware of this little twist.'

'He knows,' Pavlik whispers. 'Either you kill them right now or you grab Keyes and run. Once you get out the front I can take over.'

Aaron's first impulse is to smash Vincenzo's larynx with her elbow and drive the letter opener that is lying on a dresser beside her into Sandrone's lungs. But she sees that Varga is fully immersed in contemplating the painting, his thoughts far away.

No. He's completely relaxed.

Aaron turns, bumps into Keyes and tips wine over her blouse. 'How clumsy of me. I'd better go to the bathroom.' Vincenzo moves to accompany her, but she declines. 'Thank you, I know where it is.'

'What's your plan?' whispers Pavlik.

She rushes through the entrance hall, hears the clattering of dishes from the kitchen, and darts up the stairs. When she arrives outside Varga's study, the hairpin is already in her hand.

But the door is unlocked. Aaron slips into the room, leaving the door ajar.

The curtains are open, Pavlik can see her. 'What are you doing?'

'Not now,' she whispers back. She pivots the antique city map aside and stands in front of the safe.

One-nine-one-eight-three-zero.

Aaron enters the first five numbers.

Then stops.

She knows this type of safe. Entering an incorrect combination will trigger an alarm.

What if Varga did know that Keyes was standing in the door when he opened the safe?

Damn.

This painting is my second most valuable possession.

I haven't had it for long.

She reaches for her mobile and loses fifteen seconds on googling 'St Anthony'.

Born AD 251, died 356.

All or nothing.

Aaron deletes the numbers and replaces them with these.

She holds her breath, the safe opens.

Underneath half a dozen fake passports lies the dossier. Seven pages, packed with hundreds of names and account numbers. Aaron's breathing quickens. She photographs everything with her mobile, puts the papers back, closes the safe, replaces the map of Rome and looks at her watch.

Only ten seconds over the time limit.

She's about to leave the room when she hears quiet footsteps.

She takes off her scarf and flattens herself against the wall.

The door opens.

It's a child.

A small boy in pyjamas, three or four years old, holding a cuddly giraffe in his arm. He toddles in, turns and sees her. His eyes are big, tired, confused. Pulled from his sleep, perhaps by a bad dream.

Aaron stands there paralysed.

'Varga's coming. He's already in the dining room,' Pavlik hisses.

She reaches out her hand. 'Can't you sleep?' she asks. 'Come, I'll tell you a story.'

If the boy screams now, it's all over.

He doesn't understand Aaron, but the gentle sound of her voice calms him. He takes her hand and lets her take him back to his room, which is across the hall.

Where is Varga?

Aaron covers the child up and sits down beside his bed. Dead tired, he listens to her words. 'There once was a small tear. It belonged to a boy who was the same age as you. He often cried because he was alone a lot. But it was always just that one tear. It would trickle over his cheek and his lip and then he'd swallow it.'

Without looking, Aaron knows that Varga is standing in the doorway, watching her. She prays that he doesn't notice her trembling.

'This made the tear very sad, because it liked the boy very much and wanted him to be happy. So it thought up a little trick: the next time the boy cried, the tear ran into his nose and tickled him so much that it made him laugh. From then on, that's what the tear did every time the boy was sad.'

He's fallen asleep. His breathing is deep and calm.

She kisses his forehead and quietly stands up.

Aaron turns round and feigns surprise at seeing the Capo. 'He was standing at the top of the stairs, sobbing,' she whispers. 'Perhaps he misses his mother.'

'Just like me. She died a year ago.'

Aaron remains silent.

'Thank you for comforting him.'

They go back down. At the bottom of the stairs, Varga stops. His face is suddenly empty and grey. 'If I was to disappear one day like one of my ships, only my son would miss me. He's all the family I have.'

He doesn't expect Aaron to reply. They rejoin the others without another word.

'Honey, I'm sorry, my headache is killing me. Could we go back to the hotel?'

'Of course, darling.'

As she gets into the car, she sees Varga standing at one of the windows. Their eyes meet. Aaron thinks she sees in his a certainty that they will never meet again.

Moonlight floods the embankment road. The river is barely carrying any water. Rocks glimmer between the sandbanks. Aaron's left hand rests on the Armani bag. Inside it is a bomb that will shake Europe. Her heartbeat slows, she experiences pure bliss. Every breath is a joy.

'Drive to the Ponte Sant'Angelo and stop there,' Keyes says to the chauffeur.

Aaron looks at him. He smiles.

She knows what she is about to see and closes her eyes to allow herself to be overwhelmed. When they stop, she opens them again. Bernini's angels guard the bridge with sacred solemnity. Gazing down on Aaron they remind her that she is but a guest in this eternity.

Straight ahead of them, the castle stands radiant in streams of light like a crown of diamonds. 'What a pity you don't like operas,' says Keyes. 'This is where the most wonderful of them all is set; Puccini's *Tosca*. In desperation over the death of her lover, Floria Tosca takes her own life by jumping from that battlement there.'

Aaron smiles. 'How sad.'

'An opera has to be sad. If you don't cry, it isn't worth the money.'

They arrive back at the hotel three minutes later.

In the lift, Keyes asks: 'Will I get my life back?'

'Looks that way.'

'Shall we celebrate?'

It's odd, he doesn't seem a single centimetre shorter than her. He smells of pine resin, how is that possible? When he kisses her, she pushes up against him. He doesn't want too much and yet he wants everything. She tears off the microphone and throws it into the lift. They stagger along the hallway. Keyes drops the key card; Aaron is nestled so close up against him that she has to crouch down with him. They laugh; he pulls the card through the scanner and slides his other hand between her legs. They tumble into the suite and onto the carpet. Aaron rolls over with Keyes, then sits herself astride him.

She sees a shadow to one side.

Adrenalin rushes into her bloodstream like an express train. She catapults herself straight up and breaks the man's jaw with a rotating kick. Aaron thrusts her middle finger into his carotid artery, unhinges his wrist joint, catches the Walther P99 with silencer and shoots him in the forehead. Half his head sprays onto the wall; armour-piercing munition. The two seconds this took leave Aaron with enough time to flick fifteen grams of lead into the throat of another man, who has emerged from the bathroom.

She spins round a hundred and eighty degrees, sees the third one. The muted shots of his Smith & Wesson tear flesh from her right arm. When her Walther barks back, his bared teeth are blasted away.

The wound shock is a crimson cloud. Rotating flashes, somewhere in the living room. Shots perforate the wallpaper behind Aaron. The cloud grows and grows and dulls her senses.

Something shreds her skin. Hot lava flows over her ribs.

That fetches her back.

Two. Behind the sofa.

She draws a streak across the room with five bullets, flies out of the firing line and rolls over to Keyes, who is lying rigid where she was sitting on him just a moment ago. Aaron grabs her mobile, pockets it and yells: 'Wake up!'

As if in a trance, he lets her pull him up. The guns pierce red holes into the dark. She shoots back, carves out a few seconds, gives Keyes a shove. He stumbles into the hallway; his lungs are making a rasping sound like an alarm clock with a low battery. She storms off, driving Keyes in front of her. After twenty metres she looks back and sees the two men rushing out of the room.

Suddenly the scene is dissected into individual images, as if Aaron was watching a film played on a faltering projector. She observes every detail with care, blanking out the fact that she is sprinting down the hallway at full speed. One of the men is wearing a green jacket that jars with his blue socks. His hair is standing up in every direction as if it was under charge, sweat sprays off him. He is left-handed like Aaron and is hyperventilating with feverish gasps. When two bullets creep out of his gun, she already knows that they will hit neither her nor Keyes.

The leather jacket of the other guy is hanging open. In addition to his Glock, he is carrying a Ruger in a second shoulder holster, also with silencer. One of the laces on his black boots is loose and is flapping about. He is grappling with an overdose of adrenalin and his movements are jagged. His mouth and eyes are open wide, as if he was looping the loop on a roller coaster.

Two-Holster barks Italian fragments into a throat mic. His silencer muzzle pulsates, sending three hissing projectiles on a long journey. But Aaron has already caught up with Keyes and nudged him ten centimetres to the side with her shoulder, so that these bullets will narrowly miss them too. She analyses the weight of her gun; there are six rounds left in the 19 mm magazine.

The Walther jumps into her right hand. She shoots between her torso and her left arm.

All that in just a single breath.

When Green-Jacket slams against the invisible wall that her bullet has erected, the images flash in quick succession again.

Green-Jacket is hurled backwards, straight into his partner. Two-Holster uses the other's fall so cleverly that the lead intended for him causes a red flower to bloom on Green-Jacket's T-shirt.

A door opens next to Aaron. With their silencers the guns just whisper; the woman in the evening dress has no idea of the requiem that is being performed here. Nobody knows about it, apart from Aaron and Keyes and Two-Holster, whose Glock is already dictating death again.

Aaron pushes the woman back into her room. The bullets spraying out of Two-Holster's gun miss her head by centimetres and shred the veneer of the door frame. The woman screams, her face crumpled by mortal fear.

The click of Two-Holster's firing pin as it hits the empty cartridge chamber resounds in Aaron's ears like a fanfare.

She sees the lift. Thinks of the microphone that is lying in there. She could alert the team with it. Three are in the lobby, Vesper is in the underground car park. But the lift is moving. She looks at the illuminated display. It's coming up.

It's on the first floor.

Where will it stop? Who's in it?

Aaron's right arm is twice as heavy as her left. The Walther nearly slithers out of her blood-smeared hand. Her left takes over; now the gun is back where it belongs.

While Two-Holster rips the Ruger out of its leather case she considers sacrificing another bullet, but she only has four left and doesn't know what will happen next.

Staircase.

'Door!' she yells.

Behind them the Ruger just goes splat-splat, but the walls are shaking. Keyes throws himself against the door and staggers. Aaron sees the hole in his trouser leg. Shot in the calf. She darts towards Keyes like a steel spring, yanks him out onto the staircase and performs half a somersault with him, which puts her bones through the mill. While Keyes is still trying to understand what just happened, she is already back up on her feet, hurling the high heels away.

'Get up!'

Keyes pulls himself up by the banister, groans, sways, his face a mask of confusion and fear. Aaron drags him down the stairs. A floor below, a boot bangs against a door.

The images come in slow motion again, turning the scene into a flicker book. One floor down are two men with splat-splat guns. Both beefy, the muscles bulging under their jackets. One of them has white brows and lashes, his eyes are just pale slits. His mouth is set in a mocking sneer; he's already triumphant over a fight that hasn't even taken place yet. The other man's teeth shine out of his suntanned face as starkly as a dog-collar out of a clergyman's cassock.

'Get down!' Aaron bellows.

She scissor-jumps over the banister and flies through the central well in a whispered blizzard of shots, the muzzle flashes lighting up the gloom like a disco ball. Two of her projectiles wipe the mockery out of White-Brow's face, turning it into a crater. The final two are for Dog-Collar.

She misses him because he falls onto his knees.

Before she lands next to him with a thump, his Heckler & Koch drives a burning peg into her side. The images blur, they overlap, racing along in a time lapse. Aaron's shoulder rams Dog-Collar, preventing him from taking aim at her again. She wallops the butt of her empty Walther onto his skull and rolls him over until he is lying on top of her, face up. She loops the Hermès scarf around Dog-Collar's neck and strangles him with the piano string. He regains consciousness, fumbles with his gun, but can't do anything with it.

'Run!' she bellows up to Keyes.

He limps down the stairs, holding onto the handrail, while Dog-Collar feebly gropes the air and a strangely high-pitched sound leaves his windpipe.

Keyes has almost reached her when Two-Holster appears at the top. She lets go of the scarf, stretches out her hand, manages to grab the hem of Keyes' trousers and pulls on it with all her might. He loses his balance and tumbles head first into the blind angle.

Blood loss is turning the world into cotton wool. She ducks behind Dog-Collar. Two-Holster's bullets chirp like a flock of small birds, greedily pecking crumbs out of Dog-Collar's chest.

He's used up the second magazine, smacks a fresh one in.

Aaron pulls up Dog-Collar's Heckler & Koch and zaps Two-Holster's position with precision fire. She frees herself from the corpse. White-Brow is lying on his weapon. She tries to pull it out from under him, but Two-Holster's gun is chirping again. Aaron dives over to Keyes, grabs him, forces him onward.

Door. Ground floor. She opens it carefully. Music washes into the stairwell, laughter, a hubbub of voices.

The bar. A party.

It could bring salvation.

Or spell the death of many innocents.

The slap of footsteps from above. Two-Holster is taking several steps at a time, will surely regain eye contact at any moment.

'Basement car park!'

They carry on running. Keyes' leather soles beat syncopations into the stairwell. In Berlin, Aaron studied a floor plan of the hotel and knows that behind the next door is a long corridor which leads to the car park. Where her heart once was there is now a shredder, permitting just one thought:

What awaits us there?

Marble explodes next to her feet, Two-Holster is firing again. Suddenly the shredder stops. Aaron assesses how many rounds she has left.

Three.

Perhaps four.

She treats Two-Holster to two, which silences the Ruger. She is at the door with Keyes. Her kidney area, ribcage and upper arm are numb. She feels sleepy. The wounds are sucking up so much oxygen that she is no longer breathing properly.

Aaron can erase pain from her consciousness.

And let it in again.

She opens the barrier by imagining herself wiping the number eleven from a blackboard with a sponge.

There is no transition, a circular saw instantly tears through her body.

It wakes her up.

She sees that Keyes is about to lose consciousness. He has lost much less blood than Aaron, but for him this is a new experience; the shock has left him hollowed out.

His cheeks are sunken and pale, his eyes are the colour of dirty snow. The wall is all that is keeping him upright. He whispers: 'That's what sun visors are for.'

'Absolutely,' Aaron whispers back.

Two-Holster's bullets are playing marimba on the banisters. She puts Keyes' arm around her shoulder and pushes the door open.

Nobody.

Thirty metres.

Behind the next door is the basement car park.

And Vesper.

And the van.

She drags Keyes along with her. Her right ankle buckles under her, fractured. Sentimental music ripples through the endless tunnel; Sinatra is singing 'Strangers in the Night'.

'Wondering in the night what were the chances, we'd be sharing love, before the night was through.'

It is absolute agony. As if she was wading through a swamp. No Two-Holster behind them, just Keyes, her and Sinatra.

'For strangers in the night love was just a glance away, a warm embracing dance away.'

Aaron bellows: 'Vesper!'

The door to the car park flies open.

Two men.

Their silenced submachine guns immediately snap into action.

Aaron topples into a recess with Keyes. She pulls back the slide of the gun, sees that there is one last cartridge in the chamber. The men slowly draw near. Their Uzis with drum magazines are painting smoke columns into the air.

This is a lousy place to die. My cat won't understand why I'm staying away. Sandra and Pavlik will have to take care of Marlowe and help him grieve. My father won't cry, but he will turn to stone. Who will explain it to my mother?

Aaron looks at Keyes.

Says: 'I'm sorry.'

He can't talk any more.

Silently she counts down the seconds that remain.

Perhaps ten.

How small one is at the end.

She sees the fire extinguisher above her head.

I'll never manage it.

Still she reaches up, burnt out like a marathon runner on the home straight, her arms as heavy as concrete.

She tries to break the fire extinguisher out of its mounting.

Fails.

Doesn't give up.

Has it.

Aaron unscrews the silencer to increase the muzzle velocity and hurls the extinguisher as far into the corridor as she can.

She drops out from behind the cover and sends her last bullet on its way.

It hits home.

The explosion pushes the narrow walls apart, makes the air go viscous like liquid sap. A blast wave spins Aaron away. The sap congeals in her lungs. As she gasps for air, she stares into a white cloud of foam that is dissipating so slowly it feels as if years are passing.

Sinatra sings: 'Doobedoobedoo'.

One of the men is lying in the corridor, riddled with shrapnel splinters, dead.

The other one is kneeling on the floor, a ghost, completely covered in foam. He manages to stand up, collapses again, crawls towards the Uzi that he dropped.

Aaron tries to reach it first.

Millimetre by millimetre.

But Two-Holster is behind her. As it hits home, his bullet turns into a steely mushroom that sprouts in her shoulder. Her heartbeat is gone. She turns to ice. With unspeakable effort she turns her head towards the man she was supposed to protect.

She thinks she can see tears on his cheeks.

Foam-Ghost has got the Uzi. A spurt of bullets cuts through Keyes' body. Red mist rises in front of Aaron's eyes.

Then Two-Holster's boot hits her temple full force.

She is dreaming. With arms spread wide she's floating in a river, drifting through the night. She sees the light of a nameless city condense in the sky. A small boy is standing on the riverbank. Aaron reaches her hand out to him, but it dissolves in the waves. A man with an Oxford signet ring takes the boy into his arms. He looks at Aaron sadly and she sees the life that she will never have.

A tear tickles in her nose. She hears a flap-flap-flap sound. She opens her eyes, recognizes Pavlik, tries to form words. They dissolve like water.

Finally she manages it. 'Where?'

'Helicopter. Lissek is having us flown out.'

'Pain.'

'You're going to be OK.'

'Keyes?'

'Dead.'

'Vesper?'

'Vanished.'

'My mobile?'

'Gone.'

For two weeks, she is in hospital. Lissek comes every day. At some point he places a medal in her hand. He says he feels shabby doing it. Aaron has given everything, put her life on the line, shown what she can do. Her bullet wounds scar over; some things heal better than others. She could make herself miserable, asking herself whether she would have been caught out by Varga's men if she hadn't kissed Keyes, hadn't tumbled into the room with him, his hand between her legs. She could tell herself that she messed up, that it's her fault he died. But she's a big girl and knows that Two-Holster was that one too many.

Pavlik and Aaron keep the thing about the safe to themselves. He wouldn't have taken the risk, but he doesn't hold it against her. Sometimes you lose.

The fact that she keeps thinking of Keyes doesn't mean that he would have been right for her. For that one night, yes. After that, he would have been as good for her as a longing that can never be fulfilled. But that doesn't make it any easier.

For some time after, she hears his voice in her dreams.

Would you die for me?

And she sees him, the way he grinned when she christened the ashtray in his Porsche, the high-heeled shoes dangling from his index finger, clouds like meringue. The dreams become less frequent, and at some point they cease.

Varga doesn't fly to Norilsk. After that night, he is never seen again. The underboss takes over the clan. This mystery preoccupies Aaron for a long time. At first she assumes it's because of her mobile, because of the risk that the photo file might be stored on a server. If that were the case, even his friends in government wouldn't be able to help Varga.

But as the first leaves start to fall, it should have long become clear to him that there is no reason to worry. There have been no investigations concerning the bribed politicians, no arrests.

Varga has vanished into thin air like smoke on a breeze.

The BKA believes that his underboss had him killed. Aaron doesn't waste a single thought on that. Not because Varga was being protected like a Roman emperor. Anyone can be liquidated, even Caesar learnt that lesson. But: when Capos are eliminated, it is preferably done in full view, in front of many witnesses.

In the middle of the day in a restaurant.

At the hairdresser's.

At a wedding or a christening.

There are always opportunities.

The body is proof that the one who ordered the killing is more powerful than the victim ever was. And if it does take place covertly, the perpetrator brags about it and circulates photos of mutilations to prove that the victim died in agony.

Varga had only recently come into the possession of the Lucas Cranach.

My second most valuable possession.

Was the painting just a bluff? A trick to have the world believe that he is dead? Someone with his means can make himself invisible. There are resorts in the Caribbean and in Asia that guarantee anonymity, with facial surgery part of the package. Just a question of money.

Still.

He gave up an empire, and Aaron wonders why.

That leaves Vesper.

There are only two explanations for his disappearance: either he was killed by Varga's men and they buried his body somewhere, or the Camorra bought him. Only now do they realize how little they knew Vesper. He had a wife whom they never saw, owned a small boat onto which he never invited anyone, was paying off an apartment which contained a newly decorated nursery; he would have become a father three months later.

Lissek speaks to Vesper's wife for a long time, then comes to a decision. He obtains a death certificate, otherwise it would take ten years and Vesper's family wouldn't be taken care of.

On a rainy November day, the whole Department gathers at Oberschöneweide cemetery, where an empty coffin is lowered into the ground. The police music corps plays the Old Comrades March. Aaron tries to remember Vesper, but the only thing that comes to her mind is how she and some of the others always mocked him with 'blabbermouth'.

Barcelona

Five years ago

She wakes up, it is pitch black, and in her heart is a hole so big that the whole world has disappeared into it. She rages and lashes out and they restrain her. She drifts for an eternity. Sometimes she can see, but nothing is making any sense. It's as if she is zapping through a thousand strangers' lives. Then she is back to staring into the bottomless darkness and knows that she is dreaming, that she is being held prisoner and that they are giving her drugs to make her believe that she is blind.

Again and again she hears the echo of a shot.

Again and again she hears the bursting of steel.

Again and again and again.

The dreams last for centuries, the images for seconds.

Once, she sees the boy.

He is holding the stuffed toy in his hand; he looks at her accusingly. She whispers to him, asks him to tell her what she has done to him. But he walks through the wall and disappears.

Then, from somewhere, a voice cuts through this ocean of pain.

Warm and tender, it tells her a story; it is the same voice that used to lull her to sleep when she was little.

'There once was a tear—'

That's when she recognizes her father. She feels him drawing her close and realizes it isn't a dream.

She will hear her own scream for ever.

I

Today

Far down below her is the sea. It rolls softly against the cliffs, a never-ending chant. She clicks her tongue several times per second and gets her bearings using the echo off the rock face to her left. She chose this as her jogging route the second day she was here; twelve kilometres along the cliff coast of Fårö sound. She knows the number of steps, knows where the path she must follow bends in an easterly direction. The sound sent out by her clicks is reflected off the trees, telling her that she has almost reached the crest. Aaron doesn't like spruce trees, so she has decided they are pines.

Being blind does have some advantages.

She feels the winter sun on her face, the frosty wind. As every morning, she hopes that it will help her think.

'Please come back to the Department.'

Inan Demirci's sentence incessantly reverberates within her.

She taps her watch. The digital voice says: 'Fifth of February. Thursday. Nine a.m., six minutes, eleven seconds.'

That is the only certainty she has.

Her mobile vibrates. She doesn't answer, counts her steps. Another three, two, one – she's in the woods. Aaron knows because it's gone darker. She turns round, runs back into the light and stops, caught up in the moment. For four weeks now she has been granted this. Four weeks since the darkness of the past five years suddenly lifted.

She is still blind, but it's not the same anymore.

The day before yesterday, there was the cyclist in the village. She almost ran into him. But Aaron sensed his blurry silhouette, a blot like in a Rorschach test.

Something black is swaying about in the harbour, perhaps a boat.

Another jogger, a grey dot.

The dancing dog in powdery white, a barking whirl.

She trots back into the dark, stops again and is already relishing the anticipation of the thin light. Tentative like the intimation of daybreak it waits for her on the other side of the woods.

Aaron listens to the murmur of the trees, loses all sense of time. A woodpecker knocks on a trunk. Icy needles prick her glowing face. Onwards. Seventy-two running strides until she reaches the fork in the path. She clicks her tongue, calm and relaxed.

And lands flat on her face.

She can locate a tree, a person, a vehicle, a house. But not the branch that must have been torn down by last night's storm.

The bruise isn't a problem, but the fall has caused her to forget the number of steps. Now she has to carefully place one foot in front of the other so she doesn't miss the fork. Her mobile vibrates again.

Aaron knows who it is. She imagines the phone conversation that she has been avoiding since she arrived on Fårö.

Hello, Jenny.

Hello, Sandra.

How are you?
Good.
Have you been to see an eye specialist?
Can we talk about something else?
Why don't you come and stay with us, Pavlik would be pleased too.
Sometime.

She clicks and receives a robust feedback from the hunter's cabin to the right. Here's the fork in the path. Aaron can run again, she knows how many steps it is to the ravine. It is deep, ten metres she estimates; at the bottom is the icy stream, she can hear it burbling now. A tree trunk lies across the ravine, around forty centimetres wide, worn down by many winters, rotten and smooth as glass, a real beast.

Aaron slows down and inches towards the edge amid the sound of rushing water. She crouches down, finds the trunk.

Three metres.

Halfway across, there's a protruding stub of a branch – that's the crunch point.

She could have gone straight on at the fork. The other route is less dangerous than a stroll down Berlin's Kudamm Avenue. But this trunk and what it does to her pulse is like a bridge to her old life, and for those seconds that she balances above the precipice Aaron is once more the woman she was.

She places one foot on the trunk, then the other, standing sideways. Carefully she approaches the stub. When Aaron's right foot touches the obstacle, she notices the rush of blood to her muscles; her body is preparing itself. Aaron lifts her foot and places it back down on the other side. She shifts her weight, holds the insides of her hands in front of her body like a ballerina and executes a half pirouette. Her left foot is as weightless as light. She touches it down on the trunk and stands.

She enjoys the adrenalin, her reward.

Then suddenly the stream is no longer far below, but raging inside her.

She hears the trunk break.

Aaron jumps. She flies into emptiness and forces herself not to think of the deep drop. One of her hands closes round something, a thick root. She clings onto it and reaches out with her other hand, which finds the stem of a young tree. As she dangles in a yawning void, the trunk plunges into the gorge and shatters.

Very slowly she pulls herself up by the stem.

It gives way, she slides a metre lower.

It feels like razors are piercing her lungs. Again she fights her way up.

Her hands are numb, she can't feel her legs.

She keeps going, succeeds, and rolls herself into the snow.

Even closing her mouth, moving her tongue or blinking would require more strength than she has left. After an eternity she raises herself onto her knees, then stands up, swaying.

She sees the little boy.

He is standing in the same place as yesterday, in the middle of the path. Rays of sunshine shimmer and dance through the treetops. The boy clutches his cuddly giraffe and stares at her.

She knows that he isn't real.

She walks through him.

Minutes later, she should have reached the edge of the woods.

But the darkness doesn't yield.

She stops, feeling uncertain. Has she miscounted the steps? She carries on, her heart throbbing, stops again and clicks her tongue. No echo. Aaron varies the click and makes a popping sound with her lips.

Nothing.

She is standing on the treeless plain above the cliffs. The sea is almost quiet, allowing her to hear her breath. Seagulls laugh.

The fear that she constantly feels, the fear when she switches her bedside light on and off ten times before going to sleep, when she opens her eyes in the morning, draws back the curtains, the fear that it might again be as dark as it was for all those years, is now gone.

For it has happened.

On the remaining two kilometres down to the harbour she thinks the same thing a hundred times over:

I will never see again.

I can't go back to the Department.

I'm crazy.

'About time. I was beginning to think you'd stood me up,' she hears Lissek call out. 'Not that I've been bored, I've had a bird shit on me twice. What do you think, shall we head over to Gotland? I know a beach hut there, where they serve home-made aquavit. That stuff will blast your brain away. I once took a bottle home with me and descaled our dishwasher with it; the thing's as good as new again.'

Whenever Aaron slows down on the jetty because a final click of her tongue has indicated the harbour master's house, Lissek talks incessantly. He knows that she can get her bearings from his voice and walk towards him, so he doesn't need to meet her at the top of the jetty and lead her. They both act as though she wasn't blind. That's the tacit agreement they have.

'Worn out?' he asks when Aaron reaches him.

She just nods.

If the thirteen-metre boat were moored astern, she could get on board with a relaxed step. But Lissek always berths it bow first, so Aaron is forced to use the wobbly ladder and immediately has to hold onto the mast of the foresail to avoid falling in the water.

Coaching.

They chug away with reefed sails. She snuggles into the anorak that Lissek has given her and warms her hands on a mug of hot coffee from the Thermos flask. Aaron knows that they are the only boat far and wide. The fishing cutters have long docked, and apart from Lissek and the coast guard no one would go out onto the sound in winter.

It was only three months ago that he handed over the Department to Demirci. Aaron never imagined that he would leave everything behind just like that. But Lissek lives in the here and now. He loves his blue timber house with the sea view, his wife Conny and his boat, the *Unsinkable II*.

They sail westward. Aaron turns around and points her face towards the pallid sun that the weather forecast has predicted. No difference, same darkness. She wonders whether Lissek is watching her. He's as quiet now as he was gabby before. She feels her way to the companion ladder and climbs down.

Aaron sits in the cabin. The powerful diesel engine pounds away below her. She lays a hand on the cladding of the hull. The vibrations run through her body, mask her racing heart, calm her down. After a while she removes her hand, remembers how to breathe.

When she climbs back up, the tiny spark of brightness flashes through her as if she'd been caught in a searchlight.

'What's up?' asks Lissek.

'Nothing.' Aaron sits down on the bench at the stern and turns towards the sun. A feeling of happiness runs through her because the brightness increases a tiny bit more.

A shadow flies through the milky whiteness.

Something lands in her lap.

'Show me your bowline.'

Aaron takes hold of the rope that Lissek has thrown her. She lays a loop, pushes the rope end through, pulls it up out of the coil and tries to lead it back.

But she's done it wrong and it fails.

'It's a piece of cake,' mutters Lissek. 'The rabbit comes up out of the hole, goes round the tree and back down the hole.'

This time it works.

'Yesterday you were four seconds faster.'

He says this with the same equanimity with which he used to calculate a risk, order a mission, place himself before her. In his vicinity, she never feels uncertain or disheartened. He only demands what the other can give. And he always knows how much that is.

'Your boat,' says Lissek.

Aaron takes over the helm. Her hands just stroke the large cherrywood wheel. She senses that they are drifting to the right, adjusts the course, ten degrees to port, and points the boat into the current. They ride across the increasingly choppy waves, the bow cutting through them. It feels like flying.

'Do you remember Varga?' she asks.

'Of course.'

'Why do you think he disappeared back then?'

'Men like him know when their time has come.'

'He was at the peak of his power.'

'It's all downhill from there.'

'And Vesper?'

'I wanted to sleep well again, so I decided he was dead. It'll be ten years in September. I'll put on my good suit, lay a cartridge on his grave and remember him as a comrade.'

'Enviable.'

'You can come along.'

Or not. Lissek has no expectations of her. That is one of the reasons why she is staying with him on Fårö and not with Sandra and Pavlik. They both want her to return to the Department. Sandra because then it would be like the old days, and Pavlik because he still sees in her the woman he once knew. Lissek knows that she is no longer that woman. And he also knows not to push her over visiting an eye specialist.

But how is she going to explain to him that Varga has kept haunting her these past few days? What would he think if she told him that she has seen his son twice?

Three times, if she includes Barcelona.

'When you were at my bedside five years ago in Spain, did I talk about a small boy?'

'You weren't yourself. You clung onto me and stammered that they were trying to kill you.'

'And on your second visit?'

'We emptied a bottle of whisky. You cried the whole time. After you'd fallen asleep, your father and I emptied another one. He was a mountain of a man, but seeing you like that, it floored him.'

Her grief is a monstrous wave and the boat dances on it like a nutshell.

'Can you remember what I said at the time?' he asks.

That I am a policewoman and will never be anything else.

'Demirci has rolled out a red carpet for you. All you have to do is walk on it.'

'I wouldn't even pass the psychological test.'

'Why?'

She doesn't answer.

'OK, role play. I'm the shrink and a real smart-arse: Ms Aaron, you were a member of the Department until five years ago. What was your role?'

'Stop talking crap.'

'Ms Aaron, it appears you have no self-control.'

'Covert operations worldwide.'

'Why did you withdraw from service?'

'I was blinded while on a mission in Barcelona. After two years, I could wipe my own arse. I applied to join the BKA and have worked for them as a profiler and interrogation specialist ever since.'

'Are you good at your job?'

'I'll leave that to others to judge.'

'You don't seem to have a very high opinion of yourself.'

'Kiss my arse.'

'Tomorrow would suit, I'm free then.'

'Draw a number and join the queue.'

'Why does Ms Demirci feel that you, a blind person, would be useful to the Department?'

'Ask Ms Demirci. Or her predecessor Lissek.'

'What for? It's widely known that you were his protégé.'

'True. And he's a senile old git.'

Lissek quietly laughs. 'What can you do better than a sighted person – than me, for example?'

'Ski jumping, but I'm not as good at bullshitting.'

'Ms Demirci must have her reasons.'

'Four weeks ago, the man I have to thank for being blind returned.'

In her mind she is back there again, racing along a desolate ice-bound country road at a hundred kilometres per hour, certain that she is about to die, with Pavlik beside her, seriously wounded.

She hears the bullets grinding down the paintwork.

Suddenly, her mortal fear evaporated in a fireball, and she saw white, blurry points, more distant than Alpha Centauri, yet near. The headlights of cars.

LIGHT.

On that road in the middle of nowhere everything was hurting Aaron, even the snowflakes that drifted into her face.

It was the best pain she'd ever experienced.

'I survived it,' she says. 'The man in question didn't. That was my recommendation letter.'

'Is it difficult to say his name out loud?'

'Not at all. Ludger Holm.'

'What does that feel like?'

'Like an ingrown toenail.'

'Well, Ms Aaron, it seems to me that you're the perfect choice for the Department.'

'I'm finished with all that.'

'The tree trunk in the woods tells a different story.'

The fact that he's been watching her hits her like a sledgehammer, but then she reminds herself that Lissek is just concerned for her. Like he always has been.

'Deceiving myself is not one of my strong points.'

'And the truth is?'

'That I'm an emotional wreck.'

'In what way does this manifest itself?'

'I laugh and cry at the wrong times.'

'What do you suspect is the reason for this?'

'You're the shrink.'

Lissek puts his arm around her. 'Stop asking yourself what your life would be like if you could still see. The answer is: you'd probably be dead.'

Aaron knows that he is right. During her years at the Department, Vesper's wasn't the only coffin she threw earth onto.

They fall quiet amid the up and down of the swell.

Until Lissek mumbles: 'Dying in bed isn't such a bad thing.'

'True. Neither of us would've ever thought it was possible.'

'What does Bushidō philosophy have to say on that?'

True patience means bearing the unbearable.

'It says: "Beware of the advice of old men. They have enough trouble just squeezing out three drops of pee."'

Lissek laughs. 'Wise words. The weather is changing, we should head back. We'll save the aquavit for another time.'

He takes over the helm again and turns the boat. They're sailing eastward. Aaron opens her anorak, protects the flame of her Dupont from the wind and lights a cigarette. The smoke barely makes it into her lungs. For the next half hour, they're both lost in thought. She imagines being able to see the coast, the lighthouse, Lissek's house on the cliff top, a basalt-grey sky.

When the easing swell tells her that they are entering the harbour she breaks the silence. 'Sometimes I've wondered why Varga's men in Rome left me alive.'

'You weren't important to him. It wasn't personal.'

'It's always personal.'

'Only for you,' he points out.

'Thanks for the flowers.'

'I thought self-deception wasn't one of your strengths?'

Touché.

'Something he said has always stayed with me.'

'Yes?'

'"If I was to disappear one day like one of my ships, only my son would miss me. He's the only family I have."'

Lissek waits three seagull cries until he replies: 'Who would miss you?'

'You and Conny. Pavlik, Sandra. Not that many either.'

'More than is granted to some.'

When they moor, it is her task to secure the stern line. Lissek always approaches the post at the same angle, so that she knows how to throw the line at his command.

'Now.'

Missed.

He steadies the boat with the reverse gear. She retrieves the line, throws the loop.

Missed again.

'Anyone would think you were blind.'

Angrily, she tries again. It hits home.

She feels her way to the foredeck, making sure she always

has three parts of her body in contact with the boat, like Lissek has taught her.

'Half a metre,' he calls out.

Aaron jumps onto the jetty and secures the mooring lines.

When Lissek gets on land, he mutters: 'Wait, something's tangled there.' She knows that in truth he is tightening her knots. But that's OK.

'Hey, Gunnar,' she hears him say.

Aaron knows the man. He and his wife run the village shop and he occasionally carries out odd jobs for Lissek. The two of them talk in Swedish. Gunnar's tone is strained, muffled. Lissek's voice sounds the same as always.

He asks two or three questions, that's it.

Car door, engine, car drives off. Lissek puts his arm around Aaron and walks with her to his jeep.

'You're shivering. Conny will fix us a drink.'

'What was that about?'

'He just wanted to know when he should come to clean the gutter.'

Ten things that make Aaron angry:
  bus drivers who don't tell her where she has to get off
  the wrong change
  tactile strips that end in nothing
  when her cleaning lady moves something
  abridged audio books
  people who shout as though she was deaf
  'do you also have a dog?'
  waiting for someone who's already been there for ages
  pity
  being taken for a fool

★

She stops. 'You're insulting me.'

Lissek takes a deep breath. 'Somebody asked about me in the shop. Whether they knew me, where I live.'

'Who?'

'He didn't introduce himself. Gunnar was in the storeroom, his wife told him. He ran outside and saw the guy drive away. Black Lexus, he couldn't read the number plate.'

'How did his wife respond?'

'They don't know what I used to do, they just know that I'm a cautious man. No doubt they have their own thoughts on the matter. She told the guy that she's never heard of me.'

'He'll be back.'

'Most certainly.'

Lissek starts to walk on, but she grabs his arm. 'That's not everything.'

'You're a real pain sometimes, you know.'

'Your training.'

'His wife's quite distressed,' he grumbles. 'This morning she found her cat lying dead in the garden. Somebody broke its neck.'

The scar on Aaron's collarbone itches.

'I've still got some outstanding accounts to settle,' he comments.

'So do I.'

2

The hallway smells of warm dough and apple and cinnamon. 'I thought you'd be back early,' Conny calls out cheerily. 'You must be chilled to the bones.'

Seven steps, avoid the umbrella stand, two steps to the right, and Aaron is standing in the kitchen door. Lissek walks past her. She knows that he is giving his wife a hug, while trying to steal a bit of cake behind her back.

'Hands off, I made this for Jenny!'

'And I just get the crumbs again,' he gripes.

'Oh Conny,' Aaron sighs, 'if you carry on feeding me up like this, I won't be able to squeeze my bum into a single pair of jeans anymore.'

'Believe me, honey, I would love to have your bum.'

Lissek has done many things right in his life, but marrying Conny was his biggest coup. He was thirty and an undercover agent for the BKA when he was courting her. Conny knew what that would mean. 'And what use was it to me? All he had to do was smile at me and I was a lost cause.' She always backed him. He never talked to her about his work, she never asked him. Some people spend all their time together and share nothing at all. Conny didn't see her husband for weeks, yet she knew him inside out.

Aaron wished her mother had been like that. She had also known what kind of man she had fallen in love with as a young woman, long before Aaron's father was made commander of the elite police tactical unit GSG 9. But she never understood, all she ever knew was fear. The fact that her daughter followed in her husband's footsteps destroyed her. Aaron's mother left him and swapped one loneliness for another, until she died of grief. Right until the end, Aaron and her father fought a silent battle over who was to blame for it.

When she walked off the ferry two weeks ago, Conny hugged her and whispered: 'I was hoping so much that you'd come.' Aaron knew then that she had made the right decision.

'We have a visitor coming for dinner this evening.'

She senses a slight tension in her friend's voice.

Someone whom Conny doesn't like?

'Who is it?' mutters Lissek.

'Thomas.'

'Ah.' He turns to face Aaron. 'You'll like him. Scientist from Berlin, he has a holiday home here. Nice guy.'

'I'll go and have a shower,' she says.

Aaron runs the water so hot it is close to scalding. Still her hands and feet remain freezing cold. She thinks about the man who asked for Lissek.

Or for her.

She stands still, doesn't feel the hot water.

When she goes to her room, she knows what is in her bedside table; Aaron and Lissek don't need to waste words over something like this. She takes the revolver out of the drawer and runs her fingers over it. A Colt Python. She opens the cylinder and lets a cartridge glide into her hand – .357 Magnum. Perfect at short distance and good for a thumb-sized hole. She puts the gun back, feeling certain that Lissek's loose favourite jumper conceals a SIG Sauer tucked into his waistband.

As they drink coffee in the conservatory, Conny says: 'Sandra says hello.' All casual, between two mouthfuls of cake.

'Thanks,' Aaron replies, equally casual.

Aaron reaches for the bowl of cream, but it isn't where it should be. Other blind people wouldn't have a problem with this. Accustomed to relying on the help of sighted people in day-to-day life, they would simply ask for the bowl. Not Aaron. She had never been in this house before, so straight after arriving, she memorized the steps and asked Conny to show her how the kitchen cupboards are organized. Aaron also discussed with her how the food should be arranged on the plate and where to place the crockery on the table. Conny has internalized it. Meat at six o'clock, side dish at three, vegetables and salad at nine, glasses at two, coffee pot and bottles at twelve and pudding at eleven o'clock. As well as the cream.

Aaron can do a lot of things like a sighted person.

It's just more work.

The bowl is placed in her hand. 'Sometimes I forget you're blind,' Conny apologizes.

'I don't.'

Aaron polishes off her second piece of cake, moves to top up her coffee and hears Conny secretly push the coffee pot to where it should already be.

Aaron goes *tsk tsk*. 'Cheat.'

They laugh. As she pours, she holds her index finger over the edge of the cup so that she knows when it is full.

'I was in the shop this morning,' Conny says to Lissek. 'Guess what, someone's killed Elin and Gunnar's cat. Elin was so upset she gave me the wrong change.'

'Probably some stupid lad or other,' he mumbles.

If Aaron had to ascribe a colour to Lissek's voice, it would be bronze – mellow, warm. With almost anyone else, she can pick up nuances that would be too slight for a sighted person, tiny erosions at the edges of the words. With Lissek she fails. When he was talking to Gunnar, only the other man's worry gave it away. Lissek has worked undercover for so many years that hiding what he's really thinking has become second nature to him.

Aaron used to be just the same.

But she has left that behind her.

Oh yes? And the tree trunk?

'I'm tired,' she says.

She lies down on the bed. Aaron knows that Conny and Lissek will play a few rounds of draughts and that he will let her win because he enjoys the freedom of being allowed to make mistakes. Would her father eventually have become like this too? When her world was vaporized by the bullet from a Remington, he quit work and took care of her. His retirement only lasted three months, then Aaron was stood beside a grave that she would never see.

She takes the Colt out of the drawer. The cold steel soothes her. 'A weapon doesn't know its master,' she hears her father say in the quarry.

I didn't understand that at the time. But I learnt.

You're blind. What do you want with the revolver?

You said: 'Not seeing, knowing.'

Beware of the advice of old men.

I was twelve and you were forty-four.

Don't be a know-it-all.

She drifts off.

Aaron is in a large house and is walking up a flight of stairs. She opens a door and the only thing behind it is a dead cat. She opens a second door and the only thing behind it is a pair of red high-heeled shoes. She opens a third door and the only thing behind it is a sleeping child. The blanket is lying on the floor. Aaron goes to cover the child up, but pauses. Where its heart should be there is a beautiful safe. She knows the combination and opens it. There's nothing inside except the papers, which she wants more than anything else. Aaron takes them out, quietly, so as not to wake the child, but it opens its eyes. It looks at her with such a sorrowful gaze that she feels herself crumble. Shaking, she puts the papers back, but the safe can't be closed again.

The child gasps for air, goes blue. Desperately, she tries to close the safe.

It opens back up.

She stares at the gaping hole, the heartbeat grows weaker and weaker, and finally stops. She falls onto her knees and holds the lifeless body tightly against her. She is warmed by its blood, and there's nothing except a voice that says: 'Dying in bed isn't such a bad thing.'

She storms off with the child in her arms, runs down the stairs and out of the house, and there's nothing there except a silver Porsche. Aaron jumps behind the wheel and beds the small body into her lap. She races along an embankment road. A black Lexus edges up alongside her. A man without a face is at the wheel. His gun flashes. She sees the child for the last time. Papers are fluttering out of its chest. She smells magnesium, like from flash grenades.

Aaron is in a boat on a subterranean river, and there's nothing except darkness. She can't hear her heartbeat, and there's nothing inside her but fear. She asks the ferryman what has happened, but no sound comes from her mouth. The ferryman takes her hand and writes something inside it.

She realizes then that she is deaf and blind.

Aaron can't stop screaming.

And there's nothing except silence.

She lashes out.

Strong arms embrace her. 'You've been dreaming.'

She recognizes Lissek's voice, feels him stroking her wet hair. It feels as if her head is going to explode, it's too small for the sea of tears. In the end there's just snot.

Lissek says: 'That was overdue.'

3

When greeting people she hasn't met before, Aaron immediately sorts them into a category. Those whose voices instantly resonate with pity. The silent ones, who are scared of doing something wrong. The insecure ones, who talk too quietly or too loudly. The idiots ('My eyesight isn't too good either'). The peeved, the superior, the nosy, the schoolmasterly. There are also some who act as though she had nothing more than a sprained ankle.

The guest who joins them for dinner is flippant, which she likes. 'Hello, I'm Thomas. It's a good thing you can't see me, I've got a real shiner. I wanted to repair the garden fence, but the hammer had a different plan.'

Warm tone. Medium height, the sound tells her.

'Typical scientist, zero motor skills,' Lissek teases.

She stretches out her hand and realizes that Thomas has been waiting for her to do it, thereby saving her the embarrassment of having to search for his.

Does he know any blind people?

The others eat gurnard, Aaron has a steak because she doesn't like eating anything with scales on. She likes Thomas. Relaxed guy, British humour. She doesn't normally speculate about what people look like. She guesses him to be in his fifties, but still a bit of a college boy; perhaps he's wearing a dotted bow tie with his tweed jacket.

They chat about anything and everything. It's a lovely evening, almost carefree, until Lissek tells them that his boat is being given an overhaul next week, and Thomas asks how big it is.

Lissek quickly skims over it.

But for her it's enough.

'So where exactly is your house?' she asks.

'At the top, by the dunes,' Conny pre-empts their guest.

'Oh, so you have a view over the sound,' says Aaron.

'Yes, that's right.'

She slams down her glass. 'The dunes are on the other side of the island. Who are you?'

Silence creeps into her bones like cold damp.

Thomas clears his throat. 'Mr Lissek asked me to come and take a look at you.'

'Call a dating hotline,' she snaps.

'Professor Reimer runs an institute for treating the blind,' Lissek explains. 'He's one of the world's leading specialists. We discussed it for a long time. Conny and I think that you should talk to someone who's an expert. Sticking your head in the sand is no solution.'

Aaron stands up abruptly. '*You* think so, do you? Without asking me.'

'How much longer do you want to torment yourself?' Conny asks miserably. 'He's taken the trouble to come here.'

'And that's my fault, is it?' She walks to the door. She's so incensed that she miscounts her steps and bumps into the sideboard.

'There's toxic hope and there's toxic fear,' Reimer says calmly. 'The former is the desperate belief in a cure, although the patient fundamentally knows that it's hopeless. The latter is the refusal to face a diagnosis, so as not to be crushed by it. That will gradually destroy you. Is that what you want?'

Aaron stops. She turns.

Her soul bared.

'You won't get a diagnosis from me. That would require tests. I just have a few questions to ask.'

Where will you hide now?

Get it over with. And then you can go and blub until you feel better.

'Shall we leave you alone?' Lissek asks.

'No.' She sits back down, lights a cigarette and resists the urge to pull on it greedily.

Conny pushes a saucer in front of her.

'How old are you?'

'Thirty-six.'

'You're a policewoman?'

'Yes.'

'And you've been blind for five years?'

'Yes.'

'How did it happen?'

'I took a shot to the head while driving through a tunnel at two hundred and sixty kilometres per hour.'

Aaron expects some kind of comment, but he skates over it as though it's the kind of thing he hears all the time. 'Where exactly did the bullet hit you?'

'Behind the left ear; it went straight through.'

'What did they tell you about the damage that was done in your cortex?'

'That there were no bone splinters in the bullet channel and that the surrounding tissue was largely undamaged.'

'Yet you're completely blind?'

'Not anymore.'

'What's changed?'

'I had a light-dark perception.'

'When?'

'Four weeks ago.'

'Describe the moment.'

'Contrary to general advice, I drove a car. I had a colleague lying next to me with a belly wound. We survived it. I saw blurred lights, headlights.'

'Frontal or peripheral?'

'Frontal.'

'Has it stayed this way?'

'With interruptions,' she says after a brief hesitation.

'Give me an example.'

'When I'm under a lot of stress it disappears.'

'Are you stressed now?'

'Of course.'

Something whisks by.

'Was that your hand?' she asks.

'Yes. In which direction?'

'From left to right.'

'And now?'

'Right to left.'

'Now?'

'Right to left again.'

'What kind of stress are we talking about?'

'Adrenalin.'

'Skydiving, bungee jumping, free climbing?'

'That kind of thing.'

'I know blind people who knit,' Reimer coments.

'One doesn't always have wool to hand.'

'You look tired out. Is your sleep disturbed?'

'Sleep? What's that?'

'Have you tried melatonin?'

'I've moved on to stronger stuff.'

'Does it ever happen that you inexplicably act as though you can see?'

'How do you mean?'

'You cross a room and take a sidestep without knowing why. The other person asks you whether you noticed the chair that stood in the way. That sort of thing.'

'Sometimes. At the airport in Visby a woman approached me after I had walked around her. She thought I was a fraud because of the white cane.'

'Yesterday, I was about to put a bottle of wine on the table,' Conny chips in, 'and you took it out of my hand, just like that.'

'Really?' Aaron asks.

'I didn't even think anything of it,' Conny continues. 'Perhaps because you look us in the eye, and you move about almost like a sighted person.'

'We call that blindsight,' says Reimer.

'Is that something good?'

'It means that your optic nerve is intact.'

'I know it is. One of the doctors explained to me that my eye is the camera and the optic nerve is the cable that leads to the image processor in the cerebral cortex. The camera is still sending the recorded images as always. But they can no longer be processed because the processor was destroyed by the bullet.'

'The visual cortex makes up fifty per cent of our entire cortex. That's a bloody enormous processor. Do you think that you've lost fifty per cent of your cerebral cortex?'

'Sometimes I think it's a hundred per cent.'

A smile shimmers through Reimer's voice. 'Although it's so large, many doctors regard the visual cortex as no more than an appendage of the eyes. Strange, don't you think? In truth we mainly see with the occipital lobe at the back of the head. That's where the images are formed.'

'Nothing is getting there.'

'Our brain is a network. The cells communicate with each

other via a hundred billion neural connections. In sighted people, the visual signals are transported on super-highways. The ancillary routes wither away and lead a shadowy existence; that's where the data traffic would need to be diverted to. The crucial question is whether this can be done in your case. One thing is certain: at the airport and when you were drinking wine you perceived something, even if the images didn't make it through to your conscious mind.'

Conny reaches for Aaron's hand.

'Do you recognize my face?' he asks.

'No.'

'What colour is my shirt?'

'Black, I think.'

'Why?'

'The wall behind you is probably white. I can perceive the contrast.'

A pen scrapes across paper. Reimer takes a few notes with quick, jagged strokes.

Conny can't bear it any longer. 'Can you help her?'

'Like I said, we would need to do some tests.'

'And if I pass?' Aaron persists.

'It's not like being at university. However much you want it, you have to be ready for it.'

'In what way?'

'The visual capacity you can achieve is influenced by many factors. Not least of all your psyche.'

'Are you some kind of homeopath?'

'You mean, do I practise energy healing, babble something, prescribe sugar syrup and invoke spirits? Sorry, no, I can't help you there, even though there are one or two eye specialists who say precisely that about me. I don't want to bore you with my research at the Massachusetts Institute of Technology or boast about my Harvard diploma.'

'But you must have a professional opinion.'

'I'm not a doctor, I'm a psychologist and neurological researcher. The doctors have given up on you. To be honest, I don't know whether I should admit you to my programme.'

'Why?' she immediately asks.

'My therapy takes a holistic approach. The medical stuff is just one aspect of it.'

'What else comes into it?'

'Do you compare your current life to the one you had before?'

'Doesn't every blind person?'

'The less clever ones,' he replies.

'You have a knack for compliments.'

'Do you see your blindness as a punishment?'

'For what?'

'*You* tell me.'

'Why would I be thinking that?'

'Because you strike me as a woman who reads Kierkegaard from morning till night.'

'As an audio book. And for relaxing, Schopenhauer,' she quips.

'Are you still the same person you used to be?'

'Of course not.'

'I don't believe a single word you're saying, Ms Aaron. You immediately sized me up. You know that I'm a little shorter than you, weigh no more than seventy-five kilos and would be no kind of opponent for you. You count your steps, and I bet you use your high heels for echolocation. I've seen you walk with them. I wouldn't want to meet you in a dark alley.'

It's all true.

'Technically, you've been blind for five years. But fundamentally you haven't realized it yet.'

'Well, whatever it takes: I *am* ready.'

Reimer says nothing.

'I can endure hardship. I'll face any truth.'

Still he says nothing.

Only now does she realize: he has turned the tables and got her to take the initiative.

'You're a damned manipulator,' she mutters.

'And you have a knack for compliments.'

'How long would the therapy take?'

'Difficult to say. Weeks, months, years. It's different with each person.'

'But you think it's possible that I might see again?'

'I've had patients with less serious injuries whom I haven't been able to help.'

'You've come all this way just to palm me off with that?'

'I assume that you're extremely disciplined, eager to learn, ambitious.'

'Yes.'

'You're in excellent physical condition.'

'Yes.'

'Do you meditate?'

'Yes.'

'These are good starting points.'

'So what does the therapy consist of?' she asks.

'What was your hearing like before you went blind?'

'Exceptional.'

'And yet, no comparison to now,' he suggests.

'You have two coins in your pocket. The left one, to be precise. And outside, a bird is pecking at a feeder.'

'The reason for this is something we call neuroplasticity. Your hearing is hypersensitive because after you lost your sight, your auditory cortex hijacked more and more cells from your visual centre; cells which were intact but no longer had a purpose. That's also why your sense of taste, smell and touch are so well developed. The human brain is a hard drive that continuously defragments itself. Those few hundred grams are eager to be occupied with something. We could try to jump-start your image processor. For example with electrical stimulation.'

'And the result?'

'There are people who call me the man who lets blind people see again. That's as flattering as it is wrong. It's positional warfare, we have to fight for every pixel. Afterwards, some people can read, even drive a car. Others are happy because they can recognize colours. And often it doesn't help at all.'

'When do we start?'

'I'm flying to a congress in Taiwan tomorrow and I'll be back the middle of next week. My institute is on Rügen. That's where the therapy would take place. Make an appointment.'

He stands up.

'I'll take you to the hotel,' says Lissek.

Reimer encloses the hand that Aaron extends towards him. His next question causes the ground to tremble beneath her.

'Do you have hallucinations?'

'No,' she immediately responds.

'Sure?'

'Why are you asking me that?'

'Why aren't you being honest with me?'

'I see a small boy,' she says quietly.

'A boy you knew?'

'Yes.'

'What does he do?'

'Nothing. He just looks at me.'

'Some blind people who regain a certain level of perception have these visions. But they don't talk about it, they're ashamed, they think they'd be seen as crazy. In actual fact it's a sign that the brain is looking for images. Because none are coming from outside, it fetches some from the memory. Your network wants to repair itself. You should help it.'

She finds herself in her inner chamber, far, far away from everything. The world is nothing more than white noise behind mountains of hope.

'Ms Aaron,' Reimer's voice eventually reaches her.

'Yes?'

'You can let go of my hand now.'

The door closes. She is reeling. Conny pulls her close for a hug. The hammering of their hearts could forge iron.

Aaron disengages and whispers: 'I'd like to be alone. Is that OK?'

'Of course.'

She goes out onto the terrace. The seagull mobile made from cracked enamel is singing out under the canopy roof. Sometimes she lets it fly against her hands. She can see the wind then. But not now. Swirling snow surrounds her, the surf is battering the cliffs. Aaron takes three steps, bumps against a chair and sits down on the naked springs.

She should be freezing in her jeans and thin blouse, but she feels hot. Her thoughts are tumbling about like balls in a lottery drum.

It means that your optic nerve is undamaged. I wouldn't want to meet you in a dark alley. Your network wants to repair itself. Are you still the same person you used to be?

In Buddhism, losing one's sight is regarded as karma. It is a sign that one has done wrong in a former life.

Aaron remembers how she took the exam for her fourth Dan and then went to the temple of Nikkō with her master. Monkeys with white crests on their heads were bathing under the waterfall. The black eyes of crows gleamed from between the branches of the cedars bending in the wind. They walked up a long row of stone steps. In front of the temple they washed their hands and rinsed their mouths, for if a person does bad things, it is these they do it with. It was New Year's Eve. As the hundred and eight beats of the chimes rang out in the Three Buddha Hall, Aaron prayed that her sins of the last year would be redeemed.

That she didn't make more time for her father.

That she wasn't fast enough in Tangier.

The arrogance of thinking herself immortal.

That she hadn't visited her mother's grave.

The quarrel with Niko.

But the real sins she didn't divulge.

A year later she was blinded by Holm.

Do you see it as punishment?

She sits in the cold for ages. The mobile is silent. Her inner clock is busted, she doesn't know if it is day or night.

Being sad is so damn exhausting.

The terrace door is pushed open. Lissek sits down beside her. 'Sorry, it was the only way,' he says with a raw voice.

'It's *me* who should apologize, not you.'

'Let's both stop with this.'

'The man is expensive. I'll pay you back.'

'Aaron, there are some things you don't pay for. Sandra and Pavlik chipped in. We won't be going hungry. And you won't be losing face if we leave it at that.'

She takes his hand. After some minutes, she asks: 'Could Reimer have been the man who was looking for you?'

'No. I asked him about it. It wasn't him.'

More silence.

'When are you leaving?' Lissek asks.

'Tomorrow.'

Wiesbaden

Four weeks ago

He thought he'd considered everything. Before he goes into her apartment, he always makes sure not to use any aftershave or deodorant and washes with unperfumed soap, as she might otherwise pick up his scent. On those days and the ones before, he doesn't eat anything that could leave behind the slightest smell. Once while he was there he was thirsty, but there was no way he was going to take even a single gulp of the mineral water in the fridge, as he considered Aaron capable of recognizing even the slightest difference in the weight of the bottle. He always wears shoes without a tread. She walks around barefoot in here, and the risk of a small stone becoming wedged in a groove of his shoe and then being left behind by him on the floor is too big; it would be enough to make her suspicious.

All this he has factored in.

But not the key that is now turning in the lock.

Silently he darts next to the door.

When the young woman walks in, his knuckle jerks against

the kyusho point on her temple. She sinks into his arms before she sees him.

He lays her down, closes the door, searches through her pockets and finds a packet of rubber gloves with a receipt. Aaron's cleaning lady. He takes off his belt and lashes her arms together. He carries her into the living room, stuffs a handkerchief in her mouth and ties her to the heating pipe. The woman doesn't bother him, he'll deal with her later.

In the silence he turns his attention back to Aaron's shelves. The many books surprised him. As did the pictures on the walls, the photos, the flowers. But it all became clear when he read her notes: Aaron is still in denial about being blind.

Proof that this punishment isn't enough.

His gaze glides across the titles. Philosophy, poetry, literature, plays, art. The same books as he would have in his apartment. If he had one. He could spend days and nights talking to her about them. It would be a pleasure.

But they will have better things to do.

He lingers over Max Frisch's collected works. Frisch was convinced that the truth can't be revealed, that it can only be invented. Aaron's absolution. One of her invented truths is her claim to know the difference between right and wrong.

One lie out of many. He will make her realize this.

In Dante's first canto it says: 'When I had journeyed half of our life's way, I found myself within a shadowed forest, for I had lost the path that does not stray.'

A great, true sentence.

Aaron will have to learn the most bitter of lessons: happiness makes us blind, but pain allows us to see.

He briefly glances at the woman – she will sleep for at least another ten minutes. How many times has she dusted these books? What does she know of them? She is pretty, looks intelligent, perhaps a student. But even if she is studying literature or philosophy, he could cite passages from each book that she would never understand. Would it be right to kill her? Of course not. Would it be wise not to kill her?

The books are arranged alphabetically. Orderliness is important for Aaron. Because her world is disintegrating. Instinctively, his eye is drawn to the slim volume that attracted his attention on the very first day. Büchner's *Woyzeck*. The paper has yellowed; Aaron has marked passages in the text, it's probably one of the books she read in school.

He leafs through the slim volume without having to pick it up, just like he can do with every book that he has ever read.

Aaron can do that too.

Further proof of the incompleteness of her punishment.

In his mind, he opens it up at scene nineteen, which contains Büchner's version of the Star Money fairy tale. He was in Marrakech yesterday for some final preparations. *Woyzeck* made him smile when he was at the bank. Aaron certainly won't smile when she finds out.

He is tempted to start up her computer, as every time he's been here. But he suspects that she has secured it with a keyboard tracer, so he will have to resist the urge. Her diaries are piled up by the desk, all in Braille. He learnt to read Braille just for her; it cost him half a year.

It was worth it.

He moves over to the bedroom. Like the living room, it is sparsely furnished, helping to turn one's thoughts away from the world. That is what Bushidō philosophy dictates. Again, this room is just like the one he might have in his apartment.

He sits down on the bed in which Aaron was sleeping while he looked at her. He remembers the night she woke up, shaking, screaming, and he held his breath so he wouldn't give himself away. It took an hour before she slipped into the next nightmare. He pictured it being about him, the man who directed the events in her dreams.

He looks at the painting by Eşref Armağan. She bought it

when she was already blind. The paint has been applied so thickly that Aaron can feel it with her fingers. What does she see in it?

Another one of her lies.

He sees a winter that lasts a lifetime. Two brothers who look in each other's eyes for the last time and remember so much pain that no poet would find words for it. He sees a woman who will learn that there are worse things than being blind.

The doorbell rings.

Instantly, he is in the hallway.

He waits.

A man calls out: 'It's me, open up. I'll help you, then we'll have time to go and eat something before the cinema.'

He opens the door without showing himself and lets the man step in. He paralyses him with a punch in the governing vessel on his back and hits him over the head with the Remington. He drags the man over to the woman. She is still unconscious, but he knows what expression her face will adopt when she stares at him as soon as she wakes up.

He once pleaded like that too.

He looks at them both. So young. They're wearing friendship bands, they're a couple. What hopes might they have for their lives? None of those hopes is foreign to him. But none has been fulfilled. He never kills for pleasure or greed or callousness. With some he did it because it was easier than sparing them. This here is different. Neither of them have seen his face. He could leave and grant them their future.

But what would Aaron think when she found out?

Would she suspect that he was the man in her apartment? That he has returned? That would endanger his plans.

He attaches the silencer to his Remington. Hesitates.

Yet again, it springs to his mind that Aaron already knows. That she feels his proximity, can smell him. He even left her a little message, on the street, when he slipped the coffee bean into her coat pocket outside the cinema. That was a little conceited of him, but he couldn't resist.

Has Aaron found it yet?

Possibly not.

He hears the woman groan, she will open her eyes any moment.

The risk isn't worth his mercy.

Without thinking about it any longer, he shoots them both in the head. He puts his gloves on and gathers together some cleaning utensils. Aaron would notice if the place hadn't been cleaned. Also, this is his last visit, so it's a way of saying goodbye.

He takes care not to move anything; he dusts, washes up, smooths out the bed.

He empties the bin.

Scrubs the blood off the parquet floor.

When he's finished, he opens one of the windows facing out onto the rear courtyard. It's already dark, the moon is playing hide and seek. The back of the building is covered in scaffolding for renovation work. The chute for the rubble is just to the right. He lifts the woman onto his shoulders, carries her out onto the scaffold and lets her body slide down through the plastic tunnel. He does the same with the man. He waits a few minutes, airs the room. Then he closes the window and leaves the apartment without glancing back.

He drives into the courtyard and loads the bodies into the boot. It takes him half an hour to drive to Eltville in the car he stole today. He finds a suitable location outside the town. He gets out, pushes the vehicle over the riverside wall into the Rhine and watches as it sinks into the murky water.

For a long time, he stays standing in the stiff wind, the freezing rain. He points his face towards the sky. The rain tastes of soot and salt and the yearning for salvation. He has robbed Aaron of her sight, but there is still so much more he can take from her. Death isn't always the worst punishment.

4

Today

Everything has its fixed place in the wardrobe. White jeans at the top, blue ones at the bottom, the same with the T-shirts and jumpers. Dresses and skirts are also hung up in order of their colour. But when she is deep in thought or something is bothering her, it can happen that she makes a mistake. So to be sure, she uses the scanner that reads out the colours when packing her suitcase. She doesn't like brightly coloured clothes, so the device ought to be reliable, but it has its quirks.

'Intensive blue,' the digital voice declares.

Meaning the purple of her pashmina jumper.

'Pale grey.'

Aaron smiles. 'How many times do I need to tell you that these jeans are white?' She puts them in the suitcase and reaches for a blouse.

'Flamingo red.'

Nice description for salmon.

It's quiet in the house. Conny is visiting an ill neighbour on a remote farm. Lissek is pottering around on the boat; he and Conny will take her to the ferry in two hours.

When he came back from buying bread this morning he said: 'The business with the cat has been cleared up. It was the son of a fisherman. His father dragged him to Elin, where he confessed. It'll be a while before the rascal can sit again.'

After breakfast, Aaron had googled Professor Reimer. Thirty-nine thousand hits. Many eye specialists oppose him, his methods deviate from mainstream medicine. But astounding successes are documented in scientific magazines such as *Science* and *Nature*.

This evening she will be at Sandra and Pavlik's house in Berlin. She is looking forward to spending time with her friends, chilling out for a while. She will start the therapy in a week.

One week.

Then her new life will begin.

Afterwards, some people can read, even drive a car.

Just being allowed to dream of it almost tears her to pieces.

Often it doesn't help at all.

No. She will nail it.

She's the one-in-a-thousand.

Ten things that Aaron longs for:
   magical places of childhood
   cinema, first row, centre
   counting wrinkles in the mirror
   sunsets
   the National Gallery
   reading with her eyes
   sunrises
   buying a convertible
   the shooting range
   throwing away the cane

*

All of a sudden, she feels that she's not alone.

Aaron spins round.

The little boy is standing in the door. He turns his back to her, looks into the hallway.

'Oh, it's you,' she says. 'Soon, we won't be seeing each other anymore. I'll get new pictures, real ones.'

She reaches for her underwear.

'Black.'

For a minute she continues with her packing, without paying any attention to the boy. Until he turns round to face her. His eyes bore into her. He turns away and disappears into the hallway.

She feels her way along the wardrobe to the door. The boy is standing on the top step, six metres away. He stares at Aaron one last time, walks down the stairs and is gone.

Then it hits her: he's trying to tell her something.

She hears it.

A gentle scraping.

Downstairs.

The kitchen door into the garden.

She darts back into the room, opens the bedside drawer and takes out the revolver. She slips off her shoes. With two steps she is back in the hallway, listening.

Nothing.

She creeps to the stairs. Her pulse is racing. Aaron holds her breath and fine-tunes her hearing until she thinks she can even hear the drop of sweat that is trickling down her temple.

A floorboard bends.

Dining room, by the terrace door.

Nobody apart from her would notice this, even the person downstairs who just trod on the board. That board is a diva. With Aaron or Conny it doesn't give. But it does with Lissek.

So it's a man. At least ninety kilos.

Aaron counts the steps, knowing that she has to miss out the fourth one because it creaks.

Nine, ten, eleven.

She's at the bottom.

The intruder hasn't noticed her yet, otherwise she'd know about it. He's still in the dining room.

No.

Steps.

Left. Conservatory.

She doesn't run to the door, she 'flows' with a wave-like movement. In the two seconds that this takes her she shifts her centre of gravity five times, becomes light as a feather.

Aaron flattens herself against the wall.

It is so quiet that she can hear the man's breathing.

He isn't fit.

Good.

Half a metre away from her stands the chest with the large glass bowl in which Conny keeps stones she's found on the beach. Aaron often touches them; she loves the smooth curves that lie so snug against her palm.

She must slow down her pulse; the adrenalin is robbing her of her agility. She breathes down into her belly and simultaneously tenses her muscles to steady her torso.

She thinks of the day that Lissek appointed her a member of the Department. He offered her time to consider. Not necessary, she accepted on the spot. Nevertheless, sleep evaded her that night. She kept thinking of her father's words. 'Lissek's men would die for him,' he'd once said. 'He only seeks out those who he thinks are prepared to do so.' Would she? After all, she didn't know him. Marlowe sensed what she needed and kept poking her with his nose until she cuddled her tomcat close to her. That soothed her as always.

Six years she was there.

She would have died for Lissek at any time.

Just like now.

Her pulse is now slow and controlled. Her strength is where her breath is, in the 'Hara', two finger widths below the navel, the body's energy centre.

More steps.

Very quiet jangling.

The chandelier. He must have brushed it with his head, that sometimes happens to Lissek too.

One point nine two metres tall.

Aaron carefully lays the revolver onto the chest. She feels for the bowl and takes out the smallest stone, lying right at the top, her favourite, round as a marble.

She rolls it over the wood floor.

The man immediately starts to move. When he's in the door, her hand shoots to where she imagines his neck to be. She catches him on the back of the head, but that will do. Aaron takes a horizontal leap, hangs onto the man and brings them both down. He groans. She rams her elbow into his solar plexus to cut off his air supply and completes the manoeuvre with a finger spear strike to his pancreas. He doesn't make a single sound; his body goes limp.

When he regains consciousness thirty seconds later, Aaron is sitting on top of him and has clamped his head between her crossed thighs. Not many men are granted this. It's unlikely that he's enjoying it. She cocks the revolver and places the barrel against his forehead.

'This is a Colt .357 Magnum,' she says in English. 'If I pull the trigger, all that'll be left of your skull is bone dust. Understood?'

The man mashes some syllables.

'Deutsch? Français? Russkiy? Español?'

The answer is a whimper.

'Then talk to Lissek.' She tenses her leg muscles and gives him fifteen seconds until he loses consciousness again. She hears the key being turned in the door. Aaron maintains the pressure, it might be Conny.

'What are you doing?' yells Lissek. 'That's Gunnar!'

Confused, she releases him.

He greedily gasps for air. Lissek kneels down next to him and talks to him in a soothing voice. Aaron knows what he is saying, although she doesn't understand the language: *Concentrate on your belly. Imagine it contains as much air as a large balloon. Let it flow out very slowly. You'll feel better soon.*

In the minutes that pass until Gunnar can sit up with Lissek's help, she whispers over and over: 'Tell him I'm sorry, I didn't mean to hurt him.'

'OK, OK,' Lissek mutters, 'he's got the message.'

Gunnar settles heavily onto the wooden chest. His voice is as thin as if Aaron was still strangling him.

'He tried to call me,' Lissek explains. 'But I forgot to charge up my mobile.'

Gunnar again. The words grate against his raw larynx.

'He should have announced his presence. It was stupid of him,' Lissek translates.

Relieved, she feels Gunnar's trembling hand squeezing hers. His next few sentences sound steadier.

But Lissek doesn't translate.

'What's the matter?' Aaron asks.

'The man is back in the village. He's sitting in the pub and says he wants to talk.'

'Who to?'

'You.'

'What does he look like?'

'Banker type.'

'We'll drive down,' Aaron announces.

'*I'll* drive down. You wait here.'

'No.'

Lissek is silent for a long time. 'Give me the revolver.'

★

He stops the jeep across from the pub. She's been there twice before, with Conny. It smelled of fried fish and real ale, and of a landlord who doesn't give two hoots about the smoking ban. Aaron moves to get out with Lissek.

He puts his hand on her arm.

'I'll take a look at him first,' he says.

Reluctantly she nods.

He leaves her alone. She lights a cigarette. 'Banker type,' Gunnar had said. That doesn't mean anything. If he'd seen Holm in his tailored suit with tie and dress handkerchief, he wouldn't have thought it possible that he had the artistry of a tightrope walker. But Aaron isn't worried about Lissek. Even though he's sixty-five, he's at his fighting weight. And with a loaded SIG Sauer he can get up to things that aren't found in any textbook.

Only now does she realize.

It's pitch black again. She is back in that deep underground cavern that she's been locked into for five years.

The car door is opened. 'Come on out,' says Lissek.

She does.

'Mr Nyström – Jenny Aaron.'

The man is anxious; his vocal cords are tight, they barely vibrate. 'I'm a solicitor in Gothenburg. At the end of December, a new client came to me. He told me that you would soon be visiting Mr Lissek on Fårö.'

'Who is this client?' Aaron asks.

She already knows the answer.

'Ludger Holm. He instructed me to give you this on 6 February, so today. Personally.'

A padded envelope is placed into her hand.

'What is it?'

'I don't know. Mr Holm sealed the envelope.'

Aaron hands it to Lissek.
He tears open the envelope, takes something out.
He doesn't say anything.
'Tell me.'
'A USB stick and a contact lens.'

5

The night ended shortly after four. Next to him, Sandra woke with a start to change and feed the screaming baby. Pavlik gently pushed her back onto the pillow, whispering: 'I'll take care of it.' By the time he'd slipped the carbon prosthetic over his stump and was lifting Jenny out of the cradle, his wife was already asleep again.

Years ago, with the twins, she'd always taken care of this. Sandra had known that he needed his sleep, and he'd been thankful to her for it. But with Jenny it doesn't bother Pavlik. Perhaps it's because he's grown old. In his business, being fifty means you're ancient.

While he warmed the milk in the kitchen and changed his daughter's nappy, he quietly sang: '*What remains of you and me at the end of time, what remains of our dreams? What remains when we fall like shooting stars, lonely and forsaken?*'

Pavlik wisely keeps his passion for schmaltzy pop songs to himself. If the lads in the Department knew, they would wind him up about it no end. He hadn't even let on to Sandra. But a few months ago she'd had a clear-out and found the CDs that he'd hidden at the back of the cupboard, to be listened to when he was alone. He made her promise him faithfully that she would keep it to herself, and between fits of giggles, she solemnly vowed to do so. Weeks later, Pavlik found a signed photo of Olivia Newton-John on his pillow. Sandra's face was all innocence. Tough guys suffer in silence.

'*Let me see you smile once more, far too soon I will be gone, let us pretend it's not forever.*'

Jenny listened happily and rewarded him with those enormous eyes that always render him defenceless. Sometimes Pavlik wonders what will happen when she's fifteen or sixteen. He already knows that she will wrap him round her little finger with ease.

As he went to throw away the old nappy, he saw that the bin was full to the brim. After Jenny had glugged down her milk he laid her back in the cradle and went to take the bin bag outside.

In among the rubbish was yesterday's newspaper.

Although almost a month has passed since several men hijacked a Berlin bus and took twenty-seven schoolchildren and two teachers hostage, police are still not issuing any information on the case. Rumours have now been leaked that the leader of the gang, who was killed during the incident, was a man named Ludger Holm. No further information regarding his identity is currently available. There is also speculation that the young woman who offered herself in exchange for the hostages was a policewoman working for the BKA.

He sucked in the dry, cold air. It was a starry night, no wind. White clouds of steam hovered over the towers of the Berlin-Lichterfelde power station. Pavlik fought against the urge to search the house for cigarettes. He had weaned himself off smoking in the clinic, and he'd sworn to stick with it this time.

He cautiously stretched his torso, felt the scar. A friendship can end in many ways. That one died a miserable death in the woods, leaving an emptiness that has screamed at him ever since. Now Pavlik knows what it's like to think of someone you once loved and feel nothing but contempt.

The knife had caught him slightly below the navel, but missed the aorta. There was no damage to his organs – the worst of it had been the loss of blood. Nevertheless, the doctors wanted to keep him in for a month. Pavlik would have gone crazy, so he discharged himself after two weeks.

When Aaron phoned them last night, he and Sandra already knew how the meeting with Professor Reimer had gone. Conny had rung earlier and told them all about it.

'What does that mean?' Sandra had asked tremulously. 'Will she be able to see again?'

'Not like she used to. If at all.'

Aaron didn't mention it with a single word and just said: 'I'll be landing in Tegel at half five. Will you pick me up?'

Twice she has saved his life. Years ago in a Paris bar and then four weeks ago, when he would have bled to death without her. He didn't thank her on either occasion. That would have been too corny. And that's how she had always approached it too; in that regard they were even. There are three siblings in their family. Aaron, Pavlik and death.

Now she's coming home.

He is standing in the airport and sees her. Her wheeled suitcase in one hand, the cane in the other, she feels her way to the exit, too proud to ask anyone for help. It has been five years since Holm's bullet cast her into a world that Pavlik cannot imagine. At the time he thought he'd never be able to look at her again, or even think of her, without remembering how he demolished his hotel room in Barcelona. He was wrong. If there's a way out of this hell, she will find it.

★

Aaron senses people shifting away from her like metal filings from a magnet with reversed polarity. She hears the rattle of a display board; laughter; a child squeaking 'Mama!'; the announcement 'Mr Reeves, please contact the information desk.' When she stops, a suitcase rams into her heels. She ignores the blurted out 'sorry' and feels a hand on her arm.

Ten things that make Aaron happy:
    arriving in Berlin
    listening to sparrows
    Sandra's laugh
    standing on high mountains
    sleeping without pills
    apple cake
    having memories
    thinking of Marlowe
    being needed
    hugging Pavlik

They don't talk on the way to the car park. Nobody does silence as well as Pavlik. His silences don't emanate loneliness or distance, it's just that he is completely within himself. Aaron pictures his face, the face she last saw five years ago. The ash-blond hair that is permanently tousled, the quiet gaze, the furrows you only see when Pavlik is tired; the dimples when he laughs.

Everything about this face is warm. But not always. Many have come to know that, not all of them have survived it.

They get into the car. The light comes on. Goes out again. In the aeroplane, she had agonized for an hour, until she'd finally switched on the reading light above her head.

The brightness had increased.

Brightness.

Now Aaron has to resist the temptation to open and close the door again, just to savour the light.

'Thank you,' she says.

'What for?'

'You know.'

'You're welcome. When do you start with the therapy?'

'Ask me something easier.'

'I thought—'

'Holm has bequeathed something to me,' she explains.

Pavlik's breathing quickens.

'Drive to the Department, then you'll understand.'

He heads for the urban motorway. They're in his private car. The rear left wheel bearing is complaining, she heard the same sound four weeks ago. But something is different.

The smell.

'You've stopped smoking,' she says.

'Yep.'

'I've never tried.'

'Be glad.'

Nothing more is said for the rest of the journey. When they've come to a halt in the underground car park of Budapester Strasse he breaks the silence: 'Where are you staying?'

'At yours, I thought. But I can also—'

'Sandra has made your room ready for you.'

'Then why do you ask?'

'Never mind.'

The Department takes up four floors of the high-rise building. *Institute for Social Analysis* the information board declares. The lift has been used by somebody who forgot to brush the polish off their shoes. The only thing Aaron can't smell is the colour.

They get out on the second floor. Pavlik enters the code that provides entry into the high security zone. In the hallway she runs her hand along the wall, until it touches the roll of honour for those killed. Her index finger wanders to the last few names.

Blaschke, Clausen and Butz's names have already been engraved.

And André.

Sauntering steps. The King of Comedy.

'Hi, beautiful,' says Fricke.

'Hi.'

'Have you heard this one?' he asks. 'Two blind tramps are sitting on a park bench. One of them sneezes. The other says: "Cool! I'll open meself a can too."'

'My sides are splitting.'

You can always rely on Fricke's humour. During a hostage situation, a gunfight, at funerals. But she has also seen him coolly beating a man thirty kilos heavier than him to mush while making a phone call.

'Are you staying or just passing through?'

'Don't know yet,' she says.

'Hop on for the ride. I've missed your butt.'

'Look at Pavlik's.'

'He doesn't wiggle his as nicely.'

'You've never asked me to,' complains Pavlik.

'Is Demirci here?' Aaron asks.

Fricke stretches the words out like chewing gum, makes them into a bubble and lets it pop. 'Svoboda is with her.'

As she enters Demirci's anteroom, Astrid Helm shoots out from behind the desk. 'Jenny, goodness, this late already. I wanted to get you something from the Chinese.'

'That's kind of you, Helmchen. A coffee will do.'

'*Pronto!*'

Of all the reasons to return to the Department, she would be one of the best.

'How long has Svoboda been in there?' Pavlik asks.

'Forty-four minutes.'

Helmchen has been the director's secretary for as long as the Department has existed. She defended Lissek like a lioness defends her cubs, and now she does the same with Demirci. Aaron imagines how she greeted Svoboda, politely, but with that sharp look under which many a person has withered.

'A double espresso, please,' she says to Helmchen.

Despite the grinder, Aaron hears Demirci's door. 'Ah, the lady who holidays,' comes the nasal twang of Berlin's Senator of the Interior, who permanently sounds as if he's suffering from sinusitis.

Svoboda supervises the Department. He's a heartless careerist with an ironed crease in his pocket handkerchief. He's never had to rise up through the pain.

'May I enquire after your health?' he asks.

'I'm still alive.' *And you would have let me perish.*

'Four men were not so fortunate.'

'Nice speech at the funeral service. Well plagiarised.'

'Arrogance isn't a virtue, Ms Aaron.'

'I must write that in my friendship book.'

'We'll be seeing each other.'

'Sometimes being blind is a blessing.'

Svoboda sweeps past her so quickly she can feel the draught. When he slams the door shut, Helmchen chuckles. 'I wouldn't have missed that for the world.'

'Ms Aaron, I'm delighted,' says Inan Demirci.

She likes that voice. It is warm and sincere and there is something steadfast about it; it's like a firm embrace. But Aaron knows that the same voice can instantly turn cold and cutting. More than that: merciless.

She has never actually seen Demirci. She is forty-seven, one year older than Sandra. Pavlik has told her she is attractive, a red-haired vixen with eyes that can laugh. Aaron imagines her to be a woman who hides her steeliness behind elegance.

The espresso cup is placed in her hand.

'Helmchen, no interruptions please,' says Demirci.

She knows the number of steps to the conference table. Again, Aaron catches the whiff of shoe polish. Svoboda's brogues always shone like mirrors, she remembers. He must have been in a hurry this morning.

'How was your little chat?' asks Pavlik when they've sat down.

'There can be no dialogue between a mosquito and a flat hand,' replies Demirci.

'He said that?'

'And a few less pleasant things.'

'Let me guess: Svoboda isn't the mosquito.'

'Four weeks ago there were thirteen dead. And still the media is piling shit onto him.'

'Passes him by like a soft summer breeze,' Pavlik comments.

'Sometimes I wish I had that talent.' Demirci turns to Aaron. 'How are you?'

'Something has happened,' Aaron informs her. She plugs the USB stick into her phone and plays back the recording.

Holm's voice sounds controlled, indifferent, like it always was. 'When you hear this, I'll be dead. You showed me what pain is and I named the price for it. Now I have a surprise for you. No doubt you remember that I spoke of a numbered account. I told you that I would sooner chop off my right hand than withdraw a single cent from it. The account is with the Banque Sayed du Maroc in Marrakech. This stick contains the access data. You're to appear there personally, under the name of Judith Traherne. The contact lens enclosed is a copy of my iris, that's how you will identify yourself as the account holder. Congratulations, Ms Aaron: you now own two billion dollars.'

Through the padded door, she hears Helmchen typing away. Somewhere in the building a radio is being played, two storeys up the floor of the gym bounces under the impact of heavy steps.

Holm knew that she would be staying with Lissek to mull things over. He also knew how much time to give her to recover. He thought of every detail.

Judith Traherne.

Aaron has googled the name. Twenty-seven thousand hits. Most of them relate to the black-and-white film *Dark Victory* from 1939. Bette Davis plays the young, rich heiress Judith Traherne, an irresponsible party girl and chain smoker. When she learns that she is terminally ill, she radically changes her way of life.

Holm's humour.

Pavlik is the first to recover his wits. 'I thought the account was in Riyadh?'

'These were his words.'

'He was in an extreme situation and was facing death,' Demirci points out. 'Perhaps he was confused.'

'No, he wasn't,' says Aaron. 'He transferred the two billion to Marrakech for a particular reason.'

Perhaps because he knew that I was once very happy there with Niko.

'This money belonged to Holm's mentor?' asks Demirci.

'Yes, who has been dead for eleven years. It stems from his criminal dealings. Holm spoke of other accounts that were never closed, but this is the only one we know of.'

'Not we, *you*.'

Aaron sits up. 'Meaning?'

'There's no proof whatsoever of its existence. You're the only one Holm has told about the account. We can neither close it nor freeze it. Legally, this isn't an inheritance, it's an endowment.'

'What does that mean?'

'It means that you're filthy rich.'

Aaron is speechless.

Pavlik rocks his chair back and forth. They sit and listen to the squeaking until he mutters: 'Our roof could do with retiling.'

More silence.

'In Japan there's a fable about a blind Buddhist monk called Hōichi,' says Aaron. 'He was lauded far and wide for his songs, which told the story of the ancient Taira clan. The clan had been wiped out in a battle long before. One night, a voice spoke into his ear. "Hōichi, you've been sent for by great nobles. Follow me." He found himself in a magnificent palace, where he sang in front of high-born men and women. They were so deeply moved that many of them cried. From that night on, Hōichi went to the palace every evening; he enjoyed it very much. But when his abbot secretly followed him one night, he saw the monk in a cemetery, with devilish fires blazing all around him. Hōichi was singing alone in front of the graves of the Taira, whose wicked ghosts had lured him there; he had never been to the palace.'

'You think Holm has set a trap for you?' Pavlik asks.

'That's what I'm going to find out. I have to go to Marrakech.'

'I'm coming with you,' he instantly says.

Aaron had hoped for this.

'No, you won't,' Demirci drily states.

'Pardon?'

'Unless Ms Aaron rejoins the Department. As far as I'm aware, extreme wealth is no impediment to serving here.'

'Are you trying to blackmail me?' Aaron asks.

'No. You me?' Demirci retorts.

Aaron composes herself. 'It's not up to us alone to decide.'

'Who else?'

*

Whenever something has needed to be resolved that concerned everyone, the troop has always gathered in the weights room. Aaron loved it and hated it. She loved it when she went in there to train with a heavy heart and she'd work until she was so exhausted that only her muscles hurt. She hated it when no barbell, no matter how heavy it was, could fight off the weight she'd walked in with.

If Pavlik isn't on a mission, he comes here every morning at seven. For the next hour he's on his own, unless someone is feeling down about something. The weights room is Pavlik's therapy room. You poke your head through the door and if somebody is with him, you quietly close it again and hope for better luck the next day.

Aaron was here at seven more than once.

Pavlik's house stood open to her, it was a privilege of their friendship, but talking shop to him there seemed unfair towards the others; nor did she want to weigh down Sandra with such matters.

More often than not, it was enough just to sit next to him on a training bench with his arm around her shoulder. At times he also gave her advice. To go and watch a sad film and have a good cry. To buy herself something insanely unnecessary and ridiculously expensive. To hike up the Kreuzberg at dawn and look over the city.

Simple things.

Pavlik has called together everyone who's here. Twenty-eight men and two women. When Aaron enters the room with him, she hears voices that she knows.

'So, Black Beauty, had enough of lazing around?'

'Were you getting on Lissek's nerves?'

'Fricke knows a great blind man's joke.'

The others remain silent and wait.

Aaron hasn't had time to choose her words, yet each one of them feels right. 'For six years I was part of this gang. The first woman in the Department. I had to put up with a fair few remarks, until the testosterone surge levelled out.'

Someone chuckles. Giulia Delmonte.

'Only six of the old troop are still here. Five died during my time. Sometimes they come and chat to me, then the night is over. Six years is a lot, few have lasted longer. Still, I wouldn't have swapped it for anything in the world. When I woke up in the hospital in Barcelona, I thought about how I should do it. Tablets or window. But then I remembered that nobody in the Department has committed suicide yet, and I didn't want to be the first.'

'Not quite,' mumbles Dobeck. 'Schlüter blew his brains away one night.'

'He cleaned his shooter while he was plastered and overlooked the cartridge in the barrel,' Krupp corrects him. 'Doesn't count.'

'Just goes to show: keep off the booze.'

'As far as I know, it was Advocaat,' says Fricke.

Everyone laughs.

'Demirci wants me back, as you know. I used to be one of the big shots here. But now I'm blind.'

She almost inserts a 'still'.

Stop acting as though the therapy is a mere formality.

Stop longing for your old life.

Stop dreaming.

Aaron pulls herself together. 'It's possible that at some point someone's arse may depend on a decision I make. That's how the cookie crumbles. If that's a problem for anyone, say it. I don't want a disability bonus, and I never want to be asking myself whether people are talking behind my back, or whether someone isn't saying something because they think they have to wrap me up in cotton wool.'

Delmonte says: 'Gauder and me could do with a third woman. We'll meet for cappuccinos, gossip about fashion, celebs and lifestyle.'

'Yes let's,' laughs Gauder. 'A Tupperware party would be nice too, with cocktails.'

'Or bubbly! And after the third glass we'll agree that men are useless.'

'Ha ha!' replies a chorus of male voices.

'You wiped out Holm and his brother.' Unfamiliar voice. 'That says it all.'

'Well said, Kemper.' Another one she doesn't know. 'Pity you can't see me, Aaron. You'd instantly fall for me.'

'She could never get *that* drunk in all her life,' Fricke seizes the opportunity. 'Nickel, you have a face only a mother can love.'

Raucous laughter.

'So, Aaron, I've missed you,' mutters Peschel, whose quirk it is to start almost every sentence with 'so'. 'Especially your lousy potato salad.'

'Good against heat rash, though!' Büker calls out.

'We've been on five missions together,' says Nowak. 'You should have seen what went off that time we were in Rome with Keyes. I kinda like it when I have someone next to me who sees the bullet before the shot is fired. Any time, Aaron.'

How she has missed these cool scumbags.

Someone stands up. 'What is this – a group-hug session? I don't care how good she used to be. She can't see the bullets now.'

'Flemming, the woman has been through more than all the rest of us put together,' barks Nickel. 'Just shut your gob.'

'I say it how it is.'

'So do I. If you were blind, you'd be blubbing from morning till night. Do you get the impression that she's feeling sorry for herself? Think a moment. Great pastime, was invented some years ago.'

'Does anyone share Flemming's opinion?' Pavlik asks.

Silence.

'Some say that you're a little prick,' Fricke snarls at the man. 'But I know that deep down inside you' – pause for effect – 'there's a much, much bigger prick. That's causing you no end of stress. All you have to do is ask me nicely and I'll beat it out of you.'

Flemming replies through gritted teeth: 'We'll see each other at the next funeral.' He leaves, barging into Aaron on his way.

The door closes.

Pavlik utters the sentence with which all entrants have been welcomed into the Department for as long as it has existed: 'A ship in harbour is safe.'

And like everyone before her, Aaron replies: 'But that is not what ships are built for.'

Those from the old days hug her, whisper something friendly into her ear. The others shake her hand and tell her their name. When it's Nickel's turn, she holds his hand in a firm grip. Although she knows nothing about him, Aaron is so grateful to him that she can't get a single word out.

He mumbles sheepishly: 'I'm not a big talker.'

6

The cane bounces over ruptured joins between the stone tiles of the Department's corridor. Delicate cracks meander across the roll of honour for the dead, the lift button has a tiny bump.

All the places she thought she knew inside out now reveal things to her that she never noticed before.

Near her mother's grave, a large tree sways in the wind. Mice rustle. In spring she picks up the scent of magnolias, but only at night.

In aeroplanes there is always a faint smell of oil. The fuselage is colder below the window than above it. During take-off the plane vibrates more strongly than during landing.

Outside Sandra and Pavlik's terraced house in Lichterfelde there is an undulation in the asphalt. A distribution box hums. The kerbstone is rounded rather than square.

Aaron's heart is thumping loudly in her chest.

After losing her sight, she had banned her friend from her life for five years. Sandra had had no choice but to accept it. Four weeks ago they met again at Pavlik's birthday party, and it was as though nothing had ever happened. The next morning Aaron faced Holm. After that she hid herself away at Lissek's, again leaving Sandra no choice.

As the door opens, she anxiously wonders how her friend will be towards her. But Sandra breaks the ice with the very first sentence.

'Will you help me chop the onions?'

Perhaps that is the miracle of a true friendship. That it can bridge years as if they were seconds, and all the unsaid things suddenly seem unimportant. Aaron is conscious of this gift as she chats to Sandra in the kitchen and neither of them mention the therapy.

'Where are the twins?'

'Away in England, Brighton, been there three months already. They'll be finishing college next year. They're so tall I have to look up to them now.'

'And the little one?'

'Upstairs. She's sleeping thank goodness. She's been a right monkey since I weaned her.' She passes her the salad. 'Wash this, will you.'

Aaron feels her way to the sink.

Sandra asks: 'How's Lissek?'

'If he carries on sailing so close to the wind, he'll soon have to commission the *Unsinkable III*.'

They laugh.

And Aaron thinks: *I have no right.*

Pavlik is tinkering with his motorbike in the garage. Country music reverberates through the thin wall.

'I'll let you in on something,' Sandra whispers. 'But you have to promise not to tell anyone.'

'What?'

'He secretly listens to Eurovision song contest compilations.'

'Never!'

'I swear! I found his CDs. Nicole, Roland Kaiser, Nana Mouskouri, the full works.'

'New depths are being plumbed.'

'Deeper than you can fathom!'

And Aaron thinks: *I have no right.*

After the meal they sit at the full table, drink red wine, grappa, espresso, gossip about this and that. Her friends are fluctuating pixels in a grey fizz, as if Aaron was sitting close to a television that is set to the wrong frequency.

Still not a word about yesterday. There's so much that connects them, including the little things. She had completely forgotten how much happiness lies in the mundane.

She has the devil in her when she hums the melody of 'Marble Breaks and Iron Bends'.

'I knew it,' growls Pavlik. 'Woman, can't you keep anything to yourself at all?'

'Dum, dum – dum, dum,' Sandra joins in.

All of this feels so good.

And Aaron thinks: *I have no right.*

She hears a loud bawling. Baby monitor.

'Bang on time,' says Pavlik. He goes upstairs while Sandra warms up the milk. When he comes back with Jenny, he asks without much ado: 'Can you hold her a moment?'

Before she can even reply, a kicking, wailing warm bundle is lying in Aaron's arms. She barely dares to breathe, she's so scared she might do something wrong. But then a tiny little hand grabs her thumb and holds onto it tight, and everything is perfect. Suddenly Jenny goes quiet and pats at her nose.

Sandra touches Aaron's shoulder. 'She recognized her godmother straight away.'

Tears well in her eyes.

'We would have asked you of course,' says Pavlik. 'But that wasn't possible. You can always say no. It's quite a responsibility. If anything were to happen to both of us, you'd have to be there for her.'

'Of course,' is all that Aaron can manage.

For a minute they listen to the gurgling and cooing of the baby. A unit so tight it seems impenetrable.

I have no right.

Pavlik clears his throat: 'Who'd have thought that our daughter will have such a rich godmother.'

Sandra laughs.

'It's true. She's inherited unexpectedly.'

'Has she now. How much?'

'About two billion.'

Sandra laughs again. When the others remain silent, she realizes it isn't a joke. 'Holm?' she asks.

Aaron nods.

'Why?'

'Good question.'

'What are you going to do?'

'The account is in Marrakech. We're going to fly over there,' says Pavlik.

'When?'

'Tuesday.'

I have no right.

Nobody knows what they will find there. Ludger Holm is dead and Pavlik has settled all his scores. He has three children and a wife who would fall to pieces at his graveside.

Aaron will board the plane.

Without him.

Thoughts can speak louder than words. Aaron shivers because she knows that Sandra can see into her innermost being.

Her friend says: 'A long time ago, Ulf had to promise me three things. Never to lie to me. Never to walk out of the house or come home without a kiss. And never to abandon you. He's not going to break any of those promises, otherwise he wouldn't be the man I love.'

These are the big things.

7

Three important days in the life of Inan Demirci:
    When she was seven, her parents travelled to Turkey
with her for the first time. An uncle was getting married and
there was going to be a celebration in the Anatolian village that
her father had left as a young man. She remembers how she got
frightened on the dusty road, because men and women she'd
never seen before were tugging at her and pinching her. She
remembers that a dead goat was carried past and there was a
cloud in the sky that looked like a fist. That she burnt her mouth
on sweet milk and wondered why the bridegroom was standing
on the roof of the house, dropping apples down onto the bride.
That the village kids ogled her disparagingly and laughed at
her red patent-leather shoes and that she only understood every
other word. That she ran behind the house, where a boy with
protruding ears and buckteeth pushed her about. That she cried
because she didn't know what she had done to him. That an
aunt gave the boy a slap and cradled Inan on her lap and sang
a song that she still remembers today.

Another was the day her father left the house very early
to wash her mother's body. From above, Demirci saw how

her father suddenly crumpled on the pavement and the prayer beads dropped from his hand. She ran downstairs and led her father back into the apartment. His arm was so thin she could feel the bone. When she sat him down on an armchair and left, she knew he wouldn't get up until she came back.

Demirci asked the Imam to tell her how a body should be washed. She scribbled everything onto a slip of paper. In the end it was so densely packed she could barely read her writing.

Much had to be observed, and none of it was familiar to her.

She anointed her mother's forehead, palms and knees and still has the smell of musk and camphor in her nose. Sometimes she hears her voice, whispering and empty, as she reads the verse of the thirty-sixth surah from the slip:

'Indeed, it is we who bring the dead to life and record what they have put forth and what they left behind, and all things we have enumerated in a clear register.'

She felt ashamed then, because she hadn't enumerated anything, hadn't written anything down, ever. Friends and relatives and neighbours came and went. What they said was like smoke, by the evening she had already forgotten it all. She secretly slipped a tablet into her father's tea. He fell asleep without having spoken a single word that day. She took pen and paper and sat until sunrise, listing everything that her mother had been for her. She started with the sentence her mother had said to her when she decided to become a policewoman: 'But never forget where you come from.'

The third day was many years later again. Demirci had met her former classmates from Hiltrup College of Policing in a restaurant to celebrate the twentieth anniversary of their graduation. They seemed carefree, as if they were still the same as back then. But that wasn't the case.

It was already late when Lennard Palmer came and sat down next to her. He had been one of their lecturers at Hiltrup and he'd been invited because he had risen to the rank of BKA Commissioner and some of her peers wanted to fraternize with him. Demirci hadn't been among his favourite students, although her achievements had been exemplary. Of course it had occurred to her that Palmer was so distant towards her because of her background; it often happened to Demirci. But he had never hinted at anything; the reason may have been a different one altogether.

On that evening in the restaurant, he stiffly raised his glass to her and indicated a smile which his eyes contradicted. Congratulations, presumably she already knew, he'd said. Puzzled, she asked him what he was talking about. That's how she learnt that the Interior Ministers' Conference was going to appoint her as Lissek's successor. She remembers to this day what music was playing: Bruce Springsteen, 'Streets of Philadelphia'.

'I could hear the blood in my veins, it was just as black and whispering as the rain.'

That was her.

Palmer eyed her and said: 'There are quotas for everything.' He stood up and jovially went to mingle with others, where he still was when Demirci left without saying goodbye.

This is what she recalls as the three armoured limousines head towards the Treptower on the banks of the Spree. The high-rise building isn't situated on the actual BKA compound opposite, but it is home to the Berlin office of the BKA Commissioner, who shuttles between the capital and Wiesbaden. The five bodyguards who make up Demirci's personal security escort her into the foyer in diamond formation. She enters the external glass lift on her own. Silently it glides skywards above the river. Swans are perching on grey ice floes; a dusting of snow floats from the sky.

Upstairs are men with submachine guns. Their faces say: *We know what you're carrying under your suit jacket.* Demirci is waved past the body scanner, one of the few people permitted to approach Palmer with a loaded gun in her shoulder holster.

'Ms Demirci.'

'Commissioner.'

He indicates two leather seats and comes straight to the point. 'You've requested information from me about the Banque Sayed du Maroc. May I ask why?'

'We want to check up on an account. I'm keen to know whether the bank is involved in criminal activities.'

Palmer reaches over to the bowl on the table and laboriously selects a boiled sweet, which he tosses about in his mouth like a pinball, before he says: 'According to an evaluation made three years ago, one quarter of the loans were bad loans, which couldn't be reclaimed because the debtors were linked to terrorism and organized crime.'

'Which source?'

'One of the fund managers confided in the CIA station chief. He was prepared to provide a legally valid statement on the condition that he would be included in a witness protection programme. It never came to that – he was shot dead in his house. The Americans had the bank investigated by the Financial Action Task Force. Among other things, they found connections to Abu Sayyaf and the Russian Mafia.'

'And then?'

'The Moroccan government didn't fancy picking a quarrel with the FATF; that would have impacted on aid payments. The loans were written off and the management was replaced. The bank hasn't attracted any further attention since then.'

'Do you have a man in Morocco?'

'In Rabat, in the embassy.'

Which she knew of course. She was just following procedure.

'Two of my people are flying to Marrakech tomorrow. I need logistical support.'

'In what way?'

'Weapons, equipment, a vehicle.'

'Which prosecutor's office?'

'None.'

Palmer runs his hand over a flawless crease, tugs on the handkerchief in his breast pocket, crunches up the sweet.

Demirci expected this reaction. In the grey zone outside the official channels it's a case of give and take, and in that respect she is currently in debit. Palmer recently helped her out in Mexico and India. She needs to return the favour.

She decides to lay something big on the table.

'Your liaison officer in Islamabad is suspected of selling internal information from Western intelligence services to Pakistan's secret service and the Taliban,' she says. 'I've been asked to send a team.'

Palmer tenses his jaw. 'Why haven't I been informed of this?'

'I have no idea, but it came from the Chancellery. It seems to me, you don't only have friends there.'

Palmer is ashen-faced. Demirci knows what's going on inside him right now. One of his people is being investigated behind his back. There could be packing cases standing in this office very soon.

'Will you help me in Morocco?' she asks.

He stares into empty space, nods mechanically.

'Thank you. My logistician will sort out the details with Rabat.'

He nods again, without actually listening.

'I'd also like to discuss a personnel decision. It's about Jenny Aaron.'

'Yes?'

'I'm recalling her to the Department. I'm very keen for this to go through without delay.'

He turns his gaze to her. 'You want to take away my best woman and you just announce it as a done deal?'

'I'm sorry, Ms Aaron has already agreed.'

Palmer straightens up. 'One day it will be your turn to wonder whether your key will still fit the lock when you arrive for work in the morning. I don't wish it upon you. No matter how many times you think of it, it still comes out of the blue.'

'We are but temporary guardians of power.'

'Don't debase yourself with platitudes.'

Demirci has a caustic reply on the tip of her tongue. But she swallows it, stands up and stretches her hand out to Palmer.

He doesn't take it. 'You think I don't like you. You think that I didn't acknowledge your achievements in Hiltrup. And you've never forgiven me for what I said to you at the anniversary get-together.'

'Are you surprised?' she asks coldly.

'My comment was wrong and stupid, I apologize for it. And the fact that I've always been rather reserved towards you has nothing to do with your Turkish heritage. At least not in the way that you think it has. You were an outstanding student, it was clear that you would go on to do exceptional things. But you want to prove something to yourself and the world. We both know what it is. Eventually it will crush you, because no matter what you achieve, you will never be rid of the fear that it isn't enough.'

Demirci looks out of the window. A coal freighter is pitching through the ice floes. Swans take flight. Waves slap against the enormous steel sculpture on the river.

'It's called *Molecule Man*,' says Palmer.

Demirci remains silent.

'The sculpture. A man made up of molecules.'

Her head shoots round. 'What on earth makes you think you have the right?'

'I haven't been this honest in a long time. It feels good. You should try it sometime.'

She walks to the door.

'Lissek left big shoes to fill,' she hears Palmer say behind her. 'I know what I'm talking about, Richard Wolf was my predecessor. It isn't easy to succeed a legend – especially when you inherit their foes.'

Demirci stops and turns round.

'Svoboda is giving you a hard time,' he continues. 'In case you think it's personal: it isn't. There are some who claim that he wants to abolish the Department. Personally, I doubt that. He wants to *own* it. And that would be dangerous.'

The tone of Palmer's voice makes her shiver.

'Last year, I investigated Svoboda.'

A chill comes over her. 'Why?'

'Some of my agents were following a Croatian who specializes in corruption services for the Mafia. The Croatian was in talks with the manager of an arms manufacturer in Munich, probably with the aim of smuggling automatic rifles for Iran past the Federal Security Council. The following day he flew to Bremen. There he met Svoboda in a restaurant. Unfortunately we had no way of listening in to their conversation. But it was interesting that Svoboda had turned up without bodyguards. He normally uses every opportunity to surround himself with his super-commando; he places great importance on security level 1. Yet when he went to Bremen, he went alone.'

'Did you arrest the Croatian?'

'We assumed they were just at the initial contact-making stage, so we let him leave the country. It was a mistake. As far as we know, he has never returned to Germany.'

'And Svoboda?'

'I had to be careful. You know that my predecessor brought down a Federal Minister of the Interior and paid for it with his job. I only kept a very select few in the loop. We took a close look at Svoboda. We checked his travel expenses, account movements, tapped his phone.'

'Without a court order?'

'And this I'm asked by the head of the Department?' he says sardonically.

'Did you find anything?'

'Nothing out of the ordinary. For three months. Then Svoboda flew to Croatia for a weekend. Again without bodyguards.'

She steadies her voice. 'With company?'

'I was already skating on very thin ice, I didn't want to fall through. Sending investigators abroad without a prosecutor's backing would have meant crossing the Rubicon. I'll leave such operations up to you.'

'So that was it?'

'Yes.'

'Why are you sharing this with me?'

'Divide and rule.'

'Don't debase yourself with platitudes.'

'As yet I remain in office. I chair the commission that prepares the resolutions for the Interior Ministers' Conference. Keep me posted about Pakistan, and I'll inform you of Svoboda's activities against you.'

Demirci tries to read Palmer's expression. It's a tempting offer. But what if there's an entirely different reason for his interest in their operation in Islamabad?

Was it a mistake to tell him about it?

How much does he really know?

He smiles bitterly. 'I don't blame you for being suspicious; too much honesty can come across as a lie. You said that the Chancellery is involved. The Intelligence Service coordinator is a protégé of Svoboda's. Did you know that? I wouldn't be surprised if your people in Islamabad find evidence that I am covering up or even involved in these supposed dealings of my liaison officer.'

'You think that Svoboda has found out about your investigations against him? That Islamabad is a plot to bring you down?'

'Is that so far-fetched?'

No.

'Do we have an agreement?'

You never know until afterwards whether a deal was fair.

She nods.

'I don't want any details on Morocco,' Palmer says. 'That's how I did it with Lissek too. But I never looked away. Your men follow a code. You think you know it. But do you really?'

'What are you trying to say?'

It suddenly grows dark outside. Ice rain drums against the windows. 'Does the name Bas Makata mean anything to you?' he asks.

'The butcher of Kinshasa?'

'About eight years ago, Lissek found out that Makata was coming to Avignon. Informing the French wasn't an option. Makata had traded arms with them, they would have warned him. So Lissek dealt with it his own way. He sent a set over there to kidnap Makata and bring him back to Germany; the Federal Public Prosecutor would then be able to transfer him to The Hague. But they came back without Makata. Lissek said he'd given them the slip.'

Demirci has a rising sense of unease. 'Why do you doubt it?'

'His men were in Avignon. And Makata was there, with his wife and their young daughter. None of them has ever been seen again since that day. You may draw your own conclusions.'

'Are you accusing Lissek of carrying out a murder mission? Are you saying that the commando liquidated Makata, his wife and the child?' she asks blankly.

'I am merely stating the facts. By the way, it was Ulf Pavlik who led the operation at the time. It's important to know who your right-hand man is.'

★

When she leaves Palmer's office, Demirci finds herself in a parallel universe. A universe in which there are people like Pavlik, Aaron and herself, and yet each of them is somebody else. This other Demirci encounters the other Pavlik in the corridor of the Department and says: 'We're sticking with tomorrow.' This Demirci is so shattered that she sits motionless in her office for half an hour, before she manages to press the button on the intercom and ask Helmchen to bring her the Makata file. This Demirci finds the half-full pack of Marlboros in the bottom desk drawer. This Demirci recalls what she'd heard about the Department long before she was appointed. *That's a godless brigade.* She recalls stories she didn't want to believe. This Demirci stares at the file for an eternity, before she finally opens it.

This Demirci reads: *Operation terminated.*

She checks who was there: Pavlik, Fricke, Butz, Lutter.

Aaron.

Ten times she picks up the receiver, puts it back down again. When she drives home in the evening, the Marlboro pack is empty and Demirci is awake until dawn. She looks at the clock and knows that the plane will take off in two hours.

8

Anyone in the check-in queue at Tegel airport who happens to be listening to the conversation between Mr and Mrs Traherne from Boston, Massachusetts, learns that they have had a wonderful week in Berlin. They visited an old friend who works at the American Academy, enjoyed delicious food, went to see the musical *Dance of the Vampires* at the Theater des Westens and the exhibition *From Hockney to Holbein* in the Martin Gropius Building. Actually, Mr Traherne was there without his wife, as she is blind. She used the time to write a long e-mail to her favourite cousin, who moved to Marrakech the year before last to work as a tourism manager and who replied that she is really looking forward to spending a few days with them.

'Did I say that Helen sends her regards?' *Have we thought of everything?*

'Three times, honey.' *Stop fretting.*

'And if we decide to stay a little longer?' *Will the BKA bail us out?*

'But without your cousin.' *No, we're on our own.*

All this in the best East Coast American accent, she a little excited because she is flying to an Arabic country for the first time ('Am I allowed to smoke there?'), he a self-assured businessman, travels worldwide.

At the same time they're wondering: who is Jean-Luc Nouvel?

When Pavlik had the passenger list checked again just over an hour ago, he was told that Nouvel was the only person to have booked a seat on the flight after them. Pavlik wants to take a look at him. He has instructed Grauder to ring the airline under the pretence of being Nouvel's sister and to have him called out at half-past eight in relation to an urgent family matter.

They hear an announcement: 'Monsieur Nouvel, réservé sur AT 3387 à Marrakech, s'il vous plaît venez à notre tour.'

There is movement in the queue as someone elbows their way to the back. A travel bag brushes against Aaron's wrist. Garlic breath, cheap aftershave, heavy breathing.

'Do you remember – our neighbour in Bay Village?' Pavlik murmurs to her. 'He's the spitting image of him.'

'Which one?'

'You know, Mr Big Baby. Two hundred and fifty pounds, with the lobster-coloured face.'

We can forget about Monsieur Nouvel.

Although they remain strictly within their cover roles and maintain the casual tone of travellers, Aaron senses how shut off Pavlik is. Even at breakfast, he chewed on every word like it was a leathery lump, and on the drive to the airport he didn't say anything at all.

He too has been in Marrakech before. Aaron had only been at the Department for a week when Pavlik returned from the mission without his partner. That was the day she saw him for the first time. His skin was like parchment and his shoulders hung heavy. He called everyone into the weights room. Aaron didn't go. It didn't seem appropriate, she hadn't known the dead colleague. Later she heard that he was called Mohr and that the others called him Sarotti. She never found out what happened in Marrakech.

Today, she thought at first that Pavlik's silence was due to his recollection of the mission. But without being able to explain why, she senses that there's a different reason. It's clear he doesn't want to talk about it, otherwise he would have done so in the car. She will wait until he wants to share it with her; that's how they do it.

The US passports are fresh from the Federal Printing Office and impeccable. They take their seats in the business class of the Royal Air Maroc flight, which differs from the economy class only in so far as the seats are in rows of two rather than three.

Immediately after take-off, Aaron turns towards the window and greedily waits for the moment in which they break through the cloud cover. After some minutes she imagines the first fuzzy shrouds spinning around the fuselage, an ever denser web, until they are surrounded by an impenetrable fog.

Then it happens.

It's no more than a pale haze that settles across her eyes, but she pictures the light streaming through the aeroplane, a blazing wave, so glaring it almost hurts.

She sits motionless for a long time, her hand against the cold window, her eyes wide open, lost in a world of images that glide by like dreams. Aaron believes she can make out the inky blue of the sky, in the distance a streak, the vapour trail of another jet, below her clouds that are so downy she wants to leap down and rest on them awhile. Snug and still.

As she leans back in her seat she hears Pavlik's deep, steady breathing. He can sleep anywhere, regardless of ambient noise; something she has always envied him for. The seat belt signs go out with a 'pling'. Pavlik just grunts. But Aaron knows that the slightest noise that doesn't belong here would have him wide awake in an instant.

She closes her eyes without any hope of finding sleep. Last night even the tablet didn't work. Aaron rolled about in bed, thoughts tangled in her head as if they were plastered together with glue.

Congratulations, you now own two billion dollars. I know blind people who knit. There can be no dialogue between a mosquito and a flat hand. We call that blindsight. That's how it's laid out in the procedural rules. We can neither close nor freeze the account. Especially your lousy potato salad. The contact lens is a copy of my iris. You have to be ready for it. Be ready for it. Be ready for it.

Eventually she gave up the battle, got dressed and went out onto the terrace to smoke. She felt Holm's presence.

He had torn Aaron's heart out, just like she had torn out his. Yet he was denied his revenge. She should hate Niko, the man she once loved. The man who betrayed her. But as strange as it was, she hadn't thought about him once during the past weeks. He was no more important to her than somebody she had asked for a light on the ferry to Gotland.

But what if that wasn't Holm's revenge at all?

What awaited her in Marrakech?

Icy sleet barrelled through the darkness and scuffed her face, a miserable east wind had her shivering. Aaron's feet were freezing cold, even though she was wearing lined boots. Just like her hands, despite the gloves. It's been like that since last summer. That was also when she realized she barely ever felt thirsty, she had to force herself to drink. She is acutely aware of every change in the weather, which always brings on a severe headache. She has long been used to her exceptional sense of smell, but now it is torturous. One of the men in the weights room had eaten something with onions, perhaps a kebab. He was standing several metres away from her; in the past even she wouldn't have registered it. Now the smell was so unpleasant that it made her feel sick.

And there was something else that preoccupied her.

Many years ago, she had started to use meditation to raise her pain barrier, like the samurai used to do before battles.

In front of you, there are eleven envelopes. Each one contains a photograph. You open the eleventh and see a woman standing quietly in the cold rain. That is indifference. Take your time, memorize the photograph.

You open the tenth and see a magazine with just one cartridge left. That is adrenalin. You open the ninth and see friends laughing together. That is being almost happy. You open the eighth and see a '64 Ford Mustang. That is pride. You open the seventh and see a small girl looking for presents in the wardrobe. That is impatience.

Take your time.

You open the sixth and see a mother grieving for her dead child. That is compassion. You open the fifth and see neo-Nazis parading. That is contempt. You open the fourth and see a samurai sword made by Sengo Muramasa. That is perfect control.

Put the third envelope aside.

You open the second and see your father. That is gratitude. You open the first and see the beautiful hand of a man. That is lust.

And take your time, take your time, take your time.

Now only the third envelope remains. You know what is in it. But first look at the woman in the rain once more. Be aware that you can look at the photograph whenever you want.

Feel the rain. Once you have accepted that it's only natural to get wet in the rain, you can get soaked to the skin with a dispassionate mind. This lesson applies to everything.

Only now do you open the third envelope. You see the pain. And you're completely indifferent to it.

She has lost this gift.

Before she faced Holm a month ago, she had fully concentrated on the meditation. Yet in the fifteen hours that she had been at his mercy, he had been able to inflict so much pain on her that she thought she would die.

Cold hands and feet. No thirst. Weather sensitivity. Extreme sense of smell. Increased perception of pain.

She had searched the internet for information on these symptoms. It turned out it was highly probable that she was addicted to Crystal Meth.

Very funny.

Aaron suspects that it is some kind of disorder. She should have told Reimer about it, but she was so jumbled up at the time.

Was?

Your network wants to repair itself.

That's her mantra.

She comes to with a start when Pavlik wakes up minutes before the stopover in Casablanca and gives her a prod. On the gangway, the wind plays chase with her hair. It is warm. She enjoys the light and wishes she could see palm trees.

In the endless tunnel of the transit area she thinks of the time she came through here with Niko. His hand that felt so perfect resting on her hip, the weightlessness of every moment. They had suddenly started to run, as if that could get them to Marrakech any faster. To the riad with the pheasant fountain, the wonky squeaking bed, the breathless whirl of that one week.

Aaron's heart convulses because she realizes that she deceived herself. She hasn't got over Niko yet. She will never forget how happy she was with him, and how it all ended.

A sob rises in her. Pavlik removes her hand from his elbow, lays his on her hip like Niko did, shows her that he's there. Still it takes a thousand stumbling steps before they reach the bench in the transfer hall and she can think straight again.

They have a one-hour stopover. Pavlik strolls about. Aaron knows that he is checking out the passengers who are joining them in Casablanca for the Marrakech flight. With his sniper's memory, it's easy for him to filter them out.

She uses the time to build a sensory map of the hall and store it in her mind. Even years later, she recognizes places she has been to before by their individual sound and smell profiles.

Pavlik sits down beside her.

'Is the plane going to be full?' she asks. *Are we getting company?*

'Yes. I should have reserved a seat by the emergency exit for my long legs.' *Looks like it.*

'Perhaps you still can.' *How many?*

'But I want to sit next to you.' *Two.*

'Is the plane already here?' *What do they look like?*

'Yes, Air Maroc.' *Arabs.*

'Big?' *Weapons?*

'Turboprop.' *Holster.*

She is just wondering how they could have got the guns through security when someone barks out an Arabic command. A woman screams, bodies dart aside. Aaron gets a visit from her old friend, adrenalin. But Pavlik taps her knee and signals for her to stay calm. Suitcases tumble onto the stone floor, a bottle smashes, a whirl of voices, punches, another command, a drawn-out, muffled whimper, then several seconds of silence before a hundred people whisper like in a museum.

'You won't believe this, honey,' Pavlik murmurs, 'the Moroccan police have arrested a man. The way they laid into him, he must have done something quite bad.'

She says goodbye to her old friend. But he wants to stay a little longer.

The boarding desk opens on time. They walk to the plane, Aaron with her arm tucked into Pavlik's, feeling ruffled.

'Steps,' he says.

She puts her hand on the railing of the gangway.

Suddenly she stops.

Matteo Varga is standing by the entrance at the top. Aaron sees him as clearly as if he were real. Wide, bulky, fear inspiring.

He throws something towards her that lands directly in front of her feet.

A lily.

Then he lumbers down the stairs. Pavlik is so far ahead that she doesn't understand what he is saying. Somebody touches her shoulder. She only has eyes for Varga. There is a fresh scar on his cheek, a fiery red gash like from a knife.

He takes off his sunglasses. In his eyes Aaron reads the certainty that Marrakech will be her grave.

'Excusez-moi, Madame,' a voice reaches her.

'What is it?' asks Pavlik.

She sets herself in motion and ascends the gangway.

At the top she turns round once more.

All she sees is milky white with grey streaks.

The air conditioning is broken, the padding on the seats is so worn through that Aaron can feel bare metal under her bum. During take-off the seat judders like a jack-hammer. Pavlik draws her head onto his shoulder and breathes so calmly that her pulse gradually falls in line with his. Throughout the flight to Marrakech she thinks of Varga, his eyes, a warning not to get into the plane. She tells herself that it was just a hallucination.

Your brain is drawing images from your memory.

But why Varga? Why his son?

What did she overlook ten years ago?

Aaron sets her watch to Moroccan time, one hour back. They wait until everyone has got out before they leave the plane. The air outside feels like a cushion that is being pushed on her face. There's a smell of burnt rubber, kerosene and palm oil. Suitcases rumble along a conveyor belt, a bus engine gives an exhausted varoom. Aaron is bathed in sweat before she even sets foot on the tarmac.

Ten moments in which Aaron wanted to be somewhere else:
  during her first wet kiss
  when she put her hand on Boenisch's cold television
  that one wrong word to Sandra
  at the pond with the hole in the ice
  when Fricke asked: 'Can you hear that ticking?'
  that night on the quay in Mombasa
  after her oral maths exam
  during all funerals
  every second in Barcelona
  now

9

At the Hertz counter they are told that they're lucky, there is just one last hire car available. When the paperwork has been dealt with, a fellow employee comes running and informs his colleague in French that the Peugeot is reserved. And? The customer concerned is two hours overdue, the other replies with a shrug. After much palaver between the two, now in Arabic, they are given the keys.

On the way to the car Aaron wonders whether the BKA liaison officer has bugged it. It would have been easy enough. A little pocket money for one of the guys at Hertz, who simply had to make sure the right car was handed out. All it takes is an inconspicuous bug, and the liaison officer is all ears.

She says: 'Palmer must be curious about why we're here.'

'Well, you heard, the car was reserved for somebody else.'

'Smokescreen.'

'Sometimes one can think a little too far outside the box.'

'It's February, hardly the holiday season,' she retorts. 'And there's just one hire car left?'

'Marrakech is a conference city.'

'You booked four hotels for us – without a problem.'

'Just crash pads in the medina. The conferences take place in the Palmeraie.'

She gives up. 'What do you think Demirci told Palmer?'

'The bare necessities.'

'How does she get on with him?'

'The Department functions according to laws he doesn't understand. We give him the creeps.'

Aaron recalls the evening two years ago, when Palmer invited her to his home following her application to join the BKA. She had felt flattered. He'd sent a limousine to pick her up and take her to Wiesbaden-Bierstadt, to his villa that looked like a fortress. They drank spectacular red wine behind twelve-centimetre armoured glass. Palmer said presumably she knew that her possible appointment collided with the service law. As a policewoman she had to be physically able, which wasn't the case with a blind person. She was about to reply that she'd be happy to have that put to the test, but he continued. He owed much to her father, he said. Not only had Jörg Aaron provided the BKA with the firing power of his elite tactical unit, he had also personally taken command of the GSG 9 deployments and always taken any political flak if an operation had failed; her father had never ducked away from challenging situations.

Aaron fought against her disappointment.

Palmer saw it. 'The service law can be sidestepped with an exemption clause. I'm not interested in your name. My people are impressed by you, that's the reason you're being given the job.'

She had rarely felt so relieved.

When Palmer said goodbye to her at the door, Aaron knew that he was studying her. 'You were at the Department for six years.'

'Yes.'

'Why do you all address each other by surname only?'

'Because we hope that it'll make it easier at the funerals.'

'Does it?'

'Not for me.'

Palmer was silent for a moment. 'Some of what you learnt under Lissek you'll have to forget. Anyone who doesn't respect the law has no future with me. Am I making myself clear?'

'Of course, Commissioner.'

Pavlik's elbow steers Aaron to the left, and she is back in the car park at Marrakech airport.

'Palmer hasn't paid us a single visit since Demirci took on the Department,' he says. 'A little while ago, I was in Treptow with her because of a terrorist threat. Palmer came in. The two of them greeted each other as if they had randomly been introduced a long time ago.'

'Pissing match?'

Pavlik laughs. 'I don't imagine she can get very far.'

'You should see how far I can get.'

'No thanks.'

'She wasn't there at the final meeting. Didn't that surprise you too?' she asks.

'Hmm.'

'Meaning?'

'Not now.'

So the thoughts that Pavlik is hiding from her relate to Demirci. What can it be? She will have to be patient. How many times has she wished that this was one of her virtues?

The car smells brand new. She opens the window, wants to feel the city. They talk about trivialities for the next ten minutes or so. Pavlik may think she is being overcautious, but he isn't taking any risks either. She knows that he is continuously checking the rear-view mirror. Three times he veers off the main road and takes side routes. The fact that he never varies the speed tells her that it's just routine.

Driving with him is always a pleasure. Despite his below-knee prosthetic, he changes gear so elegantly that it barely registers. His braking and acceleration are as smooth as velvet, everything is fluid. This has nothing to do with their current leisurely pace. It's no different during a pursuit or getaway.

They're on the avenue that she once drove along with Niko. Aaron pictures the eight lanes, fringed by date palms on both sides, behind them vast stretches of wasteland, the wind prowling across it. Weathered display boards showed picture book estates that were never going to be built.

The traffic grows dense. Mopeds narrowly clatter past them, at a traffic light a donkey complains about his heavy cart. Children's shouts ring out from somewhere, a football game perhaps.

Then she hears it again.

At the airport, Aaron had noticed a Moto Guzzi with a distinctive sound. As soon as the driver decelerates, the exhaust rattles because the two-cylinder engine is drawing in air; a case for the workshop.

The motorbike overtakes and is gone.

Back again.

Very faint. It is keeping its distance.

Aaron touches Pavlik and discreetly points to the rear.

Neither of them speaks for a minute. Then he says: 'I hope the city will soon come into view.' *Don't know what you mean.*

She makes a scissor symbol with her index finger and middle finger. *Motorbike.*

Pavlik mutters: 'Looks like there's congestion up ahead, I'll try a different route.'

He turns right, left, right again.

The Guzzi stays with them.

Comes closer.

Pavlik draws a two on Aaron's jeans. *Two men.*

'It's no use,' he says and rejoins the main boulevard.

A little later they are on the Avenue Mohammed V, the city's shopping strip. Pavlik drives into a multi-storey car park.

Question: what will the Guzzi do?

If it continues to tail them, the men aren't from the BKA. It wouldn't make sense for the BKA to follow them in. The van that the liaison officer has provided for them is parked on the second level.

They circle upwards on the spiral ramp.

The Guzzi hums behind them.

Time to drop the pretence.

'Arabs?' she asks.

'Probably.'

'What do they look like?'

'Helmets. The driver is a gorilla, the other a terrier.'

'We can go into the shopping centre or settle it right now.'

'Settle it.'

He heads for the third level and parks the car. The Guzzi stops next to them, the biker cuts the engine too.

Aaron hears steps, someone is walking round the car.

'You've got the gorilla,' says Pavlik.

'Weapon?'

'Bowie knife. Right-handed.'

'Get out!' Pavlik's man orders in French.

They open the doors and get out.

Aaron's opponent is standing right in front of her. A black wall. Immediately, she pleads in a whiny voice: 'Please don't hurt us. Do you want money? Here, I have some.' She pretends to reach into her Prada bag and sees a shadow flit across as he moves to seize the bag. Aaron grabs his left wrist, shifts her full weight onto his arm and forces him to drop a curtsey. Her knee hits his crotch as if the two were connected by a taut rubber band. While he is so crazed by the pain that he can't even groan she hopes for a movement of the knife hand, but she can't detect anything. Aaron searches for it with lightning speed, only grazes it at first and then catches hold of it on the second attempt. She brutally twists the hand outward until his elbow tendon snaps with a bang, reminding him how to scream. By the time he drops the knife she has already rammed her foot against his kneecap with full force to break his balance. She hammers her heel into the bridge of his nose and sends him into the land of dreams.

Four seconds. It used to be three, but she can live with that. Aaron was so focused on her opponent that she didn't notice what went on between Pavlik and his man.

'My foot has gone to sleep,' he grumbles. Judging by his relaxed voice his pulse is still at its resting rate.

'Mine was bigger.'

'Yes, but mine was uglier.'

'They've been following us since the airport. What did they want from us?' she asks.

They briefly ponder.

'The car,' they both conclude at the same time.

Pavlik searches the car's interior and engine bay. Nothing.

He taps the bodywork, doors and wheel houses. Negative. Finally he opens the boot and takes out their luggage. He lifts up the cover for the spare wheel.

'And?' asks Aaron.

'Hang on.' Pavlik heaves the tyre onto the floor and slices it open with his knife.

'Well I never,' he mutters.

'Dope?'

'At least twenty kilos of shit.'

Aaron's man sighs. Using four fingers, she stimulates the gallbladder meridian behind his left ear and lets him have a few more minutes in wonderland.

Pavlik stows the luggage again. They leave the men lying where they are, get back in the Peugeot and drive down a level. The key for the van is under the sill. Pavlik opens the rear door, unzips the equipment bag and rummages around in it.

'Contact transmitter?' she asks.

'Check.'

'Bugs?'

'Check.'

'Transmission decoder?'

'Check.'

'Mics, earbuds, transmitters?'

'Check.'

'Rifle with sight?'

'Check.'

'Night vision goggles?'

'Check.'

'Spotting scope?'

'Check.'

'Binoculars?'

'Check.'

'Guns and reserve magazines?'

'Check.'

He thrusts a weapon into her hand.

Plastic grip, light as a feather; a Glock. Aaron sniffs the muzzle. A virgin, not a single shot has been fired from it. The bit of steel where the serial number should be embossed is roughened up. Filed off. Aaron slides the magazine into her hand, nineteen rounds. She pushes out a cartridge and fingers it. The lead core is exposed at the nose. Semi-jacketed, high stopping power. She tests the trigger, smooth, as befits a Glock, then slides the magazine back in. As she tucks the gun into the waistband under her blouse she asks: 'Yours?'

'Twins.' Pavlik hands her the luggage from the Peugeot; she throws both bags in the van. He unscrews something. Petrol fumes reach Aaron's nostrils. She hears the tyre with the drugs go up in flames.

An overpowering smell of citric acid hits her when she gets in the van. There is something else beneath it that she can't initially place, but then identifies as cough syrup. She winds down the recalcitrant window, runs her hand over the tatty seat pad. Both the front shock absorbers are bottoming out.

'We can talk,' she says.

'We can?'

'This banger is ancient,' she elaborates. 'The liaison officer must have bought it off some small-time crook, so it can't be traced back. But he still went through a whole bottle of disinfectant to wipe away its history. I reckon he's on edge; he knows we're not here to see the sights. If we get busted and the Moroccans find a bug in the van, they'll be onto the BKA in a flash. He won't want to take that risk. Plus: two virgins, filed-off serial numbers; I reckon Palmer has taken out travel insurance.'

'Makes sense,' Pavlik concedes.

'Nobody praises as euphorically as you. In any case, the liaison officer is bound to be tailing us.'

'What makes you so sure?'

'He's got a heavy cold, should be in bed,' she speculates. 'Palmer has hounded him into travelling from Rabat to Marrakech, it sucks. He says to himself: if I have to be here, coughing my lungs up, then I want to get something out of it at least. He'll probably try to draw up a movement chart on us; it'll look good at the next promotion.'

'You should become a profiler.'

'You should use your nose.'

For quarter of an hour, they wind their way through the medina, enveloped in a giant cloud of fumes, mixed with a hint of spices, sweet tea and sweat, overlaid with the chaos of building sites, engines, market criers, the clack-clack of horses' hoofs and the clanging from tinsmiths' workshops. Anywhere else, it would sound like a cacophony, but here it combines into a perfect symphony.

Aaron gets a headache, she closes the window. The reek of the disinfectant has almost vanished. 'How's the liaison officer getting on?'

'Red Seat. Falls back every now and then, is never on our lane. Evidently he's competent on the basics, which doesn't surprise me.'

'Do you know him?'

'No, but Morocco is a hot spot. He wouldn't have the job if he'd come last in the sack race.'

'Where are we?'

'At the Djemaa el Fna.'

She pictures the giant square, the throbbing heart of Marrakech, and remembers how Niko and she had to use hand signals to communicate in the pandemonium.

Pavlik takes two left turns.

Changes into the wrong gear.

Aaron's heart skips a beat. What's up with him?

But he carries on as if nothing had happened. Eventually he stops and mutters: 'Here it is.'

She knows that they are in the Rue des Berbères. Pavlik has studied satellite images of the bank. It's housed in an old building, turn of the century, smartly renovated, six storeys. From here it is fifty metres to the Djemaa el Fna, where the road ends.

'Two bored security guards at the entrance,' he says.

Aaron had called the bank yesterday and was instantly put through to the manager. It was clear from his eagerness that he knew the account balance down to the last cent. She had arranged her visit for today, 4 p.m.

'Bien sûr, I am entirely at your disposal.'

That would be in five minutes.

Aaron dials the direct number which the manager gave her.

He answers immediately. 'Badr Hamdaoui.'

'Judith Traherne. My flight was delayed. If it's convenient, I would like to come tomorrow at half-past nine.'

'Of course, as you wish.'

As she hangs up, the waiting begins. They want to know whether the bank is under surveillance, and whether Hamdaoui will pass on news of the postponement.

'I'm going to take a nap,' says Pavlik. 'Wake me up if there's any change.'

'Fuck, you're so hilarious.'

'I know.'

As they sit in the van, the minutes drip away like treacle. Somewhere a beggar is carping on, the sound of a sintir wafts over from the Djemaa el Fna.

Aaron lets her mind go blank.

Grains of sand travel with the wind – nobody knows where to.

On the summit of the mountain you can't see the summit.

What does the winter care about blooming flowers.

Car door. A vehicle pulls out, drives away.

SUV, petrol engine.

'Two women,' Pavlik informs her. 'Kiss, kiss.'

The sea moves without reason.

The sun sits wearily in the sky.

'That was it. Back in a moment.' He gets out. She hears him activate the central locking. Aaron reaches for the Glock.

Why did he mess up the gear change?

Pavlik crosses the road at a brisk pace. There is a driveway next to the bank. The stench of refuse containers drifts across from a yard, several top-of-the-range limousines are parked up. The leathery old man cleaning an Audi with a Hoover looks as though he could have had that job when the archangel Gabriel appeared before Muhammad.

A quick glance tells Pavlik that there's a security door by the rear entrance. He strolls over and knocks.

A guard opens. 'Excusez-moi, c'est privé.'

A folding chair in the hallway. Just one man.

'Pardon,' Pavlik replies. He walks along the quiet alleyway that winds its way from the yard into the souks. Looking at the satellite images, it hadn't been clear whether it's wide enough for a car.

It isn't.

As an escape route, only usable on foot.

Pavlik stops. He opens the top buttons of his trousers and pulls up his shirt. The scar hasn't torn open, that's the good news. The bad news is that it's been burning like hell ever since he took care of the dealer in the car park. It was no big thing, so it's easy to figure out what would happen if he came across a real opponent. Just a moment ago it was so bad he messed up a gear change. Aaron noticed it. He had been tempted to grumble about the gearbox, but she wouldn't have believed him.

Since she came back from Sweden she hasn't asked him once how his stomach is healing. That's how they are about injuries; they don't talk about them. Sandra knows. Still it would never have occurred to her to try to dissuade him from going to Marrakech. In her eyes, even at eighty per cent capacity he is still better than others. He wishes it were true. Just one per cent makes a world of difference.

He buttons his trousers back up. Gradually, it's calming down. He hadn't been able to train for a month. That's an eternity. The last time he'd had such a long break was when he lost his lower leg in the motorbike accident.

But he knows who he's got by his side.

He's a motorcyclist. She isn't.

She noticed the Guzzi. He didn't.

Yesterday evening, the door to Aaron's room was open a crack and he'd watched her do her exercises. Her balance had always been fascinatingly good. Now it is akin to that of an

Olympic gymnast. Pavlik would bet his last penny that she can master a stretched somersault on a balance beam.

In the car park he saw her from the corner of his eye. When she reached for the Arab's knife hand she slipped off, but instantly corrected herself and completed the procedure in textbook style.

It was the first time that Pavlik had seen her fight blind. The man weighed at least a hundred kilos. He had as little chance as a buffalo against a lioness, never mind the one-second delay.

If push comes to shove, it might be her that rescues him and not the other way round.

He goes back to the van. 'The road is our only option.'

Aaron tucks the Glock away. 'No surprise.'

'Which of the four doss houses shall we settle for?' he asks.

'None. I've booked us a suite at La Mamounia.'

'That's one of the most expensive hotels in the world.'

'I'm stinking rich, remember?'

'We must have another chat about my roof.'

10

Aaron loves the scent of luxury. Her salary is nothing spectacular, but she treats herself to nice things like the Prada bag, which was a bargain at Saks Fifth Avenue because it was from the previous season. She always sniffs at everything first, that's even more important than touching. The bag has a whiff of Blue Hour with cool jazz, the leather strap of her Cartier watch for blind people carries the scent of the jewellery shop in the Rue Balzac in Paris, which you enter as a queen and leave as a pauper, and her Montblanc fountain pen smells of the longing to use it again one day.

Although it's been twenty-eight years since Aaron stayed in La Mamounia, the lobby smells exactly the way she remembers. It smells of a giant in harem pants and a red tasselled cap, who is holding the world's biggest ice-cream cone in his hands and is bending down to a little girl, who astutely concludes that she has arrived in paradise.

When the page boy leaves them alone in their suite, Pavlik comments: 'Wow, even the entrance is bigger than our living room. Medieval wood inlay on the walls. Feel this.'

Carved roses, birds, geckos. Aaron sniffs the wood. Cedar.

She slips off her shoes and digs her toes into the fluffy carpet. Pavlik has to describe everything to her in detail: the silk wallpaper with the Berber motifs in the living room, the plump brocade cushions with Arabic characters woven into them, the two enormous crystal chandeliers with glass drops. In the bathroom, almost the size of a conference room, she sniffs essences of rosemary and argan, and runs her fingers over the hand-painted tiles, feeling lions, camels and horses. She goes into the bedroom with Pavlik and drops onto the king-size bed that is as soft as the clouds she was picturing in the aeroplane.

Everything smells of that week twenty-eight years ago.

When Aaron has had her fill, she spends half an hour memorizing the rooms, the sequences of steps, floor coverings and furniture. She hears Pavlik talking on the phone on the terrace; she can tell by the tone of his voice that he is talking to Demirci. Aaron listens, but his voice is calm, professional, as though everything is fine.

She runs a hot bubble bath. Swathed in the relaxing scent of sandalwood she stretches, concentrates on each muscle in turn and moves on to her workout. After two hundred sit-ups and fifty press-ups the enormous tub is full.

She sinks into the water. Aaron can dive under without having to draw her legs up; even when she stretches out her arms she doesn't touch the edge. On the Djemaa el Fna, the muezzin calls people to the Koutoubia mosque for the last prayer. She closes her eyes, her thoughts drift away with the singsong from the mosque's crackly loudspeaker.

When Jenny was eight, a meeting between international special units took place in Marrakech, which included Germany's elite police tactical unit GSG 9. Her father had wanted Jenny and her mum to come along, although he was going to be very busy during that week. Perhaps it was because her parents had had a big argument not long before.

She was in the plane when she heard the name La Mamounia for the first time. It sounded mysterious, like something from a fairy tale. She bombarded her father with questions and he told her it was where God went for his holidays.

The Moroccan King Hassan II had personally requested for her family to be given a suite. Although Morocco was a member of the Arab League, Hassan maintained a special relationship with Israel for strategic purposes. This earned him accusations from Arafat's close circle. The King, who wasn't generally known to indulge people, had been informed that Jörg Aaron had played a prominent role in the storming of the Lufthansa aircraft *Landshut* in Mogadishu ten years earlier. The event had been a heavy blow for the PLO, thus Hassan decided on a whim to show his reverence for Jörg Aaron.

Her father explained all this to her much later, when she was old enough. All she was aware of during those days was how respectful everyone was towards him, and that made her very happy, as he was her hero. He barely had any time for Jenny and her mother, but there were such marvels to gaze at in the city. These she excitedly relayed to him in the hour before going to sleep.

Dancing monkeys!

Sweet mountains!

Women with curtains over their faces!

Spirit conjurers!

Peppermint biscuits!

Metal benders!

She misses her father so much.

She paid for the suite out of his legacy.

After she's got changed, Pavlik watches from the terrace as she crosses the living room with assured strides, avoids the bag he lazily dropped on the floor, and comes out to stand beside him at the railing. Anyone who didn't know would never think these were the movements of a blind person.

She directs her eyes at him, giving him the impression that she is looking at him. 'Anything new?'

'No.' Pause. 'That's creepy,' he adds.

'What?'

'You.'

'It takes effort.'

'It doesn't show.'

'Good.'

'How did you do that with the bag?'

'What bag?'

'The one that was lying in the way.'

'I didn't know it was there. It's blindsight.'

'Cool.'

She smokes, enjoys the moment. Palms rustle, car doors slam. This is where she was standing with her father when the FBI director's convoy pulled up.

As he got out, his bodyguards surrounded him. Her father asked: 'What's that formation called?'

'Diamond,' she said, quick as a flash.

'What is its advantage over the wedge?'

'The rear flank is covered.'

'What do you call the bodyguard who takes care of that?'

'Tail guard.'

'And the one at the front?'

'Point man.'

'Where's the commando leader?'

'On the right.'

'Why?'

'Because the sun is shining from the left and attackers will make sure they have the sun behind them.'

'Always?' her father asked.

'Not at dusk. Then a gunman's silhouette stands out against the light.'

They hadn't noticed Jenny's mother coming out. She'd overheard them. Her mother's knees were shaking. 'Please leave me alone with your father,' she said in a tone that indicated she would not tolerate any dissent.

Her mother closed the terrace door. Jenny couldn't hear what her parents were saying, but when the door opened again her mother's make-up was smudged and her eyes were dull.

'Where are you?' Pavlik now asks.

'Just lost in thought. Come, I'll show you the garden.'

They sit down by the pool, which is deserted at this hour. In the cool of the evening they scramble into their jackets, drink hellishly sweet peppermint tea and nibble almonds. Storks clap their beaks, a peacock calls. Aaron remembers how she chased after the prancing birds until they struck up a loud ruckus, to be joined by herons, cranes, brown-necked ravens and swifts. She explored all the paths, and eventually each one would end at the big ice-cream cart with the mousey-faced page boy, who no longer needed to ask which flavour she wanted because it was always lemon, lemon, lemon!

'Is it the same as it was back then?' asks Pavlik. She had told him about that week years ago.

'Yes.'

She knows he doesn't really understand the connection she had to her father. His own father had been solitary, unapproachable. He hadn't been able to cope with the early death of Pavlik's mother, which left him alone with four kids. Pavlik had to grow up fast and assume responsibility for his younger brothers. His father didn't even make it to fifty. Pavlik had thought it wouldn't affect him, but at the funeral Sandra had to hold him up.

Sandra finds it easier to empathize with Aaron, being an only child as well. Sandra's parents are the kind of people who immediately make you feel a part of the family. Her father had worked for Siemens as an electrician, a modest man who had built something with his wife. Pavlik is pally with him. The two can spend hours sitting on the shores of the Ruppiner See with their fishing rods, even though Pavlik isn't the least bit interested in angling.

When Sandra and he bought their house they had to borrow money from her parents; Pavlik struggled with that. His father-in-law simply said: 'Children don't owe their parents anything, and they in turn owe them everything.'

Aaron thinks this sentence is all wrong. When Sandra told her about it, she'd said as much. Her friend changed the subject. Aaron left it at that. She doesn't have to share Sandra's opinion in every respect, and when it comes to their fathers, women can never agree.

'Shall we head into town?' Pavlik now asks her.

'Absolutely. There's a coffee bar on the north side of the Djemaa el Fna, the Café Argana. The terrace will blow your mind.'

'We'll go separately. We don't know if the liaison officer is the only one on our heels. I'll keep you in my sight.'

'But I'm just a poor blind woman, how shall I find my way across the square?' she asks with a grin.

'You could find your way across the Sahara.'

The doorman claps his hands twice, a taxi pulls up. Pavlik has been waiting on the boulevard in the van and now follows Aaron. She asks to be taken to the avenue that runs along the south of the square and gets out at the bus stop. Behind her is the Koutoubia. She wonders whether the blind beggars will still be sitting there this late in the evening. The Qur'an reverently tells of a godly blind man whom the Prophet Muhammad had permitted to rest on his cloak; in front of every mosque there are blind people who base their plea on this.

It is easy to find the right direction, Aaron simply has to follow the noise. In a different setting, the cane would provide her with information on the consistency of the ground, and its clacking would echo back to her as it bounces off houses and cars.

But here there is such a din that the cane simply serves to prevent her from walking into people or market stalls.

Aaron uses the avenue's kerbstone as a guide. Caleches end to end; harnesses creak, she smells horse dung, hears a snort. She stops; a velvety snout tickles her flat hand and magics away the sugar lumps she pocketed at the hotel.

Without thinking, she swerves as she walks on. She can tell from the shoulder she brushes against and the pungent smell that she has gone round a coachman.

Five minutes later she reaches the actual square and jumps onto the carousel of sounds. The high-pitched bells of the water sellers with the funny hats buzz around Aaron. One of them is cross, probably because tourists are taking a picture of him and don't want to pay for it; cash is what counts.

Next are the snake charmers. She pictures the cobras being prodded by the pungi player's foot, encouraging them to lazily raise their heads. Monkeys scream, bagpipes and mizmars join in. Caught in the cannonade of a thousand drums she approaches the street performers; soon her heartbeat mimics the wild thunder.

When she smells spirit, feels a burst of heat and somebody grabs her with a flurry of Arabic words in order to push her in a different direction, she knows that she came a little too close to a fire eater. Everywhere there are beating rhythms, screaming animals, men and women. Loudspeakers spill forth distorted music, to which the Gnawa, descendants of slaves from sub-Saharan Africa, will dance ecstatically until dawn without tiring, their bodies electrified.

Several times Aaron bumps into people as they flit past her this way and that, without paying any attention to her cane. But nobody minds, everyone here is in a haze.

She hears a loud voice whipping out words in a fast-paced tremolo. It changes tone, imperiously barks an order, then abruptly murmurs meaningfully and is interrupted by the 'ah's and 'oh's of the audience: a storyteller. Perhaps it is the fairy tale of the Berber prince who disguised himself as a travelling merchant in order to find his beloved, or the one about the poor coppersmith, who avenged the death of his parents but lost the girl who had promised her hand to him. The stories are always about eternal love, a big adventure and also cruelty.

Somebody pulls on Aaron's arm. 'Mademoiselle! Mademoiselle! I will tell your fortune! For only one hundred Dirhams!'

An instant later she finds herself sitting on a stool. She fumbles a banknote out of her jeans. The one-hundred notes are in the left, the twenties are in the right-hand pocket. Something is pushed into her hand. It's a pack of cards.

'Pick a card. Don't show it to me. Hold the card to your heart.'

She does it.

'You will encounter a man who has no homeland. He is clever and knows many things. But you must be on your guard against him. You will have a child. But not with him. You will be happy. But not yet. You will see the desert. But you will be in great danger there. You will dream, but you won't know that it's a dream. You will grow very old or die young.'

'What does this man look like?' Aaron asks.

'He doesn't have a face. He travels through time like a shadow. For another hundred Dirhams I can also read your palm. The palm often reveals more than a card.'

She declines with a smile.

Aaron leaves behind the singers, knife throwers, artists and faith healers, and is soon enveloped by wafts of barbecued meat from countless food stalls. Lanterns see-saw in her darkness, as though she was on a high sea looking at the navigation lights of distant ships.

The fray gets so thick that the cane has become entirely useless. She retracts it and simply allows herself to be pushed along by others, picking up the smell of freshly squeezed lemon juice, cooked snails, mint and spicy marinades. A man laughs into her ear and plants a wet kiss onto her cheek.

Touts badger her: 'Beautiful lady, come here, best kebab in the world! Viens ici! Tagine de bœuf! Meilleur prix! English? Français? Deutsch? You good here with me, nice girl!' A cloud of spice explodes in Aaron's nose. She feels ravenously hungry, could eat it all at once. She stumbles through this steaming cathedral in a trance and only comes to again when the throng that she is wedged into dissolves.

Dazed, Aaron stands in a sudden emptiness. The same roaring noise as before encircles her, but it no longer permeates her, it bounces off her as though she was surrounded by a shield. She feels a draught from the left and realizes that she is at the centre of the Djemaa el Fna, where it opens up towards the north, eventually merging into the souks. She now has a new guideway for the last stretch. But suddenly she is suffused with the vast energy being pumped out by this human horde powerhouse. She is the beating heart of the square, where everything flows together like in a lightning conductor.

Aaron is so overwhelmed that her legs crumple and she simply sits herself down on the ground.

Somebody kneels down beside her.

'Are you OK?' Pavlik yells.

Laboriously, she gets up again, reaches for his elbow. He battles his way through the crowd with her. Twice she loses her hold on Pavlik in the scuffle, finds him again, and finally feels him pressing her against him. Clinging onto each other tight, they make it through to the restaurant, both exhausted.

The roof terrace is jam-packed, but he manages to grab a small table next to a heater. Pavlik positions himself so that he can see the entrance. Aaron notices that he gives the table a nudge to check how sturdy it is; in the event of a gunfight a solid table offers more protection. She knows that he has memorized the back exit and is mentally moving all the obstacles around like building blocks. Next, he will apply the left-hand rule; he'll close his eyes, grab the seat and imagine how, in the event, he would move backwards to the exit while holding Aaron behind him with his left hand to protect her. Such things are deeply internalized. She catches herself placing her own hand on the chair, only with her it's the right. You never shake these things off.

The square stretches out below them, the air is trembling to the beat of the drums. Aaron feels Pavlik's finger on her lips. He reaches into the right-hand pocket of her jacket. She hears him throw something on the ground and trample it.

'Now,' he says.

'The liaison officer?'

'He was ten steps behind you all the time. He barged into you near the storyteller and deposited the bug.'

'What does he look like?'

'Big bloke, love handles, mid-forties, dark hair, beard.'

'Where is he?'

'Somewhere downstairs. The terrace is a little too risky for him.'

The waiter brings the menu. They order Moroccan beer and couscous with merguez sausage. Aaron chose this restaurant because she was here with Niko and she doesn't want the memory to exercise any power over her.

After a few minutes' silence she notices with relief that she's alone with Pavlik; there's no ghost sitting at the table.

Djemaa el Fna means *assembly of the dead.*

Nowhere would be more appropriate for them both.

She takes her ears for a walk. An American couple bemoans a stolen purse, a group from Portugal or Brazil celebrate a business deal, and a tour guide flirts with a German tourist. All the other voices are Arabic – with one exception: a man, twenty metres away from them, by the door to the bar. Aaron angles her hearing towards him like a parabolic aerial.

'Who's that standing by the entrance?' she asks Pavlik.

'Arab. Was on the phone, now he's looking for a table.'

'He spoke in French,' says Aaron. '"*Yes, I can see them well. They have ordered something. No problem.*" The liaison officer must've approached him downstairs because he doesn't trust the bug and can't be arsed to keep vigil. He probably asked the guy to keep an eye on us for a few Dirhams and tell him when we leave.'

'You were able to hear that in this racket?' he asks amazed.

'If I ever regain my sight, it'll disappear.'

'You want to think carefully about that.'

The couscous is divine, Aaron has to force herself not to wolf it down. She eats with her fingers, Pavlik with a fork. 'You may only use three fingers of your right hand,' she grunts with her mouth full.

'Says who?'

'Allah.'

'I bet he had a water bowl.'

'Rubbish. Allah wants us to lick our fingers.'

She does so. Pavlik laughs. She lights a cigarette. He laughs even louder.

'What?'

'It says on the packet: "Smoking causes blindness."'

'I'll stop right now.'

'What was the fortune teller's prophecy?'

'That I should be on my guard against a tall blond man with one and a half legs.'

'I could have given you that advice for free.'

'I wanted a second opinion.'

Suddenly she is holding a spoon in her left hand and doesn't know how it got there.

Someone at the next table says 'merci' and takes the spoon.

'Did it fall down?' she asks Pavlik.

'And you caught it as fast as you used to,' he mutters.

They let the time pass. The torch of a fire eater darts up to them, for Aaron it's just a faint line. It stays imprinted on her retina for a second, before it dies away in the darkness.

'Were you here with your father?'

'No.'

Pavlik comprehends. 'Did I ever tell you that he tried to woo me away from the Department?'

She shakes her head.

'It was ages ago, before your time.'

'Didn't you fancy the GSG 9?' Aaron asks.

'Too much time in the barracks. The drill doesn't suit me.'

'You were in the Armed Forces for five years.'

'You should have seen the file they kept on me.'

The conversation moves up a level. 'I can't figure Demirci out,' Aaron comments. 'Marrakech would at least warrant a small set. She's usually so careful.'

'She still is.'

'In what way?'

'Svoboda has tightened the reins. She has to inform him of every mission. She wouldn't be able to keep a set secret from him. In any case, you're a red rag to him, Demirci is keen to let sleeping dogs lie. We aren't really here.'

Hesitantly she says: 'Something is bugging you.'

'Flemming. The fact that he spoke out against you, it's just like him. He doesn't fit in, I can't seem to get straight with him.'

'Who has he come to replace?'

'Kalli.'

'Bigfoot Kallweit? He's dead?'

'No, damaged meniscus.'

'Why was Flemming appointed?' she asks.

'He was with the Special Forces Command, went to Afghanistan three times. He carried a wounded comrade twenty kilometres across the mountains and saved his life.'

'What – he isn't police?'

'He's a demolition ball with ears.'

'That can come in handy sometimes.'

'When he came to us, he broke the instructor's nose in the first combat training session. The great philosopher Tom Waits once said: "The way you do anything is the way you do everything."'

'Think of Baltzer. He did his own thing too, but he was as solid as a wall,' she reasons.

'And then he bit the dust all alone in front of a wall. We stand together and we fall together. Otherwise you don't belong in the Department.'

'There's something else.'

Pavlik is silent for so long that she starts to worry.

'I'm a big girl now,' she says.

'Demirci asked Helmchen to bring her the Avignon file.'

Ten things that Aaron never mentions:
chloroform
newspaper clippings
suicide letters
Chagall
retained bullets
vets

Wanjuscha
deposit boxes
Nitrazepam
Avignon

They walk across the square without a word. Drive to the hotel without a word. Aaron heads for her bedroom without a word.

Pavlik holds something under her nose. 'Sniff this.'

She can't believe it.

'I nabbed two grams.'

'You can't be serious.'

'Come on. It's good quality stuff.'

Would it be better to crawl off to bed, take a tablet and spend the half hour until it takes effect feeling as miserable as she has been for the last half hour?

While they lie on the cushions and Pavlik rolls the biggest joint of all time, she asks: 'When was your first time?'

'When I was sixteen, three mates and me. We bought the dope from a guy who called himself Dr Spaceweed. We went down to the branch canal, then we fired up the torpedo. I was so high that I took my clothes off and staggered home in my underpants. Round the corner from ours, I bumped into Birch.'

'You bumped into a *birch*?'

'No. Rudi Birch. Our neighbour. He was in his seventies, a total square. He looked me in the eyes and said: "Right, my lad, you're going to come and crash on my sofa, and when you've slept it off I'll give you something to put on." He was still a square, though.'

Aaron takes the first toke, instantly feels herself going dizzy, then sinks into a warm tingling sensation that whisks away her thoughts. She takes another pull and passes the joint on.

'And you?' Pavlik asks.

'At my school there was a boy, Tim, and I knew: *He's the one*. My parents were out. We fumbled about a bit, but we were both so nervous that we were screwing it up. He'd brought along a blim. Perhaps also to impress me. In any case, it helped.' Says: 'elbed'. 'Afterwards we counted the stars on my bedroom ceiling.' Says: 'feiling'. 'The door opened and my father walked in. He'd never even seen me with a boy before, and here I was in bed with one. And his nose was working OK too.'

'Oh boy,' Pavlik chuckles. 'That would've been a great one for the press: Jörg Aaron catches daughter in drug sex orgy.'

She inhales deeply. 'Even better: Jörg Aaron puts daughter in convent.'

They double up with laughter.

'His only comment was: "Before your mother comes back, you ought to air this room."'

'Cool.'

'Bloody cool.'

Aaron sees garish acrylic colours flow into each other, as if someone had poured a bucket of water over a pop art painting. They smudge and blur, creating a mush from which colourful bubbles rise up like on the surface of Venus.

They suddenly have a ravenous hunger for something sweet. Giggling, they raid the minibar. The chocolate bars are soon devoured and the lemonade bottles empty, so she rings room service and puts in an order for ten scoops of lemon ice-cream.

'And a cake!' Pavlik trumpets. 'Something gooey with lots of cream on top!'

She passes it on.

'Hang on! I need two litres of Coke! And some white espresso parfait with redcurrant mousse!'

She gives him a sceptical look. 'Do they have that kind of thing?'

'If not, we'll sue the hotel!'

She orders it. 'Bien sûr,' the woman on the other end of the line simply says.

They muck around with no sense of time. Aaron can weave her fingers into a plait, Pavlik sings 'Come Share the Wine'; they laugh about every silly little thing. The room service waiter knocks. Aaron's tip causes his voice to do a little skip, which she likes so much that she pops another fifty into his hand.

They flop on the bed and stuff their faces until their bellies can't take any more. Aaron snuggles up in Pavlik's arm. Her eyes close and for the first time in five years she sleeps through the night without a tablet.

11

When sighted people wake up in the morning, it gets light. For Aaron it gets dark. She knows that she's been dreaming, there were colours and images, but she doesn't know what about.

They check out at nine. Pavlik parks the van in a side road by the Jewish cemetery. They have discussed whether to drive to the bank in it. In the event of needing to make a quick getaway, Aaron would prefer the van to being on foot. But Pavlik is better placed to assess the local situation. The Rue des Berbères ends at the Djemaa el Fna, where the van is no good to them, and the other direction can easily be blocked off.

Apart from her cane, she only takes what she can carry on her person. Cash, passport, mobile, Glock. The gun is as inconspicuous under her short leather jacket as Pavlik's in his hip holster.

Aaron pictures him in his suit. The shoulder area of a marksman is extremely muscular, enabling him to neutralize the recoil of the gun. Pavlik conceals this with made-to-measure clothing, paid for by the Department. Even his sweaters and

flannel shirts come from a tailor. It takes a trained eye to notice
how well toned he is.

The alleyways of the Mellah reek of sweat, faeces and rotting
meat. Rubbish has been set alight somewhere, acrid smoke
hangs between the houses. Aaron knows this quarter. Even
with the mint leaves which she rubs between her fingers, she
repeatedly has to hold her breath. A bakery floods the lane with
the smell of warm flatbreads. Nowhere else are the beguiling
and the disgusting so close beside each other. Pavlik had derided
her when she'd asked the staff in the hotel breakfast room for
the mint. Now, as they pass through a manure – hashish – rose
petal – cat piss cloud where rancid fish is offered for sale, he
eats humble pie by reaching into her jacket pocket and pinching
the last leaf.

Children's hands continuously tug at her, little begging voices
surround her. She gave money to the first ones, but they are
growing too numerous. Pavlik has to fend off men who offer
to guide them round the quarter. One of them is so persistent
that he only lets off when Pavlik threatens to hit him. His angry
torrent of words loses itself in the howl of a two-stroke engine
coming from one of the countless moped workshops.

'Where shall we do it?' Aaron asks.

'Just up here.'

He turns right and immediately pulls her into an entrance.
They wait twenty seconds, then Pavlik leaps away from her.

A man lands beside her. 'What the hell do you think you're
doing?' he barks in surprise. His voice is heavy with cold.

Pavlik says: 'It's time we introduced ourselves.'

The liaison officer acts all timid. 'What do you want?
Money?'

'I'm Clyde, this is Bonnie. And you? Dirty Harry?'

Harry coughs, Aaron can hear every glob of phlegm. 'Are we
done?' he asks.

'We have an appointment at the bank,' she says. 'It's possible that it's being watched. We want you to keep an eye on the road while we're in there. If you see anything, call one of us. You've got the numbers.'

'Dream on.'

'I know your informant leader. He'll be over the moon when he finds out how clumsy you've been.'

'Screw you.'

'You wouldn't enjoy it,' she retorts.

'We'll be seeing you,' says Pavlik. He takes Aaron by the arm. They head off into the haze of grilled sardines, fresh dog shit, vomit, washing powder and patchouli.

'What do you think?' she asks.

Pavlik's answer goes under in a sudden staccato of hammering and chiselling.

But Aaron knows anyway: it's pointless.

They round a corner and a fresh breeze sweeps down a wide road. Buses thunder past, mopeds are buzzing around like hornets, interspersed with three-wheeled tuk-tuks with rattling seats and squeaky horns. Soon the hammering from dozens of copper and brass forges swells to a mighty chorus, travelling far into the distance. They are at the Place des Ferblantiers.

'Taxi stand,' says Pavlik.

The car smells as if rancid fat was congealing inside it. Aaron sinks so far into the worn-out seat that her knees are angled steeply upwards. It takes three attempts to start the engine. They're just setting off when something crash-lands on the bonnet. The driver slams on the brakes and fires off a cannonade of expletives, which is met by counter-bombardment.

'What's up?' she asks Pavlik.

'Melons. A donkey cart has shed its load.'

The driver reverses, wrestles the car into a forward gear and hurtles through an obstacle course of potholes. The Glock is pressing into her back. A whistle warbles.

'C'est parti! C'est parti!' Traffic policeman.

Aaron can feel the sun on the back of her neck, they are heading west. According to Bushidō, that is where paradise and salvation reside. But Bushidō isn't always right.

They're not talking anymore, both are fully absorbed now. Ten minutes later Pavlik tells the driver to stop. They walk to the bank. Aaron has unfolded her cane, her movements are hesitant. It wasn't previously arranged, but Pavlik instantly plays along and stops a good distance away from the entrance.

'There are steps ahead, honey.'

Aaron carefully feels her way towards them with the cane. She moves so anxiously that a passing tourist offers to help.

'Est-ce que je peux vous aider?'

'Merci,' Pavlik fends him off, 'ce n'est pas nécessaire.'

It's cool in the lobby. The clacking of the cane comes back as a clear, sharp echo: marble. To her right, the sound ripples unevenly: counters or desks, quite far away; the hall must be large.

'I'll let them know that we're here.' Pavlik moves away.

He returns and has somebody with him.

'Mr Hamdaoui is expecting you,' a woman says.

Aaron fusses about with the cane. After forty-three short steps they reach the lift. She adds them to the nineteen she took from the entrance and knows that she could sprint out onto the road from here in four seconds.

Even the lift is air conditioned. The woman is wearing something white. She loves Shalimar and too much hairspray. 'Is this your first time in Marrakech?' Judging by her English she has lived abroad for some time.

'Yes. It's a beautiful city,' Aaron replies.

The woman's silence contains the question how a blind person can gauge that.

Long corridor, twenty-eight steps. Anteroom, eleven.

The director's voice comes out of nowhere. 'Badr Hamdaoui. Mrs Traherne, Mr Traherne, pleased to meet you.'

You could oil hinges with his intonation. Peppermint disguises the smell of booze on his breath. Something with figs, probably Mahia. Aaron knows the liquor. Eighty per cent, a widow maker. Either Hamdaoui has a serious alcohol problem or he is very nervous.

A drop of spit flies onto her cheek. 'If you please—'

A deep pile carpet swallows all sound in his office. Pavlik directs her. Aaron waves her stick about, bashes it against the steel table legs a few times and analyses the echo. Surprisingly small room. Two windows. Muffled reverberation from the right, perhaps a wall hanging.

They sit down. 'A small formality first,' says Hamdaoui.

Something is pushed towards Aaron.

Pavlik had helped her earlier to insert the contact lens. It feels strange to have a copy of Holm's iris on her eye. As if he was a part of her now. But hasn't he always been?

The scanner silently sweeps her eye.

'Thank you.' Hamdaoui gives a little cough. 'Pardon me. The procedure by which the funds were transferred to you was very unusual.'

'Please describe it to me.'

'Well, Mr Woyzeck opened the account on 4 January.'

Woyzeck.

Büchner's drama, the subject of her college thesis.

'On the same day, the remittance arrived from Riyadh. A remarkable sum.'

Aaron withdraws into her inner chamber. What's the reference? Woyzeck beats his lover Marie to death out of jealousy. That isn't it. His humiliation at the hands of the captain and the doctor?

No.

Wealth. Inheritance. Giving.

That's it: the Star Money fairy tale.

There once was a poor child that had no father and no mother. Everything was dead and there was no one left on earth.

In Büchner's version the girl isn't rewarded with silver coins. Instead she travels to the moon, which is just a rotten branch, to the sun, which turns out to be a withered flower, and the stars, which are nothing but impaled insects.

What's the message?

A warning?

'Mrs Traherne?'

'Sorry, what did you say?'

'Mr Woyzeck informed me that he didn't have much longer to live and that you were his sole heiress. For the sake of simplicity and in order to avoid the bureaucracy of a testament, he said you would prove your identity by means of an eye scan. I must confess that I was a little surprised. But I can't think of any reason why I should question it. In the eyes of this establishment, you're the owner of this account.'

'Which bank did the money come from?'

'From the Al Jeddah Bank in Riyadh.'

'And this was the only time you had any dealings with Mr Woyzeck?'

'It was our only encounter.' Tinny rustling. She realizes that Hamdaoui is stretching out his hand. 'Would you like one?'

'What is it?'

'I beg your pardon, how silly of me.'

'It's a mint pastille, honey.'

'No thanks.'

The director's voice turns a shade more oily still. 'Mr Woyzeck thought you might be interested in investing.'

'Do you have any suggestions?' Pavlik asks.

'Indeed. Bonds issued by the Kingdom of Morocco, for

example, offer a guaranteed 5.375 per cent interest. Tax-free, of course.'

She smiles. 'Aren't interest payments prohibited in Islam? What do you call it – ribā?'

'We're not an Islamic institution, madam.'

But the Jeddah Bank in Saudi Arabia is. That's why the two billion never increased.

'Of course there are also investment opportunities that offer considerably higher returns,' says Hamdaoui. 'Such as the Russian Anadyrneft Group, a rapidly expanding energy company with enormous price potential.'

Aaron and Pavlik can happily believe that. The group is owned by the Smirnowskaja; Interpol has had its sights on it for some time.

'Or you might want to get involved in the American construction industry. Ambrose & Draytons would be a good choice. We have it from a reliable source that the firm will soon be given the contract for three new casinos in Las Vegas and Atlantic City. That will drive up the shares.'

Part of the Cosa Nostra portfolio.

Hesitantly, Hamdaoui adds: 'Mr Woyzeck also had a suggestion. He said it might interest you.'

'What exactly?' asks Pavlik.

'C&B Global Basics.'

'What's that?'

'It's a closed fund, it's being managed in London.'

'Closed – that means project-linked?'

'Yes.'

'What project?'

Hamdaoui clears his throat in embarrassment. 'To be honest, I don't know. I've tried to obtain information about it, without success. The initiator of such a fund is under no obligation to make its purpose public.'

'And who is this person?' Pavlik asks.

'That is also beyond my knowledge.'

'I'm not very conversant with these things,' says Aaron. 'Closed? Doesn't that mean one can no longer invest?'

'Only in the second phase. Currently shares are still being offered, that much I was able to find out.'

Pavlik stands up. 'It's likely we'll stay in Marrakech for a few days. We will have a think about it and we'll be in touch.'

'Here, if you please. This is the card with my private number,' Hamdaoui says. 'You can ring me any time.'

Aaron extends her hand, his is slippery.

'Perhaps you would like to view your safe deposit box.'

'I didn't know I had one.'

'Mr Woyzeck had it arranged for you.'

The same woman takes the lift down with them. This time she doesn't make conversation. Although it's cool inside the building, sweat is ruining her perfume. Aaron loosens her muscles.

Earlier, she counted the seconds it took the lift to reach the management floor. This time their journey takes six seconds longer.

Basement.

Marble, sharp echo. Aaron locates an alcove and receives a few deeper responses from it. No stone. Wood, presumably chairs. Twenty steps. The woman stops and enters a five-digit code. A heavy door opens. Aaron's cane maps the room behind it.

About thirty square metres. Steel along the walls. Safe deposit boxes. In the middle is a large table.

'I need the scan. If you wouldn't mind—'

She feels her way towards the table and sits down. Pavlik leads her hand to the scanner. Aaron places her chin on the rest. A lock snaps; scraping noises, clicking.

The box is set down on the table and unlocked.

'I'll be outside.' The woman leaves them alone.

Pavlik opens the case.

'What's inside?'

'An ancient Walkman with headphones.' He gives her one of the two earbuds.

'Wait a moment.' She runs her fingers over the cool metal of the box, feels the embossed number, forty-seven, steadies her breath.

Then she nods.

Pavlik pushes the playback button; they hear Holm's voice.

'Ms Aaron, I knew you wouldn't be able to resist my invitation. Now you're in Marrakech, a city that holds some very special memories; you were here with the two most important men in your life. Of course you will already have met the manager. An unpleasant man with moist articulation. Was he nervous? Of course. In case you're wondering about the Walkman: it was all I owned when I left my parents' house with my brother. I kept hold of it all those years, perhaps the only sign of sentimentality that I permitted myself. How does it feel to be this rich? Assets aren't important to you. That's another thing that connects us. The two billion disgusts you because many people paid for it with their life. But be honest: I'm sure you've wondered what good you could do with it. How about a charity for blind people in Third World countries? Or you could finance innovative therapies? Neurological research? Don't deny it. Kenshō is one of the commandments of Bushidō, and it demands that we explore our inner nature. But the question is: can you keep the money?' Holm is briefly silent. 'Regarding that, I have to tell you that my adoptive father stole it off someone. Now—'

Pavlik stops the tape. 'Not here.' He closes the box, pockets the Walkman and activates a buzzer.

The woman returns. 'Was everything to your satisfaction?'

'Yes, thank you.'

They take the lift to the ground floor. Forty-three steps. The woman stops in the same place where Aaron was met by her. 'Please excuse me, I have an important appointment.' Her voice sounds strained.

'No problem, we know the way out,' Pavlik replies.

The woman quickly walks away.

'She's scared,' Aaron whispers.

'Come.' Pavlik walks back with her and turns right after a few metres, then left. She throws away the cane, takes a headscarf out of her jacket and puts it on. Her mouth is dry. A pneumatic hammer drives adrenalin bolts into her chest. Pavlik shoves her onward. He opens a door, immediately closes it again. Next door. Locked. He quickens his steps.

'Monsieur?' A man's voice, ten metres ahead of them.

'We seem to have got lost,' says Pavlik in French, without slowing down.

'You can't come through—'

She feels Pavlik's whirling movement. The man collapses without a sound. A door flies open, they're out in the yard.

12

Aaron sprints along the alleyway beside Pavlik, her hand on his elbow. Shouts ring out from the Rue des Berbères, Arabic commands.

'Five,' he reports. 'Guns. No one else.'

They draw their weapons. Pavlik dodges obstacles, Aaron follows suit as if she were running on parallel tracks. Shots strike a wall, mortar sprays against her cheek. They both turn mid-run and fire.

Aaron showers the void with bullets, hears a plaintive sound, perhaps fifty metres behind them.

'Three.'

They rush forwards into a wall of mobile ringtones, bike bells, the sputtering of mopeds, schmaltzy pop music, Babylonian voices. They are in the souks, the city's main artery, a straw-roofed labyrinth of bazaars that branches out in all directions like capillaries and meanders towards the medina.

It's as if Aaron is staring into a furiously fast solar eclipse. The shadow of the moon is pushing its way in front of the star, covering it completely, producing a sparkling corona of white light that is abruptly extinguished, leaving nothing but gaping blackness behind.

Her shoulder smashes against something hard. She stumbles, reaches out to steady herself, clawing her hand into a mass of metal parts.

Nails. Hardware stall.

'Two from the right,' Pavlik shouts.

Her fist closes around a nail.

People scream, fly past her, take cover. Aaron tucks the Glock into her waistband, stands beside Pavlik as if in an arena. Then she's yanked away from him.

She makes herself light.

The attacker was expecting her to resist and gasps in surprise. Aaron collides with him, feels his breath in her face. She tries to ram two fingers under his chin but misses because he throws his head to the side. Aaron hears shots, gets hold of the man's ear and gives it a brutal twist until the cartilage snaps. He howls, thrashes about senselessly, grazes her with a left hook.

Even if he knew what she intends to do with the nail, he wouldn't be fast enough to prevent it.

Next to her, Pavlik is returning the fire from the second attacker, until Aaron obscures his view mid-fight. When she drives the nail into the Arab's eye and he drops down screaming, Pavlik throws himself onto the ground. In the split second before Aaron's man hits the floor, Pavlik shoots through her legs and drives a bullet into the second man's ankle. He howls like an animal, topples over; Northern European, blond.

Before he can fire another shot, Pavlik leaps up, grabs an axe from the hardware stall's display and hurls it into the blond man's forehead.

With a quick glance he sees that their pursuers from the alleyway are only twenty metres behind them now. Gunfire, flashes, his left hip is suddenly numb. His Glock sends out three express deliveries. One of the men collapses, the other two take cover.

'It's me.' Pavlik clamps his hand round Aaron's arm like a vice. He drags her through a maze of noise, heat and burning muscles. A shout rings out. She senses a passage opening behind them, people are moving aside. More shots, screams. Pavlik runs in zigzags like a hare; Aaron trips, struggles to keep up.

'How many?' she pants.

'At least two.'

She notices that Pavlik is running unevenly.

'Jump!' he yells.

Aaron takes a leap but her right foot gets caught in something. She crashes into one of the stalls, reaches out for support and tears half the goods down with her. A flood of saffron, chilli, cinnamon and cumin pours over her and into her open mouth. She can barely breathe, she retches and is immediately yanked back up by Pavlik. He drags her onward while a woman sends a hailstorm of curses after them.

Right, left, right, he pulls her through countless shops. Soaps, oils and fried foods mingle into a single sour smell. Textiles slap Aaron in the face, then bead curtains and carpets. She spits out the spice remnants in her mouth. The adrenalin is stealing the oxygen from her lungs.

When Pavlik suddenly stops and turns on his own axis, she knows: dead end. Her hand closes around the Glock.

But then a man whispers in French: 'Here, quick!'

Pavlik pushes her head down. She crawls through musty-smelling clothes with him. Second-hand, dry-cleaned, stiff as a board. Aaron lies still, pressed against Pavlik, her left hand on his hip. She feels something wet. Blood? Hers or his?

Then they're there. It's clear just from their pounding steps: more than two. One of them thrusts a reserve magazine into his gun, one whispers into his mobile, one curses, one barks at some tourists to make themselves scarce.

All four are panting like a pack of dogs on a fox hunt.

The breath of the fifth flows soft and steady. He addresses the trader in Arabic. His voice has the nonchalant melody of cruelty, even the softest syllable spreads fear. The trader replies haltingly, as if every other word is sticking to his tongue. Mr Cool issues commands, the men run on.

Aaron still has that voice in her ear.

She has heard it before. When?

Back then it wasn't speaking Arabic, which has alienated the sound.

It's not his mother tongue.

The clothes are pushed aside. 'Come.'

Aaron and Pavlik follow the trader.

After twenty steps he comes to a halt: 'This way.'

'Thank you.'

'Good luck.'

Pavlik walks at a swift pace, but not so fast that they draw attention. His arm is around Aaron's hip, she keeps her head low. Mopeds race through the narrow gorge of the street, one of them so close that its mirror bashes against her hand.

'Did you see the one who spoke?' she asks.

'Just his shoes,' he forces out. 'Brown, Italian, not a single fleck of dust on them. He must be on one of our lists.'

'Did his voice sound familiar to you?' she asks.

'No. You?'

'Yes, but I don't know where from. What's the matter with your hip?'

'Graze wound.' He pulls her headscarf further down over her forehead. 'They're trying to kill me, but you they want alive.'

It's as if Aaron is clinging onto a rock face and an avalanche is sweeping away all her thoughts, hurling them down into a bottomless abyss.

But she can feel it.

Behind her, still at a distance, the jostling, thronging mass is separating. The stream of bodies stutters, then comes to a halt. Fear rides on the air like spiders' threads. Fear of men with guns.

'They're onto us again,' she says.

'Where?'

'Behind us. More than fifty metres.'

Pavlik turns his head.

'Can you see them?' she asks.

'No.' He quickens his steps.

'They must've separated, it's probably just two of them,' she pants. 'We can't shake them off. Let's do it like in Nicosia.'

Anyone else would have said: 'Back then, yes. But now, blind?'

Pavlik says: 'OK.' He slows down, lets the pursuers come closer.

Loud shouts: 'Go! Go! Go!'

The men are clearing the path with brute force.

Pavlik turns round again and starts running. 'Yes. Two.'

She responds to the slightest movement of his elbow, which she is touching with two fingers.

'Hulks,' he slings her way. 'Bigger than me, Europeans.'

He tugs Aaron sharply to the right. The Arabic Techno that is pumping through the bazaar grows quiet; there's a strong smell of leather, they're in a shop.

'Out, out!' Pavlik bellows.

Somebody hurriedly squeezes past Aaron.

'Left,' Pavlik murmurs.

She perceives him silently moving into cover. Under a shelf, between racks, into an alcove, whatever. For Aaron it's just important that he is on her left, hiding away low down, and that she knows what he's got in his hand.

She hears heavy boots, the exhausted panting of the two men, then a badly pronounced: 'Where is the man?'

English, stumbling on the *th*; he thinks she's American.

Aaron holds up both hands. 'Who do you mean?' she replies in her best East Coast accent, remaining in her role.

His accomplice takes a step forwards. He should be within Pavlik's reach now.

She hopes.

The first one again: 'You're coming with me. Come on.'

She doesn't move, feels her muscles firing up and enjoying the oxygen supplied to them by her perfect breathing.

'Didn't you hear what I said?' he barks.

It is harder when an opponent stands to the side or behind, and points the weapon at one's temple or the back of the head. But she can deal with that too. At the Department, they practised it blindfolded.

This guy here does her the favour of placing the barrel of his gun squarely on Aaron's forehead.

She's had to do this seven or eight times.

Rule one: move out of the line of fire.

Aaron ducks away below the gun.

Rule two: get control of the gun.

She grabs the barrel of the gun with both hands, so fast that the man's eyes are unable to follow.

Rule three: secure the gun.

Aaron uses her hands as levers, yanks the gun to the side and simultaneously twists it like a Rubik's Cube, forcing him to let go of it.

Rule four: don't hang about.

This took her half a second.

Rule five: keep the attacker at bay.

Or kill him.

When Aaron shoots him in the face, his accomplice is already going down with a scream; Pavlik has severed his Achilles tendon with a knife. He thrashes the man's head on the stone floor, jumps up, pulls Aaron back out into the bazaar and drags her into a wide alley.

A moped thunders out of a side lane and sweeps past them, chasing people aside. Aaron and Pavlik attach themselves to its rear. They sprint through the swathe that is being cut for them, they no longer have to run in zigzags.

'What about the others? Have we lost them?' she gasps.

Shots answer her question.

They follow the moped into a bend. Aaron feels wind on her face, the echo of the clattering engine tells her that they are on a small square. Something wet brushes against her face. It is wool, they're in the dyers' souk. To their right, a second vehicle races towards them, squeaky horn, three-wheeled transporter. Pavlik fires off a string of shots, buys them time.

The transporter is almost level with them; the pungent smell of ammonia hits Aaron's nose.

'I'll find you.'

Before she can react to this, Pavlik has grabbed her like a doll and thrown her through the air.

Aaron lands on something soft, damp and foul smelling.

'Pavlik!' she shouts.

Rapid shots grow faint and diminish to a whisper as the vehicle she's in lunges into the seething flow of a wide road. A crescendo of police sirens rings in her ears. Aaron feels around her, she's lying on half-tanned furs. She forces herself to blank out the urge to vomit, crawls under the load and covers herself with it.

She curses Pavlik for stealing her last mint leaf. She curses him for having forced her to leave him alone.

She curses the frantic fear she feels for him.

The transporter swerves, the driver is pushing his way through chaotic traffic. Several times he slams on the brakes, pounds the horn and swears like a trooper. After an eternity, during every second of which Aaron is sure she's about to throw up, he stops and gets off.

Steps move away, the driver greets someone.

Aaron crawls out from under the furs and gasps for air. But what hits her is far worse. She just manages to jump off the platform, then she's bent over double and vomits until her stomach is sore.

She knows where she is. In the tanners' quarter. She was here with Niko. She remembers the enormous stone vats, filled with urine and excrement, in which men stand submerged up to their chest, scrubbing tissue remnants off the skins. Aaron stumbles forwards, realizes the stench is getting even more abominable, turns round and plods in the opposite direction.

She clicks her tongue.

She's in an alleyway, locates doorways, a car.

Aaron no longer has her cane and takes very small steps. She trips over something bony, which emits a sleepy growl, dog. She feels her way along the wall of a building and manages to reach a driveway. A little further along there's a busy square, she hears people and bus engines.

She squats down and slowly breathes through her mouth, holds her breath for five seconds, repeats the process ten times. Gradually she notices her diaphragm moving lower, allowing her lungs to expand.

Her phone vibrates. She fumbles it out of her jeans.

'Where are you?'

Aaron is so relieved to hear Pavlik's voice that she forgets the stench. 'Tanners' quarter. Big square with buses. Alleyway.'

'I'll be there in ten minutes.'

She clings to her phone.

He calls again. 'Set it to loud and switch off the answer service.'

It rings twenty times, then she hears quick steps.

Pavlik kneels down beside her. 'Are you OK?'

'Yes. The men?'

'Dealt with.'

'Was the one with the Italian shoes among them?'

'No. We have to get out of here.'

Aaron stands up.

'Wait.' Pavlik takes off her scarf and uses it to wipe her face. 'Sorry, there's no other way.' He spits onto the fabric and rubs away the spice remnants that have mixed with her sweat and congealed to a mask.

'Where are we going?' she asks.

'Van.'

They get hold of what is probably Marrakech's only taxi with functioning air conditioning. The driver still opens his window; Aaron doesn't blame him. The radio tootles 'habibi, habibi'. She prays that there are no news broadcasts on the short journey. They have killed five men, perhaps six, in front of a million witnesses. Every policeman in Marrakech will now be looking for them.

13

They tumble into the van. 'Duck down,' Pavlik hisses.

Aaron slides down in her seat. 'Police?'

'Patrol.' After a minute, he carefully peers out. 'OK.' He calls the first of the four doss houses in the medina where he has booked a room for the week. 'Dumont. My wife and I have a reservation with you but we couldn't get here until today. One question: do you have internet?— Thank you, see you later.'

Pavlik repeats this three times. With the last one, they strike lucky. No internet; the man at the other end only speaks broken French.

It is next to the Ben Youssef madrasa. They park the van around the corner. Pavlik carefully wipes down the vehicle's interior and door handles. They take the three bags inside.

In the house, Aaron is greeted by a fug of old mutton, damp walls and cheese she never wants to try. The man at the counter doesn't even ask for the Belgian passports they are now using. For two hundred Dirhams, less than twenty Euros, they are given accommodation on the first floor, facing the street.

The room smells as if it hasn't been aired for years. The

ceiling fan plaintively sets itself in motion, whisking together dust, decay and bad karma.

'Almost like in La Mamounia,' Pavlik comments.

'Take off your shirt and trousers.'

'Joke?'

'Let me see your hip.'

He lays down on the bed. Aaron runs her fingers over a bulging welt covered in dry, crumbly blood. Pavlik doesn't make a sound.

'Graze wound.'

'My words exactly.'

She hears him opening the equipment bag. 'Complete?'

'Yes, nurse.' He whacks an antibiotic into his thigh, disinfects the lesion and sticks a dressing over it.

'How's your belly?'

Now she has asked after all. Aaron wanted to ask when she first arrived in Berlin, when they drove to Sandra, yesterday before their departure. But she stuck to their ritual.

No. You were scared of the truth.

'It'll get better if I lie down for a bit.'

'You shouldn't have come along.'

'It made a difference just then.'

'Don't ever do that again,' she says.

'What?'

'Face them on your own.'

'It was the only way.'

'Promise me.'

'I promise.'

Aaron grabs her bag, goes into the bathroom and stuffs the stinking clothes into the bin. The lukewarm water doesn't bother her. She scrubs herself down with curd soap until her hand hurts.

She thinks of the safe deposit box number.

Forty-seven.

As if there weren't more important things.

She turns off the thin stream, crouches down in the bath and stares into her darkness. Up until now, it has always gone away as soon as the adrenalin has dissipated. Not this time.

Aaron draws up a hit list of her current fears.

What is hiding behind the account?

How do we get away from here?

Why is it staying pitch black?

Only in third place.

She towel dries her hair, applies a generous amount of deodorant, brushes her teeth and puts on fresh clothes. Something tickles her foot and disappears with a rustle. Cockroach.

Welcome back to the Department, Aaron.

She gets on the bed and lights her first cigarette since yesterday.

'Go for it,' she says.

Pavlik hands her an earbud and rewinds the Walkman cassette a bit. They hear Holm again. 'But the question is: can you keep the money? Regarding that, I have to tell you that my adoptive father stole it off someone. Well, patience is a revolutionary virtue. This man has been waiting eleven years for the day he'll get it back. You've heard him mentioned many times before. He's known as *the Broker*.'

Pavlik stops the recording. Aaron composes herself.

The Broker is a terrorist.

Wrong.

He is *the* terrorist.

More precisely: he brings together terrorists and financial investors, who place stock market bets on share price crashes or the collapse of entire economic sectors after an attack. He supplies assassins with targets, logistics and finance and is said to have made vast fortunes by short selling stocks.

September 11 is attributed to him. His consortium bet that the shares of reinsurers and airlines would plummet, and made huge profits.

'They've thought up many horror stories in Langley, at MI6 and at the Intelligence Service,' says Pavlik. 'I doubt that he really exists.'

'The bomb in the Manchester City football stadium. Seven thousand dead. The stock market value of the Premier League was pulverized. That's another one he is supposed to be responsible for.'

'They never managed to prove it,' he points out.

'Dar es Salaam, Sydney, Athens,' she continues.

'You know something.'

'Last year, that planned poison gas attack on Frankfurt airport. The BKA seized a member of the terrorist cell.'

'I was told they'd all been killed during the operation – apart from one, who escaped,' Pavlik says slowly.

'He was turned.' Pause. '*I* turned him. He's now in Peshawar and is supplying information to our Intelligence Service. He told me that a businessman had contacted them and had presented them with a finished plan. Of course it wouldn't have been the Broker himself, but the profile fitted his consortium to a tee. The attack was to take place at eleven p.m., two hours before the Tokyo stock market opens. It would have been perfect, the following morning the shock wave would have gripped the markets in Europe.'

'Was there any short selling?' he asks.

'It's not clear.'

'Surely that could have been traced back.'

'It's not that straightforward. The Broker spreads the transactions across countless banks around the world. He knows how to outwit financial regulators and who has to be bribed. Also, he doesn't just bet on falling share prices. Every catastrophe has its winners: armaments and technology groups, construction firms and so forth. Then there's the currency fluctuations, which can be used to rake in vast sums. Nobody has the means to monitor all this.'

Pavlik pushes play again. 'Ms Aaron, as you know, my adoptive father was involved in illegal commodity trading. Eleven years ago he took part in a joint venture with the Broker. It concerned the attack on the Yamal natural gas pipeline that runs from Siberia to Europe; you remember, no doubt. I was involved in the preparations and instructed the Chechen Islamists, who served as useful fools.

'It was a complicated financial scheme, I won't bore you with the details. Put simply: it was a bet against Gazprom, based on the certainty that its market value would nosedive after the attack. The Broker and my father made a deal to share the profits – as well as any possible losses. To allow for the possibility that one of them would die beforehand, they each provided a two billion dollar security, deposited on accounts to which they would have reciprocal access.

'The attack was a success, but in business terms it was a fiasco. Gazprom announced they were tapping vast new fields along the Volga. The gas would be pumped to Europe via the Soyuz pipeline, which would more than compensate for the Yamal pipeline being out of service for several months. On the same day, they also announced the merger of Gazprom with the state-owned Rosneft Group. Instead of collapsing, the share price shot to a record high.

'Much can be learnt from this disaster. Two extraordinary men were prepared to take a huge risk. They demonstrated the cold-bloodedness that is required in order to rule. But for what? For a tremendous rate of return. At the end of the day, it was just greed.

'Ten years earlier my father wouldn't have let himself in for it. Even though he valued money, he saw it merely as a means to attain power. By the time he met the Broker, he'd grown old and stubborn. He should have been alert to the Rosneft-Gazprom merger, there were signs. He knew about the natural gas fields along the Volga, but he thought it would be too costly to exploit them.

'The Broker knowingly took this risk; he needs it as a stimulant, it's his drug. It's one way to establish a global empire, Alexander the Great demonstrated as much over two thousand years ago. Gamblers like the Broker win and lose billions. There are many lucrative targets for him, below the line he's always in the black. That's not to say that he doesn't care about losing his entire stake. And that's what happened back then.

'When the short positions had to be closed, my father was in custody awaiting trial – for reasons that had nothing to do with this deal, but a lot to do with you, Ms Aaron, as you know. Before he died in prison and all his Russian accounts were frozen, he managed to transfer the two billion from Moscow to Riyadh.

'The Broker could no longer get to my father's money. The investors in his fund recouped their losses from him, and that was enough to blow even his capital.

'He knew that I had access to the Saudi account. I could have given the Broker his money. But I loathe people who are so greedy. All those years, he has been looking for me. That didn't trouble me; I don't need to tell you that I have a gift for making myself invisible.

'Yesterday, I transferred the two billion to Marrakech. By the way: I am currently sitting in the park of La Mamounia, enjoying its delights. It's exactly how you described it. There's much that would be worth staying alive for. The paintings by Georges Noël, a Château Lafite 1959, Bach's cello suites, the birch forest near Lubichowo, the mercy of oblivion. But what I long for even more is death.

'The Broker knows nothing of these things, all he desires is adrenalin and money. I'm sure he's already found out where his money is. He'll have bribed someone in the bank, heard that a Mrs Traherne is the new account holder, and is waiting for you.

'Perhaps he already knows who you really are. If he does, then not from me. At any rate: if I were in your shoes, I'd be careful when I leave the house.'

Bloody bastard.

'Ever since you received my message on Fårö, you'll have been asking yourself why I'm doing this. Of all your theories, only one will have remained plausible to you: that these two billion are part of my revenge and that I've set a trap for you in Marrakech.

'I am going to surprise you one last time: you're wrong. The reason for your inheritance is a sentence that I found in your diary. It's from Browning. Isn't that ironic, Ms Aaron? A poet that shares his name with your favourite gun. Your father quoted the sentence during your time of deepest sorrow, when you were blind and helpless, and you doubted his love because he wouldn't allow you to take your own life.'

Aaron shivers.

Take away love, and our earth is a tomb.

These words saved her.

'One can despise a person and yet respect them at the same time,' Holm continues. 'There's nobody I've had more in common with than you. It's our life sentence.' He is silent for a moment. 'You thought it was about revenge? It is. But not mine. I've already had that. Bushidō states that to take revenge, one has to know who on and why. I will tell you, because you should know. The Broker, the man this money belongs to, the man who is now looking for you, is the man who had your father killed.'

14

Ten things that Aaron won't recall later on:
    that she screams
 throws the Walkman across the room
 digs her fingernails in her arm
 Pavlik grabs her and doesn't let go
 her heart rips her breath to shreds
 she smells her father's cigar
 she goes weak and just whimpers
 she thinks there are dragonflies on her shoulder
 a red sun explodes in her head
 her eyes are melting snow

The first thing is darkness. Then the taste of rust. Then Pavlik's voice: 'I'm here.'

'Holm is lying,' she whispers. 'My father died of a heart attack. Butz was with him.'

'I can carry on listening alone in the bathroom.'

'No. I want to know.'

'Sure?'

'Yes.'

Pavlik picks the Walkman up off the floor and lets the tape run on. 'Your father had heart problems; nothing serious, but he took an antihypertensive drug. His killer gained access to his house and swapped the drug with digitoxin, an extract of the Digitalis plant. Your father must have felt unwell for days, without having an explanation for it. Loss of appetite, impaired colour vision, nausea.'

The evening before, he was with me in the rehab clinic. We practised Braille and he couldn't concentrate. At nine he said he was tired and wanted to go to bed. We hugged and he left. I could have asked: is something the matter? Could have said: let's call a doctor.

Instead of laying my hand on his cold forehead the next day.

'You don't want to believe it, I know,' she hears Holm's voice again. 'When someone as important as your father dies, they usually carry out a post-mortem. Presumably the digitoxin wasn't detected in the blood; they would've had to look for it specifically. Nevertheless, there's a way to verify what I'm telling you. Digitoxin metabolizes in the liver. The transaminase enzyme levels must have been raised. Not so high as to arouse suspicion, but high enough for you to believe me.

'You're wondering how I found out about the murder. Well, we share a small world. A few years ago, I was involved with a man who was keen to impress me, so he told me about it. Your father was very important to the Broker; the man I'm talking about was a professional killer with astronomically high fees. He boasted that he was only in Sankt Augustin for three hours. He broke into the house without leaving a trace, found a prescription and obtained the false drug. An hour later he was on the plane to Los Angeles. When the media reported the death of your father, he was sipping on a cappuccino at the Beverly Wilshire and writing out an invoice for the final instalment of his fee.

'There are perhaps a handful of people in the world who are in the know regarding the Broker's identity. I'm one of them. Please forgive me for not telling you who he is. I could give you the key to the enigma, but we shouldn't pretend that we're friends. I've already laid a trail for you; you know what I mean. And now I'll give you one thing more: there's a man living in Marrakech who is of interest to you. His name is Veit Jansen.'

Holm is silent for so long, she thinks the recording has come to an end. Then she hears him one last time.

'You remember my prediction: you're my destiny and I'm yours. Only now does it fulfil itself. You and I, Ms Aaron, have been on a long journey together that took us into hell. You've had to stay there, while I found my way out. Perhaps you'll find your way out too some day. Farewell.'

Even before the tape stops, she grabs the iPhone that she only uses for this mission. 'Telephone,' she says to Siri. She dictates the number for Burkhard Mehrtens. He was her father's GP and one of his few friends.

'Mehrtens.'

'It's Jenny here.'

He sounds pleased. 'How are you? Are you in Sankt Augustin?'

'No. I need some information: when they performed the autopsy on my father, did they do a digitoxin blood count?'

'I don't think so,' he replies puzzled. 'Why?'

'Do you have a copy of the report?'

'But what's the matter? You sound all wound up.'

'Do you have a copy?'

'Yes, here in my practice. Give me a moment.' He covers the receiver, talks to someone, then he's back again. 'They didn't test for digitoxin. Why would they? Jörg had high blood pressure, Digitalis would have been counter-productive.'

'What were his liver function readings?'

'One moment – normal. Apart from the AST, which was slightly above the borderline.'

'Is that the transaminase?'

'Yes.'

It's as if Aaron's fingers are made of stone. She can barely hold the phone. Her chest, neck, mouth, everything is stone.

'Jenny?'

'I'll get back to you.' She ends the call and whispers: 'Why didn't he get himself checked out?'

'He intended to go to the doctor,' says Pavlik.

'How can you know that?'

He struggles for words. 'Because I was with him.'

'What do you mean "with him"?' she asks confused.

'Your father had asked Butz and me to go and see him. It was about Barcelona. He was convinced that you'd been lured into a trap there. He felt nauseous, he mentioned he was having trouble with his eyes and that he was going to see a doctor. But then he collapsed dead in front of us.'

'You were there.' She repeats it: 'You were there.'

'When you arrived, I wanted to let you know, but I couldn't do it. It broke my heart to see you like that.'

'Of all the days on which I needed you, that was the one!' she screams at Pavlik. 'I was bawling my heart out and you buggered off!'

'I'm sorry.'

'That's not enough!'

She tries to run round the bed, forgetting that her bag is lying in the way. She falls headlong, crawls into the bathroom and locks the door. Aaron is doubled over on the floor and cries until everything hurts and her spit tastes of bile; like it did back then, when Butz had gone and had left her alone in the empty house that smelled of her father, his Havanas, his whisky, his aftershave and her childhood certainty that nothing could happen to her here, ever.

She feels around for her wash bag, finds the detested tablets, swallows one and longs so much for that smell to disappear.

When she wakes up on the tiled floor, the whole of her body is numb. She feels cold. Her eyes are hurting. She taps on the Cartier.

'Eleventh of February. Wednesday. Seven p.m., eleven minutes, twelve seconds.'

It is quiet. Aaron hears her own breathing. She thinks of Butz. He didn't want to leave her alone that day, but she sent him away. Nobody would have been able to console her. Nobody would have been strong enough to save her from the ruins of her life.

Not even Pavlik or Sandra. Aaron would have pushed them away, the same way she had already done.

He had to promise me never to abandon you.

That day, Pavlik broke his promise. And how many has she broken? To share everything, be it pain or happiness. To be truthful. Not to risk her only friend's life in the interest of egotism.

She pushes herself up, unlocks the door. It's silent in the room. She feels her way to the bed and lies down. Pavlik is emanating heat like a fire brick. She hears his heart beating in the darkness.

'There were two things that I kept secret from you,' he whispers. 'That was one of them. The other is that Sandra and I were at the funeral. We respected your wishes. But after we saw you at your father's grave we didn't say a single word all day. I went to the Department, which was pointless, I was just pretending to be there. Lissek sent me home. The twins kept asking about you. They were too young to understand why you didn't come to visit us anymore. Leo said: "But *we* can see for her."

'One night I woke up and Sandra wasn't lying next to me. Her car had gone, she didn't answer her phone. I was going mad with worry. It was already light when she came back. She had driven to the Tegeler See, to the little beach where we had that picnic, do you remember? There she buried all the photographs we had of you. She told me that she had to stop looking at them all the time, because it made her so sad that her heart wouldn't beat properly anymore. Last Friday, when you were in bed, we bundled Jenny into the car and dug the box with the photographs up again.'

Ten perfect moments for Aaron:
  the intro to 'Purple Rain'
  her first gun
  meeting Sandra
  suddenly standing in front of Magritte's *Empire of Light*
  biting into a pastrami sandwich
  hiding in her grandparents' cherry tree
  the first sentence in Frisch's *I'm Not Stiller*
  bungee jumping
  the final image in Hitchcock's *Vertigo*
  in this filthy dump with Pavlik

They lie motionless for a long time.
  Then Aaron sits up. 'Have you called Demirci?'
  'First we should consider our options.'
  'You have to get the hell out of Morocco. I have an appointment with Veit Jansen.'
  '*We*,' he corrects her.
  'I can't ask that of you.'
  'Don't go silly on me.'
  'How do we get out afterwards?' Aaron asks. 'We're being sought for several murders. There may be facial composites of us in circulation.'
  'There are. I've had a look at them online. I'm one metre seventy, with a potbelly and Mediterranean appearance, most

likely Italian or Spanish. You've got chubby cheeks like Renée Zellweger and a tendency to warts. It hasn't occurred to anybody that you're blind.'

'I feel a little hurt.'

'Don't be so sensitive. The police aren't our main problem, it's the Broker. He has unlimited financial means. Using the large airports and border crossings is out of the question.'

'Lissek's piggy bank,' she says.

'That's what I was thinking.'

Lissek practised creative housekeeping and siphoned a little bit off every year. Over time, a seven-figure sum had built up. This secret fund served to pay for operations which were so expensive that Lissek would have had to replace a first-rate strategy with a second-rate one. Aaron remembers how Krupp once had to buy a Ferrari 599 in Dubai because it was part of his cover story. Lissek reluctantly released the three hundred thousand Euros. Things took a turn for the worse when Krupp wrote the racer off on his very first outing and it emerged that he had forgotten to insure it. Legendary sentence: 'It was all in Arabic.' Lissek was truly unbearable for weeks. During this period, it was also Lissek's birthday. The troop clubbed together. When they gathered at the Irish pub, the Ferrari they had hired was parked outside. Pavlik handed Lissek the keys with a grin: 'You can drive around in it for twenty-four hours. That's twenty more than Krupp had.' Lissek cracked up.

'Does Demirci know about the piggy bank?' she asks.

'Yes. Lissek told me how she reacted to the information.'

'Calmly?'

'It was eleven in the morning, she asked him to hand her the office booze.'

Aaron has strength again for a quiet laugh.

★

Demirci owns three encrypted phones. A work one, a private one and one on which you can *always* reach her, even if she's in a meeting at the Chancellery.

She answers immediately.

Pavlik puts the phone on speaker. 'It's us.'

'One second.' Demirci whispers to someone: 'Not now.' She closes a door. 'I'm listening.'

Pavlik provides her with a rundown of the past ten hours.

She asks the right questions:

How is Aaron? How much is Pavlik handicapped by the injury? Is the hotel safe?

'I've looked at a map,' he eventually says. 'There's a town on the edge of the Sahara. Erfoud. It has a small airfield. Send us a jet.'

'When can you get there?' Demirci's voice is so calm one would think she was arranging a business lunch.

'That depends on Veit Jansen,' says Aaron. 'We need information on him. All we know is that he lives here.'

'That can wait. First we get you back.'

'No. We can use him to get to the Broker. We might never have this opportunity again.'

'Why should we trust Holm?' Demirci interjects.

'Because I know him better than anyone else does.'

There is silence at the other end.

'The fund he made us aware of is important,' Aaron adds. 'A large-scale terrorist attack is being planned.'

Demirci says: 'Assuming you find Jansen, how long would you need to get to Erfoud?'

'Eight hours,' Pavlik calculates. 'But not with the van. The engine sounds as if it's about to die. We can rule out car hire, no doubt they're monitoring every rental place. The Peugeot is standing in the car park, but we hired it with our American passports, so they'll already be looking for that. I have to steal a car.'

'Too risky. The registration would be forwarded to all patrol cars.'

'Do you have a better idea?' Aaron asks.

'The liaison officer will take care of it.'

'He just let us walk into the trap at the bank.'

'Leave the BKA to me,' Demirci insists.

'Something else: I need to know which operations my father carried out in the two years before he retired. At some point during this time his path crossed with the Broker's.'

'OK. Ms Aaron?'

'Yes?'

'I'm very sorry.' Demirci ends the call.

'She didn't even break a sweat,' says Aaron.

'That's why she's got the job.'

'And not a single word about Bas Makata.'

'She will have her own thoughts on the matter.'

'Do you still think about it?' she asks.

'Sometimes it catches me out when I wake up.'

'Our doubts don't count, only our actions.'

'That's Lissek's line.'

'And true.'

They both leave it to the other to tear open that particular wound.

But for today there are wounds enough.

Pavlik rings Sandra. He tells her how things stand, doesn't gloss over anything, he's as honest as she demands. Then he goes into the bathroom to clean the guns; it's compulsory after a fire exchange, to avoid the risk of the gun jamming. And it stops them going round the bend.

Aaron goes to stand beside him. He silently hands her one of the guns. She takes it apart, places the breechblock, spring and barrel in the basin alongside the parts of the other Glock and carefully rubs Ballistol onto everything. The smell is as familiar to her as that of her skin. She grows calmer with each action. When everything has been rubbed dry, they put the guns back together without taking heed of which part belongs to which weapon.

The notion pleases her.

Aaron lays down on the bed while Pavlik showers. She finds herself thinking about the safe deposit box number again.

Forty-seven.

It reminds her of something, but she can't lay her finger on it. Is it another encoded message from Holm? He loved playing mind games.

Woyzeck.

Judith Traherne.

Forty-seven.

I am overwrought. It probably doesn't mean anything at all.

Her ears are bored. She hears a bed rhythmically creaking overhead. The fan is whining. A television is on somewhere. Tourists out on the street. Time stands still like a guard in front of the Royal Palace.

One hour. Two. Three.

There's a knock. Pavlik draws the Glock. 'Oui.'

'It's me.'

He lets the liaison officer in. 'Ah, what an honour.'

'Seems I'm your dogsbody,' Harry forces out.

'Like in the Rue des Berbères?' Aaron asks.

Harry's cough suggests a case of pharyngitis. 'You left five bodies behind in the souks,' he wheezes. 'I had to turn down the invitation to that party. In case you've wondered: the false personal descriptions are down to me. I know a few people in the police here. Cost me ten thousand Euros, Palmer will send the bill.'

'Fair enough,' she says.

'Don't get chummy with me.'

Something lands on the bed. A paper bag with sandwiches. Aaron smells chicken, curry, saffron. She realizes how hungry she is.

Pavlik grabs one too. 'Have you got the car?' he asks with a full mouth.

'BMW 5 Series, it's outside. Why don't you take the next plane? You won't have any trouble getting through customs.'

'Not an option.'

'Tangier? Ferry to Gibraltar?'

'No.'

'I could organize something in the south, straight across the desert, then over the border to Mauritania. We use the spot to shift informants out every now and then; we're financing the house building of two customs officers down there.'

Pavlik decides to be straight with him too. 'We're doing it via Erfoud. Do you know it?'

'You mean the airfield?'

'That's the one.'

'It's just a sand dune with a windsock. Resupply flights into the Sahara, geologists, hippies and Algerian smugglers. I would avoid Algeria if I were you. If you end up in prison there, you'll have to hold onto your balls with both hands. And as a woman, I'd say you're better off in Iran.'

'We've booked a direct flight,' Aaron replies.

'Right.' Harry is gripped by a coughing spell. 'We'd have to take the road over the Atlas. On the side roads you often have to slow down to walking pace, sometimes you can't drive at all. The pass is at fourteen hundred metres. Up there, it either rains cats and dogs or it snows like at the South Pole. Avalanches, landslides, mud. It's a frigging donkey path.'

'You're OK,' says Pavlik, 'but that was it as far as you're concerned. We'll sort the rest. You should hit the sack with that fever you've got.'

'I wouldn't dream of trying to change your mind.' Harry throws him the car key. 'I've heard you're looking for Veit Jansen.'

Aaron pricks up her ears.

'Demirci called Palmer, who called his deputy, who called the group leader, who called my informant leader. I just earn my living chewing on dry crusts at the end of the food chain.'

'You know who Jansen is?' she asks.

'Half a year ago, we were keeping tabs on an import-export firm in Würzburg. One of the deliveries to Casablanca caught our attention. I went to take a look. During the night, a lorry drove to Agadir, where they handed crates of explosives to an ISIS sleeper cell. I used the information to bring my account with the Moroccan secret service into the black. They shut down the cell and shared the results with us. A few months earlier, one of the terrorists had repeatedly phoned a man in Marrakech.'

'Jansen,' says Pavlik.

'Why are you interested in him?'

'The answer wouldn't be conducive to your convalescence.'

Harry laughs silently. 'He was a lobbyist for the German arms industry in Berlin until the end of the nineties. We didn't cross paths during that time. By 2008, he had withdrawn from his activities and had bought a villa in Marrakech, out in the Palmeraie. Nothing had been heard from him after that. Until half a year ago.'

Aaron gets an uneasy feeling. 'You're talking about him in the past tense.'

'They found him in the souks. Jansen was sitting on a chair as if he had nodded off, with an ice pick stuck in his back. A perfect job.'

The Broker.

Damn.

'Perhaps his wife will be of use to you. Layla al-Jazari. Twenty years younger than him, she has Tunisian roots but is a German citizen. I ran a quick update: she still lives in Marrakech.'

15

The BMW is parked in an unlit car park behind the madrasa. Nobody takes any notice of Pavlik, apart from two fighting cats, which slink off hissing.

He aimlessly drives through the winding streets of the medina. He can hear the distant drums on the Djemaa el Fna. They grow quiet, until they are just a notion, a reminder of an evening on which the world hadn't unravelled yet. Dark buildings stare at Pavlik. A cobalt blue night sky, the kind you see in old Hollywood films, stretches out above him.

His left calf itches, although he lost it on a country road eight years ago. He's got used to the fact that it helps if he scratches his right cheek.

Sometimes it's good to feel what you've lost.

On several occasions, he chooses a narrow lane in which pursuers would have to show themselves. When he is sure that he doesn't have company he enters Layla al-Jazari's address into the navigation system. He chooses a roundabout route, which will first take him south and then northwards along the Circuit de la Palmeraie. Minutes later, he's accelerating on the arterial road. The rich varoom of the two hundred horsepower engine gives him a fake sense of security.

Aaron wanted to come along. Pavlik persuaded her to stay. She should get some sleep, wouldn't be able to do anything anyway, will be safer in the hotel.

All good reasons.

In truth he simply needed to be alone.

The two of them are bound by the strongest friendship he's ever known. Perhaps friendship isn't even the right word. They have wrested each other away from the maws of death, that stays forever.

Her father was so much more for her.

Pavlik knew of Jörg Aaron long before he met his daughter. Mogadishu was part of the syllabus when he was being trained as a lone fighter and sniper with the mountain troops. Whenever it had been paramount to think of every contingency, and not to leave anything to chance, his sergeant used to say: 'Do it like Jörg Aaron.'

In later years, they came across each other professionally. Pavlik soon attracted the older man's attention during joint training sessions between the GSG 9 and the Department. When he couldn't entice Pavlik away, Jörg Aaron accepted the fact like a gigolo swallows the rebuff of an attractive woman. Though the next time they met, he did greet Pavlik with the comment: 'Ah, here's the man who kicked me in the balls.'

He was jovial without being chummy, witty without the need for smut, and he commanded respect without putting others down. Yet there was something about him that Pavlik didn't like. It took him a while to figure out what it was: ruthlessness.

This didn't manifest itself through domineering or irresponsible behaviour towards his men. But it was Pavlik's impression that Jörg Aaron made decisions on his own, and would cast any objections aside. In his position that was dangerous. That was why Pavlik hadn't let himself be wooed. He wasn't going to tell Aaron this; in any case she wouldn't want to hear it.

Her father noticed that Pavlik treated him with reservation and therefore did the same in return. They were professionally respectful towards each other, but that was all. This changed when Aaron joined the Department. It was just nuances, a long handshake, a glance. Jörg Aaron didn't need to spell it out: he hoped that Pavlik would keep an eye out for his daughter.

Was he a good father? Aaron wouldn't understand the question. He was everything for her and she for him. But what should Pavlik think of a man who puts a gun into the hands of a twelve year old and drills her until she outperforms him with it?

She was still a babe in arms when Jörg Aaron decided she would become a policewoman. He plunged her mother into misery. Pavlik remembers her clearly, a woman who must have been beautiful once, but who had aged prematurely. She never stopped seeking the little girl with plaits in her daughter.

He thinks of what his father-in-law said to him once while they sat fishing: 'Children don't owe their parents anything, and they in turn owe them everything.'

That is true.

Aaron's mother didn't hold it against her daughter, she accepted that she followed her father, became a tiny speck on the horizon and finally disappeared altogether. She punished her husband by leaving him. If it hurt him, he certainly didn't show it. But there came a day when even Jörg Aaron had to look into the mirror. Pavlik remembers walking down the endless hospital corridor in Barcelona with leaden steps, and seeing Aaron's father. He was sitting on a bench, clinging onto an empty coffee cup, all life drained from his face.

His wife had already been dead for two years. She was saved from witnessing this. Yes, he gave up everything for his daughter then. Without him she would be dead. But without him she would also never have become the woman whose ambition earned her a mortal enemy in Holm.

She fulfilled each one of her missions with an unrelenting drive. The point when one has to give up because it has become futile doesn't exist for her.

Aaron's father is one reason for this.

The other is the serial killer Runge.

She chased him when she was still a fledgling police cadet, but eventually gave up for the sake of her own sanity. The three women that Runge went on to murder afterwards haunt Aaron to this day. She feels accountable to them.

She is merciless.

Nobody can take everything away from her and think he'll survive it. Pavlik will have to decide whether he is going to take this possibly final journey with her too.

No words were needed.

She wants to kill one of the most powerful men in the world.

When she said 'Get the hell out of Morocco,' she built him a golden bridge supported by glass pillars. If he had consented, it would have been their farewell. Even if Aaron would never hold it against him, it would always stand between them.

Pavlik isn't like that.

Rather than killing the two men he traded fire with in the souks, he just incapacitated them.

He isn't on a revenge campaign.

That's easy to say. You haven't lost everything.

It would be too simplistic to tell himself that he promised Sandra. Supporting Aaron isn't the same thing as going into battle with her.

He doesn't owe her that.

But he owes himself the truth.

Our doubts don't count, only our actions.

The moment he had entered the Palmeraie into the navigation system, his mind was made up.

★

He has long left the city and the last street lights behind. Sand is blowing across the road in streaks. The headlights pluck white scraps out of the darkness; Pavlik hasn't seen another car for several minutes. At one point he spots the reflection of a camp fire, camel herders that have settled down for the night.

Then he sees distant lights, dumped in the middle of nowhere.

The Palmeraie welcomes him with a parade of flags. A toothless Berber is squatting beside a guard's hut. His braces rest against his pointy ribs as he sucks on a watermelon. The oasis was wrested from the desert in the nineties and is now home to the luxury resorts of large hotel chains. Pavlik zips along. The satnav leads him past a golf course and into a residential estate, where some of the plots are so enormous that the villas can't be seen from the road.

Jansen's house is large without being swanky. Compound wall, closed gate. Two floors, no light. The opposite side of the road is undeveloped; a palm grove.

Several cars are parked on the street. One of them contains two men. A grey Range Rover. Pavlik can look across without worry as he passes it, as his tinted windows hide him. The guy behind the wheel is an Arab, the other one he can't make out. There are a hundred reasons for a car to be passing at this hour; provided he doesn't stop, he is of no interest.

As he drives round the block, he registers another three inconspicuously parked vehicles.

Their positions are straight from the surveillance manual.

Eight men.

Pavlik drives on, doubles back and parks the BMW behind the palm grove. He shoulders his equipment bag and silently disappears into the dark. The knife scar is no longer bothering him. The graze wound stings, but barely impedes his movement.

He stops at the edge of the grove. Opposite is the south face of the villa, with the gate.

Pavlik looks around. There are two refuse containers partially covered by palms. He climbs onto one of them. The Rover is thirty metres to his left; for the men inside Pavlik isn't even a shadow. He takes the night vision goggles out of the bag and takes a closer look at them. He recognizes the one on the passenger side. He's the supposed tourist who offered to help yesterday, when Aaron was shuffling about in front of the bank. Nordic type, wiry, awake, busy cracking nuts. The other has neck muscles like a wrestler; a real bulldozer.

Pavlik switches to thermal mode and focuses his attention on the villa. On the first floor, he receives the heat signature of a person lying down, probably Layla. She is tossing and turning, wakeful. He changes back to night vision. The front door and the gate have electronic locks. A Smart car and a Mercedes are standing in a carport. He briefly considers attaching a camera to one of the palms, but it might be discovered.

He thinks of Aaron on the terrace at the Djemaa el Fna, the unbelievable moment when she told him what the man had whispered into his phone. That's better than a camera.

Pavlik reaches into the bag and slides a dummy and two magnetic miniature tracking devices into the magazine of the compressed air rifle. He selects a parked car on the other side of the road. Renault, hundred metres.

Pavlik sends the dummy on its journey. The shot is silent, but the alarm system of the Renault starts to wail when the rubber projectile hits the radiator grille. The men immediately leap out of the Rover. Nutcracker speaks into a walkie-talkie; Bulldozer draws a revolver and runs along the compound wall.

Pavlik fires off the tracking devices. The gentle smack of the magnets as they attach themselves to the number plates of the Smart car and the Mercedes in the carport can't be heard in the noise. He has placed the GPS trackers right on the digits, only very close inspection would reveal their presence.

In the house, a light comes on upstairs. Pavlik catches sight of a woman's outline behind the curtains, but he hasn't got time to look more closely right now.

When Nutcracker runs into the palm grove, Pavlik is already a hundred metres away. He gets into the car and drives southward without having been discovered.

As he cruises along the Circuit de la Palmeraie, the only thing in the rear-view mirror is the moon, a bright disc that rolls out from behind the clouds. Pavlik switches on the radio and finds a station that plays schmaltzy pop songs. All that's missing is a cigarette and it would be perfect.

16

Finding sleep is impossible. She lies there for an hour, rigid and stiff, as if trapped in an iron lung.

My birthday, I was so disappointed when I had unwrapped my presents, so sad when I went to bed. But then came quiet steps, a package with a bow, a beautiful Starfire 9 mm. His smile. 'I'll keep it safe for you, your mother mustn't know.'

She spends a further hour trying to cry. The few tears she manages to squeeze out are as hard as grit.

She remembers what her father once said: 'If you're hurting, buy yourself a pair of shoes that pinch.' Sometimes an ache can help to take your mind off the pain.

Aaron feels around for her mobile and asks Siri for the time difference to Taiwan. 'The time in Taipei City, Taiwan, is zero nine hours and twelve minutes.'

Thomas Reimer should have had breakfast by now. She knows his number off by heart.

'Yes?' he mumbles sleepily.

'Jenny Aaron. Did I wake you up?'

'No problem at all. I have to get up in four hours anyway.'

'I thought you were in Taiwan?'

'Until yesterday. Now I'm in Nairobi.'

'I'm sorry. We can talk another time.'

'I'll have room service bring me a coffee, then I'll call you back.'

Her telephone number is withheld, so she gives it to him.

Aaron lights a cigarette, counts the seconds. She can't concentrate, starts again, and again and again, and only ever makes it to ten.

Finally the mobile rings.

'What can I help you with?' Reimer asks.

'For several months now, I've had specific symptoms. I wanted to tell you about them in Sweden, but it was all too much that evening.'

'What symptoms?'

'I almost constantly have cold hands and feet. I'm never thirsty, and I have a low pain barrier.'

'Do you react to weather changes?'

'Yes.'

'Vibration sensitivity?'

'Yes.'

'Do smells sometimes make you nauseous?'

'Yes again.' She takes a deep breath. 'Am I ill?'

'It's the Flammer syndrome.'

'What's that?'

'You have an unusual name. Are you related to Jörg Aaron?'

'He was my father.'

'Thought so. Flammer mainly affects women of your age who are extremely ambitious, overexert themselves to the point of exhaustion and have a compulsion to be in control. Those affected are often unable to process grief and pain, and have a tendency to try to struggle through it alone. The super-ego dominance plays an important role. Given who your father was, I don't need to ask who shaped your super-ego.'

'Is that all you can offer? Kitchen sink psychology?' she asks sharply. 'How disappointing.'

'Direct hit?' he replies.

Angry silence.

'Have you tried to live up to his expectations all your life?' he continues.

'Given how little you know me, you're surprisingly quick to pass judgement.'

'And you denounced me as a phoney in record time.'

'I just wanted to know whether I'm ill.'

'No, you're not. The Flammer syndrome is an indication of the permanent stress you're under.'

'Thank you. I'm sorry that I got you out of bed,' she says frostily and is about to hang up.

'My secretary has told me that you haven't registered for the therapy,' she hears Reimer say. 'I'm wondering why.'

'Something came up.'

'I see. One has to set priorities,' he drily replies.

'I'm on a mission in Morocco.'

'Have you noticed any changes over the last few days?'

She doesn't answer.

'I'll take that as a yes.'

Reluctantly she says: 'It used to take about half an hour before my eyes responded to light again. But today it's been pitch black since lunchtime.'

'Are we talking adrenalin?'

'Yes.'

'I've tried to explain to you that adrenalin is counter-productive. You have to reduce your exposure to it.'

'If you jump in the water, you get wet.'

'And if you don't climb out, you stay wet.'

Her heartbeat is taking her on a merry-go-round.

'Imagine you're flying over Amsterdam and you see lots of large and small canals. That's your blood circulation. The aorta, arteries and veins are the main channels, they don't care if they are flooded with stress hormones. Unfortunately, your retina and your brain are full of very delicate capillaries, which are extremely sensitive to stress. It causes the cells to go into hibernation.'

'For how long?'

'Come on, you're an intelligent woman.'

The merry-go-round is spinning so fast she feels dizzy.

'Stress is a pick-pocket, but adrenalin is a killer. For a while, your cells can protect themselves against it by shutting down. That's what I mean by hibernation. The Flammer syndrome is an indication that your blood supply is dysregulated. That's why you permanently have cold hands and feet. The adrenalin is causing a spasm in your cerebral vessels, which is cutting off the oxygen supply to the cells. If it continues for too long, the cells die off. That's permanent. I don't know whether my therapy would be successful with you. But I know with absolute certainty that you will never be able to see again if you carry on the way you have been.'

She hears the echo of a drop thundering into the bathroom basin.

The dynamo on a bicycle whirs past outside.

A key jingles down in the lobby.

Continental plates are shifting under the Atlantic.

All she keeps thinking is: *Never Never Never.*

Reimer asks: 'Are you still there?'

'That's bullshit. That would mean everyone who's under permanent stress would go blind,' she blurts out.

'People deal with it differently. Somebody who has been on an adventure trip down the Amazon, during which he was nearly strangled by an anaconda, had to flee from natives with blowpipes and survived a crocodile attack, isn't going to get in a lather when he comes back and finds there's a scratch on his car. His neighbour, who fights his way through the urban jungle of Berlin every day, also finds a scratch in the paintwork. And this man goes berserk.'

'I'm more the Amazon type.'

'No, you're not. You've snapped at me twice, just in the course of this phone call. You're a ticking bomb. It depends on how often a person is exposed to adrenalin, for how long, over what time span and, most importantly, how they dispel it. You've been living at the limit for a long time, without compensating for it, Ms Aaron. Now it's coming back to roost.'

'For five years I was totally blind, and then suddenly I was able to differentiate between light and dark. That means something in me has improved, not worsened.'

'There are spontaneous recoveries. We're a long way from knowing everything about the human brain. Sometimes coma patients wake up after years. We have to acknowledge that. It doesn't mean that the laws of biology are erased.'

'I can't pick and choose my stress levels right now.'

'I've never had a patient for whom the terms we use have such a different meaning. It's as though we have insufficient command of each other's language. You speak of stress and mean adrenalin. I speak of meditation and you of combat training. It's about time you find out who you are. When you're on your deathbed, it won't matter whether you were able to see or not, only what kind of person you were.'

'There's something I have to see through,' she whispers. 'After that I'll be all yours. You can ask of me whatever you want. If the therapy involves standing naked on one leg in the pedestrian zone all night, then that's what I'll do.'

'What I expect of you isn't important. What do you expect of yourself?'

'You said that my visual centre is able to protect itself against the adrenalin for a certain amount of time. How long for?'

'Ms Aaron—'

'Please!'

Reimer takes a deep breath. 'I'm not going to give you an exact figure. That would be unscientific. And you would count the minutes.'

'How could I prevent this spasm?'

'No doctor in the world would support you in doing that.'

'You're not a doctor. The doctors have given up on me.'

It feels like his silence will never end. Then he grumbles: 'An endothelin blocker would improve the blood flow and relax the blood vessels.'

'Is it sold as a medicine?'

'Yes. For the treatment of epilepsy, for example.'

'What is it called?'

'Endothelinac. It has strong side-effects. Headaches, mood swings, tiredness, vertigo.'

'Sounds as though I've been swallowing it for years. What dose do I have to take?'

'There's no way I'm going to tell you that. When are you coming back to Germany?'

'I don't know.'

She wants to cry.

She wants to so badly.

'I should turn you down as a patient. You ride roughshod over everything that would be conducive to a successful therapy.'

Her heart is pushing against her cold chest.

'And are you going to?'

'Take care, Ms Aaron.' Reimer ends the call.

Minute after minute she waits in vain for tears.

She capitulates, goes into the bathroom to wash her face with cold water and hears the door.

Pavlik pokes his head in.

He can see something is up, but he doesn't ask.

'And?'

'The villa is guarded like Fort Knox. Eight men outside. I've marked Layla's two cars.'

'Are they her guys?'
'They'd be on the premises if they were.'
'Does she know about them?' she asks.
'Probably.'
'Did you see her?'
'For a second, behind the curtain. It looks like she's alone in the house.' He runs his hand over her hair. 'It's going to be a long day. Even fireflies need to sleep sometime.'

Ten words that Aaron loves:
  wistful
  smarty-pants
  shenanigans
  crux
  sunset
  fiddlesticks
  clean
  firefly
  woebegone
  sweet-pea

She's been listening to Pavlik's quiet breathing for an eternity. Now he's mumbling something in his sleep, incomprehensible, but gentle, without fear. Who is he talking to? Perhaps he's in a place where the dead console the living. Aaron wishes she could slip into his dream.
  I speak of meditation and you of combat training.
  It's not that she doesn't know how to do it.
  It's just that it's been a while.
  Aaron imagines walking through a museum where the world's most complicated paintings are on display. Dalí's *Galatea of the Spheres*, *Berlin Linocut* by Mark Webber, Jackson Pollock's

The She-Wolf, Giorgio Vasari's *Battle of Marciano*; the big commentators. She stops in front of a Hieronymus Bosch.

The Wrath of God.

She studies the painting, then fades it out.

Aaron pictures herself in front of a white canvas and starts to fill it with the motifs of the painting: the burning palace, the winged two-horn rhino, the archangel on the mount of perdition, the waterspout made of gilded masks, the Cardinal with the tongues of fire, the Medusa in the mirror and the man without a face, the amorous couple with hair of locusts, the cat playing with a severed hand.

She contemplates her work. She sees that something isn't right and ponders what it is. The waterspout. It belongs on the right, next to the beautiful woman in the cage of thorns, the dragon fish and the one-legged executioner.

The cat winks at her. 'See, you're dreaming already.'

I'm not.

'You are.'

The water pouring out the spout is cool and fresh. Aaron quenches her thirst and looks across the harbour to the blue timber house, which is as one with the blue firmament and the blue sea.

Pavlik is standing on the jetty.

But he says: 'You're not here for me.'

She turns and sees her father. 'I was beginning to think you'd stood me up,' he tells her. 'Not that I was bored. We're never bored here.' His eyes laugh sadly; seagulls fly out of his Havana and up into the sky.

They head out on the boat. It is warm, the air tastes of seaweed. The wind dunks a lonely cloud into the yolk of the sun. They set the sails and glide into a perfect summer's day, and Pavlik remains behind on the jetty, motionless.

Aaron can see far into the distance: the whitecaps of the swell, the boisterous ballet of the dolphins, and on the horizon a ship with three funnels.

'Your boat,' her father says and hands her the rudder.

She sets course for the dolphins, races across the crests of the waves, standing in the spray.

Her father looks back at the blue timber house that is getting smaller and smaller. 'I should have the roof retiled.'

Suddenly Aaron's heart beats so hard that it leaps out of her chest and sinks to the bottom of the sea. She listens to the thump-thump until it is lost among the rushing of the waves.

'Why didn't you tell me that you were unwell on our last evening?' she whispers.

'I thought I was immortal. We all do, don't we?'

'I don't. Not anymore.'

'Because death is your friend. But it's a false friend. It only thinks of itself.'

'When did you come across the Broker?'

She can't bear his gaze, which speaks of the nights at her bedside in Barcelona.

'I don't want you to find him,' he replies. 'Even if you survive, what would you gain?'

'Peace.'

'Didn't you hear what the professor said? You have to let go of me, otherwise you will never regain your sight.'

'What will I do with it?' she asks. 'See your grave for the first time and breathe the same air as your murderer?'

'Isn't it cowardly for a samurai to seek death?'

'Not if he dies for his lord.'

'Head back, there's a storm brewing,' her father says.

But Aaron holds the course.

She sails out onto the open sea. Under black clouds, over black water, surrounded by the cries of black sea birds she heads towards a black sun.

Her father is gone. She feels a small hand inside hers.

The boy whispers: 'I know who you are, even if you don't know who I am.'

She thinks about this, but she knows exactly who the boy is. Aaron tries to say his name, she struggles and struggles, but cannot utter it.

Suddenly she understands. She has been saying it all along, she just can't hear it.

Because she is deaf.

But it doesn't frighten her. She is perfectly calm. The hand of the boy is cool and firm. She feels safe and secure because she realizes in this moment that he is her guardian angel.

17

They set off before dawn. The street smells of last night's rain, of dust sticking to asphalt. The city is already noisy. It's cool. Horses pull heavy carts along the roads, lambs in a cattle truck bleat against the siren of an ambulance.

Aaron's temples are throbbing. She thinks of how she crept into the bathroom, leaving Pavlik to sleep. Her finger hovered over the switch, until finally she flicked it and the neon burst into her eyes. She stood in front of the mirror for a long time, staring into the blinding white wall of light. She lost track of time and jumped when Pavlik said from the door: 'We're running late.'

She let minutes pass, lost in the one second when he turned round and left her alone. She could still see his movement, his shoulder was a veil, his head a pale dot like in a Pointillist painting.

It's back. For how long?

Now, in the car, she wonders what awaits Pavlik and her today. She can guess: a tsunami of adrenalin. She needs the epilepsy drug. But the pharmacies aren't open yet.

The Magic Tree air freshener dangling from the rear-view mirror reeks of synthetic apple. It's giving Aaron a headache, but she doesn't chuck it out; the smell is a welcome distraction.

'What if Layla doesn't know anything?' she asks.

'The Broker wouldn't have put the house under surveillance if she didn't.'

'What's he scared of?'

'She might know his name.'

'Then why isn't she dead yet?'

'He probably thinks we can't knock off that many men,' Pavlik replies. 'That's a mistake, but every mistake finds somebody to make it.'

That is true. If you doubt that you can defeat any enemy with your spirit alone, then you also doubt that water extinguishes fire.

But Aaron isn't convinced. 'Perhaps she's a lure.'

'By the way, did I ever tell you about the little dude in my head?' he retorts.

'No. How do you get on with him?'

'Some days better than others. Ever since yesterday, he's been knocking on my skullcap and telling me that this woman is a top prize.'

Once Pavlik has made a decision, he is immune to all doubts. This gives her courage, as always.

He stops at a bakery and buys mineral water and a warm flatbread. They don't know when they will next get something to eat. As he accelerates on the arterial road, she asks: 'How large is the property?'

'Seven thousand square metres. Palms, argan trees.'

'Wall or fence?'

'Wall, three metres high, stone.'

'Any protection?'

'Glass shards along the top edge.'

'Motion sensors?'

'Didn't see any.'

'And the gate?'

'Smooth steel, with prongs at the top.'

'How far is it from there to the front door?'

'Twenty-one metres.'

Aaron can rely on that. As a sniper, Pavlik is able to accurately determine distances and sizes; he can do it standing on his head.

Paved path, four metres wide, lined by cedars. No steps in front of the door. Rose beds, a fountain, on the left the carport. The house has a living area of about three hundred square metres. Modern architecture, pale stone. Going by the windows, there are probably seven rooms. Three of them are on the first floor, which is narrower, an elegant superstructure with a terrace along each side. They only know the function of one of the rooms: Layla's bedroom on the right.

These are the bare facts.

Aaron breaks off some bread, chews reluctantly, and drinks some water because common sense tells her to. After about half an hour Pavlik slows down. They're here. Aaron feels his calm. She too has brushed off all insecurity and nervousness. It's a familiar transition. It's what happens when there's no turning back.

He turns off the road and stops. She knows that they're in a small car park; Pavlik chose it last night. It's two hundred metres to the house, as the crow flies. There's no visual contact; that would be too risky because of the men keeping watch on it. Layla is probably still asleep. They will know if she leaves in one of the cars, as the bugs on the number plates are linked to Pavlik's mobile.

He starts up the wireless decoder. The device scans every electronic impulse within five hundred metres and stores the signals of car keys, household appliances, TV remote controls, telephones, radio alarm clocks, timers and all kinds of transponders.

For them, however, only Layla's gate is of interest.

When it opens, Pavlik can copy and decrypt the signal with the decoder, and can then control the gate as if he had Layla's sensor. Most of these locking systems operate with a single algorithm. That would mean that they could also unlock the front door of the villa.

But in order to find the right one among the flood of received signals, they have to know when exactly the gate is being opened.

Without Pavlik being able to see it.

This is Aaron's job.

'Do you think you'll hear it at that distance?' he had asked.

'Perhaps.'

She opens the window and ramps her cortex up to operating temperature. She hears distant cars on the Circuit. A quiet staccato, plop-plop-plop, golf balls on the driving range. Somewhere a coffee machine gurgles behind an open window. Fluttering flags, probably a hotel. Several lawn sprinklers are hissing. Small birds shyly chirrup. There's a clatter from window shutters, but not on Layla's street.

'It would help if you could breathe more quietly,' Aaron says.

The man with the resting heart rate of twenty-eight bpm huffs.

Time is a sated, fat snail. Nothing in the world is harder than concentrating in a complete void.

Paths to infinity.

Clouds wander aimlessly.

No traveller knows the hut over there.

Aaron diligently analyses every sound and archives it. If one of them repeats itself she doesn't pay any attention to it, her subconscious has already stored it away as unimportant. Thus, the world around her grows more and more quiet.

She sinks into the waiting like into sleep.

What if Layla doesn't leave the villa at all?

Not today, not tomorrow, not in a hundred years?

Dawn slowly breaks. Pavlik's belly grumbles. Gusts of wind kick an empty can over the street. Two or three times a car passes. A muezzin calls people to morning prayer, so distant it's no more than a notion.

The river cleans fish.

When you reach the horizon you see the next horizon.

There.

Electric motor.

Aaron raises a finger, Pavlik sits up.

No, it's not a sliding gate. Different house.

Just as she is about to signal *false alarm*, she registers a squeaking and scraping. It's barely more than a suggestion.

Right distance, right direction.

'That's it,' says Aaron.

Thirty seconds later, cars are started up and driven away. The gate closes again.

'Have you got the signal?' she asks.

'Yes. How many cars are following her?'

'Three or four.'

She knows that this isn't precise enough. One of the vehicles may have stayed behind to keep an eye on the villa. They will have to find out.

'I'll go and have a look,' says Pavlik.

He avoids going through the palm grove.

A bear doesn't piss in the same bush twice.

There's no one about, the neighbourhood isn't awake yet. A glance at his mobile tells him that Layla is heading southward. She has taken the Smart car, she's probably heading into the city.

Pavlik reaches her road and peers around the corner. He sees the Rover, as expected.

Two men have been left behind.

He goes through their options: they could repeat the game every day until the Broker thinks that they've left Marrakech and calls away the guards. How long might that take? Weeks? Months? Another possibility would be to try to get at Layla in town.

Not yet.

All they know about her is that she was married to Jansen. That's not enough to put pressure on her.

One step at a time.

First they have to get into the villa.

Then they'll get hold of Layla.

Pavlik hopes that the two men in the Rover are still the same ones as last night. That would mean that they've got a long shift behind them and their reaction speed won't be as fast as that of a rested team.

And how rested is he?

He's about to find out.

Layla drove off four minutes ago. Pavlik has to wait until she has reached the city, to ensure the surveillance commando is far enough away.

He crouches down behind a palm. A bit of shade and greenery are all he needs to make himself invisible. He checks the decoder and sees that the binary code of the sensor signal has been decrypted.

Pavlik calls Aaron. 'Two.'

'Can you get at them?'

'Not on the street.'

'Lure them onto the property.'

'Too early.'

'Where's Layla?'

'Heading into town. I'll be back in touch.' He ends the call.

He's concerned about Aaron. When he got back to the hotel at three, she had that 'don't ask' look he knows so well. She came and laid down next to him to sleep. He had left the light on in the room, forgetting that this wasn't necessary with Aaron.

She didn't switch it off.

When she heard him get up to switch it off she quickly said: 'Sorry, forgot.'

He knew then that she couldn't differentiate between light and dark anymore. He lay there with his eyes open for a long time. He pretended to be asleep, mumbled something, as if he was dreaming. At some point he drifted off. When he woke up at five, he felt like he'd spent the night downing a bottle of vodka and having a bar fight.

While she was in the bathroom, he did something that he's ashamed of. He checked her mobile. She had rung an unfamiliar number during the night. The phone call was very brief, but then the other person had called her back. They had talked for twenty minutes.

Pavlik dialled the number.

He heard the other person say 'Reimer' and ended the call.

It took a lot of effort not to let on. Aaron is so sensitive that even silence could have given him away.

As they left the room, he wanted to check one last time. Somewhere inside him there was a glimmer of hope that he'd got it wrong.

He deliberately left the light on.

Aaron said: 'Switch the light off.'

He kept his confusion to himself. Perhaps it's wrong to wait until she opens up. She can be so unbelievably secretive. Damn, she probably thinks exactly the same about him. For two people who share so much, they share surprisingly little.

Pavlik looks at his mobile. The Smart car has reached Marrakech's city centre and is standing in the Rue el Jahed.

Hivernage. He knows the area. 'In Hivernage, even the beggars wear Gucci,' someone once said to him. Someone he has been trying not to think about for the past two days.

Sarotti, who always wanted to fly first class.

He returned to Berlin in a zinc coffin.

Pavlik severs the recollection with a glance at his watch. If anything happens at Layla's villa, the two men will inform the surveillance commando. Then one or possibly two cars will be sent back. It takes at least twenty-five minutes to get here from the city.

He walks back to the street corner. Using the decoder, he opens the gate to the villa. The men immediately leap out of the Rover and draw their guns.

It's the same two as yesterday: Nutcracker and Bulldozer.

He studies them.

Nutcracker moves like somebody for whom a few minutes' sleep in a cold car are plenty. As he runs in a zigzag towards the property he remembers to protect himself; he keeps in the shadows, swerves round a lamppost which could provide some cover if need be, and oscillates his upper body so as not to provide a fixed target. None of his movements appear rash or frantic; he even finds the time to instruct his partner with whispered commands.

Military or police training, of the elite variety.

Bulldozer is the sort of guy whose last thought will be to wonder what he's done wrong. The answer would be: pretty much everything. He doesn't cast a single glance into the palm grove, he leaves his rear uncovered, storms towards the gate in full frontal position and doesn't work the slide of his gun until he gets there. The man doesn't have much experience with situations such as this one. Brute force is probably his thing. Bouncer, debt collector, bone crusher. It's hard to find good people, even for the Broker; reassuring to know.

When they have vanished out of sight, Pavlik sprints forwards. He's at the gate in ten seconds. They are nowhere to be seen, have probably split up and are running round the house to the left and right.

He attaches the silencer to his gun.

Option one: he waits until they reappear and engages in a gunfight with them.

Not good.

He needs at least one of them alive.

Nutcracker.

Option two: he hides on the rear seat of the Rover, sends Bulldozer warmest regards from the Glock family and knocks out Nutcracker. Also a gamble. He doubts that the latter will fall prey to a trick like that.

Third option?

He thinks of Lissek's retirement do. After the steak house, the Irish pub and the karaoke dive, they had ended up in a go-go bar. Lissek had married Nieser off to one of the strippers, wearing nothing but his underpants and a table cloth, which he had fashioned into a cassock. And that was more than the bride and groom were wearing.

Heaven knows how the photo ended up in the hands of Nieser's wife. She gave him a right dressing down. Fricke was there. Apparently Nieser stammered: 'Sweetheart, I was briefly distracted on the street, and as I turned round, there was this door standing open. I just traipsed in after the others, I swear.'

Thanks, Nieser.

Pavlik runs to the door, unlocks it with the decoder and leaves it wide open. He doesn't know whether there are any staff in the house; presumably not, otherwise someone would have come to see what was going on with the gate.

The entrance hall has a closet that serves as a cloakroom. He makes space for his ninety kilos and pulls the door to, leaving just a crack.

Pavlik waits.

He hears heavy breathing.

Bulldozer is the advance party.

Good.

Behind him Nutcracker whispers in English: 'Steady now.'

He has an accent. German or Scandinavian.

The first time Pavlik killed someone was shortly after he had started working for the SEK Special Enforcement Commando. He was deeply moved by the event, even though it was pretty repulsive. The guy, a Lithuanian, was crammed to the eyeballs with Ecstasy. As they stormed the dealer's apartment he grabbed a sawn-off shotgun. Pavlik's bullet shredded his aorta, but the guy still managed to pepper the ceiling with lead, that's how close it was. Dying is only quick in films. Most of the time it's an agonizing struggle, an endless grind. The Lithuanian emptied his bowels and it stank of shit as he clawed at Pavlik's uniform and called for his mother. Many have followed him. It hasn't made Pavlik indifferent, but it's no longer the same.

In the seconds it takes for Bulldozer to creep past the closet, Pavlik reflects on the fact that his opponent wouldn't give him the slightest chance. For this he gets a death of which he will barely be aware.

Important rule: make it simple and make it fast.

He shoots Bulldozer in the back of the head and throws himself against the closet door. It smacks Nutcracker squarely in the face and sends him reeling. As Pavlik flies towards him, the man numbly tries to evade him, haphazardly fires in his direction, but misses him. Pavlik slams Nutcracker's lower arm onto the knee he sends darting up. The man drops his gun with a groan and staggers as Pavlik rams his fist into his face.

So far, it's been a piece of cake. As he stabs his Glock into Nutcracker's jugular notch he wonders whether he overestimated him.

He didn't.

The man bats aside the weapon so fast that to Pavlik it looks like an abrupt cut in a film.

Nutcracker grabs the silencer. Both try to gain possession of the gun, twisting their hands at mind-boggling speed, while belting kicks and any free fist into the other's face, eyes and genitals.

A tiny window opens in Nutcracker's cover. Pavlik slams his palm onto his opponent's lips, which sends an electric surge shooting through the man's body.

But it's a pyrrhic victory. Nutcracker has simultaneously levered the gun out of Pavlik's hand. The Glock tumbles to the floor.

They stand facing each other, one metre apart.

The guns are lying between them. They read in each other's eyes that neither of them is going to try to reach them.

Nutcracker spits out blood. 'Tired, old man?'

'Let's find out.'

Pavlik's shifts his weight onto the balls of his feet, draws his chin down onto his chest to protect his jaw and opens the debate with a swift right-hand jab, which Nutcracker neatly blocks, replying with a double hand against Pavlik's sternum. He responds with a reverse punch, driving his shoulder and hip forwards to give the blow a brutal power. Normally this is a knock-out argument, but it shows no effect. Nutcracker just shakes himself off, continues the conversation with a kick to Pavlik's neck and even stays relaxed when Pavlik drives his knuckles into his spleen. They swap anecdotes with humourless upper cuts and jabs. Nutcracker's fist makes an arrogant assertion against Pavlik's sinus node, which Pavlik contradicts with rollicking liver shots. The ridgehand that his opponent fires off could have buckled his windpipe like a straw, but it dissipates like chatter because Pavlik ducks down.

He could spend hours chewing the fat with Nutcracker, but time is ticking away. Three minutes have passed since he opened the gate, and he is sure that his opponent will have already informed the others in the city.

Pavlik has to end the fight. Now.

The axe kick with his carbon prosthetic has the force of a sledgehammer.

But Nutcracker dodges it with lightning speed. With stiff fingers he stabs into the neuroplexus of Pavlik's pelvic organs.

And straight into the scar below his navel.

The pain thunders towards Pavlik like a steam train and tears him into a black tunnel. In the void, a thought spins past him: he should have drawn his knife. In a blind reflex he pushes his thumbs into Nutcracker's eyes, but there's no strength in it.

Far away, he hears the voice of his instructor: *You're always engaged in two battles. One against your opponent and one against yourself. When everything inside you yearns to give up, you haven't even reached half of your potential.*

Nothing but mere theory; Pavlik slides into a big silence.

Nutcracker has done everything right. Except one thing: he rams his knee into Pavlik's hip wound. Beside this pain there can be no other.

It's like an adrenalin injection into his heart.

The train races out of the tunnel with him. Suddenly he sees everything in razor-sharp detail: Nutcracker's white knuckles, the thick blue vein pulsating on his neck, the perfectly twisted shoulder as he prepares the final farewell with a kick to Pavlik's head.

But no matter how much he can take, the knife that Pavlik drives into his thigh up to the plunge line, while simultaneously slamming his elbow onto the bridge of his nose, is too much.

Nutcracker keels over.

He stays down. He's gone.

Pavlik once read that in Stalingrad they carried out amputations with the lids of tin cans. Without anaesthesia. That must have felt like his hip just then. He doesn't sink to his knees, he falls. For half an eternity he just breathes to fend off the blackout that threatens to engulf him. His entire body consists only of this damned wound.

Pain does not exist. It is a fairy tale told by our nervous system, they've had drummed into them.

This particular fairy tale he will remember for ever.

Groaning, he pushes Nutcracker's gun into his waistband. He pulls the knife out of the man's leg, wipes it on his jeans and tucks it into the sheath under his jacket.

He pats down Nutcracker and finds the phone in his leather jacket. German display. He checks the last call. Five minutes ago, Moroccan number.

Pavlik checks the location of the Smart car. Still in Hivernage, now in the Rue du Temple. But at least one car is on its way over here.

He inserts a flash drive into Nutcracker's phone and loads the app that Krampe, the Department's technician, has developed. Pavlik grabs the Glock and slaps Nutcracker in the face until he wakes up.

When he opens his eyes they are blood red because Pavlik's thumbs have caused the veins to burst.

You probably look better than I do.

He kicks the phone to Nutcracker. 'Press the button and read out the text,' he says.

'Fuck you.'

'Read it without altering your voice, or I'll do the same to you as I did to your mate.'

'The hell I will.'

Pavlik shoots him in the right knee. The man doesn't make a single sound, but red tears trickle from his red eyes and over his stark white lips.

'I've changed my mind,' Pavlik growls. 'First both knees, then the elbows, then your balls.'

Nutcracker takes the phone.

The app will generate a mirror pattern of his voice. Krampe has a penchant for poetry and has chosen a poem that contains all the necessary sounds for a perfect clone.

It is by Robert Gernhardt and is called: 'The Intercity Has a Brake Failure After Karlsruhe.'

Grudgingly, Nutcracker starts to read: 'Framed in the lilac's purple blaze stands a cottage—'

Pavlik shoots off his left earlobe. 'Like I said: read it with your normal voice.'

He makes more of an effort now. 'Framed in the lilac's purple blaze stands a cottage / The rusting tub is immersed in blooms / A path runs dry and dusty / Unceasing, the wind tugs at the grass / All is enraptured: the swallows, the blossom / All is steady: the fences, the hedgerows / All is illuminated: the ballast, the sleepers / All is buggered: the brakes, the schedule.'

'Good boy.'

Nutcracker slides the phone back over to Pavlik.

'Stand up,' he says.

The man tries to get up. He uses his kneecap as an excuse, failing artfully. Pavlik wouldn't dream of helping him.

When Nutcracker realizes that Pavlik isn't falling for it, he pushes himself up.

'Turn round.' Pavlik hits him over the head with the butt of the Glock. Nutcracker collapses. He drags him to the closet, shoves him in, locks the door and calls the number on the screen.

It is answered immediately. 'Yes?'

'Where are you?' he asks in English. For the person on the other end he now sounds like Nutcracker.

'About halfway. Anything new?'

'You can turn round. It was the cleaner. I've disposed of her.'

'Oh boy.'

Someone with Nutcracker's abilities would be a leader in any elite unit. Correspondingly, Pavlik acts self-assured. 'Go cry to your mama. What's Layla doing?'

'She's taken the boy to school.'
A child. That complicates matters.
'Stay on her,' Pavlik says coolly.
'She's having breakfast on the terrace of the Royal Mirage. Three are with her. Shouldn't we still—'
'You've heard me,' he snaps.
'OK. Where shall we send her afterwards?'
His pain is abruptly numbed by a realization:
Layla is receiving orders from them.
'To the Palais Badi, tell her to go for a walk,' he forces out.
The other man ends the call.
He senses it even before the gate to the road closes.
Behind him.
He drops the gun and raises his hands.
Very slowly he turns round. He sees highly polished Italian shoes and hears a voice from the realm of the dead.
'Hello, Pavlik.'

18

At eight on the dot she called a pharmacy. They didn't have Endothelinac in stock. Aaron got the same answer from the next two she rang. She could carry on trying, but it's clear that the earliest she will get the drug is the day after tomorrow. She has ordered it nevertheless. She doesn't know how long she will have to stay in Marrakech. How quickly they can get to Layla.

'Twelfth of February. Thursday. Eight a.m., ten minutes, forty-seven seconds,' says her watch in the car.

Forty-seven.

Forty-seven.

Forty-seven.

As far as she's aware, the number hasn't played any significant role in her life. Did it have a special meaning for Holm? If yes, it would have to relate to something that connects them.

Suddenly it's so simple that Aaron can't understand why she didn't think of it straight away.

Bushidō.

The forty-seven rōnin. Of course.

The feudal lord Asano Naganori once came to the court of the shōgun in Edo. When a master of ceremonies insulted him,

Naganori sliced open the master's forehead with his sword. For this, the shōgun ordered Naganori to kill himself by seppuku, which caused his samurai to become leaderless rōnin.

Forty-seven of them decided to avenge the death of their daimyō. Because the master of ceremonies suspected this, he had his house protected by the shōgun's household guard. The rōnin still managed to force their way in. They killed half an army. Their leader decapitated the master of ceremonies with Naganori's sword, and the rōnin laid his head on their lord's grave in the temple of Sengakuji. Then they turned themselves in to face the shōgun's judgement and also committed seppuku.

Like Aaron, Holm followed Bushidō philosophy.

He knew of the legend.

He insisted on having the safe deposit box number forty-seven.

What is Holm trying to tell her?

That her revenge will bring about her death?

Perhaps it was also intended as a consolation. The rōnin died honourably. If they had accepted their fate, nobody would remember them today.

She pushes it aside and concentrates on the present.

It's been thirty-eight minutes since Pavlik phoned her. Thirteen minutes ago the gate opened. He lured the men onto the property in order to eliminate them. He needs one of them alive, which presents a particular challenge.

Nevertheless, she should have heard Pavlik drive the Rover onto the premises by now.

It's not going to plan, something is holding him up.

Of all the things that Aaron hates about being blind, waiting around and not being able to do anything is the worst.

Perhaps the Broker already knows who you really are.

If he does, then not from me.

Was that a hint that the Department has a leak?

It could also have been conjecture.

Aaron tries to crawl inside the Broker's head. She is sitting on his two billion. He is wondering why Holm has made her the heiress, and can't find an answer. The men who survived in the souks will have told him that Aaron and Pavlik can handle their weapons and are well versed in close combat. He will assume that they have been sent by an international police authority or a secret service.

A thought clings to her like a leech.

What if Layla is long dead, and the woman we think is Layla is in fact on the Broker's payroll?

Aaron reaches for the equipment bag and rummages around in it. She finds the larger magazine for the Glock and whacks it into the grip. As if a few rounds will make a difference.

She hears the gate.

It's closing again.

And the Rover hasn't moved.

Aaron's muscles tense, her heart does what it wants. She fixes the silencer onto the gun, tucks it into her jeans and gets out with the spare cane.

The shortest route would be through the palm grove. But she wouldn't be able to get her bearings there, she'd be stumbling about.

She has to go along the road.

The first hundred metres she runs with her cane folded up. She is far enough from the villa for her clicking not to be heard. The echo guides her. Crossing the car park, Aaron dodges the cars, lampposts, signs, a refuse bin.

But not the flower tub.

The wretched thing was hiding in the reverberation off a palm. She suppresses a yell. At first she thinks her shin bone is broken. No. It can bear weight, it's only bruised. She limps on, carefully at first, then faster again.

The change in the wind tells her that she has reached the road. Where's the kerbstone? Got it. She sprints to the other side.

Her shin bone plays along. Aaron counts the steps, assuming a standard road width of six metres.

It's six-and-a-half. She realizes this as she takes a leap onto the pavement, jumps into empty space and is thrown off balance. She gets caught on the kerbstone, almost tumbles over, catches herself and darts to the left.

Her tongue issues fast power-clicks.

The echo is broken in front of her.

Twenty metres, in the middle of the pavement.

A person.

She doesn't reduce her speed, but reaches under her jacket. She feels the Glock. Aaron is so full of adrenalin that her skin is burning.

She clicks her tongue again.

The person isn't moving.

Just standing still.

As she comes close, her eyes burn, her lips, even her hair. Then she hears an aggressive yapping. Dog walker. Harmless, her mind tells her.

But fear is tarring the world.

Ten steps on, she allows herself a final click.

Any moment now she will be at the turn-off. There she has to keep to the right. Fifty metres to Layla's road. She slows down and lets the cane snap open. The speed at which she is rushing along the footpath while swinging the cane across the pavement would be described as crazy by other blind people. Aaron feels as though she is barely moving.

It always feels that way, because she can't see her destination. Fifty metres is an abstract size, it is only the number of steps that tells her she is making progress.

A lowering of the footpath signals that the next corner is ahead. Aaron stops. She holds her breath and boots up her receivers. Her heart is doing somersaults. The wind is rustling the palms. Far away, the little dog yowls. Nothing else.

Lissek says: fear makes the wolf bigger than he is.

She sprints across the roadway. This time she allows for six-and-a-half metres and lands on the footpath with perfect balance. After two quick steps she comes to the boundary wall of the compound. She runs along it, one hand on the stone, until she feels metal.

The gate with the recessed door.

In everyday life, perfect breathing is a luxury, a pleasure. Now Aaron's life depends on it. And perhaps Pavlik's too.

She focuses on the centre of her body and allows no other thought than *breathe. Breathe, breathe, breathe.* She visualizes the breath flowing into her, how it permeates every muscle, every artery, every cell, making her light as air.

When she feels that her pulse has dropped to under eighty bpm, she puts down her cane, takes off her ballerina shoes and feels for the door handle. Carefully she pushes down on it. Locked. She hoists herself up by the brickwork and with a wide stride she places her right foot on the door handle, then wedges the toes of her left foot into a gap. She stretches up a hand and feels for the steel teeth along the top of the gate.

Aaron can only use three fingers of each hand for this move because she has to grip the gate between the steep prongs. She heaves herself up, swings to the left and braces her feet against the wall. She is now suspended horizontally, three metres above the ground. In her mind, she is floating above herself like a drone. She sees herself pushing off forcefully with her feet, thrusting herself upward and turning simultaneously to change into the cross grip.

For a moment she is vertical, like a gymnast on the bar. She balances her weight on her fingers and performs half a stretched backward somersault, landing on her feet.

She's on the premises.

Aaron draws the Glock and silently runs towards the house. The paving under her bare feet is a four-metre-wide runway that leads directly to the front door.

Twenty-one metres.

The door is open.

For seconds, Aaron stands motionless.

She hears whispering in the darkness.

As she creeps through the entrance hall with arms outstretched, her foot bumps against something soft. She knows it's a corpse. Naked fear flips her stomach upside down.

She squats down.

Runs her fingers over the body.

He's wearing a leather jacket.

Not Pavlik.

Slowly she advances towards the whispering.

It turns into a voice.

All of a sudden it's as if Aaron is in a desert, staring at the horizon, where a silhouette is appearing. It takes shape. A face emerges. It shimmers like a mirage, a ghost from her nightmares.

It is the man who never uttered more than five words. The one none of them knew. Who left behind a wife and an unborn son. Whose empty coffin she had stood beside.

Vesper.

'I would have ended it sooner, but I was curious to see whether you've still got it in you,' she hears him say.

'Give me my Glock, then you'll find out,' Pavlik mumbles. 'Or put yours aside. Either suits me.'

Vesper laughs coldly. 'You've kept in good shape. Let me guess: plenty of sleep, not much booze, no tarts?'

'You're already dead. Aaron will be here soon. You know what she's like. I pity you.'

'I already died ten years ago. Remember?'

Aaron flattens herself against the wall. She carefully stretches out her right hand and feels the edge where the hall opens into the living room. The echo tells her that Vesper is standing about six metres away. He is totally fixed on Pavlik, his eyes are trained on him.

'I know your tactics. You were just a diversion. Aaron is trying to snatch Layla in town.'

He doesn't know that I'm blind.

'I'm sure she isn't alone,' says Vesper. 'Lissek will have sent a small set at least.'

'Lissek isn't around anymore.'

'Has someone finally snuffed him out?'

'Retired.'

'I hope he has three strokes and ends up in a home.'

'I'll pass it on to him.'

'Ha ha. I have to admit, that was quite something. Aaron pretending to be blind. She put on a good show outside the bank. Who came up with that one? You?'

'Should I feel flattered?'

'But then in the souks, the whole fabulous cover story fell apart. Show me a blind person who moves like that and I'll fuck a camel on the Djemaa el Fna.'

Don't make promises you can't keep.

Aaron slides forwards a few centimetres. She can pinpoint Vesper precisely, the room has good acoustics.

'How much did you pocket in Rome?' Pavlik asks.

'It's not all about money. A new life was worth far more to me. I can't tell you how sick I was of it all. The mortgage for the apartment, the wife with the belly that kept growing fatter, the cheap perfume, painting the nursery. But most of all I was sick of you. I don't know what happened to Sarotti that time you were here in Marrakech. I just know that you were covering something up. He was my friend. It made me sick to see the others looking up to a guy like you. Whenever I left the Department, I'd shower for an age. Your drivel about decency and honour was like muck that wouldn't wash off. Why do you think I barely opened my mouth anymore?'

'It wasn't my fault that Sarotti died.'

'I bet.'

'Lissek didn't want you and the others to find out the truth.'

'It's great to have a pal like that.'

'Sarotti thought with his dick and signed his own death warrant.'

'You're lying.'

'Make it easy for yourself.'

Aaron can hear from Pavlik's voice that he is injured. His breathing is flat. He is sitting to the right of her. Vesper is looking down at him.

'Time to speed things up a little: you're going to ring Aaron now and tell her to come here.'

'If you're looking for a seal to juggle your balls, go to the circus.'

'I would do it if I were in your shoes.'

'I'm sure I'll get something really great in return.'

'A quick death.'

'As enticing as nine Euros ninety-nine.'

'Otherwise Hakim will take care of you. If I ask him nicely, he'll be here in fifteen minutes. He was with ISIS. He'll cut off your leg as if it was a slice of bread.'

Aaron hears Pavlik rolling up his jeans. 'I hope he's got a good knife.'

'Oops,' says Vesper. 'Did it hurt?'

'I got a new leg, but you'll die the arsehole you are. Pity, you could have made something of yourself.'

'Yeah? Like what?'

'Trial patient for the pharmaceutical industry, slopsucker, spittoon cleaner in a Cambodian brothel, rent boy outside Kassel station. All of them better than what you've done with your life.'

Aaron takes a silent step into the room and aims where she guesses Vesper's head to be. 'If you move, you'll be dead faster than you can blink,' she says.

Silence.

'You took your time,' Pavlik grumbles.

'Sorry, I had to stick a finger down my throat first.'

'Hello, rich woman,' Vesper forces out.

The sound of his voice tells her that he is still aiming at Pavlik and hasn't dared to turn his head.

'Carefully put the gun on the floor.'

He doesn't move.

'So you prefer to wait for the others? That's fine. I'm sure Nowak, Fricke and Krupp will have lots to tell you,' she says.

'I'm bored already.'

'I cried at your graveside, do you know that?'

'I was there a few years ago. A tasteless stone, a stupid bible quote and some kind of green stuff. I took a look at the kid too. I'm not even sure it's mine. Looked like the type that gets knocked around at school all day. I did everything right.'

'Right now you're doing everything wrong,' she says icily.

Aaron is bluffing. Even with a direct hit to the heart, Vesper would still be alive for five seconds. In order to neutralize him so quickly that he is dead before he can bend his finger, she has to knock out an area of his brain the size of a tennis ball.

Blind.

It's impossible.

But he doesn't know that.

She gives her voice an arrogant tone. 'You've seen me shoot often enough. I can do it at fifty metres.'

'You used to be attractive *and* clever. Give my boss what belongs to him and you'll both stay alive.'

'Says the guy who carries out a mass murderer's dirty work,' Pavlik sneers.

'You might get out of this house alive. Perhaps even out of the city. But never out of Morocco. This is the best offer you'll get.'

'I'm offering you a bullet to the head.'

'Think about it,' he says. 'None of us has to die.'

Even if I land a chance hit: then what?
He knows who the Broker is.
No matter what I do, I'll lose either way.

Vesper mutters: 'The thing with your father, that was a job, no more.'

The world stands still.

Vesper.

'I shouldn't have told Holm about it.'

When I lost everything, you were sitting in the Beverly Wilshire, sipping on a cappuccino.

'Why?' she hears herself ask.

'Didn't concern me.'

She swallows down the fear like spit. 'Holm wasn't your only mistake. You were in Sankt Augustin for a laughable three hours. That was stupid of you. If you had watched my father, you would have known that he drove to a rehab clinic every day to visit me. Because he loved me more than anything in the world. His blind daughter. Who is going to kill you now, blabbermouth.'

She feels the air move as he throws himself in her direction. She catapults herself onto the carpet and fires until her magazine is empty.

Pavlik bellows: 'You've got him!'

She doesn't stop.

She carries on shooting until the firing pin just clicks.

Aaron crawls to Vesper, tears the gun out of his limp hand, rams it into his face and discharges all the rounds in his magazine too. She smells the blood and is quiet and feels nothing.

Pavlik sits down next to her and lays his arm around her.

Nothing, nothing, nothing.

'Cry,' he whispers.

'I can't.'

He pulls her head against his shoulder. 'It's like riding a bike.'

But she's forgotten how.

19

Things that need to be done:
Pavlik drags himself up to the first floor and empties the medicine cabinet in the bathroom. Back in the living room, he tips the contents of a bag onto the table, lies down on the sofa and opens his jeans with a groan.

'Has the blood soaked through?' asks Aaron.

'Yes.' He takes care of the wound.

'If we survive this, I'll teach you a meditation. It's called: *The lesson of the rainstorm.*'

'And what will it teach me? How not to get wet in the rain?'

'Pretty much.'

'Damn, all that money I could've saved on umbrellas.'

'What kind of painkillers has she got?'

'Aspirin, Ibuprofen and Palladone.'

She knows that last one. It contains morphine.

'Take a Palladone.'

'I already have.'

'How many mg?'

'The highest dose. She's got four boxes of it.'

Either Layla is in chronic pain or she's addicted.

'Any tranquillizers?'

'Enough Valium for half an army.'

She can smell cigarettes. 'Vesper didn't smoke, did he?'

'He used to find it disgusting.'

'Can you see any photos of Jansen and Layla?'

'Several. And one of her child.'

'She has a child?'

'A son.'

Her thoughts are running themselves ragged. 'How old?'

'She's just dropped him off at school, so he's at least six. In the photograph he's about four or five.'

'What does he look like?'

'Black curly hair, freckles. He'll break some hearts one day.'

'What is he doing in the picture?'

'He's sitting on the floor, playing.'

'What with?'

'A stuffed toy.'

Her voice almost buckles. 'Is it a giraffe?'

'No, a lion. There's something strange about that boy.'

'How do you mean?'

'He's got a very serious expression. As if he's—'

'What?'

'—grown up already.'

Just dreams, nothing more.

'Describe Jansen and Layla to me.'

'He was blond, good-looking. Rimless glasses. Seeing him on the street, you might've assumed he was a professor. Layla is graceful, a beauty. She has a birth mark above her lip, a little blot planted there by a heavenly hand. Blue eyes, unusual. On one of the photos she's laughing, but she looks lost.'

'How old is she?'

'In the photos I'd say mid-thirties.'

'Is she the woman you saw at the window?'

'Why shouldn't she be?'

'Because Layla may not be alive anymore.'

'She is. The guy on the phone was talking of Layla.'

'Are she and Jansen touching each other in the photos?'

'She is nestled up to him, as if she's seeking protection.'

'And he?'

'Cool. He has this I'm-better-than-the-rest kind of look.'

'Where were the photos taken?'

'In the villa here and in the garden, the others seem to be holiday pics. Coney Island, Golden Gate Bridge. The boy is in those ones too.'

'Take a picture of one. I'll send it to Omar Al-Saud.'

'Who's he?'

'He's the Federal Intelligence Service informant in Pakistan. He can tell us whether Jansen was the man in Frankfurt.'

Pavlik pulls up his jeans, stands up and takes the photo.

The smell of blood is making Aaron feel sick.

'That's your father's killer lying there,' says Pavlik, his voice coarse. 'Why don't we just get out of here?'

'Vesper wasn't his killer. He was just a weapon.'

'You really want to go through with it?'

'Your last chance to step away.'

Things that need to be done:

'I have to take care of the guy in the closet.'

'What do you want to do with him?' she asks.

'Tie him up.'

'We might see him again.'

'You can't kill every guy you might see again.' He hobbles into the hall. She hears him opening a door. The man wakes up as Pavlik gets to work on him.

His voice is full of hate: 'One day I'm going to rip out your guts and drink your blood from your skull.'

'Cheers.' He knocks the man unconscious again.

Aaron taps her watch. 'Twelfth of February. Thursday. Eight a.m., thirty-six minutes, three seconds.'

Pavlik comes back.

'What's Layla doing?' she asks.

'She's having breakfast, we've got time.'

She feels her way to a seat. 'Varga hired Vesper in Rome. It could be that he's the Broker.'

'Just because Vesper let himself be bought by him ten years ago? He became a contract killer. Anyone could hire him.'

'Holm talked about the possibility that the Broker knows who I really am. Perhaps he was referring to Vesper, Varga's troubleshooter.'

'I know that you've never believed that Varga is dead,' says Pavlik. 'But I'm not convinced.'

'Why?'

'He loved his son. Think of what he said about family. If he'd stayed alive, he would have taken his son with him back then.'

Aaron turns to Pavlik in surprise.

'The boy was taken to Varga's brother,' Pavlik continues. 'I thought you knew that.'

'No.'

'A week later he was killed on the way to kindergarten by a car bomb. The Italians assumed it was a revenge act by another clan.'

A scythe cuts across Aaron's breath.

She sees the boy. He is hugging his giraffe, staring at her with sleepy eyes, then takes her hand. He listens to her story until his eyes close and she kisses his forehead.

And then he is dead.

Varga's face is empty and grey.

Aaron whispers: 'I dream about him.'

'The boy?'

'Yes.'
'Since when?'
'For the past ten years.'

Things that need to be done:
Aaron asks Pavlik to describe the house. They start in the living room. 'Sixty square metres. Persian carpets, glass table, sofa and seats with Arabic calligraphy. Cupboard, chest, television, music system. Well-stocked house bar.'
'How full are the bottles?'
'Just a few drops left.'
'Any paintings?'
'Three landscape pictures of the Atlas, plus two Impressionists. Hang on.' He looks at them more closely. 'Degas and Monet. Secured with an alarm system. Origina—'
Aaron puts a finger to her lips.
A car.
Driving fast.
It comes closer.
Turns into the road.
Drives past.
'Are there any personal belongings lying around?'
'German magazines, fashion and lifestyle stuff.'
'What else?'
'An old-fashioned organizer, bound in leather.'
'Has she noted down any appointments?'
Pavlik opens it. 'A workman, twice, something to do with the kitchen; visit by someone called Esther, who stayed for four days; parents' evening at the school; dinner at the Al Fassia with Ramiye and Bashar; eight doctor's appointments, all of them with a Dr Yousif; last week an estate agent came round. That's all since the beginning of January.'
'She wants to sell the villa,' says Aaron.

'Probably. Let me see if I can find out anything about the doctor.' He scrolls on his mobile. 'Consultant for internal medicine in the city.'

'What language does she write in?'

'German.'

'Any phone numbers?'

He skims through the pages for some time. 'Poor, lonely Layla.'

'Let me guess: she barely knows anyone here.'

'Ten people, mainly women,' Pavlik confirms.

'What kind of music does she listen to?'

'Classical.'

Bach's cello suites, the mercy of oblivion.

And still you force me to think of you.

Are you even dead?

'Any Bach among it?'

Pavlik doesn't answer.

'Please have a look.'

'There's no point.'

'Holm could have been here,' she says. 'Perhaps he left behind a clue for us.'

'He didn't know that Jansen is dead. He's probably never been in this house. And if he has, then not in the past six months.'

'Do it anyway.'

'No.'

'Why?'

'Because Holm is controlling you like a puppet even from his grave. It's time you got him out of your head.'

Tears well up in Aaron, but they don't find their way and get lost in nothingness.

'Ask me what's in the cupboard,' says Pavlik.

'What's in the cupboard?' she replies mechanically.

Pavlik opens it. 'Bits and pieces.'

A phone rings in the hall; the answering machine switches on. A female voice says in French: 'Hello, it's Ramiye. I'm ringing to ask how you are. Call me back sometime.' The call ends.

Pavlik opens a sliding door. 'His study.'

Cigar smoke cloaks the furniture and walls.

'Leather sofa, two seats, desk. Expensive paraphernalia: Montegrappa fountain pen, silver curved dagger, cigar cutter, Art Deco lighter, ashtray, illustrated book on Casablanca, photos of Layla and the child.'

'Drawers?'

'No. The book is lying open. A half-smoked cigar is still sitting in the ashtray. She's left everything exactly how it was the day he died.'

'What about books?'

'Just the one on Casablanca.'

'No documents, records?'

'No.'

What's that sound?

'Vesper has been here for days,' says Pavlik. 'If there was anything interesting—'

'Shhh.'

She concentrates.

She can hear it quite clearly now. A buzzing, extremely high-frequency, above twenty thousand hertz.

'There's a jamming transmitter here.'

'I can't hear anything.'

'You'd either have to be blind or have four legs and a tail to hear it.'

'Neither option sounds very tempting.'

'The jammer didn't block the gate signal,' she says. 'So it has some other role.'

'Counter-eavesdropping.'

'Yes. Who installed the thing? Vesper?'

'It's possible.'

'Or it was Jansen?' Aaron speculates.

Pavlik mutters: 'If the system is hidden well, Vesper may not have known about it.'

'Exactly. In which case there's only one person who could have switched the transmitter on.'

'Layla.'

'That would mean two things: she knows that her husband was a criminal, and she's looking for an opportunity to secretly attract attention.'

'And she suspects that Vesper's lot are tapping the phone,' he agrees.

'She might not know for sure. She's probably thought about picking it up a hundred times, but hasn't found the courage to do it.'

'Meaning: she's only cooperating out of fear.'

'If what we're thinking is right. How's your hip doing?'

'Like new. And I'm pretty high too.'

'Let's go on up.'

He stops at the bottom of the stairs. 'There's a golf bag here.'

'With gloves?'

'Yes, lying on top.'

'For a man or woman?'

'His.'

They start with the master bedroom. Aaron inhales the smell of the room. Beeswax and a hint of lilac.

'Double bed, two pillows, both sides are made up. There's a photo of Jansen on the bedside table.'

She clicks her tongue: there's a second door. 'Dressing room?'

'Yes.' Pavlik goes in with her. She runs her fingers over cashmere, linen, mohair, silk.

'Elegance for every occasion,' he says. 'Chanel, Kenzo, Armani and all the rest. And a few sporty things too; I bet Layla looks like a lady even in those. About a hundred pairs of shoes, most of them with high heels.'

'What colours?'

'Muted, you'd like them.' He opens a sliding door. 'His stuff is still hanging up.' Pavlik crouches down. 'There's a box here.' Aaron hears rustling. 'Letters from him, sorted by year.'

'Where's Layla now?'

He checks his mobile. 'As before, Hivernage.'

Aaron feels her way back into the bedroom and sits down on the bed. 'Read out the letters.'

'Vesper's already had these in his hands. There won't be anything about Jansen's dealings in them.'

'Vesper was only interested in whether they were a risk to his boss. I'm looking for the key to Layla's head.'

'How long will that take you?'

'However long it takes.'

'I hate to seem impatient, but we've got stuff to do.'

Aaron asks: 'What do we think we know about Layla? That she takes tranquillizers and painkillers, drinks too much, is receiving medical treatment, that she loved her husband and wants to leave Marrakech. Are we sure about these things? Perhaps she's a teetotaller, and Vesper drank like a fish. Is that her medication? It could have been Jansen's. Perhaps there's an offer on the villa, but Layla doesn't want to sell. And the photos? What if Vesper told her to have them on display, in order to create the semblance of a happy marriage? The appointments and contacts in the organizer: are they real or fake? Jansen's clothes: just for show? Is Layla's son still alive, or is the boy she took to school a different child, a decoy? You have to question everything. Even so-called facts are never a certainty; if you change your perspective, the house of cards can collapse in an instant. At the BKA, we locked ourselves in for days. Once, a colleague addressed me with "Jenny" and I said: "I'm not Jenny." It's the ideal job for someone who wants to gradually drive themselves round the bend. At the moment, you're my entire team. Just try to contradict me on everything – even if you agree with me.'

'No way.'

'Wonderful, you've grasped it.'

20

The first letter is sixteen years old. Jansen wrote it on paper from the Four Seasons in New York. Layla is living in Berlin, on Mexikoplatz. An area patronized by the wealthy who don't wish to brag.

'"Dear Layla,"' Pavlik reads out, '"you will be wondering how I got hold of your address. Well, I have ways and means. I've been thinking of you a lot since we met in the airport café. I will be in Berlin next week and would like to meet with you. You can say no of course, but until then I remain hopeful—"'

Jansen suggests the Grand Slam, a two star restaurant in Grunewald, on a Tuesday evening in April.

'What was his handwriting like?' Aaron asks.

'Confident, a cocksure kind of guy.'

The next letter is dated two weeks later, sent from Jerusalem, for collection at the post office: 'Dear Layla, it was a mistake to tell your husband about us. But it can't be helped now. The bastard beat you. You have to leave him, right now. A single word from you, and I will be at your door. I will talk to him in a language that he understands—'

Another two weeks later, Singapore: 'My darling, I don't understand why you're still scared of him. You say that he disappeared three days ago. Believe me, he won't be back. I know his type, he's hooked up with someone else already—'

'Jansen had him eliminated,' says Aaron.

'Speculation.'

'Probability calculation.'

'Perhaps he just went out to get some cigarettes,' Pavlik suggests.

'Yes, where the Wannsee is at its deepest.'

After that, there is post from Oslo: 'My darling, I hate to leave you alone, especially at this time. But a lot depends on this conference. Let us forget about the ugly quarrel. There are questions one simply doesn't ask. You know that I love you. Nothing else matters—'

Pavlik mutters: 'I take back the cigarette theory.'

Layla and Jansen become a couple and live in Geneva and Monaco. The age difference isn't an issue; if it is mentioned at all, it is in a playful manner.

From Milan, Jansen writes: 'When I was your age, everyone over forty seemed ancient to me, and today everyone under sixty is a spring chicken. That means that at forty-six, I am virtually still a child.'

They want to marry – which isn't possible because Layla would first have to get divorced and her husband is unlocatable. Once, Jansen lets drop a sarcastic remark about the fee of an interior designer, mainly to tease her; money is not a problem. On her twenty-eighth birthday he surprises her with a jet that takes them to the Virgin Islands. They watch the sun set as they picnic in White Bay and must have spent their days in rapture, as a few weeks later Jansen confesses: 'That night in White Bay I could have died and my life would have been complete.'

On letter paper from the Mumbai Plaza he quotes Rilke: 'Everything that touches us, me and you, takes us together like a violin's bow, which draws one voice out of two separate strings.'

Aaron thinks of the study without books. Jansen had probably never read Rilke's 'Love Song', he probably discovered the lines by chance. But well chosen, he was clearly a romantic.

He travels continuously, jetting around the world, and her happiness suffers from it. Any mentions of his work are incidental and vague. He speaks of conferences, meetings, deals, without ever specifying a sector or providing a name. Both of them want to have children. For Layla this becomes increasingly important; Jansen implores her time and again not to lose hope. He now tenderly refers to her as *Amari*, 'my moon'.

'There's no way he was a lobbyist for the German arms industry,' Pavlik mutters. 'He never spent any time in Berlin.'

'You think Harry told us a fairy story?'

'One Thousand and One Nights.'

'Why?'

'The answer to that is probably unpleasant.' He picks up a new letter. 'This is where it gets interesting. In October, eight and a half years ago, he writes from Alexandria: "I've met someone very influential and I've invited him to Boca for two days."'

He means Boca Raton in Florida. They know from previous letters that Layla and Jansen had a holiday home there.

'"Amari, I know we wanted to have that week to ourselves. But he's an important man. He's got amazing ideas, you can never think too big. I'm sure you will like him; he is phenomenally well educated and an art lover. Just imagine—"'

'Why have you stopped reading?' asks Aaron.

'"Just imagine, he owns a Lucas Cranach."'

It is very quiet for a long time.

Varga.

It's true.

Varga is alive.

Varga is the Broker.

Aaron composes herself. 'Sinking ships got him the necessary spending money. He had completely repositioned himself once before already, when he gave up arms trading. Someone like him gets bored if he stays with the same thing for too long.'

'He doesn't seem to be bored at the moment.'

'I've never underestimated anyone as much as him. I realized that when I stood in front of the painting. He knew that I had been at the safe. It didn't worry him. He could've had me killed in the house, but that would have been too distasteful for him. He set ten men on me at the hotel, including Vesper. I didn't stand a chance.'

'He let you live.'

'I've often wondered about that.'

'Certainly not for sentimental reasons.'

'Lissek thinks it's because I was of no relevance to him.'

'The attack on the Yamal pipeline happened eleven years ago. So Varga must have already been involved in the terror business when we were in Rome with Keyes,' Pavlik reflects. 'Why didn't he leave his clan much earlier?'

'Perhaps it was only then that he asked himself what use it still was to him. From his time as an arms trader he'll have had contacts to terror organizations all over the world. That and his wits were all he needed.'

She falls through time.

'When I was about thirteen or fourteen, my father asked me what true power was. I didn't know. He said: "An empire that nobody knows about."'

Did Varga want to protect his son, and therefore placed him in the care of his brother?

In Bushidō, relinquishment is the ultimate form of love.

No.

It was all a big lie. His son was unimportant to him. He played with me the way he plays with everything.

'Vesper went through the letters,' she says. 'Why didn't he destroy that one?'

'Varga is convinced that we already know.'

'From Holm.'

'Yes.'

'In any case, Boca Raton was the start of the collaboration between him and Jansen,' says Aaron.

'Is it OK if I don't contradict you?'

'Just this once.'

Jakarta, the following month: '"Amari, your text worried me greatly. What does that mean: they found something in your kidney? What kind of a statement is that? I wanted to fly back immediately, but the local air traffic controllers are on strike and I can't get away. You're not answering the phone or replying to my messages. Why are you leaving me hanging like this? I'm sure I'll be home long before these lines reach you. It's ludicrous to write this letter, but I have to do something—"'

'Jakarta – Hang on.' Aaron reaches for her mobile. 'Search in Google: Jakarta 2007 terrorist attack.'

'I didn't find anything. Sorry about that,' replies Siri. 'Do you perhaps mean: Jakarta 2008?'

'Yes.'

'Twenty-one thousand two hundred and four hits.'

'Read out the top hit.'

'Spiegel Online, 29 January 2008. Yesterday's explosion at a research facility of the pharmaceutical company PT Kendari Chemical has claimed a further two lives. This brings the death toll to two hundred and ninety-one. The terrorist organization Masar Al Islami has since claimed responsibility for the attack, which destroyed the entire test series for an Alzheimer's drug that had been hailed as groundbreaking by PT Chemical Kendari. The share price of the company has collapsed, causing stock exchange trading to be suspended today.'

'His first job for Varga,' says Pavlik.

'No discussion.'

Jansen spends a lot of time at home that year. Layla needs him. She has a kidney tumour, is operated on and has to undergo radiotherapy. Her greatest fear is that this will damage her ovaries; she is still hoping for a child.

The six journeys that Jansen makes that year take him to Africa and North America. From Montreal he writes that they could adopt a child. He is distraught and worried for the woman who means everything to him. Jansen indicates that he is thinking of retiring, but it remains vague, just empty talk.

At the end of August he has to go to Nigeria for two weeks, which, as he insists in a letter from Lagos, could not be postponed. Evidently, he had tried in vain to persuade Layla to stay with her mother in Berlin for that time. Jansen tells her off. He says he doesn't understand why she finds it so hard to accept help. Why she never thinks of herself, only of others.

The radiation therapy is successful, the letters express great relief.

In December 2008 he writes from Kathmandu: 'Amari, my first letter to Marrakech, how wonderful. I am so glad that you love the city and the house as much as I do. I will be with you tomorrow and I'm already curious to find out what you and the interior designer have come up with. As always, this letter won't reach you until I'm already holding you in my arms again. I really am an old-fashioned guy. But you say, that's exactly what you love about me—'

He was wrong, she doesn't feel at home in Marrakech. She grew up in Germany, that is her culture, even though her family is originally from Tunisia.

Jansen writes many letters, and each one of them mentions a quarrel. Layla is climbing the walls with loneliness, she doesn't feel safe in the city. Her Arabic isn't good, she continually feels that people are talking about her behind her back. She thinks of leaving him. That drives him crazy. Losing Layla would be the end of the world for him. Jansen is financially sorted for the rest of his life, why doesn't he retire? For fear of Varga? He talks of something 'very foolish' that she has done. A half-hearted suicide attempt?

Then there's wonderful news: Layla is pregnant. They can both hardly believe it. A boy! She is worried and prays that her child won't be affected by the cancer therapy. Jansen reassures her with heartfelt words. If he shares her dark thoughts, he doesn't let it show. Three letters focus on discussing names.

Until he writes from Dar es Salaam: 'This evening, I spent a long time sitting in the hotel bar with my partner. He asked me what I thought of the name Luca. Well, I think it's a great name! What do you think?'

'Varga,' says Aaron.

'Could've been someone else entirely.'

'Luca. Like Lucas Cranach.'

'Coincidence,' Pavlik asserts.

'What seems like a coincidence is nothing other than fate.'

'Let me guess: says Bushidō.'

'No, says my horoscope.'

Luca is born and is healthy. In his next letter Jansen brims over with joy: 'I'm so incredibly proud. I tell everyone that I've become a father, regardless of whether they want to hear it or not. Yesterday somebody asked me what it was like to be there at the birth. I thought about it for a long time and then said: "It's as if you're really tiny and really enormous both at the same time."'

Pavlik mutters: 'I know exactly what you mean.'

In the following years, Jansen travels more than ever before. But it no longer puts a strain on the relationship. At last, Layla is not lonely anymore. Her husband is declared dead. She and Jansen marry in Locarno. The wedding is a low key affair with a select few guests. It is their happiest time.

Pavlik picks up a new envelope. 'Hello.'

'What?'

'When exactly is that businessman supposed to have met with the terrorist cell in Frankfurt last year?'

'On 4 March.'

'"Frankfurt, 3 March. Dear Amari, be glad you didn't come with me, the weather in Germany is truly awful. Thank goodness you talked me into taking the coat, otherwise I would be miserably cold—"'

Silence.

'You needn't bother contacting your man in Peshawar,' says Pavlik.

Jansen's last letter is dated 2 July, a week before his sixtieth birthday. It is written in London and ends: 'Soon I will be home. The decision has been made, I'm pulling out of the business. When a man of my age looks back, he should be able to do it without regrets. But all I see is the time I wasted, when I should have been at your side all along. Do you remember, Amari, how it all started? How I took your suitcase from the conveyor belt, thinking it was mine? You've never since looked at me as angrily as you did then. For this I am grateful to you. I am yours for ever and I'm thinking of you and Luca full of tenderness. Your Veit.'

They are silent for a while. Then Pavlik says: 'That bastard has almost got me to like him.'

'Apparently Josef Mengele played the piano most beautifully. Did that make him a likeable person?'

He is only listening with half an ear. 'Jansen wrote to her from London to say that he's retiring. He couldn't have done that without Varga's consent. That isn't the kind of thing you discuss over the phone.'

'The fund that Holm suggested to us is managed there,' Aaron continues his train of thought. 'A city in which you can make yourself invisible, after cosmetic surgery for example.'

'Too vague.'

'But it's a lead,' she insists. 'It took us a day to find out who he is. And now we might know *where* he is.'

'It's all happening too easily,' he objects.

'Those three downstairs would have a different opinion. So would the ones in the souks.'

'You wanted to see the kid's room. Come.'

He crosses the hallway with her and opens a door.

Aaron smells crafting glue, intermingled with caramel; Luca likes sweets. She forms her lips to make an E sound and clicks her tongue until she gets a rough picture. The bed is on the left. She touches a set of shelves. Toy cars, stuffed animals, picture books. What is that by the window? A desk? As she steps towards it, she knocks something over with her foot. Toy soldiers?

Aaron stops.

She feels bad.

Pavlik says: 'The walls and the ceiling are decorated with painted clouds, birds, aeroplanes and a Zeppelin. There's an enormous sheet hanging above the bed; looks like he uses it to build a den. Lots of toys and stuffed animals, but he's put those away.'

'Is there a giraffe among them?'

'I can't see one. Reach above you.'

Aaron stretches out her hand and sets in motion a mobile. 'What kind is it?' she asks.

'Seagulls.'

The scythe is back, cutting short her breath.

'By the window, is that a desk?'

'Yes.'

'What's on it?'

'Exercise books, a ball of wool, a pocket knife, a magnifying glass, a paper hat, glue, a fire engine and a picture he's drawn.'

'What's on the picture?'

'A steamship with three funnels.'

Seconds pass, Pavlik touches her shoulder and she is back in the boy's room. 'What did you say?' she asks numbly.

'That everyone needs to keep papers somewhere. Bank statements, ID, insurance, vaccination records, that kind of stuff. I could rifle through every cupboard and drawer in the house, but I already know that there's no point.'

She thinks. 'They've probably taken her passport away from her.'

'Her husband must have made arrangements to ensure that Layla and the boy are safe if something happens to him.'

'You mean a fallback, hidden away somewhere?'

'Exactly. Safe?'

'Can be broken into,' Aaron reflects.

'She could have deposited it outside the villa. For example at the house of this Ramiye.'

You never think of yourself, only of others.

'Layla wouldn't endanger her friend like that. It doesn't fit with her character. She's very conscientious.'

'Where would you hide something like that?' Pavlik asks.

'In the house, where I could get at it quickly. But not in a fixed place. Inside something that just lies around most of the time. Something that a person searching the house might walk right past countless times, without paying any attention to it.'

'Wait a second.' He disappears.

Aaron feels her way to the desk. She runs her fingers over the top and picks up the drawing.

A ship with three funnels.

Pavlik returns. He dumps something onto the floor. She hears metal clanging. It's the golf bag. He empties it and gets to work on it, slicing open the leather.

'Hole-in-one. Two forged Canadian passports for her and the boy, under the names of Louise and Noah Gagné. Credit cards, driving licence, and a key for a safe deposit box.'

'Good, that's it then.'

Pavlik uses Nutcracker's phone to ring the man he spoke to three hours ago. 'How's it looking?'

'She's been shopping. The boy's only in school till half eleven. She's about to pick him up. What next?'

'Tell her to drive to the Jardin Menara. The boy can feed the fish there and you can keep an eye on her.'

'Yeah, yeah, don't you be busting your balls now.'

'Go fuck yourself.' He hangs up. 'I'll pack a bag.'

'Remember to pack some warm things. And Valium and Palladone.'

'Not necessary.'

'We have to play it safe. If she's dependent on that stuff she'll go round the bend without it.'

'Then she'll have enough with her.'

'Pavlik?'

'Yes?'

'The profiling is over.'

'Sorry, it's become a habit already.' He leaves her alone.

Aaron picks up the drawing again. She fingers the fat lines of wax crayons.

Is that a lonely cloud? And is this the yolk of the sun? And on the horizon a blue timber house above the cliffs?

21

How is it possible not to notice the darkness, when darkness is all around? How is it possible to pretend she had firm ground under her feet, when she is sinking into the maelstrom of darkness? How is it possible to long, hour after hour, for a glimmer of light, and not despair of the darkness?

'Where are we?' she asks.

'Dual carriageway.'

'Not on the Circuit?'

'We don't have to make the detour anymore.'

'Describe it to me.'

'Salt, salt and more salt. Not even cactuses grow here. Everything is plastered with billboards. Beer, cigarettes, McDonald's. They have a McKebab here.'

Her hunger for images is so enormous that she switches on the cinema in her head. She is driving through the desert on a Harley – *Zabriskie Point 12 Miles* – and is looking across an endless glittering plain. She stops, climbs off the bike and walks towards the glitter. It is near, but doesn't draw nearer. Her boots crack the white crust that covers everything like hoar frost. She bends down, crumbles the crust between her fingers, licks them and tastes salt. Aaron runs and jumps into a mirrored wall of heat and stares into the sun that melts like a blob of butter.

Used images that will have to last her a lifetime.

'Can you see the city?' she asks.

'It looks like an enormous wedding cake that has fallen from the sky, with the Koutoubia as the candle.'

'Is there much traffic?'

'It's congested going the other way. Tomorrow's a holy day, they're already ringing in the weekend.'

'What does the sky look like?'

'Allah is counting sheep.'

'What colour are the cars?'

He is silent.

'Black and white?'

'Aaron, what's going on?' Pavlik calmly asks.

She wants to tell him about the adrenalin that has raged in her cortex like an apoplectic seizure, the black web that is growing inside her, the dried-up, useless cells that she has to lug around with her for evermore. No, she doesn't *want* to tell him, she desperately *longs* to. Then he will console her, he's so very good at it. But if he knew what she is putting on the line, he wouldn't allow this to carry on for another second.

That's your father's killer lying there.

Vesper was the first she's killed out of revenge.

She has never felt so indifferent about taking a life.

Because the one that she grieved for ten years ago is lying in an empty coffin in Berlin. Because the one whose blood is drying on Layla's carpet was nothing more than a hireling and the man who commands pain is still alive.

She could tell herself a thousand lies, she knows them all: that Layla only has to tell her where Varga is. That the Department will hunt him down. That Varga will go to court. That she starts the therapy and invents a new life for herself. And another lie, and another and another.

Bushidō states: *Revenge is the highest court.*

She wants to place her hand on Varga's chest and feel that his heart is no longer beating.

Pavlik turns off the road and stops in a parking bay. He switches off the engine. 'Let me into your head.'

'I've misplaced the key.'

'What exactly did Reimer tell you in Sweden?'

Aaron tenses up. 'I've already told you that.'

'No you haven't. We've just been pretending that you have.'

'He has to do some tests.'

'Sandra read an interview with him. He says that the therapy can only benefit those who still have some sight left. Being able to perceive light and dark would be an absolute minimum requirement.'

Pavlik can't know. It's impossible.

'Yes, that's why he's taking me on as a patient.'

'How much can you see? Now, for example. Can you see that the sun is blasting straight onto the windscreen?'

'Yes.'

'The sun is behind us.'

Aaron feels paralysed.

'I looked at your phone. I feel lousy about doing that, but I stand by it. Something is happening with you. You wanted to keep it secret from me. It hasn't worked. Why did you ring Reimer last night? And don't tell me that you swapped cake recipes.'

'How could you do that?' she screams at him.

'What exactly?' he yells back. 'Be worried about you?'

'You had no right to do that!'

'Oh but I did. We're heading for a ride on a nuclear warhead. Nobody else would do that for you. We have a one-in-a-thousand chance of succeeding. That's OK, you don't need to thank me for it. But I need to know what you can and what you can't do. My life depends on it. And so does yours.'

'Two hours ago, I saved your backside.'

'Which I risked for you.'

Her voice is shaking. 'You want me to apologize for it?'

'I'm so sick of your self-righteousness.'

'Then why don't you just bugger off!' Aaron gets out and slams the door. Shivering, she stands in a wind that travelled glowing hot from the Sahara and was transformed by the Atlas range into an icy beast.

Pavlik gets out too.

She closes her thin jacket. 'We don't tell each other every stupid little thing. We never have done,' she barks.

'You call that little?'

Anger seals her mouth, the wind chills her to the bones. Pavlik lays his arm around her. She pushes him away. They repeat this twice, then Aaron leans into him.

Freezing is more fun together.

'The adrenalin is killing the cells in my visual centre,' she whispers. 'I need to reduce it, otherwise that's it for me. There's a drug that would help. But I can't get hold of it here until the day after tomorrow.'

She knows what's coming. He wants them to drive to Erfoud straight away. Because nothing in the world, no promise and no revenge would be worth risking that much.

So this is where our paths will part. Fly home to Sandra and your children. Don't worry about your promise. I'm releasing you from it. I won't hold it against you.

And another three lies.

'We've known each other for eleven years,' Pavlik mutters. 'You've done some crazy things, but I've never told you what you should or shouldn't do, and there's no point starting now. For me, the therapy would be more important than anything, but you're not me. We'll go grab Layla and grill her. If it all goes well, we'll be boarding the plane first thing tomorrow morning and you'll have the drug by the afternoon.'

His energy radiates so much heat that it feels to Aaron as if she's wearing a thick coat.

They drive on for five minutes without a word. Then she scrapes up a memory that has defied all the boozing. 'What happened that time with Sarotti?'

Pavlik is silent for a long time. 'Does Adrian Sydow mean anything to you?'

'The steel baron?'

'Steel, electrical industry, company stakes. He only had one child, Zoé, the apple of his eye. She was twenty, squandered his money and thought style icon was a job title. She had supposedly received anonymous calls, although there were no witnesses to this apart from her. Sydow developed a fixation that someone was trying to abduct her. He wanted personal protection and ran to the BKA. Palmer politely explained to him that his people had better things to do. Sydow rang the Chancellor and reminded her of his campaign donations. She passed it on to Lissek. He cursed like hell. None of us believed that there was anything to it, so he only put Sarotti and me on the case. We travelled to Saint-Tropez, New York and Miami with Zoé. She bought jogging shoes with laces made of braided gold for four thousand dollars. She knew nothing about life, apart from that it is shit without coke. Sarotti was crazy about her, he hopped around her like a canary. I took him to task countless times, but he wanted more than his three balls of ice-cream with sprinkles on top. We flew to Marrakech, her father has a villa in Hivernage. She dragged us to a party where the guests included David Bowie, Whitney Huston and Yves Saint Laurent. The host was a Russian oligarch who kept dolphins in a pool. I had never seen that many deranged people in one place. Sarotti was glowing as if he had a fever. He'd have licked the sweat out of Zoé's décolletage if I hadn't kept him in check. I rang Lissek. He said: "I want you two out of there tomorrow, the Chancellor can stuff it." At four a.m., I crawled into bed. I dreamt that I was falling. I was woken up by a gunshot. I stormed into Zoé's bedroom to find Sarotti lying naked in a kilo of snow. She had blasted away his skullcap with his SIG Sauer. Zoé looked at me, laughed, stuck the gun into her mouth and pulled the trigger. Merry Christmas. Give me a cigarette, will you?'

'Pavlik—'

'Don't. I leave you your sorrows, leave me mine.'

They both light up.

'Sarotti was buried in full honours,' mutters Aaron.

'Lissek thought up a story. He said: "I appointed the jerk to the Department and I'll decide what is written on his gravestone."'

'It's not your fault,' Aaron consoles him.

'That's what I told myself too. Five or six thousand times.'

She imagines him blowing bitter smoke rings.

'Do you know what's so fucking brilliant about cigarettes?' he asks.

'That you can't develop smoker's leg on the left anymore?'

'That with each one, you can tell yourself: this is the last.'

The city comes humming towards them. They have to cut through the centre. 'Reimer asked me something,' says Aaron. 'He wanted to know whether I compare my current life with the one I had before I lost my sight.'

'Do you?'

'Don't you mourn for your leg?'

'What leg?'

Aaron chucks the Magic Tree out of the car. In return she gets a full broadside of rotting fish up her nose and quickly closes the window again. 'Why the Jardin Menara?'

'Have you ever been there?'

'No – you?'

'Zoé had a photo shoot for some sort of gossip magazine there. It's an olive plantation, one hundred hectares. In the middle of it there's an enormous water basin with a pavilion built on top of three archways. A pedestrian avenue leads from the entrance to the basin, and there are stalls selling knick-knacks.'

'We'd make a perfect target on the avenue,' she comments.

'On the north-west side there is vehicle access for gardeners. After five hundred metres you have a good view of the basin.'

'And you can just drive in through there?'

'No, there's a barrier with guards. A bit of pocket money will sort that.'

'Have you got enough on you?' she asks.

'I thought you might lend me some.'

'Typical, as soon as you've put a little aside, people start hitting you up.'

The traffic noise ebbs away. They are on the outskirts. Pavlik slows down. 'We're passing the main entrance. There's the Smart car. Layla's escort has parked up too. They're in the park.'

He turns off the road, stops and lowers his window. After a brief negotiation with a man from security there's a rustling sound as bank notes change hands.

'Merci beaucoup, Monsieur, et bonne journée.'

They trundle on at a walking pace. Pavlik stops and cuts the engine.

'Can you see them?' Aaron asks.

'She's standing at the basin, putting a jacket on the boy. He's running off now to feed bread to the carp. She's lighting a cigarette, turning round. She's even slimmer than in the pictures, she's lost weight.'

'How far from here?'

'Hundred metres.'

'And the men?'

'Good quality stock. One and two are sitting on a bench and pretending to read the papers. Three and four are standing in one of the archways, half in the shade, you can only see them from here. Five and six are hanging around the souvenir stalls and keeping an eye on the avenue. Oh, and number seven, coming out of the shrubbery. I'm almost flattered.'

'Is there much going on?'

'It's pretty dead. A few joggers, an ice-cream seller, a gang of OAPs and two young lovers.'

'How do you want to do it?'

'I'll call Varga's man and invent a story that will make them leave without Layla.'

'Such as?'

'That we've been collared outside the villa and they should come to the Palmeraie. I'll tell him that Layla would be in the way there, that it's going to get ugly.'

'They won't risk her running to the police.'

'There's no way she'll do that. For one thing, they will have made it clear to her that it would be her death sentence. Also, her husband was a criminal, he'll have told her countless times never to trust anyone. And anyway, without her fake passport she can't get away.'

'The blokes have no idea about the passport. They won't leave Layla and Luca here.'

'I wasn't talking about him. They'll take Luca with them. For that reason alone she won't budge.'

'We're not going without him.'

'He isn't important to us.'

'He's important to *me*.'

'Why?'

She is silent.

'The boy stands between us and Layla,' he says. 'They won't do anything to him. They even let him go to school, that's how safe they feel. He doesn't know anything, he's only a child. They'll have instructed Layla what to tell him. That Uncle Vesper is a relative, something along those lines.'

'He won't have believed it.'

'He's six years old. He still believes in Father Christmas.'

'Not Luca. He's afraid for his mother. That's the only reason he's playing along.'

'You talk about him as if you've known him for ages.'

Perhaps I have.

'Would I understand if you explained it to me?'

'No.'

She thinks.

'They'll probably let him live. But as long as they have him, Layla won't say a single word. We have to prevent her being separated from Luca at all costs.'

'Fear is useful when you want to soften somebody up.'

'My strategy is based on empathy, not fear. And I've got a better idea.'

'Excellent timing.'

'In autumn, the streets of Osaka are covered with empty nutshells, especially near the traffic lights.'

'That's great.'

'Japanese large-billed crows are the cleverest birds in the world, did you know that?'

'It's getting better by the minute.'

'They wait until the traffic lights change to red, then they place the nuts in front of the cars and let the tyres crack them open.'

A light comes on in Pavlik's head.

'All we need is a nutcracker,' says Aaron.

She pictures his grin.

'Let me guess,' he says. 'First word starts with an L, the second with an O.'

Ten things that Aaron likes in people:

    passion

    quiet confidence

an honest laugh
implicit trust
self-deprecation
the ability to listen
dry humour
loyalty
strength of nerve
fast thinking

22

A hard cough barks out of the phone's speaker. The liaison
officer sounds as though somebody has removed his
larynx. 'Yes?'

'It's me,' Pavlik says. 'Are you still in Marrakech?'

'No, I'm in Rabat. I'm guzzling a disgusting tea that some
quack hoisted on me and tucking into aspirins as if they were
Smarties. Where are you?'

'Jardin Menara. You need to do us a favour.'

'Your balance is sliding heavily into the red.'

'It's no big thing. Just ring one of your mates in the police
force and tell him that seven guys with guns are hanging round
the basin. Two are passing the time by the pavilion, two are
reading the papers, and the other three are standing by the
souvenir stalls at the end of the avenue. Tell your pal to send a
couple of unmarked cars.'

'What should they arrest them for?'

'Let your imagination run wild, I'm sure you'll think of
something. But listen, these guys—' Pavlik has to wait while
Harry's inflamed bronchial tubes challenge the loudspeaker.
'These guys are professionals. Tell the police to use the rear

gate, and no turning up with howling sirens. The three at the souvenir stalls will try to flee via the avenue, so they'll need to position some people at the entrance.'

'And what would you call a *big thing*? No, don't tell me. I'd never rest easy again.'

'You're a good man.'

'Up yours too.' His lungs rattle. 'Have you spoken to Jansen's wife? Not that it's anything to do with me, I'm just curious.'

'Drew a blank. He didn't talk to her about business.'

'I see a 1998 Saint-Émilion,' Harry suggests.

'Are you hallucinating already?'

'My favourite wine. Don't worry about the ribbon, I'll drink it straight away.' Harry puts down the phone.

'He's feeling shit, he has a fever, yet he asks about Layla,' says Aaron.

'Yep. I smell a rat.'

'One thing I don't understand: if the BKA has information on Jansen that they are keeping from us, why lead us to him in the first place? Harry could have said: Jansen? Never heard of him.'

'I've given up speculating about what I might find in a woman's handbag or the BKA's secret files.'

'Anything new with Layla?'

'All quiet on the western front. She's smoking her third cigarette.'

'How is she wearing her hair?'

'Loose.'

Aaron undoes the clasp that is holding her mane of curly hair in a ponytail. 'How tall is she?'

'One seventy with shoes.'

'What kind?'

'High heels.'

'What is she wearing?'

'Black knee-length skirt, padded blue jacket.'

'Can you get out without the men seeing you?'

'Yes.'

'Fetch me the skirt and the high heels from my bag.'

He gets out and opens the boot. She takes off her jeans. Pavlik returns. She pulls on the skirt and changes her shoes.

'Is she wearing make-up?'

'Hang on.' He raises the binoculars. 'Only lipstick, I think.'

Aaron picks up her Prada bag from the back seat. She puts on lipstick and can tell from the sound of Pavlik's breath that he is staring at her. 'Now you know what's in a woman's handbag.'

'I've never seen anyone put on make-up without a mirror.'

'Me neither. Are Layla's nails varnished?'

He reaches for the binoculars again. 'Yes.'

Aaron rummages around in her handbag and hands him a small bottle. 'Try your best.'

'Oh boy.'

She extends her left hand. 'I won't tell anyone.'

He gets to work.

'You're taking too much,' she comments.

'How do you know that?'

'Because you're dribbling.'

Pavlik briefly lets go of her hand. She hears the sound signal of his mobile. He puts it on loudspeaker. Demirci answers. 'Where are you?'

'Still in Marrakech,' he says as he tackles the next fingernail.

'What have you found out?'

'Jansen is dead. But his wife lives here. We've been in her villa. We eliminated two men there. One of them used to work for the Department. He high-tailed it ten years ago in Rome. Varga had bought him.'

'Are we talking about Matteo Varga, the Camorra Capo? The one who was liquidated by his underboss?'

Pavlik is silent. He shares his thoughts with Aaron.

You *decide whether we tell her.*

She weighs it up and comes to the conclusion that it's OK to tell Demirci what they know about Varga. This is just about his identity, not his whereabouts. Aaron won't mention that he could be in London.

'Wrong,' she says. 'He's alive. He's the Broker.'

Demirci takes a moment to gather herself. 'And that's certain?'

'Yes.'

'Who was the man in Rome?'

'Henning Vesper.'

'He's on the roll of honour,' Demirci says flatly.

'He's not the only one who doesn't belong there.'

'What does Jansen's wife know?'

'Good question. Jansen may have been Varga's closest confidant. He arranged terrorist attacks for him all over the world. Varga had him eliminated. We're trying to induce Layla to cooperate.'

'Does she have personal security?'

'She's being used as bait for us,' Pavlik replies. 'We're in the process of fixing the problem. If all goes well, Layla will be sitting in the car with us in half an hour and we'll be heading off to Erfoud.'

'She's a German national, but she's using a Canadian passport,' says Aaron while Pavlik changes over to her right hand.

'Does this mean that you intend to bring the woman with you?'

'Her and her young son.'

'If she cooperates,' Demirci qualifies.

'Otherwise we'll force her.'

Demirci's voice could cut through armoured glass. 'You'll do no such thing.'

'She's our—'

'It's possible that Lissek would have handled it that way,' Demirci interrupts Aaron. 'But in case you haven't noticed, he's retired. The woman will either get in that plane of her own free will or not at all. This is not up for discussion. Is that clear?'

'Perfectly clear.'

'Nor will you kidnap her and carry her off to some hiding place to make her talk. I don't want to be taken to court for false imprisonment.'

Damn.

'When is our taxi due to arrive?' Pavlik asks.

'You won't manage to reach Erfoud before nightfall. That's too dangerous, we don't know whether the airfield is safe. You'll have to spend the night somewhere. We'll speak again this evening. If everything goes to plan, the jet will land tomorrow morning at eight your time.'

'The liaison officer tried to make us believe that Jansen was a lobbyist for the German weapons industry until 2008. That's definitely a misinformation.'

There is silence at the other end.

'We've read the letters Jansen sent to his wife. He was engaged in dubious dealings long before he met Varga, and he kept well away from Berlin.'

'Allegedly, the BKA only came across Jansen last summer, through phone calls from a terrorist cell in Casablanca,' Aaron adds. 'I don't believe that for one minute. I'll guarantee you they've got records on him, filed under U for unlocatable.'

'We'll speak this evening,' is Demirci's only comment.

There's a click as she puts down the phone.

Aaron waves her hands about to dry the varnish.

'You heard her,' Pavlik says, 'you have to crack Layla here, otherwise we're scuppered.'

'How much time do you reckon we have?'

'From the time of arrest perhaps half an hour, maximum an hour. If Harry can buy Moroccan policemen it'll be a doddle for Varga. They'll soon be back on the road.'

'Pass me the headphones.'

'What exactly are you going to do with her?' he asks.

'I will create a rapport.'

'What kind of rapport are we talking about?'

'It's a psychotherapy technique that's also used in fighting terrorism. I'm going to get Layla to trust me. I'm going to make her believe that I understand her, that I'm similar to her in many ways. First of all, I need to convince her to fly to Germany with us. For that I'll need you.'

'In what way?'

'Watch her facial expressions. Tell me about every change in her body language. Where she's looking is also important. I can detect a lot from the way someone is breathing, but not the nuances. If I brush a strand of hair off my forehead it means radio silence. Hand on chin means communication back on.'

'OK.'

'And steal her cigarettes.'

Theft by trickery is part of basic training at the Department. André was the uncrowned king. He once filched Lissek's tie – while he was wearing it.

Aaron takes all but three of the Marlboro out of her half-full pack and hands them to Pavlik. 'No need to scrounge anymore.'

Nothing is happening.

The waiting erodes their conviction.

The police should have got here ages ago.

Has the liaison officer bottled out? Or has he got different orders?

Directly from Palmer?

A plane thunders past above them as it takes off. Aaron imagines looking at the city one last time, saying farewell to this place where she has experienced such happiness and such sadness, where she marvelled and loved and suffered and killed. As if she could leave behind the fear and the guilt and the pain, forget the unspoken and the unspeakable, travel to a different time, a different world, in which everything ends well, like in the fairy tale of the little boy and the tear.

Pavlik lays a hand on her cheek, calm and warm.

'How do you do that?' she whispers.

'What?'

'How do you always know what's going on inside me?'

'And you of all people ask me that?' he replies.

'With you it's magic.'

'You don't reveal all your tricks to me either.'

'Tell me something nice.'

'The sky is vast and open, you can see all the way to the Atlas. The snow on the peaks is sparkling in the sun.'

Like meringue on a cake.

Standing by the Fontana dell'Acqua Paola, Aaron felt that the world was her oyster. She can remember how the hairs on her arms prickled when Keyes told her what was in the safe. Then the man who had her father killed kissed her hand. Then the man who had her father killed chatted to her about art. Then the man who had her father killed dished up one lie after the other.

And she believed them all.

She will no longer call him Varga. That would make him human. She will call him only the Broker.

Aaron wishes she hadn't taken the Broker's child back to bed, had waited for the Broker instead, a shadow behind the door of his room, where she would have strangled him with the Hermès scarf.

So many would still be alive.

Her father.

And Leon Keyes.

She has wondered sometimes whether there could have been something between them after all.

Of course not.

Still. He was a wily rascal with style. She has a soft spot for those.

'Here they are. Five black SUVs.'

She hears them drive past. They stop. Doors open quietly.

'Uzis, balaclavas, Kevlar vests,' Pavlik remarks. 'They aren't ordinary cops, looks like an anti-terror team. Nice, well-rehearsed movements. First the boys in the archway. Turn round, cross your hands behind your head. That's the way. Now the two on the bench. Lie down, arms and legs well apart. Someone ought to be doing a training video of this.'

'And the ones by the souvenir stall?'

'Running to the exit, where a welcome party is waiting.'

'What's Layla doing?'

'She's calling the boy over to her.'

The cards are all on the table. Apart from this last one. If they've bet the wrong way and Layla goes to the policemen the game is lost.

No, you're not going to do that, Amari. You want to take Luca far, far away from here, no matter where.

She hears doors opening and closing.

The men are being bundled into the cars.

Quick departure.

'Is Layla still there?'

'She hasn't moved an inch.'

23

She leaves the cane in the car, places a hand on Pavlik's elbow and hurries to the basin with him.

He starts to run. 'They're almost on the avenue.'

Aaron is so focused that she no longer takes in her surroundings. She blanks out everything that might distract her, every thought, every smell, every sound. Her lungs are working as evenly as if she were connected to a respirator.

'Ten metres,' says Pavlik. He slows down. 'Mrs Jansen? Wait a moment, please.'

She lets go of his elbow. Her senses leap back into action and transmit information to her cortex. Layla wants to flee with the child. Heeled shoes on smooth stone, the rattling of keys. Luca's steps are short and clumsy, Pavlik's strides are wide and energetic. A trace of perfume is floating in the air where Layla stood a moment ago, Cruel Gardénia.

Heels smack. Layla has stopped because Pavlik is holding onto her.

Aaron analyses the echo. Deeper reverberation at two o'clock, six metres away. Medium-sized object of low height.

Park bench?

'What do you want?' Fear is making Layla's voice shrill.

She calmly walks towards her. 'I just want to *talk* to you.'

'What about?'

'Hey, young man, do you want an ice-cream?' Pavlik asks. 'I'll buy you one.'

'Luca, you stay right here!'

Aaron knows that the woman is stiff as a board because the adrenalin is paralysing her. There are two ways to start with the rapport. She could use gestures, a relaxed body language or a smile to signal that her intentions are friendly.

Or she can immediately start to mirror Layla, even if she is being defensive.

Aaron decides on the latter.

We'll do everything in unison, Amari.

She tenses her muscles and adjusts the pitch of her voice to the shaky timbre of her opposite. 'We *won't harm* you and Luca. It was *us* who informed the police. *We* made sure that these men were *arrested*. Spare me a few minutes of your time, after that you're *free* to leave with your son. Agreed?'

Layla is silent.

'There's only the two of us. Just follow your *feeling.*'

A nice word, warm and soft, don't you agree, Amari?

'Those ice-creams look good. I'll get myself one too,' says Pavlik.

Let him go. What could you do about it anyway?

'Mama?'

'It's OK. I can see you from here.'

Little and big steps grow distant.

Layla's breath falters. Her larynx is tense, which makes it difficult to mirror her.

Aaron probes her way towards the syncopations. In order to engender a feeling of trust, it is vital to accurately copy the other's breathing rate. Later it will help her to perfectly match the register of Layla's voice. The problem is that the woman is twenty centimetres shorter and her lungs do not have the same volume. This means that Aaron has to breathe much faster. When she tried it for the first time at the BKA, she got so short of breath after five minutes that she had to stop. But it's just a matter of practice, now she can do it in her sleep.

'Who are you?' Layla asks.

'Shall we sit down, Mrs Jansen?' She doesn't want Layla to have to look up at her. 'Please.'

Layla hesitates, then starts to walk.

Aaron follows her steps. She was right: park bench. She nudges her leg against it and sits down next to Layla. 'My name is Juliane Marquardt. We're from the German police and we're here to *protect* you.'

You and me against everyone else, Amari.

'Protect – who from?'

'Those men that frightened you and Luca work for the man who murdered your husband. Did you know that?'

'She's crossing her arms,' Pavlik's voice comes through the earbud. 'Her chin is jutting out, shoulders are drooping. She has a dry mouth, she keeps running her tongue over her lips, which are pressed into a thin line.'

'You're mistaken. Listen, we were just out for a walk.'

'I *understand*. I would react exactly the same way.'

Understand. Let the word resonate within you. Note how I'm emphasizing it. It's not just a throwaway remark.

Only now does she respond to Layla's body language. Aaron approaches it softly softly; mirroring her opposite in a very obvious manner would seem like mimicry. Bit by bit she will copy the movements more closely, but always with a delay, so that it doesn't attract attention.

Imitating facial expressions is easy. The other person can't see their own face and therefore doesn't notice it. Aaron gently juts out her chin and moistens her thin lips. She completes the mirroring by placing her hand on her left arm. It isn't as glaring as crossing her arms, but carries the same message.

'Those men are very dangerous. You're *right* to be afraid.'

'You're just mistaking me for somebody else.' Layla rummages around in her handbag.

'She's looking for her cigarettes,' Pavlik whispers.

Aaron whips out her Marlboro. 'Please, help yourself.' She gives Layla a light. That is one of her best tricks. Unfortunately no sighted person can appreciate it. She smokes too, brushes aside a strand of hair and observes Layla's breathing. Layla is sucking so hard on the cigarette that there is a quiet popping sound when her lips let go of the filter.

But the nicotine calms her.

We could have killed you ages ago. We're the good ones.

With greedy puffs, Aaron gets the last out of her cigarette. She touches her chin and ends the radio silence. 'I keep telling myself that I should give it up. I just can't manage it,' she says.

'She's looking straight at you for the first time.'

'Who are you talking to?' she hears Luca.

'Oh, I sometimes just talk to myself. Come, let's buy some fish food. Do you have a favourite carp?'

'The one with the white dot.'

Luca's voice sounds like that of a boy who likes his own company, but isn't afraid of strangers. Hearing him conjures up a world full of wonderment and toffee sweets in rustling bags.

Concentrate on Layla.

'You're not well. You've been seeing a doctor. Nothing serious, I hope.'

I'm worried about you, Amari.

'Who told you that?'

There's no point in hiding from her that they've been in the villa. On the contrary, Aaron is using it. 'We were in your house earlier. Please don't be alarmed. We've taken *considerable risks* to save your *life*.'

273

I'm being honest, I don't have any secrets from you.

She surfs on the wave of Layla's breath and expects that her voice will soon return to its normal pitch.

'These are all just lies.'

Then why is your breath slowly settling down, Amari?

Why does your voice sound almost natural?

Warm note, smoky.

Mirroring that is as difficult for Aaron as chewing gum. 'The man who was in your house is *dead*. He *can't harm* you and Luca anymore. How long has he been with you? Three days? Four?'

'Three,' says Layla unintentionally.

Applied neurolinguistics.

'Did you know him from before? Did your husband bring him to your home once? Or did he invite him round for dinner?'

'I don't know anything about the people my husband was involved with. I never heard anything about them.'

She talks fast, which means that she's also a fast thinker. These things go hand in hand.

'We led a quiet life. He was robbed in the souks. His wallet was stolen. He was killed just for that. For nothing.'

Layla's voice cracks. She's breathing into her chest because she's afraid that Aaron won't believe her.

Aaron adopts the same breathing pattern.

Right from the start, she listened out for filler words in Layla's speech; superfluous add-ins that everyone uses. With Layla it is JUST. So Aaron makes lavish use of it too.

'There's no point in arguing over why your husband had to die. That's *just* going to cost us time.' She talks at precisely the same speed as Layla. 'You look tired. I can sympathize with that. The only way to get any sleep, even *just* for a few hours, is with Valium. Then the next day, you *just* have this dreadful hangover, it's like wading through treacle. *Believe me*, I know what I'm talking about.'

I'm sharing something with you, Amari. We have so much in common.

'The men will be back. Luca and you can't go back to the house.'

'She's looking past you, at me and the boy,' Pavlik whispers. 'He's feeding the fish. He's standing at eight o'clock, thirty metres from you. Layla is tired, she's rubbing her eyes.'

Aaron points her face in Luca's direction. She runs her index finger over her cheekbone. 'You have your son to consider. You're very lucky to have him. I gather you had him quite late.'

I won't tell you about the letters, Amari.

'I envy you. To be *honest*, my husband and I can't have kids. It isn't easy. I used to feel that if I could *just* have a child, my life would be complete.'

Aaron is careful never to link any phrases with BUT. The word always introduces doubt, while AND signals affirmation. That is a fundamental rule when building a rapport, even if what is said is contradicting.

'*My husband* is away a lot on business, you see. And so am I. Going out to work does help. You must have *loved* your husband very much. One can tell *just* by looking at the photos. And his study. I can *understand* that you haven't changed anything. I don't think I could either, if something happened to *my husband*. And now *your husband* can't help you anymore.'

Layla gets angry. 'Just because you broke into my house, you think you can comment on my marriage?'

'She's crossing her arms again.'

Aaron folds her hands in her lap, that's enough. The same as it's enough to raise her voice by a fraction, to let Layla's indignation resonate. 'We didn't break in, we were *just* there because we were *worried* about you. We know you *just* want to sell the house and move back to Germany. The thing is, how's that going to work? Without passports?'

Layla's breath darts away like a little mouse.

While Aaron mirrors this, she says: 'You know, it could be so *easy*. We've found the fake passports. They're in our car, in a bag that we've packed for you both. We've also packed your *medication*. You and Luca could be in Germany tomorrow, in *safety*. Doesn't that sound good? It's *just* up to you, nobody is going to make you come.'

'She's looking you in the eyes, she's thinking,' Pavlik whispers.

Amari, do you know that the man who was so affectionate towards you, who showed you the sunset in White Bay and quoted Rilke, was in Frankfurt a year ago to instruct five ISIS terrorists so they could gas a thousand people in Terminal 1? When our Pakistani informant sat opposite me for the first time, he spat at me and said: 'Whores like you are sold for a basket of fruit on the market in Rakka.' Three weeks later, before boarding the flight to Peshawar, he hugged me. He was in tears and he said: 'My sister, I thank you so much.'

'And then?' Layla asks.

Aaron acts as though she is returning her gaze. 'Then we will see. It's possible that you have no idea what your husband did professionally.'

Stay away from BUT.

'Here and there you may have picked up on something. Perhaps some of his business acquaintances came to visit, or you may have overheard part of a phone conversation, heard a name for example.' Aaron invents three. 'Sandro Dazieri, Sebastian Volkerts, Bob Wilkins.'

She pauses briefly.

This once I will still refer to him like that.

'Or Matteo Varga – one of those perhaps?'

'She didn't flinch with any of them.'

That doesn't mean anything. He goes by a different name now. Amari, you know this man. Don't make it so hard for yourself. He ordered the killing of the two people we cared most about in this world. You want to tell me about him. Fate has brought us together.

'I've never heard of them,' says Layla. 'We rarely had guests. It was always just friends.'

'If that's the case: no problem. We will *just* talk things through. We *just* want to consult you on a few details.'

'It's been twenty minutes now,' Pavlik urges her.

'Can I have another cigarette?'

'Of course – help yourself.'

'It's your last one.'

'Doesn't matter.'

You're important to me, Amari.

Aaron gives her a light. 'You're just very cautious, and I would be too *in your position*. You could have alerted the police earlier, yet you decided not to. Surely you've wondered how you're going to get out of this situation *alive*, and you *just* kept arriving at the same fear. It's like a silent scream. No one else would be as *honest* with you as I am. It's time you finally allowed yourself to *trust* someone.'

'I have friends.'

'Where are they?'

Such a simple question. And such a bitter answer.

'I'm here for you. You have my word.'

'The word of a stranger.'

'It's odd, I *feel* as though we've know each other for ages.'

Surely you do too, Amari.

Aaron tests whether she is ready. She slows down her breathing until it corresponds to her own rhythm. Layla has never breathed this slowly before. If she involuntarily follows her lead, the rapport has been established.

Layla says nothing for a long time.

Let go, Amari, you're like me.

After thirty seconds she notices that it's working. Layla starts to breathe at the same pace as Aaron.

The calm flow of trust.

Perfect.

'If you want, you and Luca will be given new identities in a country of your choice. You'll never hear from any of these men again.'

Say it, Amari.

What do you have to lose?

'Luca!' Layla calls out.

Little and big steps.

'We're going on a journey,' she says to him.

He looks up to Aaron. 'What's your name?'

'Juliane.'

'No, that's not your name,' he declares in a matter-of-fact way.

Her heart gives a lurch.

'Did they take your phone away from you?' Pavlik asks.

'Yes.'

'I need to scan you.' He runs the detector over her. The Broker's men may not have believed that Layla and Luca could escape them, but Vesper worked for the Department for five years.

Shit happens.

That is drilled into each one of them there from day one.

The detector responds.

And again.

There's a bug in Layla's jacket pocket and one in Luca's hood.

Pavlik stamps on them with his foot.

It's possible that they are also carrying nanotransmitters inside them. These can be administered with a drink or a yoghurt, invisible and tasteless. Tiny parasites that keep on working for twenty-four hours.

That risk remains.

'Our car is parked over there,' Pavlik says.

Aaron hooks her arm round his. She briefly hopes that Luca will reach for her hand, but he takes his mother's.

A phone rings. Unfamiliar melody.

Pavlik moves away so that Layla and Luca can't hear him.

But Aaron still can.

'Yes?' he asks. 'What, police?' He is silent. Then he barks: 'That woman was important. You've messed up. If I set eyes on any of you again you're dead. Let me give you some sound advice: get the hell out of Morocco. Save me the work.'

Aaron hears him throw the mobile into the bushes.

They carry on walking.

'Have you been blind for a long time?' Luca asks.

'Yes. A very long time.'

Layla's steps falter.

She hadn't realized.

24

Since her phone conversation with Aaron and Pavlik, Inan Demirci has been stacking up thoughts like building blocks. And every time the tower ends up collapsing.

She leaves her office. 'Helmchen, is Palmer in Berlin today?'

'Always on Thursdays.'

'I need to meet with him. At four.'

'Oh. That's very short notice.'

'Tell his secretary that it's about Veit Jansen.'

'And where? In Treptow?'

On no account. The meeting mustn't become a home game for Palmer. She could ask him to come to the Department. But what if Svoboda has a mole at the Federal Police Office? Svoboda is well aware of Palmer's views on Demirci; he knows that the BKA Commissioner wouldn't come to the Budapester Strasse unless there was some grave reason.

The safe house near Potsdam would be a good choice. It is situated in extensive grounds by the Templiner See and is equipped with the latest technology. The conversation could be recorded, which would be an advantage.

But the building is currently being used to house two

computer specialists who have defected from the Russian secret service and are being questioned by the CIA; a favour that will be returned by the organization when a suitable occasion arises.

Another option would be the Mill, the Department's instruction and training centre near Beelitz. It's a long drive though, up to seventy minutes, depending on traffic. Not a convenient solution.

'Somewhere outside the city centre, where we'll be undisturbed,' says Demirci. 'But not out in the sticks.'

Helmchen ponders. Born and bred in Berlin, she knows every location that would be suitable for such a conversation; Lissek occasionally had a need for this kind of setting too. 'The Pfaueninsel. At this time of year there's hardly anyone there. You can stroll around there in peace. There's a rustic inn by the ferry stop.'

'How long will it take me to get there?'

'With the helicopter?'

There's a heliport on the roof. The aircraft is provided by the Federal Police.

Not secure enough. Don't trust anyone.

'With the car,' she says.

'They're still digging up sections of the Avus road. You would have to allow three quarters of an hour.'

'Arrange the meeting. And I want to see Mr Janko in ten minutes.'

She takes the lift up to the roof terrace. Sometimes the cold helps her to get her head straight. Freezing, she sucks the bitterness from two cigarettes. It doesn't calm her. She thinks of the two Marlboro packs she saw in the waste bin this morning and feels sick. Helmchen had wordlessly placed a bowl of sweets on the desk. She hasn't touched them.

★

Björn Janko is waiting in the anteroom. He is the Department's logistician, a lank ageing hippy with a long grey mane and a tattoo on his forearm: *Shit happens.* An indescribable chaos reigns in his office, underpinned by a system which only he understands. In the midst of it all stands an enormous aquarium, which he lovingly tends. Janko's nickname is Guppy.

Demirci was sceptical at first; the logistician plays an important role in the Department's operations. He is responsible for the organization and technical planning and for providing the equipment. He has to consider every possibility and ensure that the on-site team has everything they need. What should Demirci think of a man who talks to his fish and has even given them names?

He soon put her right. Guppy plans every mission as though his own life depended on it. The men and women trust him implicitly. As Demirci now does.

'Come on through, Mr Janko – you too, Helmchen.'

Demirci goes into her office with them. They sit down at the table. 'We need a jet,' she says. 'It has to be ready early tomorrow morning.'

'Destination?' Guppy asks.

'Erfoud. A small airfield near the Sahara. Arrange the landing rights.'

'What time is take-off?'

'How long will the flight take?'

Guppy makes a rough calculation. 'Four hours.'

'Morocco is an hour behind. Let's assume five a.m.. We won't be sure until this evening.'

'That's outside the core flying times, we'll need special authorization for that,' says Helmchen. 'Are we running this via the Interior Senate?'

Very diplomatic. Helmchen, switched on as always.

'How can we avoid it?' Demirci asks.

Guppy mutters: 'I'll sort it out with the airport operations manager in Schönefeld. It won't be the first time we've wangled it that way.'

'Good. I'll be on the flight. Helmchen, please cancel all appointments for tomorrow.'

'Are we getting Aaron and Pavlik out?' Guppy asks.

'Yes.'

'Which passports will they be using?'

'The Norwegian ones. Malin and Erik Jøndal.'

'Who do you want to have in the team?'

'Fricke, Kemper, Rogge and Nickel.' After a pause she adds: 'I'll leave the fifth open for now.'

'Which equipment set?' he asks.

'Rescue.'

'In that case I'll book the jet with Sierra Security.'

They're a private security firm based in Scotland. The pilots are trained for such operations.

'Is that possible at such short notice?' Demirci asks.

'Depends how much we're willing to fork out.'

'Price is not an issue.'

Guppy takes notes. He will make use of a spy satellite to get an exact idea of Erfoud. When they land, each member of the team will know the location inside out.

'We might be taking two additional people on board,' says Demirci.

'Who?'

'A woman and a child. I still have to clarify that.'

'I need their nationality for customs.'

'Canadian.'

'Do you want to have a medical team in the plane?'

'Yes.'

Helmchen is very quiet.

'Mobile operating theatre?'

'As a precaution.'

'I'll sort that with Sierra too.'

'If the woman and the child come back with us we will have to take them to a safe house. Which ones are free?'

'Frankfurt on the Oder, Cottbus, Rügen and the Teufelsbach hill farm.'

'Where exactly is that?'

'In the Alps, by the Walchensee. It's at fifteen hundred metres, arse end of the world.'

'We'll use that one.'

'I'll sort out landing rights for Munich.'

'Good. And an armoured transporter.'

'Is that all?'

'Yes.'

Guppy leaves.

'Helmchen, just a moment, please.' Demirci waits until he has closed the door. 'Any news from Palmer?'

'His secretary said that she'd ring back. Two minutes later she confirmed the appointment.'

Aha.

'Shall I notify the Five?' asks Helmchen.

Demirci's bodyguards.

Officially she is at the highest security level and has personal protection available around the clock, but that is more symbolic. The public know of the Department's existence, but that is all. Nothing about their missions, their successes and failures leaks out. Not even the location is known. If anyone was to ask what goes on in this obscure Institute for Social Analysis that takes up four floors, they would be met with shoulder shrugging. Searching for Demirci's photo on the internet is a futile exercise. All that can be found in relation to her name are links from her time as head of the Dortmund Homicide Unit.

She is Germany's most invisible woman.

Except for Aaron.

'I'll drive on my own,' she says.

'OK. I'll enter the address into your satnav.'

'One last thing, Helmchen: we aren't keeping any records of this flight, the operation never took place.'

'No problem.'

'And we're not paying for the jet out of our budget,' Demirci adds.

'You mean the piggy bank?'

'Yes.'

How easily it trips off Demirci's tongue already. When Lissek told her about it during the office handover she was speechless. She decided she would discreetly feed the money back into the regular funds bit by bit and dissolve the secret account. That was on 1 December. Since then she has resorted to it twice, and both times it made all the difference. The next budgetary round is due in May. Demirci has already secretly been thinking about how she can smuggle imaginary costs into the calculation, to replenish the piggy bank.

The Department has a strange effect on people.

'Please send Mr Flemming to me.'

Helmchen hovers in the doorway. 'How are they both?' she asks quietly.

She is the mother hen of the troop. All the Department's men and women are like family to her, but her relationship with Aaron and Pavlik is special. Demirci doesn't know what this link was forged by. Perhaps she will ask her secretary one day. Would she get an answer? Helmchen is as secretive as a Trappist nun.

'As one would expect under the circumstances,' Demirci replies.

Helmchen nods.

She doesn't look very relieved.

Inan Demirci lights a cigarette and leafs through Flemming's file again. It is unusual for someone to be appointed to the

Department from outside the police service. But Lissek defied all bureaucratic barriers and headhunted Flemming from the Special Forces Command of the German Armed Forces last year.

The main tasks of the Special Forces Command are reconnaissance, combating terrorism, evacuation and operations behind enemy lines. Only the best of the best can join the elite unit. Their mantra is: *Facit Omnia Voluntas, the will decides.*

That would also predestine Flemming for the Department.

He demonstrated exceptional capacity in Afghanistan and was awarded the gold cross of honour. His evaluations were outstanding.

But Demirci wouldn't have appointed him.

He didn't make use of any therapeutic help when he returned to Germany. He had gone without food or water for thirty-six hours as he battled his way through Taliban-infested territory with a severely wounded comrade over his shoulders. Nobody gets through something like that unscathed. Flemming passed the psychological aptitude test for the Department, but one of the passages in the interview transcript perplexed Demirci.

Question: Are you a team player?
Reply: As long as there is a team.
Question: What do you mean by that?
Reply: In the end, we all die alone.

The psychologist didn't go into it any further. Unfortunately.

What speaks in his favour? His physical abilities.

And what speaks against him? The opportunities for deployment are limited. Freeing hostages is more or less the only thing she can use Flemming for, as he lacks the police training required for undercover operations. Also, Flemming is single. Demirci prefers the men in her troop to be married, or to be in a stable relationship at least. They have more to lose and are therefore inclined to switch on their brain.

Lissek didn't care about all that.

Lissek is Lissek.

Regarding Flemming she might have left it at that, if it hadn't been for the 'jolly get-together' that Pavlik had proposed.

'Four of us are dead,' he'd said. 'The lads really need to let off some steam. I'll see about organizing a punch-up. That'll clear their heads.'

Demirci had shuddered at the thought of it, but Pavlik was better versed in such matters. Helmchen had known exactly what type of beer joint was suitable for this kind of thing.

'What shall I wear?' Demirci had asked when they were alone.

'Something that can go in a hot wash to get rid of the booze and blood stains.'

Not a very encouraging reply.

The place Helmchen chose was in Moabit, near the central market. Peanut shells covered the floor of the bodega. The walls were plastered with posters of Zapata, Pancho Villa and a man not known to Demirci, who had a machete clenched between his teeth. Probably because he was standing behind a woman dressed only with two crossed-over ammunition belts, and he needed to have his hands free to grab her breasts.

Mexican punk was blaring out of the loudspeakers; Corona and brown Tequila flowed freely, also some kind of brew called 'Macke' that was probably excellent against plaque. Cryptic toasts were proposed (*To the red ape! Death to the Greenlanders! There's no winter as cold as Sandy!*), and Demirci felt as though she had chanced upon a previously undiscovered jungle tribe during an expedition.

By midnight they were all legless.

Apart from her and Flemming.

She watched him furtively. While the others roared out dirty jokes that made her blush, performed party tricks among which the farting of the national anthem was the most harmless, and generally knocked back drinks as if there was no tomorrow, Flemming sat apart and sipped on his second beer. He didn't seem to be the least bit interested in what was going on around him, and none of the others took any notice of him.

She was just about to go and sit down next to him, when the first chair flew through the room. Demirci just managed to dive under the table, before the inevitable took its course. For minutes she cowered there, listening to the shouting and swearing and the sound of splintering wood. All of a sudden, Kleff's face was close in front of hers. He gave Demirci a red-nosed grin, was dragged backwards by his feet and yelled to her: 'They're animals!' Then some kind of flying object hit the stereo system and everything went quiet.

Cautiously she crept out from under the table.

Fricke was hanging from the ceiling fan by one hand and holding a chair leg in the other; Delmonte, swaying gently, was rearranging her bust; Dobeck and Peschel were bleeding from nose and mouth; Nickel was crawling about on the floor searching the peanut shells for one of his contact lenses; Pavlik's sweatshirt only had one sleeve left; and the rest of the troop didn't look much better.

Demirci didn't know what had triggered it. Peschel muttered something about a stupid joke; Rogge slapped Nowak on the back of the head and told him to watch where he put his feet in future; and Marx snarled at Krupp never to mention Sarajevo again.

'I only wanted—' Nieser mumbled three times at no one in particular.

'I only wanted a nymphomaniac with a brewery,' bawled Fricke and let himself drop. 'Didn't work out either.'

They laughed themselves to tears and Pavlik ordered a new round.

Flemming had disappeared.

Around three a.m. the hard core staggered off. Everyone agreed it had been a great evening, and Kleff was even moved to plant a smacker on Demirci's cheek.

She stayed sitting with Pavlik for a little while. He was cooling his chin with a bag of frozen chilli con carne.

'Helmchen didn't promise me too much,' she said.

'It was very civilized, I thought.'

'Yes, like that time in Verdun.'

'Anyone would think you're plastered.'

'Since when does humour come in bottles?' She pulled a tooth out of the tabletop.

Pavlik took it from her, examined it and chucked into a corner. 'Not mine. I'm missing a molar.'

'What do you think about Flemming?'

'Problem.'

'What's up with him?'

'No idea. Perhaps he needs a woman. Or a dog. Or a smack in the face. If he hadn't exited with an Irish goodbye, the last one would have already been taken care of.'

'Do you think you'll be able to get him round?'

'I've been trying for a year. Afghanistan can make a man as brittle as glass.'

'Why did Lissek want to have him?'

'Kallweit's knee wasn't playing along anymore. He was a bull of a man. Lissek always wanted to have at least one battle ram in the troop.'

'You don't?' Demirci asks.

'I'm too drunk to philosophize.'

'I'm thinking of sending him back to Special Forces Command.'

'They wouldn't take him back.'

'Why?'

'That lot are just as stuck up as we are. Once you've left, you've left. That would be catastrophic for Flemming. He would have to go to an ordinary Armed Forces unit. He wouldn't be able to handle that. Some comedian or another once said: "Once you've shagged Angelina Jolie, you don't move back home to Mama."'

'What can we do?'

'Talk to him,' Pavlik suggests.

'I don't have enough testosterone for that.'

'He's used to order and obedience. For him you're his commander. Not much outranks you, apart from God himself perhaps.'

She thought about that while Pavlik's chilli slowly defrosted and a puddle formed on the table. As they left, the landlord grumbled: 'Two thousand for the furniture, that's mates' rates. Your club already has my account number.'

Helmchen announces: 'Mr Flemming is here now.'

'Send him in.'

Flemming, a man next to whom Wladimir Klitschko would appear dainty, makes himself small in the doorway. Demirci knows how smoothly he can move, but he walks in stiff as a board.

'Please take a seat.'

She offers him a cigarette. He shakes his head.

She always feels as if he is standing to attention when she talks to him.

'Mr Flemming, why did you join us?'

'Because I was asked.'

'That isn't an answer.'

'Is there a problem?'

Demirci watches the seconds dissipate into vapour. 'I believe you're from Hanau?' she eventually asks.

'Yes.'

'That's only a few kilometres from my home town, Babenhausen.'

He doesn't know where this is leading.

'My father owned a small tailor's shop there,' she continues. 'When I was seventeen, he was burgled. The two men quickly realized that he didn't have much that was worth stealing. They wrecked the whole shop and beat my father to a pulp. Two policemen came. They noted down what had happened, but they didn't even ask for a description of the perpetrators. It was clear straight away that they weren't going to do anything about it. My father was just some old Turk, he didn't matter to them. The fact that he was hospitalized, couldn't work for a month and had to borrow money from the bank in order to feed his family didn't worry them. That's when I decided to become a policewoman. So that people like my father wouldn't be without rights. Do you understand where I'm coming from?'

Flemming nods. He searches for words. 'The Special Forces Command was supposed to fight the Taliban. But the people there don't want to live like us. It seemed more and more pointless to me. Lissek said: "The Department is the front line of our state of law." I liked that.'

'Will you tell me about what happened in Afghanistan?'

'No.'

She briefly leaves this hanging in the air. 'What's your opinion – was it the right decision to accept Lissek's offer of appointment?'

'May I speak openly?'

'Always, we aren't the military.'

'I know that Pavlik wants me to get the boot.'

'Why should he?'

'I'm not a cop, I'm not one of the gang. For the others I'm just Rambo on holiday. We don't have anything in common. Half the time, I don't even know what they're talking about.' He looks at her with a firm gaze. 'Perhaps it will be best for everyone. So just get it over with.'

Demirci stubs out her cigarette. 'Mr Flemming, how would you feel about taking part in a one-year schooling programme at the Berlin State Criminal Police, where you would be given police training? I've spoken to the programme leader, he's agreeable to it. You'll continue to receive the Department's full pay and should I require your assistance for a particular operation, I'll call you in. After the training, you'll rejoin us. You can start on the first.'

Flemming swallows hard.

'Do you want to sleep on it?'

He clears his throat. 'No. Count me in. Thank you.'

'Good.' Demirci looks at her watch. She takes her coat and accompanies Flemming into the anteroom. 'Helmchen, I'm going for that lunch engagement now. I'll walk. Ask someone to park my car by the ROCA café and bring me the key.'

'Will do.'

Demirci extends her hand to Flemming. 'You're flying to Morocco with me and a team early tomorrow morning. Mr Janko will brief you on the details. Regarding Ulf Pavlik you're wrong. He spoke out in your favour.'

25

The Budapester Strasse is one long traffic jam. The Emperor of Japan is in town for a two-day state visit, and he is residing at the InterContinental across the road. Demirci subconsciously counts the armoured limousines that are pulling up outside the hotel. The Emperor will rest, before driving to the Hotel Adlon for this evening's gala dinner, to which she had also been invited.

She declined. These events are not her world, she feels one tends to sell oneself short during small talk. Of course it isn't wise of her to withdraw so frequently from Berlin's schmoozing events. There is much that she has to pick up on if she wants to stay abreast of the gossip. You never know what kind of chit-chat is circulating about you.

A couple of days ago she was at a reception hosted by the American embassy. 'Attending that is compulsory,' Lissek had told her. The CIA station chief likes to invite an illustrious group to the fireside lounge, where off-the-record conversations on security policies are held.

'It's a proper congregation of dickheads,' Lissek had said. 'Each one of them thinks he's got the biggest. If you allow them to belittle you, you'll never get a look-in. Wear something with a low neckline.'

Palmer and Svoboda were there too.

She walks along the perimeter of the zoo. The stone elephants beside the gate brace themselves against the harsh wind that is throwing damp snow into her face.

Demirci buttons up her coat.

She thinks of Ellen, whom she has arranged to meet.

They've know each other since their school days. Ellen is the only one of her schoolfriends she is still in touch with, perhaps because the two of them both followed a similar path; Ellen is a public prosecutor in Düsseldorf.

She married when she was thirty, but got divorced soon after. The reasons were only vaguely mentioned. After that, Demirci never saw her with another man.

They didn't need anyone else and they had a lot in common. It wasn't just the nonchalant certainty that they were better than most, but also their interest in art and classical music, and their memories of a time when everything seemed so easy.

Men were never a topic, ever. They factored them out as if matters of the heart were utterly irrelevant to their lives.

Demirci is experienced in being unhappy. Her relationships always had a short half life, and she is honest enough with herself to recognize that this was down to her. She never accorded any man the same importance as she did to her career. In fact, there was only one to whom she had truly opened her heart. He was a boy in her tutor group. Demirci was so nuts about him that on the day after they had slept with each other, her head was full of shooting stars and she messed up her final maths exam. She would have followed him anywhere, but he left to study in Norway without saying goodbye. For six months she was so distraught she thought she'd never get over it.

Others that followed helped to get over the loneliness for a while, but she didn't share her life with them. To avoid any feelings of guilt, she automatically sought out men who were as wrapped up in their jobs as she was.

They didn't even notice that she didn't talk about her work; men prefer to talk about themselves anyway. One of them was married, which she only found out after several months. It alarmed her to realize how little she knew about him.

It was many years before she began to understand why Ellen had remained single.

There were little signals. The way she hugged Demirci when they met up, the tenderness in her voice, and then the glance she happened to catch in a bar mirror as she went to the toilets and Ellen thought herself unobserved.

Demirci's heart grew heavy. She didn't want to lose her friend, but she couldn't give her what she longed for.

The next time they met, Demirci was uneasy. Ellen didn't notice it and was brimming over with excitement. There was something to celebrate: she had been appointed Director of Public Prosecutions. Demirci felt happy for her, despite everything. But now that she knew Ellen's secret, the old intimacy was lost.

Around nine, she invented a toothache. It happened out on the street. Ellen tried to kiss her. It failed because Demirci turned her face away; Ellen's lips slid into her hair. Awkward and clueless, they stood facing each other while it started to rain and no words would come. Then Demirci walked away mutely.

That was a year ago. They haven't seen each other since then. They've spoken on the phone twice, on their birthdays. Anything else would have meant admitting that the friendship was over, and she was as fearful of that as Ellen was. They acted as though that confounded situation outside the bar had never happened, and they both grew sadder with each word.

Twice Demirci has been to the Federal Intelligence Service in Cologne, when previously she would have got in touch with Ellen instead. It's only twenty minutes to Düsseldorf by train, and it wouldn't have been a problem to stay overnight either. But she didn't.

Yesterday, Ellen rang. Demirci instantly felt pangs of guilt. It might be nonsense, but it felt to her as if she'd betrayed their friendship when she turned her face away on the street. Ellen said that she was in Berlin for business and asked whether they could meet. Tomorrow at two? Demirci was tempted to cite existing commitments as an excuse. Instead she suggested the ROCA in the Waldorf Astoria.

She had briefly toyed with the idea of having her bodyguards accompany her. As if five muscle-bound men could make Demirci feel more self-assured.

Ellen is already there and is labouring on an uneasy smile. The hug is just hinted at, their cheeks briefly brush against each other; to use the word touch would be to exaggerate.

'How are you?' Demirci asks after sitting down. She realizes that her voice is brittle and clears her throat. 'My goodness, what weather.'

'So-so. And you?'

Ellen is wearing a lot of make-up. Her face bears the signs of a sleepless night.

So does mine.

'I'm smoking again,' she sighs. 'And I hate myself for it.'

The waiter brings the menu.

'Thank you,' Ellen says. 'We're not eating.'

Demirci looks at her friend perplexed.

'What would you like to drink?'

'We haven't decided yet.'

The waiter leaves the menu on the table and leaves.

Demirci has a lump in her throat.

Her commando leader enters the restaurant. He gives her the sensor for the Daimler. 'It's parked across the road.'

She nods. He disappears again.

'I didn't want to tell you over the phone,' Ellen says, 'and I didn't want you to find out via the official channel either.'

'What?'

'In April I will assume control of the police department in the Interior Senate. The intention is for me to be appointed Commissioner of Police next year.'

A group of tipsy tourists is making a racket on the other side of the window. A car slams on the brakes because a homeless man is pushing a shopping trolley across the road. Snowflakes are melting on the glass, leaving behind a shaky matrix.

Demirci doesn't say a word.

'Svoboda brought up the fact that I'm from Babenhausen and asked me if I knew you. He intimated that the relationship between you and him is difficult and wanted to know whether that would be a problem for me.'

Demirci scrapes together the words. 'What did you reply?'

'That he needn't worry.' Coolly, Ellen adds: 'Our friendship won't survive it. But then we've just been dragging that around with us anyway.'

Demirci stands up. 'You needn't have been concerned. It would have been enough to tell me over the phone.'

She takes her coat from the chair.

Ellen holds on to her arm. 'You don't know what it's like to dream of something that's beyond your reach. You know nothing of other people's unhappiness, other than what you've read in files. I used to envy you for it. Now I feel sorry for you.'

The first time Demirci becomes aware of her surroundings again she sees that she is on the Kurfürstendamm. People rush past with bags from luxury boutiques, their faces marked by shopping stress. It has stopped snowing, the sky is the colour of freshly poured concrete.

Some people can find solace in hate. That was never her way. Even the dealer whose ricochet shot killed her mother outside the discotheque many years ago only triggered a feeling of contempt in her. She felt some satisfaction in attending court as the judgement was passed, but after that she rarely thought of him.

In the crisp cold of this day, the shadows drawing out already, she wishes that Svoboda was lying in the snow in front of her, begging her forgiveness for what he has done.

She mustn't allow herself to feel like that.

Demirci has to keep a clear head, otherwise she will run straight into the trap. She doesn't believe for one second that Svoboda found out about the connection between her and Ellen by chance. He has looked into her past and deliberately chosen Ellen. Svoboda doesn't know of her feelings for Demirci. But it was clear to him that he would drive Ellen into a conflict of loyalties that would shatter their friendship.

Sadism, interesting character trait, weak point.

Would Svoboda have treated Lissek in the same way? Hardly. He underestimates her. Presumably because she is a woman.

Good.

Everyone was scared of Lissek. It was said that he had a file on everyone. There is a room in the Department that is secured with armour steel and lasers. The reports on every mission and every secret operation are stored there.

Fitted into one of the walls is a safe that can't even be cracked with explosives. When Demirci opened it for the first time she was prepared for anything.

The safe was empty, apart from a handwritten note that Lissek had left for her.

Our doubts don't count, only our actions.

She looks at her watch. It's another fifty minutes before she has to drive out to the Pfaueninsel. As she walks along the boulevard she has no eyes for the displays of the designer shops.

Perhaps Lissek took the files with him, as life insurance. A kind of dead man's switch, that would be just like him. Or he has destroyed them. One has to let go sometime.

There's one that he's bound to still have: the one about Svoboda.

Aaron told her about it. Years ago, the Italian Mafia tapped Svoboda's office landline, which nearly cost Aaron her life during a mission.

Demirci could ring Lissek.

No. Even if he gives her the file and she leaks it to the press, Svoboda would only have to resign at worst.

That wouldn't be enough.

She wonders whether the Mafia tapped his phone without him knowing.

'Svoboda wants to own the Department,' Palmer had said.

What use would it be to him?

Demirci is entrusted with highly volatile investigations. Terrorism, international organized crime, counter-intelligence. If Palmer is right about Svoboda and he does have criminal energy, then control over the Department would indeed be useful. He would have a very sharp scalpel in his hand, which he could render so blunt that it would become entirely useless for any kind of operation.

This is how Richard Wolf must have felt when he set his guerrilla troop against the Federal Minister of the Interior.

Wolf won the battle. But at what cost?

She will have to think carefully about her next move.

Palmer is the Joker in this game.

Can she trust him?

At the American embassy, she saw him and Svoboda engaged in an animated conversation. The men rakishly nodded in her direction, then Palmer threw a comment to the Senator of the Interior and laughed with him.

Later everyone was sitting down with brandy and cigars,

Demirci the only woman, her cigarette in a silver holder. ISIS is on the retreat, the hacker attacks by the Russians are amateurish, three terrorist cells have been shut down in France, yet another Taliban leader has been eliminated with a drone, organized crime is an unavoidable evil, everything is hunky-dory.

'You look sceptical, Ms Demirci,' Svoboda commented in a nasal voice as he artfully sniffed at his brandy glass. 'Are you of a different opinion?'

'To know where we stand, I only need to look at what's on my desk,' she replied.

Lennard Palmer gave a wide grin: 'The bits and pieces lying around between the make-up.'

The gentlemen laughed.

'And what lies around on your desk?' she asked.

'I wouldn't like to say in front of a lady.'

'What makes you think that I am one?'

'The stuff coming from your desk that lands on mine.'

They laughed even louder.

This time she refrained from replying.

When Demirci had her coat on, Palmer joined her by the cloakroom; they were alone for a moment.

'I hope you understand,' he said quietly.

Demirci felt like kicking him between the legs.

She is already at the Olivaer Platz. Time to turn back and get the car. As she passes the delicatessen on the Bleibtreustrasse she realizes that she hasn't eaten anything since yesterday lunchtime. She buys herself a tuna sandwich although she doesn't feel hungry. It tastes like polystyrene; after one bite she throws it in a bin.

Before she gets into her car, she looks across to the ROCA. Ellen is still sitting at the table, a glass of red wine in front of her. Demirci thinks she sees tears, but perhaps it's just the snowflakes on the window.

26

She drives up the Kantstrasse. Illuminated signs are already flashing along the Asian Mile. Bare trees shiver on the banks of the Lietzensee. Sleet sprinkles the windscreen, the wipers leap into action. At the Messedamm, the beacon light of the radio tower flits about in the clouds like a thunderstorm.

Without the satnav, Demirci would be hopelessly lost. She has only lived in Berlin for two months; the city is a behemoth and everything beyond the government district is unexplored territory. On the Avus road she joins an endless column of traffic that crawls past the construction site.

Her bones feel leaden. Hating is a tiring business.

How tired must Aaron be feeling?

Her relationship with her father was exceptionally close, that much she knows. When Demirci attended the police academy, she spent a lot of time researching Jörg Aaron and wrote a paper on him. A father like him can be a millstone. But his daughter must have loved him very much.

There is nowhere that Varga would be safe from her. She wants to kill him, Demirci has no illusions about that.

Can she prevent Aaron from going through with it?

That will be difficult. Aaron knows more than her. What other information might Holm's recording contain? What did they find in Jansen's house? What if she succeeds in getting his wife to talk?

Will Aaron share all the information with Demirci?

She doubts it.

She has to rely on Pavlik to prevent a retaliation campaign. To whom does he feel the greater loyalty? Aaron or her?

If he decides to help Aaron, Demirci will be powerless.

He is the toughest man in the Department.

She is still a weapon on two legs, even now.

Varga has every reason to be afraid of those two.

Demirci knows Aaron's file inside out. There have been several internal investigations against her. The last one followed an operation in Helsinki. A taxi driver was killed during an exchange of fire with a group of Hells Angels. Something had prompted Lissek to copy the initial dialogue of her interrogation and to include it in the report.

Ms Aaron, are you aware of the gravity of the accusations against you?

Of course. Do you know what we call this room at the Department?

No.

Pyongyang. I'm through with every one of your types. The pally ones who feign understanding. The sexually needy ones with their pervy innuendos. The wide-legged machos. The bookkeepers, therapists, sycophants and sewer rats. I can't wait to see which category you belong in.

Aaron was comprehensively exonerated, the death of the taxi driver was not her fault. Each one of the investigations against her was shelved. For Demirci, Aaron embodied the Department's motto more than anyone else.

It's never easy.

She didn't know about Avignon then.

She ardently hopes that there is some other explanation for the disappearance of Bas Makata and his family.

She has barely thought of anything else for days.

Aaron and Pavlik.

Why does it have to be those two?

Demirci will have to ask them what happened. She is dreading it.

She turns off the Avus road by the Wannsee. Gulls are balancing on a stormy gust which has the boats lurching in the marina. After a few kilometres, the navigation system directs her onto a small winding road that leads through some woodland.

There is only one car parked outside the inn. Palmer has also come alone, of course. She gets out and considers him for a moment; the brown hair, the professor's nose, the soft cheeks, the eyes of a colour she can't discern. Nothing about this face fits, and yet it is attractive.

'Commissioner.'

'Ms Demirci.'

Sets of antlers have been nailed to the inn's wooden façade; an extractor pumps the stench of old chip oil into the open air.

Palmer's voice is businesslike. 'Are we going in?'

She looks over to the ferry. 'Let's cross over to the island.'

'You'll spoil your shoes.'

'You're spoiling my entire day.'

He holds his umbrella over her. It feels too close for Demirci, but she would get soaking wet otherwise. The ferryman isn't bothered by the weather, he's busy playing Skat on his phone.

Palmer glances over his shoulder. 'That isn't a suit game, that's a grand.'

'What d'yer dream of at night?'

'You put the wrong cards back down. The two clubs need to go down. If you do that you'll win with sixty-one,' Palmer informs him.

'No bleedin' way.'

'Oh well, it's your money.'

Palmer and Skat. Demirci's powers of imagination are finding their limits.

They buy tickets.

'Last crossing's at five,' says the ferryman.

'Thank you, that's fine for us,' she replies.

He takes them across; it's only a short hop to the island. Country music wafts out from the bridge. Demirci lights a cigarette, she's freezing. They step off the boat.

'At five, not five past, don't you be forgetting!' the ferryman calls after them.

Wordlessly, they walk along the waterside. The sky is tumbling onto the treetops. The peacocks that gave the island its name have crawled away into the undergrowth.

To the right is a clearing with a knight's castle, it looks like a film set. Demirci stops.

'Frederick William II had it built for his mistress Wilhelmine von Lichtenau,' says Palmer. 'This is where he discreetly met with her. It's a good place for secrets.'

'I don't think we're likely candidates for an amorous liaison,' she replies.

'It was an infelicitous affair for Wilhelmine. After the death of the king, his son had her banished.'

'A simple solution. Surely that would appeal to you.'

He smiles bleakly. 'I don't know what you've inherited from Lissek. Wolf left me a safe that contained things which robbed me of many a night's sleep. If you're interested in knowing the real reason for Uwe Barschel's death – just ask.'

'Other things interest me more.' She steps out into the sleet so that they are looking at each other. 'Who was Veit Jansen?'

Palmer's gaze is empty. 'His real name was Olaf Berg. He was one of our undercover agents and played a significant role in the arrest of Ilich Ramírez Sánchez.'

'Carlos the Jackal.'

'Yes. You know what happens to men who are undercover for too long. Wolf had him checked out at the end of the nineties. Berg was living beyond his means. He saw it coming and disappeared. After that his trail went cold.'

'Until the terrorist cell in Casablanca was shut down,' she surmises.

'The name Jansen meant nothing to us. My liaison officer went to Marrakech and took pictures. When Berg was identified, he was already dead.'

Demirci shakes her head. 'That's nowhere near everything. You wouldn't have needed to keep that from us.'

Palmer looks across the water. No light, anywhere. 'Somewhere over there is the Cecilienhof Palace, where Truman and Stalin divided the world up between them. It was all very simple back then.'

'I'm waiting,' says Demirci.

'After Berg disappeared, Wolf's people turned his house upside down. They found an old notebook stashed in a hiding place. He was in contact with Yigal Amir. Ever heard of him?'

'No.'

'He was the Israeli right-wing extremist who murdered Yitzhak Rabin in 1995.'

Demirci holds her breath.

'Berg had met with him on several occasions, the last time was shortly before the assassination. There's reason to believe that he was the mastermind behind the attack. We never found out who was behind Berg. Rabin had many enemies.'

Icy water trickles down Demirci's collar.

'Wolf buried it,' Palmer said hoarsely.

'To save his own skin,' she comments.

'No. He feared that it would put the reconciliation between Israel and Germany on ice for a very long time if he made it public. Wolf left it to me to decide how I should deal with it. I came to the conclusion that he was right.'

'Why did you help us in Marrakech?'

'I decided to take my chances. Now that you know the truth, does it change anything?'

Demirci stares out onto the lake. A police boat is pitching through the churning water.

No. But I wish I hadn't asked.

'Did you find anything out about this fund?' she asks.

She had passed it on to him yesterday.

'It's being managed by a man called Peter Lockhart,' says Palmer. 'He's a financial tycoon, stinking rich. I've brought MI5 on board, they've put him under surveillance.'

'What's being invested in?'

'European shares. Biotechnology, arms, chemical industry.'

'Short selling?'

'No, call options. They're betting on rising prices.'

'Europe – that doesn't necessarily mean that the terrorist attack will take place here.'

'Correct. It only means that these firms would profit from the attack, which could happen anywhere.'

Palmer has been honest with her. It's time to share something big with him. 'We know who the Broker is,' she says.

He inhales sharply.

'Matteo Varga.'

'Varga is dead,' Palmer counters.

'Apparently not.'

'Could there be a mistake?'

'I fear not.'

'We once had an informant called Leon Keyes, must be at least ten years ago,' Palmer mutters in a daze. 'The Department protected him for us in Rome. Or as Lissek would have put it:

he took care of my dirty laundry. Jenny Aaron killed seven of Varga's men, but she couldn't save Keyes. We thought Varga had been eliminated by his own family. The bastard has made fools of us all.'

'This stays between us,' she says. 'No manhunt. Varga has links to Interpol. We have to let him believe he's safe.'

'Sounds like the punchline is yet to come.'

'We may have a state witness.'

'Who?'

'Berg's wife.'

'I was told she doesn't know anything,' Palmer replies slowly.

'And I was told that a certain Veit Jansen was a lobbyist.'

'You'll catch your death.' He holds the umbrella over her and tucks his chin into his scarf. 'It would be helpful if I knew more about this account.'

Yes. But if Aaron kills Varga and Palmer knows why, there would be nothing I could do to help her. I need to know what happened in Avignon. So much depends on it.

'Let's wait and see how things develop,' she says evasively.

'Jenny Aaron is in Morocco. She's still on my payroll. Don't you think that would warrant a little more candour?'

'Do you really want to discuss the service law with me?'

They are silent.

'Did you ever meet her before she lost her sight?' he asks.

'No. What was she like?'

'It was the first time I saw a beast of prey in the wild.'

'That didn't stop you hiring her for the BKA.'

'It would have been stupid to forgo the opportunity. And you're not stupid either. That's why she's back with you again.'

'Sulking?'

'I'll be over it by the time I'm on my death bed.'

He's quite charming. She'd never noticed that before.

Demirci says: 'Svoboda should be under surveillance. I can't do that without him knowing, but you can.'

Palmer's eyes grow darker than the Wannsee.

It's a big ask. He won't do it.

'It was initiated last week,' he informs her.

So much for my insight into human nature.

'Who's in the loop?'

'My best people.'

'Have you got anything yet?'

'The world never turns as fast as one would like.'

Demirci looks at her watch. 'We should head back, otherwise we'll have to spend the night here.'

'Tempting.'

Is he flirting with me?

Palmer grins. 'I just wanted to see the look on your face.'

She hooks her arm round his. Her toes are frozen numb inside the soaked shoes.

'Is there any news from Pakistan?' he asks.

'We're tailing your man. I received the first report yesterday. Nothing out of the ordinary so far. We'll see.'

'Will I be the first to hear if anything comes to light?'

'You have my word.'

She doesn't tell Palmer that they have passed false information to the liaison officer concerning a CIA operation. Fodder for the Taliban. Should they receive it, it would result in a movement of troops in the west of Afghanistan. If that takes place, they will arrest the liaison officer. Demirci doesn't think that Palmer is involved. But then nor did she think that something like Avignon was possible.

'Svoboda has got some kind of ace up his sleeve,' he mutters. 'He was bragging at the reception in the embassy. He said it was your birthday soon and he was going to send you a nice present.'

Ellen. I hope you choke on it.

'The Interior Ministers' Conference was in session a couple of days ago,' she says. 'Was there any talk about me?'

'Of course. Svoboda is stirring up opinion against you. She says you're incapable, have sacrificed four men, the usual.'

'Do I have any friends there?'

'Those who voted for your appointment won't distance themselves from you that fast, that would mean losing face. The others are watching the show. I cracked a lads' joke at your expense. Bavaria laughed the loudest.'

As they cross back over, the ferryman says to Palmer: 'I replayed the grand. Bugger me, you were spot on! I'd have won with one point.'

'A clever horse only jumps as high as it has to,' replies the BKA Commissioner.

They stop by the cars.

'Was it a good one at least?' Demirci asks.

He looks at her questioningly.

'The lads' joke.'

'It served its purpose.' Palmer hesitates. 'I fear I have some more bad news for you. There's been a hacker attack on the embassy in Rabat; we don't know who's behind it. They listened in on the phones. It's possible that the liaison officer's landline calls were affected.'

An icy shiver runs down her spine. 'Calls to the BKA?'

'Yes.'

'Was Erfoud mentioned?'

'I had that checked immediately. All the phone calls between liaison officers and informant leaders are recorded. There was no talk about Erfoud.'

'Were any names mentioned?'

'No, no names either. The liaison officer called them Bonnie and Clyde; don't ask me how he came up with that one.' Pause. 'That's not the problem.'

'Then what is?'

'He said they were intending to head over the Atlas. You should be prepared for anything.'

27

They had reached the first foothills two hours ago. Now they are climbing so steeply that Aaron can feel pressure in her ears. There is barely any traffic on the wide road they are following. No commuters live this far out, and the settlements between Marrakech and Erfoud are tiny. It must be getting on for four o'clock.

Layla is sitting in the back with Luca. Aaron can feel the woman's fear, but Luca is very calm. He has placed his hand inside his mother's to give her courage.

Pavlik's phone vibrates. He listens wordlessly. Shortly after, he pulls into a parking area. He indicates to Layla to stay in the car and says to Aaron: 'Let's have a smoke.'

The cigarette already tastes of a cold night. Pavlik tells her what Demirci learnt from Palmer.

Olaf Berg alias Veit Jansen is interesting.

The tapped phone calls are bad.

Does the Broker suspect where they are heading? Erfoud is one possibility among many. He has to consider the possibility that they want to cross into Algeria, or that they are avoiding the big roads leading north and taking a detour across the Atlas to reach the Mediterranean. Three other small airfields are also dotted along this route. For the Broker it's a lottery.

Still: Pavlik has chosen Erfoud because it's in the middle of nowhere. Their enemy may be thinking the same. Erfoud is perfect. That's why it's dangerous.

They could go with the liaison officer's suggestion and be smuggled through the Western Sahara to Mauritania. That would cost them at least a day, possibly two. And they don't know whether it would be any safer.

They weigh up their options in silence.

You will see the desert.

But you will be in great danger there.

Aaron directs her eyes where she believes the sun to be. She imagines looking into a valley. Livestock grazing on lush green pastures are herded across a ford in a mountain stream. She pictures the herdsmen standing in the stream, the sparkling glacier water from the Atlas reaching up to their knees. Behind them there might be a village, squat blocks of clay clinging to the rock face, with windows like arrow slits. All of this below a sky that looks as if it is made of wafer-thin glass.

'It's beautiful here,' she says into the stillness.

'Yes, if you turn round. Where you're looking there's a rubbish dump.' Pavlik stamps out his cigarette. 'You've dispatched Vesper, Varga's best man. Without the leader, the chain of command falters. Let's drive on.'

He informs Demirci. She makes no attempt to persuade him otherwise. It is easy to find out that a jet from Germany is intending to land in Erfoud early tomorrow morning, so to disguise their intentions, Guppy is obtaining landing rights for all Moroccan airports plus two Algerian ones, and has booked tickets for the seven o'clock ferry from Tangier to Gibraltar under the name of Traherne.

Pavlik will turn off the main road near a place called Aflou and take a side road heading north-east, which will lead them high up onto a mountain pass and then southward from there. They can afford the extra four hours for the detour; the jet is due to land at eight, there's plenty of time. If they are lucky they will find a hotel somewhere. If not, the BMW will have to do for the night.

Back in the car, Aaron locks herself away in her inner chamber. No bunker in the world has thicker walls.

She thinks about the safe deposit box number again.

Some elements of the rōnin legend are like a mirror. The house of the master of ceremonies was heavily guarded. To avenge the death of their lord, the samurai had to subjugate an almost overpowering household guard.

This and other things suggest that Holm chose the mythical number forty-seven for that reason.

But sometimes so much evidence tallies that one can get completely caught up in it. During her training at the Department Aaron was warned of this kind of intoxication.

Her instructor called it 'evidence binge'.

Look at it from a different angle.

If it was intended as a metaphor, it is somewhat askew.

Her father wasn't her lord. She isn't a rōnin, she wasn't cast out. She doesn't need this revenge to reinstate her honour. Or her father's.

Holm knew that.

The simplest explanation would be that it was just any old deposit box, and she is trying to imbue it with some kind of meaning.

Aaron inserts the earbud of her phone and says: 'Search in Google forty-seven.'

Pavlik will be thinking what's the point, but he doesn't say anything.

A little later she knows that the tropics of Capricorn and Cancer are forty-seven degrees apart, that Rasputin died at the age of forty-seven, and that the year 47 BC brought a whole host of key historical events, including the end of the Alexandrian war, Herod's appointment as governor of Galilee and the introduction of the Julian calendar. Forty-seven is also the name of an agent in a video game, the dialling code for Norway, the average age of German schoolteachers and the atomic mass of a titanium isotope.

The number is everything and nothing.

It's time you got Holm out of your head.

How?

To take revenge, one has to know why.

Of all the things her father gave her, what could Aaron cite as entitlement? What would be worth it? That night when the spiders' webs sparkled in the moonlight and he explained the stars to her, starting with the North Star because it leads the way through the darkness?

As precious as that is, does it justify revenge?

When she was four, he taught her how to do magic. They quickly got past the simple things, like making a coin disappear, guessing cards or pretending to cut a piece of string in two. Jenny learnt to perform 'the invisible hand', 'the secret chamber', 'the horse without a tail'.

As precious as that is, does it justify revenge?

His stories always contained a flaw in the logic, which she then had to find. That a tear cannot run into a nose, a bumblebee can't swim, a stone can't hover in mid-air. And each had a moral. Many of them were consoling. They told her that it isn't bad to cry, that physics can't explain miracles and that one should dare to attempt the impossible. Others were bitter and cruel, yet true nevertheless. The most important lesson was that she should only rely on someone whom she would trust with her own life.

As precious as that is, does it justify revenge?

Aaron remembers how they looked at search-and-find picture books. Her father would give her a minute to memorize the details before he closed the book and asked her to list everything. If she hadn't made more than three mistakes she was allowed to choose a reward. Her absolute favourite was the pillow fight.

Once he showed her pictures of a department store. He asked her to tell him what would be the best way to break in. All her plans were doomed to fail, as there was always something she had overlooked. The watchman with the twirly moustache, the large, well-fed dog, the twinkle of the camera, the lock with seven seals. In the end she still managed it, and her father didn't raise any more objections. He asked her what she would steal, and she said: 'A princess dress.' He threw her up in the air and caught her, and it was as if she were five years old again.

As precious as that is, does it justify revenge?

One summery Sunday they sat by the quarry pond, letting their thoughts bounce free. Crane flies were weaving black lace over the water and the air fizzed like sherbet powder.

Her father took a small phial out of his pocket and drizzled a liquid onto her shoulder. 'Look what's going to happen now.' Soon a swarm of dragonflies surrounded her and each one of them tried to get a place by the nectar. Jenny was so awestruck in the midst of this shimmering rainbow that she held her breath. Today she knows that the pheromone he used is fired at sniper positions in order to mark them and irritate the enemy gunmen as they take aim at their target.

On that day by the quarry pond this was far, far away, and all that existed was the magic of a perfect moment.

As precious as that is, does it justify revenge?

The following summer they went to a disused industrial site by the Rhine. Her father took her into an empty factory building. Inside it, there were no machines, no stones, no hole in the floor, nothing one could have used to hide behind. He told her to close her eyes, count to ten and then look for him. After twenty minutes she gave up and called out for him, full of fear that he had left her there alone.

That was her first experience of adrenalin; she was six years old.

Her father stepped out of the shadow of a soot-stained window and brushed off the chalk he had coated himself in. 'A little while ago, you were standing right in front of me. You didn't see me because you relied only on your eyes. Close them. What do you notice?' She puzzled over what it might be, until she became aware of her father's body heat. 'And now?' he asked. She didn't hear anything, but she felt a change in the air; her father had moved. He said: 'Sometimes you have to close your eyes in order to see.'

As precious as that is, does it justify revenge?

He showed her how to mend a bicycle. She had to teach herself how to ride it. He showed her how to find her way in a forest. She had to figure out herself how to get out. He showed her how to creep up on a fawn so that it wouldn't pick up her scent. She learnt by herself how to run away from a stag. All these things she made her own before she was seven.

As precious as that is, does it justify revenge?

The trip to the quarry when she was twelve marked the start of a new period. It was no longer a game. 'It's not the gun that kills,' her father said before he handed her his Beretta.

Aaron remembers how proud she was when she had placed a series of ten shots into the inner ring of the target for the first time. The last shot wasn't completely in the centre, it scratched the circle.

So what?

Her father looked at her sternly and said: 'With the tenth guy you only shot off his earlobe, and now you're dead.'

The tricks he showed her over the following years had different names to the magic tricks of the past. They were called

'The five-legged spider', 'The cold kiss' or 'The burning man'. She learnt to replace physical strength with leverage, to become as good with the right as she was with the left, to move silently like a blade of grass in the wind, to recognize the strongest among several opponents with a single glance. This and this and this later saved her life and that of others.

As precious as that is, does it justify revenge?

She and her father never even once spoke about her becoming a policewoman. That would have been like saying there's a thunderstorm while watching the lightning.

At home, she saw the look in her mother's eyes. Jenny would snuggle up to her and have a cuddle to stop her feeling sad. But in her mind she was still in the quarry.

Only Pavlik, Sandra and Lissek know all of this. None of them has ever expressed any opinion on it. She can imagine what they think. That she never had a childhood or youth, was never carefree, never knew the bliss of not having to meet an expectation. That isn't true. She can recall so many things that had nothing to do with weapons or training.

Aaron remembers the sorrow she had felt at fifteen. She was a head taller than her classmates, a spindly beanpole with breasts the size of mouse fists. She wept into her pillow for hours and it didn't help much when her mum said that everything would even itself out eventually.

But when her father took her into his arms and muttered 'Every butterfly was once a caterpillar,' it was OK again.

The first boys who came to knock on her door were scared of him. He would study them silently from top to bottom, and there was only one he let pass. That was Tim, and he was the right one.

As precious as that is, does it justify revenge?

Her father wasn't perfect, she knows that. Aaron is no longer the little girl who idolized him in La Mamounia twenty-eight years ago. He failed as a husband, he barely had any time for his few friends, and even for Aaron he wasn't always there when she needed him. He didn't give her the choice to do something different with her life. She might have become a linguist, a psychiatrist or opened a gallery. She wouldn't have any scars, wouldn't be blind and lonely. To ponder this is as pointless as writing her name in water. She is who she is.

It's down to her father, and she owes him more than she could have ever repaid him.

Pavlik stops. 'Petrol station.'

'I'd like to smoke a cigarette,' says Layla.

Aaron takes a new pack of Marlboro out of the glove compartment and hands it to her. 'Luca and I will wait in the car. I'm sure we've got plenty to chat about.'

This is unprofessional, she should be making use of every opportunity to strengthen the rapport. But she wants to be alone with Luca.

Pavlik and Layla get out.

'So, how old are you?' Aaron asks.

'Nearly six and a quarter.'

'Ah, you're almost grown up then.'

'No, not yet for a long time. My papa said: "If you want to become a proper man, you first have to be a proper little boy."'

'He must have been very clever.'

'Yes. And ticklish. On his tummy.'

They are silent for a moment.

'Are we going to be in Germany soon?' Luca asks.

'Tomorrow. We have to go in an aeroplane. Have you been there before?'

'Yes. At my grandma's funeral. I was just little, but I know that it was cold.'

'It's nice there, you'll like it.'

He doesn't reply to this. She senses that he wants to be left in peace, so they are silent. The others return. When Pavlik opens the car door, moisture wafts in. Ozone. It will rain soon, Aaron can smell it in the air.

They continue their journey. She hears Layla pushing tablets out of a blister pack and washing them down with water. It must be Palladone, the Valium tablets are in a small tube. She doesn't think that Layla is addicted. She is receiving medical treatment, and Pavlik mentioned that she had lost weight. Two Palladone. How serious is the illness? How could Aaron use it for the interrogation? She immediately feels ashamed. Compassion is one of the seven virtues, and she is behaving like a rōnin.

Shortly after the petrol station they turn off the main road. Loose gravel drums against the car's underbody. They wind their way up into the mountains, driving into the rain. At first it's just splatters, then large drops fall fast and hard onto the windscreen.

Aaron sinks into the rhythm of tight bends and steep inclines, and plans Layla's interrogation. Some things will be easier than in the Jardin Menara. She is already familiar with the other woman's breathing rhythm, her favourite filler word, her speaking tempo, her vocal tones.

And she already knows which of the four basic types Layla is. In visual people, perception is dominated by the eyes. This is reflected in the language they use.

Typical words are: hazy, clear, imagination, insight, form.

They love phrases such as: Shed light onto the matter. Establish clarity. You have to see it to believe it. I'm of exactly the same view.

Auditory types, on the other hand, primarily perceive the world via sounds. Ask, tell, true, loud, silent, ring a bell, harmoniously, have a row.

They tend to say things like: We're on the same wavelength. Listen to me. Screaming out for attention.

For kinaesthetic people, taste, touch and smell are enormously important. They often use words such as: hard, warm, cold, heavy, bitter, light, smooth.

Typical figures of speech might be: I can't grasp that. It's dragging me down. Firm ground under my feet.

Aaron is such a person. She always has been. Being blind, this helps her.

Lastly there are the neutral types. Their language sounds academic and is the hardest to interpret, because much of what they say remains abstract. Intend, decide, know, assess, change. They are a nightmare for the interrogator.

Luckily Layla is an auditory type.

I never heard anything about them. We led a quiet life. Who told you that? You think you can comment on my marriage. The word of a stranger.

Auditory types are usually slower and talk with deliberation, contrary to the kinaesthetic and visual types, which tend to be fast in everything. Layla is different, but exceptions prove the rule. Gesticulation often occurs at diaphragm level. Crossing the arms in front of the chest fits this pattern precisely. Because their hearing is so dominant, auditory types are easily irritated by sounds. If they are interrupted, they quickly lose the thread.

Language is the most important aspect.

Aaron will aim to use words that are geared towards Layla's primary sense, thereby strengthening her feeling of being understood.

She had already started doing it at the park.

There's no point in arguing about it. I can understand that you haven't changed anything. We just want to consult you on a few details. Doesn't that sound good? It's like a silent scream.

At the petrol station she'd continued where she had left off.

I'm sure Luca and I have got plenty to chat about.

All of a sudden, a strong beam of light cuts through the darkness like a blowtorch.

'He's not dipping his main beam,' Pavlik mutters.

Aaron already has the Glock in her hand.

'Duck down!' she hisses to the rear.

Pavlik slows down. Aaron knows that he has drawn his gun too. She opens her window and hears, just centimetres away, a steep rock face. The blowtorch keeps cutting new, sparkling islands into the blackness, until suddenly everything is light. The other car speeds past them, a booming echo in the rain, then it is dark again.

What remains is Aaron's hammering heart.

What remains is cold sweat.

What remains is the moment when the light reappeared.

28

The village only consists of a few houses. They belong to Berbers who make a living from trekking tourism, but there is also a hotel. Aaron has a queasy feeling in her stomach as she gets out of the car. It reminds her that she hasn't eaten anything since the flatbread this morning. For a samurai it is shameful to feel hunger. She doesn't obey every one of the principles.

The innkeeper comes running out, calls for his wife and his daughters and shoos them to the stove. Full of joy over the unexpected income he dishes up couscous with a happy Arabic singsong. Aaron doesn't like mutton, but she takes a large helping nevertheless. She is so happy that she can see the light of the lamp that is swaying gently in the draught of the ceiling fan. When the others order a dessert to please Luca, she stands up to memorize the steps.

The hotel only has one dormitory, which is crammed full with plank beds; they are the only guests. If Aaron stretches out her left arm while lying down she touches Luca's bed. She walks over to the window, four steps, and opens it. A rain shower washes the tiredness from her face.

She clicks her tongue. In the rain all sounds are muffled, it's as if the world was made of wax. But afterwards, when the air has been cleansed, the tiniest sounds carry across great distances.

It's only a few metres down to the ground. Going by the woolly echo there isn't anything else down there; perhaps a barren plain.

Aaron closes the window and feels her way to the door with her cane. The hallway smells of cold mutton fat. Eleven steps to the staircase. She puts her hand on the banister with its peeling paintwork. The stone steps are so roughly hewn that she can feel the striations through the soles of her ballerina shoes. She can hear women's laughter and the clattering of plates coming from downstairs. A stern male voice brays from a radio, perhaps it's the king. On the left is the small dining room where the others are sitting.

And back, the same again.

On the third run through, she no longer needs the cane and can move around the house at great speed. She goes outside and smokes a cigarette under the porch roof. Her heart is beating fast in the thin air.

Aaron knows that Fricke will be among the team tomorrow. He is too good for Demirci not to include him.

She calls him up, hears loud music, a babble of voices.

'Hi.'

'Just a sec.' Fricke goes somewhere quieter.

Is he in a pub? No, not before a mission, not even Fricke is that crazy.

'Where are you?' she asks.

'Pub.'

For a moment Aaron is lost for words.

'It's Delmonte's birthday. I've been guzzling non-alcoholic beer for two hours. At eleven I'll make my exit.'

'Who else is on the team tomorrow?'

'Kemper, Rogge, Nickel and Flemming.'

'Flemming,' she instinctively repeats.

'Don't worry. He's an arsehole, but his hundred and thirty kilos, spread across two and a bit metres, can be very useful. No matter what you women say when there's a man around: sometimes size does matter.'

'I've got a favour to ask: I need a medicine, Endothelinac. The stuff is only available on prescription, but I'm sure you can find a way round it.'

'How do you spell that?'

She spells it out for him.

'What's it for?'

'It helps against stupid questions.'

'OK.'

'This is just between us.'

'Of course. How are you?'

'Like a moth in an empty wardrobe.'

'And the old man?'

'Looks like seventy.'

'How can you know that?'

'Imagination is the keen eye of the blind.' She ends the call.

The rain is hissing on the road like fat in a pan. Her jacket isn't keeping her warm, the leather is creaking in the cold. Pavlik comes out; she recognizes him by the nature of the silence.

'How high up are we?' she asks.

'Almost fifteen hundred metres. It's two hours to Erfoud.' He helps himself to one of her cigarettes.

Aaron gives him a light and bends over the Dupont lighter.

She pauses, keeps it burning.

'Is something the matter?' Pavlik asks.

'I can see the flame,' she whispers. 'Well, not exactly see it. But it's there. It's flickering red. And a little bit blue. Now the wind has blown it out.'

He lays his arm around her. Ten seconds of intimacy.

She snaps the lighter closed. 'Where's Layla?'

'Putting the boy to bed.'

'Has she taken any more tablets?'

'One Palladone.'

'How is she looking?'

'As if she'd grown up in a china shop. If she had five kilos more on her ribs she'd be thin. She barely ate or drank anything. I don't know what's wrong with her, but she needs to go to a hospital.'

'In Germany.'

'If we make it.'

She shrugs her shoulders. 'Everything's gone fine so far.'

'Said Danton on the steps to the scaffold.'

Pavlik is right. Of all the exit points Erfoud is the most likely option, and the Broker's men will have put it right at the top of the list.

'What's the bullet wound doing?' she asks.

'Keeping me awake.'

'Minx.'

Pavlik flicks away his cigarette. 'Why did you google the number forty-seven?'

She could say: no particular reason. That would be ludicrous.

'The number of the bank deposit box. I think Holm was trying to tell me something.'

'Haven't we been there already?'

'Have you heard of the forty-seven rōnin?'

'You mean the film?'

'It's based on a true event.' Aaron tells him the story while she smokes another cigarette. Then they listen to the rain.

'Almost everything Holm has said could contain a message,' he argues. 'Alexander the Great, Château Lafite, Judith Traherne, the paintings of that French guy, Bach, the Beverly Wilshire, the Russian village—'

'Lubichowo,' she says.

'It won't get you anywhere. It'll just drive you round the bend.'

'Georges Noël.'

'Who?'

'The painter. I once saw an exhibition of his at the National Gallery. I doubt that Holm liked his work; they're abstract paintings, but Holm was a mystic and a poet. I'd say he liked Dalí, De Chirico, Kubin, Velázquez, Munch, and of course Chagall.'

'You know far more about Holm than I do,' Pavlik says. 'For me, the most important thing is this: I know that he was sick in his head and that he enjoyed destroying people. I won't allow him to do that to you all over again.'

'You're mistaken about him. For everything he did, even the most terrible things, there was a reason.'

'You sound like Pol Pot's defence lawyer.'

'I'm trying to think like him.'

'He led us to Olaf Berg. That was a message. If there had been anything else, he would have wrapped it in a clear sentence.'

'From the very first moment, Holm wanted to compete with me and I with him,' Aaron replies. 'Even if you'll never understand it: we were alike, we recognized each other. He's challenging my intelligence, anything else would have been too banal for him. It's a brain-teaser. You know what he said: "I could give you the key to the enigma."'

Pavlik is silent for a while. 'I've got no idea about the painter, I know too little about art to gauge that. Let's stay with the number. If your theory is correct, he'll have specifically asked for deposit box number forty-seven. Right?'

'Yes.'

He taps a number into the mobile. 'Good evening, Monsieur Hamdaoui, Jack Traherne here. Forgive me for troubling you so late in the evening, but I have a question. Did Mr Woyzeck express any particular wishes concerning the safe deposit box?'

For a long time, Aaron only hears the rain. She knows that Pavlik is keeping an eye on his watch; after a minute their location could be traced.

'Thank you,' he eventually mutters. 'Good night.'

'And?' she asks apprehensively.

'Holm wanted to have that specific deposit box,' Pavlik concedes. 'He instructed Hamdaoui to keep it to himself, unless you specifically asked him about it.'

He takes the SIM card out of the mobile, snaps it in half, throws it away and inserts a new one. The wind is chasing the rain under the roof. Somewhere a dog yowls, a window shutter is closed, a door shakes on its hinges.

'It's not about the rōnin,' she says. 'That would have just been a gimmick. Holm plotted it all. There's more to it. The Broker's hiding place. Why he had my father killed. The target of the terrorist attack. Something on that scale.'

Pavlik ponders awhile. 'The forty-seven is probably only part of the puzzle. There's something missing. From scratch: Alexander the Great, Georges Noël, Château Lafite, Browning, Judith Traherne, Bach, Beverly Wilshire, Lubichowo.'

'Don't forget the Walkman,' she adds.

'He explained that: sentimental reasons.'

'An alien concept to him.'

'The Beverly Wilshire. Varga's abode? Room number forty-seven?' he muses.

'Too simple. And the Broker isn't stupid enough to show himself on a stage like that.'

'Judith Traherne – wasn't Judith a biblical figure?'

'I'm not very well versed in the Bible,' she replies.

Pavlik looks it up on Wikipedia. 'She decapitated the Assyrian commander Holofernes and stole his head.'

'That would be irony at best. Like choosing Woyzeck.'

'Didn't the samurai have a thing about heads too?'

'They kept them as trophies and treated them with great

respect, they even styled the hair and applied make-up to them,'
says Aaron. 'Before a battle they would perfume their own
heads, so that the victor could delight in the fragrance.'

'How dashing of them.'

'But that isn't it.'

'What about Noël?' Pavlik asks. 'The French term for
Christmas.'

'Christmas 1947. A date of birth? Someone who is sixty-
eight now?'

'No. Too far-fetched.'

'Holm used a quote,' says Aaron. '"Patience is a revolutionary
virtue." I've heard that somewhere before.'

'Rosa Luxemburg. Every sniper knows that saying.'

'It's odd that he referred to her. He despised zealots.'

'Luxembourg. The target of the attack? Perhaps a bank?'

'Or it's a reference to Rosa – pink. Pink triangle? That's how
they identified homosexuals in the concentration camps.'

'Varga isn't gay.'

'You're right. If there's any significance in it, then
Luxembourg.'

Layla joins them. 'Luca has asked for you.'

Aaron walks to the bed without needing to feel her way and sits
down on the edge. In the twilight everything looks black to her.
'Can't you sleep, young man?'

'How do you do that?'

'What?'

'Make it look as if you can see.'

'I cheat. Don't you cheat sometimes?'

'When we're playing cards. Mama always sees it, but she still
lets me win. And in the car you took out your gun. But you're
blind.'

'My father said: '"It's not seeing, it's knowing that matters."'

'What's it like to be blind?'

Aaron searches for words. 'It's like standing in a harbour and waiting for a ship that never comes.'

She senses that he is pondering something.

'Do you want to touch my face?' he finally asks.

'Why?'

'Because that's what blind people do. I saw it in a film.'

She smiles. 'I don't need to do that. I know exactly what you look like.'

'What do I look like then?'

'Like a smarty-pants.'

But Aaron stretches out her hand nevertheless. She has never done this with anyone. Yet it's so nice. She barely touches him, as if fearful her hands are too rough.

'You have to use two hands. Otherwise you don't see anything.'

Aaron does as she is told. She enjoys it, then a sadness grows. She gives him a nudge. 'You have even more freckles than I do.'

'What's your real name?'

'Jenny.'

'I wasn't scared when you took out your gun.'

'One can be brave and still be scared.'

He thinks about this. 'Really?'

'Yes.'

'My papa once said that the thing we are the most frightened of is fear. But I don't understand that.'

'You must miss him a lot.'

'And you miss yours.'

He says that so calmly, so matter-of-factly, that she forgets to breathe. She flinches when Luca puts his hand in hers.

'Do you think that he's in heaven?' he asks.

'If there is a heaven, he was there,' she whispers. 'And then he was reborn. Perhaps as a person. Or an animal. Sometimes I think: a lion.'

'Can you tell me a story?'

She doesn't answer, she just feels his hand.

'Don't you know any?'

Aaron clears her throat. 'There once was a small tear. It belonged to a boy who was the same age as—'

'Not that kind of story,' he says. 'Tell me one that's true. One about you and your papa.'

There are so many she could tell.

Tender ones, funny ones, dangerous ones, sad ones.

But none are like this one.

When she was in Barcelona, when she recognized his voice and screamed, it wasn't an end and it wasn't a beginning. In that second she knew what had happened. And in the very next she denied it again.

'At first I didn't want to believe that I'm blind,' she says quietly. 'When I was in the hospital I acted as though I could see. I ate with my fingers so that I wouldn't make a fool of myself with the cutlery. I only got out of bed if I could hold on to my papa's arm. I claimed that I couldn't manage on my own because I was having dizzy spells. When the doctors wanted to talk to me, I made out that I didn't understand what they were saying.'

'What does "made out" mean?' Luca mumbles sleepily.

'It's sort of like pretending. One of the doctors was very clever. He brought me a German newspaper and said he thought I'd be pleased to have it. I told him that I was too tired to read and that he should take it away again. One morning I even asked my papa to close the curtains in the room, I said the sun was hurting my eyes. He didn't close the curtains, instead he got me dressed and climbed into a taxi with me.'

She thinks of the journey and how she kept her eyes closed throughout. The world had crackled like the distorted and infinitely distant signals of a short-wave radio station.

'Where did he take you?'

Aaron fights back the tears. 'Is there something that you're so good at that you think nobody else could do it better?'

'Climbing a tree,' he mutters, already drifting off.

'With me it was shooting. My papa took me to a shooting range. When we got there, he gave me a gun. I said that I didn't feel well. I said that I needed to lie down. I begged him to take me back to the hospital. But he didn't give in and said that he would take me there every day, until I would finally do it – I—'

Her voice fails.

There's no sound. Just Luca's tranquil breathing. Aaron takes his hand out of hers and kisses him on the forehead. She walks to the door as quietly as a mouse.

Then she hears him once more, softly, as if he was talking in his sleep. 'I dreamt about you.'

Aaron feels as though she's walked into a wall. 'What happened in your dream?'

'There was lots of fire and smoke and a big animal that wanted to eat us up. But you weren't scared and I wasn't either.'

Her heart stops beating, the world is banging against her ribcage.

At some point she closes the door. Aaron sits down on the hallway floor. She thinks back to that time in Barcelona, when her father placed the Browning in her hand. The grip felt as cold as if the gun had been lying in the snow all night long. Aaron held it like a thousand times before.

And yet like never before.

The cold crept up her arm and froze everything inside her. She didn't feel it when her finger pulled the trigger. When the shot rang out, she started. She heard the echo and was shaking so much that she dropped the gun.

Her father led her to the target. Fifty metres, it felt like a dream. A dream in which she was walking through bursting mirrors. He took her hand and laid it onto the paper.

Aaron searched for the bullet hole.

There was none.

In that moment she realized for ever that reality can't be invented. She sank to her knees and implored her father to let her die.

He said: 'I can't do that. Because I love you. If you take away love, our earth is a tomb.'

As precious as everything else is, this alone is the reason why she will kill the Broker.

29

The innkeeper pours the tea. Aaron can tell from the gurgling that he is lifting the pot as high as his head, lowering it and lifting it back up again several times; a ceremony that requires a lot of practice before it can be mastered.

The man warbles something in Arabic.

'He's asking when we want to have breakfast,' Layla translates.

'We're heading off at five. Tell him that it's enough to just put some tea and pastries on the table for us.'

Layla passes it on. He replies with a torrent of words and then leaves the two women alone in the dining room.

'He doesn't mind, he'll wake us at half-past four. May I?'

'Of course.'

Layla reaches for the cigarettes and lights one up.

They both smoke.

The rapport begins.

Pavlik whispers into Aaron's earbud: 'She's twisting her wedding ring and looking you in the eyes. She probably still can't quite believe that you're blind.'

Aaron can hear the rain pelting down on his jacket.

The courtyard is the only place from which he can observe them without Layla noticing. The next hour is going to be very uncomfortable for him, but as a marksman he's used to that.

She wishes he had been a little more precise. To mirror someone you have to invert everything. On which hand is Layla wearing the ring? She grew up in Germany. Most continental Europeans wear theirs on the right.

Aaron brushes across the back of her right hand, that is enough.

Layla's breathing is a little faster than normal, but within the tolerance range for nervousness. Aaron imitates it and pretends to return Layla's gaze. 'You have an extraordinary son. I'm sure you already know that.'

'Yes.' Hesitantly she adds: 'He likes you.'

'Perhaps because I'm blind. It makes children inquisitive.'

'No, it's not because of that. Or at least not only because of that.' Layla's voice is uniform. She keeps to one single note, as if she were striking the same piano key over and over.

'Was he planned?'

'She's squeezing her shoulders together,' Pavlik reports.

Aaron lets a few seconds pass before she stretches the back of her neck, as if she had some tension there.

'Surely you already know that,' says Layla. 'From the letters.'

'I'm sorry if I've hurt your feelings. We just needed some information. It's our work. That might sound trite. I really do mean it. The letters are in the car. They're yours, I won't tell my superiors about them. They mean a lot to you, I respect that.'

'You cunning beast,' mutters Pavlik. 'And what will you do if she wants to see the letters? Drive to the villa and get them?'

Oh Amari, it's so much easier to believe me than to torment yourself, wondering whether you can trust me.

Layla says nothing for a long time. To Aaron, her face is a blurred patch, as grey as shale.

'We first met in Paris,' she finally says.

Her voice stumbles into the memory. Aaron has difficulty imitating Layla's shallow breath.

'I was visiting a friend. When he took my suitcase off the conveyor belt in Orly I barked at him. Veit just laughed and said: "We'll share the suitcase, agreed?" He was so outrageously charming. For a split second I imagined what my life would be like if I was with him. My heart was thumping with fear. I was married, after all.'

'And unhappy.'

'She's putting her hands around the tea glass. She feels cold.'

Aaron takes a sip of her tea, runs her fingers over the edge of her glass.

'Is your father still alive?' Layla asks.

Yours must be dead, he isn't mentioned at all in the letters. Luca said that he was at his grandma's funeral. So you no longer have any parents, Amari.

'He died years ago, shortly after my mother,' Aaron replies.

'My father was from Tunisia. Germany remained alien to him right until the end, much of it seemed godless to him. He didn't even learn the language properly. I have two brothers, they're exactly like him. I was just a girl. Still, I did my best to be a good daughter.'

Aaron sinks a little lower on her chair in order to be at the same eye level with her opposite. She magics some of Layla's sadness into her voice. 'My father left my mother when I was little. Every now and then he would ring me up, most of the time he was drunk.' She almost lets slip a BUT. 'And even as a young woman I constantly asked myself whether he would approve of this or that. It's like an ear worm that you can never get rid of.'

And what if Luca tells her about Barcelona? Then she will know that I lied. No, he won't do that. It's our secret.

'Hello?' Pavlik pipes up. 'Did she just smile?'

'My father owned a grocery store,' says Layla. 'We were doing OK. On my twentieth birthday he introduced me to a man who owned several Arab restaurants. He gave me an expensive gift, but his words were cold. I cried a lot, then I married him. My father was very proud.'

'Surely you had other plans for your life, dreamt of doing something. Wouldn't that have been possible?'

'You mean: go against my father's wishes?'

'Yes.'

'There's an Arab proverb: "If you speak, your speech must be better than your silence would have been." I would have liked to study architecture. That wasn't possible. As far as my father was concerned, post-sixteen education was unnecessary.'

What fits with that?

Design? No, too close.

'I wanted to do something with horticulture,' Aaron says. 'It's still my passion. Every park calls to me.'

'Surely you were free to choose.'

'I had to earn money, I couldn't afford to go and study. A schoolfriend of mine joined the police. He said to me: why don't you come too? It sounded quite good.'

Careful. She never had any money trouble.

'When my training was finished, I inherited,' she adds. 'From an uncle I had barely known. After that I could have done all kinds of things. Only I'm not the type that constantly wants to change everything.'

Neither are you, Amari.

'Yes, I can understand that.'

'It must be difficult to share your life with a man you don't love.'

'I know it sounds like a violation, but I didn't see it like that. He was away a lot and rarely slept with me. And if he did, it went by like a visit to the dentist.'

Time for some unpleasant truths.

'He hit you. It's mentioned in one of the letters.'

'For years, he barely looked at me. But when I told him about Veit, he reached for the belt. I didn't—'

Aaron realizes that Layla is biting her lip. 'You didn't tell Veit that detail,' she finishes the other woman's thought. 'Because you were afraid of what he would do.'

Layla lights up another cigarette. The thought of smoking another one so soon repulses Aaron, but she follows suit.

'I know what you're getting at,' Layla says stiffly.

'There was no sign of your husband after he disappeared, not a single peep. His restaurants, the beautiful house on Mexikoplatz, do you really think that he gave it all up to start from scratch somewhere else? Especially after you confessed to him about Veit? Surely you didn't believe that?'

'She's counting her fingers,' Pavlik mutters.

Aaron gingerly starts to breathe in the tensed-up manner of her companion. She waits, she doesn't press her.

'Some of my husband's regulars were men from a Lebanese clan,' Layla claims. 'In the back room, things were talked about that I didn't want to know anything of. Those men were quite capable of doing that kind of thing.'

'Oh come on. You told Veit outright about your suspicions. The two of you had an argument about it. He wrote: "There are questions one simply doesn't ask."'

Suddenly Layla shouts at her. 'He was a good husband and a good father! He protected us, always! You just want to persuade me that he was a criminal!'

The rapport demands that Aaron shouts back in a high voice. 'I don't hold it against you that you defend him, just don't take me for a fool!'

'She's shaking,' Pavlik informs her. 'She looks like she wants to jump up and run off. Do something.'

Aaron gradually works towards the rhythm that she has memorized as Layla's relaxed breathing pattern. During a long silence, her companion's tension gradually dissipates, her pulses falls in line with Aaron's.

We can tell each other everything, Amari, even if it hurts.

She smiles. 'Finally you've come out of your shell, Layla. You don't mind if I call you Layla, do you?'

'What kind of business is Veit supposed to have been involved in?'

Aaron can tell by the sound that her opposite is looking at her again.

'I'm interested in what he told you about it.'

'Only that it was about import and export.'

'Which sector?'

'Construction machinery.'

'Was there a headquarters? An office? Employees? Were there Christmas holidays, dismissals, calls from secretaries, tax returns? Did he ever bring anything home from work? No? Isn't that odd?'

'But that was exactly how it was,' Layla burst out helplessly. 'I don't know anything about the people my husband was involved with.'

Aaron registers that Layla is using the precise same wording as she did in the Jardin Menara. A clear indication that she is lying.

'Why should someone who has led a blameless life deposit false passports for his wife and his child? Why did he have a jamming transmitter installed at your home? Why did he have overseas accounts? Why are there—'

She breaks off.

She hears it.

Pavlik hisses: 'A car has pulled up out front.'

'Please stand up,' Aaron says calmly.

'What's the matter?'

'Come over this way. Quietly. Switch the light out.'

Silently, she positions herself beside the door. She hears the light switch being pressed. Layla scurries next to her. Aaron draws the Glock and pushes the other woman against the wall with her right arm.

Steps. Two male voices. Arabic.

She knows that Pavlik is already in the house. He could be standing just a metre away from the men and they wouldn't notice him. If he wants, they'd be dead before they got through this door.

But they will need to report to their commando leader at regular intervals, otherwise the next lot will soon be here. It's the same as in the Palmeraie. They need one of them alive. The one who sends the messages, the leader. As a rule, that's the man who walks in second. If necessary, he can use the first man as a shield, and increase his fire power with the other's weapon. Pavlik will only concern himself with the leader, she will take care of the other one.

No matter how good the man is, in the dark she is a nightmare, an invisible slayer. She swiftly runs through the moves in her mind's eye. First she will flatten the bridge of his nose and his cheekbone with her elbow, then perform a quick roll and aim at the biggest target area: stomach and chest. Three shots. The semi-jacket projectiles will expand inside the body, tear apart the tissue and eat their way into the soft parts like starved rats. Even if Aaron doesn't hit any vital organs, he will die of the shock.

Just then she hears laughter. It's the innkeeper. Words fly to and fro.

'Invitation to a birthday party,' Layla whispers.

Aaron puts a finger to her lips.

The chatting carries on a little while longer, then the visitors take their leave. It's only when the car drives off that the copper taste disappears from Aaron's mouth.

She puts away the gun. 'You did well.'

Layla switches the light back on. When they've sat down, Aaron holds out the packet of cigarettes to her. Now she needs one too. She helps her companion calm down by using her breath, assuming an open, relaxed posture, giving her a smile.

It's a good opportunity to insert an anchor. She reaches for Layla's hand and squeezes it. At the same time she hums a little melody to herself, *Somewhere over the rainbow, way up high.* If she repeats this later, Layla will associate it with a feeling of safety and the knowledge that Aaron will protect her and Luca.

Layla's hand is shaking in hers. The body needs longer than the mind to come back to normal.

'Are you OK now?' Aaron asks.

'She's nodding,' Pavlik mutters.

'I'm blind. You have to talk to me.'

'I'm sorry. Yes, thank you.'

Aaron takes her hand away. 'Layla, do you think that all of this is happening because you led a quiet life and your husband traded with construction machinery? Just because his wallet was stolen in the souks?'

Silence.

'Veit Jansen wasn't his real name, by the way,' she casually mentions. 'His real name was Olaf Berg.'

'She's staring at you,' Pavlik says. 'She didn't know.'

This will make it easier for you. From now on we're no longer talking about the man who made you laugh, cared for you when you were ill, held your hand during Luca's birth, wrote old-fashioned letters and called you Amari. Now we're talking about a man to whom you owe absolutely nothing. You never knew this man.

'That's not true,' Layla whispers.

'Would I invent a thing like that? Haven't I been open and honest with you so far?'

Aaron breathes as fast as Layla. She suspects that her mouth is dry and moistens her own lips. Aaron steadfastly directs her gaze at the other woman's eyes. She plants a sympathetic expression on her face. 'I know that this is a shock for you. It's often easier to tell the truth than to hear the truth.'

'She's returning your gaze,' Pavlik tells her. 'I think she's ready.'

'Layla, we're only interested in *one* man. He's in his mid-sixties now. He's not tall, but he's large. He has thick hair, which he may have dyed. On his forehead there are two vertical furrows that look as though they'd been carved in. Everything about him appears coarse, even his face and hands. In actual fact he is well educated and knows lots about painting and art. It's possible that he's had cosmetic surgery to change his appearance. Perhaps he's shaved his head or grown a beard. But one thing always stays the same: the voice. He talks loudly, speaks fluent American English with an Italian accent, and when he laughs it sounds like a thunderstorm.' Aaron briefly pauses. 'You know this man. He came to visit you and Olaf Berg in Boca Raton in October 2007.'

It's no effort for her to breathe as nervously as her opposite.

She had expected Layla to concoct a story, to stall for time, but the reply comes without hesitation. 'I didn't fly out with him. I developed severe back pain shortly beforehand. I could hardly move. I should have gone to the doctor, but – I didn't think it was anything serious. Veit didn't want to leave me on my own. But the man he was going to meet was very important to him. I told him that I would manage. I didn't know that it was the first symptoms of kidney cancer. For weeks I struggled on, until I went to the hospital.'

Layla hasn't repeated herself a single time. She didn't extend the vowels, she spoke fluidly, in short sentences.

It's the opposite of a liar, who builds endless cascades of words, for fear that he might be interrupted.

She is telling the truth.

'There will have been other occasions. Berg worked for him for many years. He probably spent more time with him than with you.'

'I swear to you, I never met him.'

Her voice catches on the end of the sentence.

What is it you want to tell me? Were you about to let something slip?

Aaron senses that Layla is wavering.

'Veit was very self-assured,' she finally says. 'But he never boasted with it. I liked that. He never looked up to anyone, except this man. When he was on the phone to him, he was almost submissive. That puzzled me.'

Aaron waits patiently.

'In the hospital, he sat at my bedside day and night.' The words begin to crumble. 'It gave me strength. I miss him so much.'

Everything disintegrates into sobs.

Aaron feels for Layla's hand, gently squeezes it and, barely audible, she hums *Somewhere*.

Layla whispers: 'The cancer is back. It's the other kidney. I don't know if I – what will happen to Luca, if I—'

'We'll get you to Germany and you'll have the best doctors, I promise,' Aaron says.

Somewhere...

'When I was in hospital – once, when he thought I was sleeping, he spoke to the man on the phone.'

'What about?'

'They talked about someone. He had a strange name which I've always remembered.'

'What name was it?'

'Bas Makata.'

Aaron freezes.

Pavlik gives a quiet groan.

'They wanted to meet with him. In Avignon.'

Berlin

Over eight years ago

Large seat in the Astor Lounge, first row centre, popcorn, Coke, nachos with salsa, watching *Blood Diamond* and drooling over DiCaprio: a perfect Saturday evening in October.

Aaron is seeing the film for the third time. Once again she is waiting for the moment in which DiCaprio, mortally wounded, rings the love of his life and mutters: 'I have a small problem.'

Not today. When they're on call and their phone vibrates, midwives have to go to the delivery room, firemen have to slide down a pole, plumbers have to head to the burst water mains, and Aaron has to abandon her popcorn because there are two corpses in a bar by the East Side Gallery.

Everything within a radius of a hundred metres has been cordoned off. The police have barricaded themselves behind two dozen patrol cars and unmarked vehicles. Fricke is on site with four men from the department. He briefs Aaron:

The BKA was pursuing a Frenchman who is pumping heroin from Marseilles to Germany. It is mixed with fentanyl, an analgesic which, even on its own, is potent enough to blow away a person's brains. In combination with H it's a free flight to Saturn.

The BKA tapped the Frenchman's calls and learnt that he was going to come to Berlin. He intended to relax in a Kempinski suite with a few luxury whores and meet a Bulgarian who was pitching for the distribution. A mobile BKA operations unit was tailing the Frenchman.

When he went into the bar, he only had two guys with him. The operations unit thought seizing him would be a breeze. If they'd been better prepared, they would have known that the Bulgarian had come with five people. Inside, his men immediately opened fire.

Two BKA officers are dead, the rest have pulled back onto the street. The Department has been asked to sort it out.

It takes them seven minutes. Three Bulgarians leave the bar in body bags. The Frenchman is hospitalized overnight at the Charité under strict security measures, where he is diagnosed with cerebral concussion. Anything else would have been a medical miracle, given that Krupp had planted a heavy ashtray between his eyes.

Aaron mourns the lost evening. Her mood sinks even further when Lissek puts her and Fricke in charge of interviewing the Frenchman the next day. It was a BKA case originally, but Lissek has a simple philosophy: he who clears the weeds also gets to harvest the grapes. Palmer reluctantly hands over the file; since his people have acted like dilettantes he will have to miss out on the bounty this time. Aaron and Fricke devote half the night to the case. Sleep is a luxury granted to others.

At eleven o'clock the Frenchman is brought to the Department in handcuffs. He is a mountain of a man. He's a little out of shape, but you can still see the signs of ten years of weight training in a Corsican prison. He doesn't say a word and is as relaxed as Obelix in the face of a Roman shield wall. After an hour, Fricke goes to get himself a coffee and a sandwich. Aaron looks at her watch. She is supposed to meet Sandra at half-past two. They have arranged to go to a Cartier-Bresson retrospective at the C/O Gallery.

Aaron has sat opposite many men like Obelix. But none of them knew how to dislocate their thumb joint and reset it again. He manages to get his hands free behind his back, jumps over the table and tries to grab her round the neck.

She pushes herself off and tips backwards with her chair. Obelix clutches at thin air. As she falls, her kick shows him how swiftly a guy can lose his manhood.

He is still immersed in the concerto of pain when she leaps up, places a hand on his shoulder for support, takes two steps up the wall and sits herself on top of him. His speed surprises her. Before she can spin him down onto the ground he storms off, with her riding piggyback. He turns and rams Aaron against the door with his hundred and twenty kilos. It feels as though she is trapped in a hydraulic press.

Her phone rings. It's a little inconvenient right now.

Unable to breathe, she has to let go of Obelix. As she lands on the floor, he tries to stamp down on her face. She rolls away, his boot heel treads into empty space.

Aaron drives a three-knuckle punch into the ankle joint of his standing leg. His foot is instantly numbed, he loses his balance and crashes down. She yanks over the steel table and lets it drop onto Obelix's calves.

Then she jumps onto the edge.

Bones break. Horrible noise. If he had managed to stamp on her head it would have sounded exactly the same.

Fricke comes in. He pays no attention to Obelix. As if the latter had always lain there, screaming like a pig.

He just says: 'Something has happened.'

★

They race to the Benjamin Franklin Clinic in Steglitz. The Indian summer has painted the trees with glorious colours. Fricke is speeding along the western ring road at full throttle, choking on the silence. Aaron calls Sandra back. She can barely understand a word because her friend is crying so much.

In the corridor of the surgical ward Sandra tumbles into her arms. Pavlik had been out on his motorbike, somewhere in Brandenburg, just for a spin.

His Honda is a beast. Just once, Aaron has sat on his pillion. Never again.

Pavlik was flown to hospital in a rescue helicopter; he's been in the operating theatre for the past hour. The doctors aren't telling Sandra anything.

They wait and wait. Thankfully, the twins are spending the day with their grandparents. Sandra rings her father and asks him not to say anything to the kids. They're desperate to talk to her, they want to tell her about the water slide at the leisure pool. Sandra can't manage it. Aaron takes the phone and tells the boys that their mother is busy making lunch. Somehow, she manages to act normal. Eight-year-old lads shouldn't have to fear for their father's life.

Lissek arrives with Helmchen. Then Nowak, Krupp, Lutter, Butz. Soon the corridor is crammed full. Everyone who isn't on a mission is here. None of them speak. Death is a familiar figure to all of them. They have watched it take comrades, criminals and innocents. If it takes Pavlik, it would be the cruellest of all.

Two beat officers turn up. They say that Pavlik's bike came off the road in a bend. It hasn't been established yet why. But that isn't all. A couple was out on a cycling trip with their little daughter. The woman was hit full force by the Honda. She died at the scene of the accident.

Sandra tries to say something. Doesn't manage it.

Lissek motions down the corridor with his chin. Everybody leaves quietly, apart from Aaron, Fricke and him.

Finally a surgeon. Coming from his mouth, it sounds like a routine event: Pavlik will survive. The tip of the motorbike's side-stand cut his lower leg clean off. Before he lost consciousness, he used his belt to apply a tourniquet to his leg. That saved his life.

Pain and relief battle with each other on Sandra's face.

He is sleeping, but she's allowed to go to him. She only wants Aaron with her. They stand outside the door and cling to the image of a man who played football with his sons.

Pavlik's heartbeat is the only sound in the room. At the foot of the bed, the left side is empty. They sit at his bedside and hold each other's hands. He wakes up. His eyes search for the missing leg. Years pass between his breaths.

Two words: 'The woman?'

Sandra shakes her head. Pavlik closes his eyes. By eight in the evening there's been no change. Aaron goes out. Lissek and Fricke are still there.

Fricke mutters: 'So what – if it's off, it's off.'

Lissek punches him and leaves. Fricke wipes the blood off his chin as Aaron puts her arm around him. Pavlik is Fricke's best friend. He would pull the devil by the tail for Pavlik.

The friendship came about after Fricke's wife left him for another man. Fuelled by three days on vodka, Fricke had the brilliant idea to steal his rival's car. He drove it to a scrap yard and had it pressed into a cube, which he deposited outside the man's house the following night. When he had sobered up, he realized that he was in big trouble. An investigation against him was launched. There weren't any witnesses, but his solicitor didn't give him much reason to be hopeful.

He would have to appear in court. Even if he managed to avoid a prison sentence, it would still mean a dishonourable discharge from the Department. Pavlik calmed Lissek down, went to Fricke's wife and her new partner and had a sensible conversation with them. He convinced the man to drop the charges. Fricke coughed up four hundred Euros every month for five years, until the car had been paid off. Something like that stays with you for life.

When Aaron leaves with Sandra after midnight, Fricke is still sitting in the same spot. They take him with them. Back at the house they drink something or other, eat something or other, then wordlessly go to find a bed. Aaron lies down with Sandra in their marital bed, on Pavlik's side. She can't bear it. She slides over to her friend and snuggles up to her. They can hear Fricke crying in the next room.

The investigation establishes that Pavlik carries no blame. He wasn't driving too fast, the motorbike simply skidded on a patch of oil on the road. When Aaron reads it out to him, he just stares through her. Presents are piled high all over the room. *Playboy* magazines, a games console, sports journals, lads' stuff. He hasn't touched any of it.

He sleeps a lot. Sandra finds scrunched-up sheets of paper in the bin, dozens of pages. He has tried again and again to write to the woman's husband. Aaron wishes the man could know Pavlik the way she does, could know that he would gladly sacrifice his second leg if it would bring the woman back to life.

Two months pass. He is at home. He moves around so awkwardly on the provisional prosthetic that Aaron has to force herself not to look away. Officially he is on sick leave, but what is going to happen? They don't talk about that. They pretend it isn't an issue. Nor do they talk about the fact that he hardly ever leaves the bed and that there are empty whisky bottles in the bin.

Aaron takes Marlowe with her to their house in Lichterfelde. Marlowe and Pavlik are mates. In the car, she sees her tomcat happily sitting on the parcel shelf. He blinks at her: *Let me handle this.*

Marlowe pulls out all the stops. He jumps onto Pavlik's lap and flops down, belly side up. He purrs as loudly as a sewing machine. He nibbles Pavlik's nose, tickles him with his whiskers. When nothing helps he resorts to his sharpest weapon: the staring game. No one has been able to resist him yet.

Pavlik nudges him off; even Marlowe is at a loss.

Ten things that Aaron doesn't like in people:
    beating around the bush
    false modesty
    lack of self-control
    fake courage
    insensitivity
    going with the flow
    obedience
    arrogance
    self-pity
    staying down

In the Department, telephones ring, meetings are held, suspects are interrogated and missions are planned as always. Pavlik's name is never mentioned. Everyone is waiting for Lissek to do the inevitable.

He doesn't.

He acts as if nothing had happened.

Helmchen knows that Aaron spends a lot of time in Lichterfelde. In the beginning she asks after Pavlik every morning. After a while she stops. She has a smile for everyone, but when she thinks herself unobserved, she switches it off like a light.

On the first day of Advent, Pavlik hands Aaron a letter addressed to Lissek. When she tries to talk to him about it, he chucks her out.

She considers throwing the envelope away. But what would that change?

Lissek reads the letter and gives it to Aaron. The last few sentences are enough: *To daydream and overlook an oil patch isn't the same as being blameless. But that's not what this is about. The Department is as strong as its weakest link. So there's no other option. Concerning you and me, Lissek: we don't need to spell out what we think of each other. You haven't been standing on the doormat every other day, claiming that you happened to be in the area. I give you great credit for that. Don't be tempted to go mushy on me. We'll wait awhile for my farewell bash. Then we'll party hard.*

The following night, Pavlik is lying awake next to Sandra. It was three in the morning the last time he looked at the clock. He listens to her breathing. Feels her warmth.

Aaron gave him a book last week. It contains wisdoms from Bushidō philosophy. Not his scene. But there was one story he liked: A young samurai visits a wise old man who has spent half his life living in a mountain cave. The samurai asks how long it will take for him to achieve completion. Perhaps ten years, comes the reply. The samurai professes that he is prepared to undertake even the most brutal tasks in order to reach his goal as fast as possible. The old man looks at him with sorrowful eyes and says that in this case it may well take forty years.

Pavlik only ever wanted to give his best. If the inscription on his headstone were to read *Here lies a pragmatist*, it would be OK with him.

The Department has always been more than the sum of the missions, the extent of the risk, the number of funerals. Pavlik never pushed himself forward, others chose him as leader. Sometimes it was a burden to him, mostly it wasn't. It's in his nature to think of others as well as himself.

The ten years were good. He met people who made it worth it. Some are no longer alive; he couldn't help that.

Everything has its time.

It's better to leave like this than in a box.

A storm is raging outside. The rain is beating against the windows like so many steel pins. He hears something rattle downstairs; perhaps it's the terrace door, the lock is a bit funny. Pavlik sits up in bed. He looks at the stump. He's never been vain. Seeing and touching the red, scarred flesh doesn't disgust him. He feels more complete without the prosthetic than with it.

He reaches for his crutches, pushes himself up and quietly hobbles out of the room. The door to the boys' room is open. They're staying with Sandra's parents, as they so often have in recent times. Pavlik would like to tell his sons that he is still the same. But he has brought them up not to lie.

He opens the landing window. Within seconds he is soaked by the rain. The sky is as black as a chimney. The wind is punching the bare trees. A thunderstorm is brewing, although it's December. Unstable air masses, high influx of cold air, relatively warm ground temperature. A sniper knows these things. He hears the sirens of fire engines. North-west, three to four kilometres away. Yet more knowledge rendered futile.

Pavlik struggles down the stairs. It would be faster if he hopped on one leg. Yesterday he did it on his hands. Would be good training. But what for?

As soon as he's downstairs, he senses it.

No sound. No voice. No movement.

But somebody is in the house.

He stands still. He hears a quiet shuffle.

Living room.

A whisper.

Two.

Another whisper, from a different corner.

Three.

Pavlik has never deluded himself. Despite the secrecy, if someone really wanted to find him, they could. He has given many men reason to hate him. He dismisses the question of who it might be. If he thought about it now, he'd be as good as dead.

They're professionals; at four in the morning most people are in the slow-wave sleep phase. The perfect time for an attack.

He hears steps approach. Pavlik is standing to the left of the door. The men will barely be able to see anything. For him, the white of another man's eyes is all he needs.

He wishes he had the Glock that is lying in the weapons safe. He puts that out of his mind too. Three against one disabled man. Who has barely got out of bed during the last few weeks. That's the way things stand.

The first one creeps into the hallway. He's probably intending to go upstairs. Where he expects Pavlik to be.

Where his wife is sleeping.

Where his children could be.

Pavlik gives himself thirty seconds at the most. He doesn't have enough stamina and stability for a longer fight. He balances on one leg and brings his crutch down hard on the masked man's head. His opponent topples over like Foreman in the eighth round against Ali. Before he hits the ground, Pavlik is on his knees and has the gun. He sees a shadow flying towards him and pulls the trigger.

He knows that he can't miss.

The shot doesn't stop the man. He tries to kick Pavlik under the chin. He blocks the move with both hands and brings the attacker down. Pavlik grabs the crystal vase from the side table and smashes it onto the man's cranial base. Before the third one can advance, he catapults himself into the living room on one leg.

He rams the man and takes him down with him. Pavlik drives his fist into his opponent's solar plexus. The man's arms go limp, he's unconscious.

Pavlik tucks the Beretta into the waistband of his pyjama trousers. He pulls himself up by the sofa.

He hops to the light switch.

The three men lie motionless.

Steps.

Sandra is running down the stairs.

Pavlik shouts: 'Stay upstairs!'

He looks at the two in the hallway, supports himself against the wall and shoves the third gun out of reach.

Groaning, they regain consciousness.

Pavlik points the gun at them. 'Take off your masks. But keep it nice and steady now.'

Sandra is at the bottom. She doesn't pay any attention to the men, walks to the front door and opens it.

Aaron and Lissek walk in.

Dumbfounded, Pavlik watches as Fricke and Krupp pull off their balaclavas. In the living room, Butz comes to and croaks: 'Whose stupid idea was this?'

Fricke looks up at Lissek. 'Good thing it was just blank ammunition. But I wish Sandra had replaced that stylish vase with a plastic one.'

'My God, what a bunch of pussies you are,' Aaron comments.

Krupp massages his sore head. 'You keep out of it, you cheated when we were drawing lots.'

She grins. 'Of course. I don't have a death wish.'

'Can I just get a word in here?' Pavlik barks. 'What the hell is going on? They almost—'

'Yes – *almost*,' Lissek interrupts him. 'And why didn't they manage it? Since when are you so slow on the uptake?'

Pavlik doesn't reply, steadies his breath.

'I'll make some coffee,' Sandra says.

'Woman, you're breaking my heart,' he mutters.

'The whisky is ruining us,' she retorts.

When the coffee is made, she goes back to bed. Pavlik and the others sit mutely around the table.

Lissek speaks up. 'Ten years ago, I was asked to take a look at someone who stood out at the Special Enforcement Commando like an aircraft carrier on a lake. I had them send me your file, I read it, closed it and asked Helmchen to draw up a contract. You're the only one I've ever appointed without interviewing them first. And in these past ten years you've proved to me every damned day what a clever chap I am. If I had to, I could manage without my boat, my house in Sweden and, if it came to it, contact with my son. Everything. Except my wife and you. I'm giving you three months, then I want you back on track. And for God's sake go and get that whisky, this coffee needs pepping up.'

Lissek's best speech ever.

Aaron and Sandra drive to Hanover with Pavlik. The city is home to a firm that manufactures high-tech prosthetics. There are artificial limbs that perform as well as real ones, and in some aspects even surpass them. Steel springs provide tremendous bounce, greater than any muscle. Indestructible carbon that draws its energy from the leverage effect. Constructions for top athletes that can take half a ton of load. Pavlik's knee joint is undamaged, below it there are still fifteen centimetres of muscle, sinew and bone. That is a blessing.

He has to wait until January, the stump needs until then to fully heal. Eventually he gets to try on his custom-made limb. He walks up and down with it.

He's a little unsteady at first.

Then he jumps up high.

Damned high.

'Not bad for a stork,' Pavlik decides.

He works on his own. Whenever Aaron is at Sandra's, she hears him lifting weights in the garage. She knows what drudgery it is. It's the same for people like Pavlik and her as it is for painters, who have to stand at the easel every day in order not to lose their skill. For every day you don't train, you need two to compensate.

In the beginning it's all about strength and stamina. Every morning, he puts down twenty kilometres in the Grunewald before breakfast. Stoically, like a machine. He devours carbohydrates and protein, goes to bed early and doesn't drink. Then he adds bag work, shadow boxing, skipping. His movements grow smooth and fluid.

There's a basketball hoop above the garage door. Aaron sees him play with the twins.

Pavlik performs a slam dunk from standing.

He buys himself a new motorbike, an Agusta. It has even more HP than the Honda. On a bitter cold February day he sets off at dawn and doesn't come back until after dark. Sandra rings Aaron. There are fresh scratches on Pavlik's knee protectors.

That's what a winner looks like.

In March he starts his combat training, at the Mill near Beelitz. The lads keep popping by to take a peek. At the Department, they stick a photo of RoboCop on his locker door. Pavlik is a big spectacle, his left jumping kick is something to be feared. Aaron visits. Pavlik has chosen the toughest cookie among the trainers, the one they call Chuck. She wouldn't want to be in his shoes.

March turns to April, spring is nudging winter aside. Sandra talks to Aaron. She wants her to fight Pavlik. Only then will she believe that her husband is ready.

They do it. They redefine pain.

The following evening, Lissek invites himself for dinner at their house in Lichterfelde. Aaron has difficulty holding her fork; Pavlik is limping with his right leg. When they've finished their meal and Sandra has left them alone, Lissek says: 'Do you remember the Frenchman whose legs you broke six months ago?'

Avignon

Eight years ago

The Frenchman is called Jean Morel. He's just a middleman,
no big shot. He gets his heroin from the Mandalay cartel
in the Golden Triangle. Guys like him are taken to court and
locked away for a few years, then they are released early for
good behaviour and immediately build up a new business that
is just as dirty as the old one.

Lissek had a better idea.

One day in October, when Pavlik was still lying in hospital,
he invited Palmer onto his boat. It was a rough day and
Lissek sailed so hard round Eiswerder Island that the BKA
Commissioner fed the fish with his breakfast. The proposition
that Lissek put to him was a credit to the old fox.

How would Palmer feel about letting Morel go? They could
ascribe Morel's release to his savvy lawyer, who claims bold as
brass that his client ended up in that bar purely by chance and
has never seen the Bulgarian before. In return, Morel would
agree to inform them when and where the Mandalay cartel's
next distribution meeting was going to take place.

Palmer fed the fish all over again. Two of his officers were dead because of this man. And even leaving piety aside, it would mean that others got to reap the benefit of seizing the cartel. What would the BKA or the Department get? They'd have to watch the feast while going hungry.

But Lissek wouldn't be Lissek if he hadn't kept a sweetener in store: Mandalay's leadership always holds the distribution meetings in rewarding destinations. The world's top hotels, superb food, the classiest whores, the best of everything. In a relaxed atmosphere, they meet with dealers from all over the globe.

The point being: Morel had picked up that it was due to take place in Germany next year. In August. The exact location had yet to be announced.

Palmer's face returned to a healthier colour. But he saw a big problem: Morel's business would have to continue operating until August, otherwise Mandalay would grow suspicious. Were they just going to sit by and watch while he brought filthy smack into Germany?

Lissek had been expecting this objection. He drew up a calculation: they would have to let Morel carry on for ten months. They would be the sole buyers of his H, at cost price of course; and would then destroy it. Morel would only be given enough to operate his premises and pay Mandalay. Lissek estimated the total bill would come to eight hundred thousand Euros. A laughable investment, considering what they would get in return.

Palmer took a large swig from the hip flask that Lissek held out to him. He suggested that this would best be achieved via a special budget from the Ministry of the Interior. Lissek knew this of course. But he wanted Palmer to think that it was his own idea. They had a deal.

Palmer persuaded the Ministry of the Interior, and Lissek liaised with the Public Prosecutor to ensure the arrest warrant against Morel was suspended. He was allowed to leave Germany with the prospect of immunity from prosecution, which he would be granted subject to full cooperation. An ambulance transported him to Marseilles. For the next few weeks, he had to conduct his business from bed.

Lissek has since learnt that the cartel's meeting will take place on the Baltic Sea. The Severin Palais and a conference hall at The Grand Hotel Heiligendamm have been block booked for a weekend. The hotel's management has no idea what lies behind the 'Bago Corporation' that is splashing out on such a scale. The BKA will have a feast seizing the cartel.

But this isn't what Lissek has come to discuss with Pavlik.

He has come to talk about an eighteen-year-old African boy. Jerôme.

He is one of the grunts that labour for a pittance in Morel's lab in Marseilles, where the smack is cut with fentanyl. Butz and Fricke were there two weeks ago to keep an eye on Morel; after all, since their deal six months earlier, the Department practically owns the business.

As far as Morel's people were concerned, they were partners of the boss, some guys from Germany.

Jerôme attracted their attention; a small, skinny fellow with sagging shoulders, who was stirring the contents of a vat. One of the other men, at least two heads taller and twice as heavy, gave him a shove for some reason. Jerôme knocked him down and went wild. It took three guys to prise him away from the man. Morel just laughed and sent Jerôme to get sandwiches.

Butz and Fricke watched the lad walk away.

He came back just as they were getting in the car. They then witnessed an odd scene. A plainly dressed African woman, about forty years old, raced across the road towards Jerôme and shouted his name. He froze on the spot. She hugged him tight and wouldn't let go, kissing him repeatedly. Both of them cried.

After two minutes, the chauffeur of a Bentley with mirrored windows sounded his horn. The woman whispered something to Jerôme and let go of him. She ran to the Bentley, got in the front and was driven away. The boy stared after the ostentatious car as if the Pope himself were seated inside.

Butz and Fricke had nothing better to do and decided to follow the limousine. The journey took them a hundred kilometres north on the motorway.

The destination was Avignon.

The Bentley drove onto the Île de la Barthelasse. The island is situated in the Rhône, opposite the historic city. Fields and plantations alternate with dense forest. The expansive stretch of land is a refuge for people who seek a rural, secluded life. Most of its inhabitants are citizens of Avignon, whose families have owned an estate there for centuries.

After ten minutes the Bentley turned off onto a side track, where a gate opened and immediately closed again. Butz stopped. Fricke climbed onto the car roof and was able to look over the wall. It was secured with razor wire and motion sensors. Floodlights were positioned in the trees, so that at night the enormous property could be illuminated as bright as day. Not the kind of thing you would expect on the Île de la Barthelasse.

Fricke watched as the Bentley stopped outside an imposing country house. Outside, an elegantly dressed African woman was playing with a girl, about eight or nine years old. The woman from Marseilles gave her a gift box. The other shooed her away with a wave of her hand.

Fricke took photos of the elegantly dressed woman. He mailed them to Berlin, where her face was run through a biometric recognition programme.

It was Chloé Makata.

Married to Bas Makata, the butcher of Kinshasa.

Aaron and Pavlik exchange glances. They know who he is. Makata was a general in the Congo before he became an arms dealer. He has killed more people than the Taliban. He never appears in public, his whereabouts are unknown. Years ago, he was thought to be dead, but then a photo of him was made public. He had been photographed outside a hotel in Paris, getting into a limousine. A spokesperson of the French government expressed surprise and stated that they had not had any knowledge of it.

Aaron remembers the picture. Makata had thrown a white scarf over his suit, as though he was going to the opera. A shiny bald head crowned his plump face. His mouth looked like a scar that had just opened up. It was set in a smile that could slice through concrete. His eyes were buried in the fat. Aaron remembers wondering what those eyes had seen. And for how many people those eyes were the last they saw.

Butz and Fricke shadowed the woman who had clung on to Jerôme in Marseilles. Evidently she was a servant of Chloé Makata.

She lived in the feudal country house. Every morning she cycled to Avignon, where she bought groceries. The third day she seemed to have off. She bought a train ticket to Arles. There she met up with Jerôme in the Roman forum. They talked for hours. They cried, exchanged kisses. Butz and Fricke noticed the striking resemblance between the two.

On the return train journey to Avignon they sat down next to the woman and showed her fake badges of the French police. She was very frightened and claimed that she was Jerôme's older sister. Fricke and Butz didn't believe her, due to the great age difference. The woman insisted that she was only twenty-seven. They couldn't check this, as she didn't have any identification on her. They made it clear to her that her brother was working for a drug dealer. That could get him a lengthy prison sentence. There was, however, a way around this. She only needed to provide them with information about the woman for whom she was working. Jerôme's sister was caught in a trap.

In desperation, she agreed.

Butz and Fricke warned her not to tell Jerôme about any of this; they would be keeping an eye on him. They waited a further week until she had her next day off, booked a hotel room in Nîmes and recorded the whole interview with a camera.

Lissek plays the video to them on his laptop. Aaron sees a woman who is sitting on a chair and doesn't know where to put her hands. Tears stain her face. Her French is good. Time and again, her voice falters as she searches for words. The recording has to be stopped and restarted several times because the woman is unable to continue.

She says: 'My name is Adaja Bilenge. I come from the Congo, from a small village in the east. There were three of us: my brothers Jerôme and Louis, and me. They were nine and eleven, and I was eighteen, when rebels attacked our village. I was at the edge of the forest, to harvest fruit, and I hid there. I heard the screams and closed my eyes. They burnt down the village and killed all the men and women and girls and small children. They took all the boys who were older than eight with them.

'On many of the bodies the arms had been hacked off. It was the same with my mother and father. I buried them, and next to them our neighbours and four friends. I didn't have a shovel, so I did it with my hands. It took me three days.

'I didn't pray for their souls. If there was a God, he wouldn't have allowed that to happen.

'Then I started to walk, I followed the sun. I saw death many times and other people's grief that was as big as mine. I had no idea where to go so I just carried on walking. After six months I arrived in Kinshasa. I begged on the streets and slept in a park until I found work in a street kitchen. The people liked my cooking. After a while, a man came and said he had something better for me. He took me to a house in which everything was made of gold. It belonged to Chloé Makata.

'At first I was just a kitchen help. I was given clean clothes and a bed, but I slept on the floor because the bed was so soft. In the beginning I wondered whether Chloé had a husband. Others told me that she was married to Bas Makata. I had never heard the name before. People said that he was a great general who was fighting against the rebels. So I vowed to work very hard, so that everything would be to his satisfaction.

'After a few months, he came to the house for the first time. He never laughed and paid the servants no attention. The cook became ill, so I was told I would have to do the dinner. The night before, I couldn't sleep. But Makata enjoyed my manioc stew. He had me called in to him and asked me where I had learnt to cook so well. "From my mother," I said and I started to cry. He wanted to know what was the matter with me. So I told him what had happened to my parents and my brothers. Makata said that the war would soon be over and that the rebels would get what they deserved. But Louis and Jerôme were long dead, he told me, nobody would be able to change that.'

Adaja's cheap wristwatch is visible. Aaron can see from it how long the recording was interrupted each time. After she had described the attack it was almost five minutes.

Now ten.

'The cook got well again, but Chloé dismissed her. After some years, we had to pack many crates with valuable things. One of them just had diamonds in it. Makata and his wife wanted me to go with them.

'At first we lived in Switzerland, I didn't know the name of the town. The people there talked about such unimportant things, and I never saw a single beggar. Then we were in Paris, it was very cold there in winter. For the past two years we've been in Avignon.

'I don't get paid. If I've bartered well at the market I keep the change. Chloé Makata doesn't notice it, although she looks very closely. She's very strict. Everything has to be done exactly how she says. She often tells me off and hits me. Most of the time I don't know why. Once she screamed at me because I broke one of the plates with the crest on it. She asked: "Were your brothers also as clumsy as you?" I've never forgotten that.'

Two minutes' break.

'I never spoke about Louis and Jerôme again, not to anyone. But I thought about them every night. It came to me that it might be easier if I accepted that they are dead. So I tried to do that. Until I – until – in Marseilles—'

This time the break lasts for half an hour.

'Makata's wife sent me to Marseilles because the shop there sells the best macaroons. I recognized him straight away. And Jerôme recognized me too. It was like – as though I was falling from a high tower. I whispered to him that we would meet up in Arles. He's eighteen now. The same age I was back then, a man already. But I still see him the way he was on the day before the attack, when I consoled him because Louis had knocked one of his teeth out while they were playing.'

The words pile up in Adaja's mouth, until they become a lump that seals it. The recording is stopped for fifteen minutes.

'He's told me what happened. It wasn't the rebels that took him and Louis away. It was Makata's men. They were just dressed like rebels, so that everybody would think that. Makata said to the children: "You have no family now. The Kalashnikov is your family."

'They had to get up in the middle of the night to train, they were only given food every other day. If one of them tried to run away, another boy had to beat him to death with a club or punish him with the machete.

'Those who had been punished were left with long or short stumps, depending on whether just the hand or the whole arm had been chopped off. They were given brown brown, that's cocaine mixed with gunpowder, so that they didn't get to think about anything.

'They attacked villages and had to search them for food. Before attacking, they were given oil to rub onto their body. They were told that it was magic oil that would protect them from injury. But they didn't believe that, because so many of them died. The first person that Jerôme killed was an old man who wouldn't tell him where the food was. Jerôme still sees his ghost today. He can't remember how many others there were.

'They rarely saw Makata. Sometimes he was in one of the camps for a few days. Jerôme saw him throw a small girl out of his tent as though she was a piece of rubbish. She was naked and had welts from being whipped. When she tried to crawl away, Makata shot her in the head.'

The recording is stopped. This time Aaron can't tell how long the break was, as the watch is covered. Adaja has her arms wrapped tightly around her body, as if she is cold.

'Louis always looked after Jerôme,' she whispers, 'being the older one. But then he lost a part of a radio. Makata passed the sentence. Three of the children had to – had to – Jerôme was forced to watch and then he had to throw his brother's body in a river.'

The sobs are cut off by the stop button.

It's an hour before Adaja can continue.

'The next night, Jerôme and a few others were sent off to search for firewood. They ran until they collapsed from exhaustion. Three of them were caught, but Jerôme made it to a

United Nations support point. There's some kind of programme. That's how he came to France. That was six years ago, he was twelve then.

'I can't believe that I've found him. He lived in a home in Toulon, but he ran away from there. I don't know what he's had to do in order to survive in France, bad things perhaps, but he isn't a bad person. He's just a boy, it isn't his fault that all this has happened. My mother said that I had to look after my little brothers. On that one day I didn't do that. Jerôme only knows that I cook for rich people. I can't tell him that it's Makata.'

Adaja is asked a question for the first time. Aaron can hear from Butz's voice that he is having trouble sounding matter-of-fact. 'Have you told anyone about Jerôme?'

'No.'

'What about the chauffeur? He saw the two of you.'

'I said that I knew him from years ago, that he's the son of friends.'

'Does Makata live in Avignon?' Fricke asks.

'No, he's only ever there for a few days.'

'When was the last time?'

'A month ago. He was in a bad mood. He constantly quarrelled with his wife.'

'Do you know when he'll be back again?'

'Yes, I think I do. It's his daughter's birthday soon. She'll be ten. Makata loves her very much, she means the world to him. How can you be like that with your own child and do such things to other children?'

Lissek closes his laptop. They are silent for a long time. He clears his throat. 'The birthday is in six days. Tomorrow, you will drive to Avignon with Lutter. Butz and Fricke are waiting there. The French are doing arms deals with Makata, they won't touch him. You will bring the bastard to Germany. The

Public Prosecutor is in the loop, he will hand him over to the International Court of Justice.'

Thirteen hours on the motorway. Pavlik is driving the Mercedes, Aaron and Lutter are in the Ford Transit. The back is stuffed full of equipment. The Ford also has a space for their passenger. They will pump Makata full of drugs, so that he doesn't wake up until they are back in Berlin.

For Aaron it isn't the first operation of this kind. She was involved in the kidnapping of the Munich multiple child murderer, who had been granted asylum by the Belarusian dictator. His secret service wanted to milk the man because he had previously worked for the Federal Intelligence Service. Back then, it all went like clockwork.

This here is much bigger.

She knows why Lissek waited another two weeks after Adaja's statement before he gave the go-ahead. He wanted to give Pavlik as much time as possible to get back in shape. As a strategist he is indispensable to Lissek. Anyone else might have carefully introduced Pavlik back into the job, instead of chucking him in at the deep end. But anyone else wouldn't have fetched Pavlik back.

Pavlik, Butz, Fricke, Lutter, Aaron. The best team that Lissek can mobilize. Kvist and André would have been among them too, but they have been in Spain for weeks.

It's important to have good people at your side. Even though it's no guarantee that you will survive. In Rome, they were a top-class troop. They still lost.

She likes Lutter. Just thirty, he's already got three kids. Thank goodness he isn't the kind of parent who constantly passes round photos and makes spectacular announcements along the lines of 'My eldest won third place in the long jump!' He always seems deeply relaxed. When Pavlik told him about their assignment he just nodded. Although Lutter is fast, he also thinks things through; Aaron is happiest working with people in whom she recognizes something of herself. He doesn't talk much, nor does he remain silent for hours; he strikes just the right balance. Better than sharing a long journey with Fricke, who chatters away like a hedge sparrow.

After Saarbrücken the motorway takes them through the Lorraine industrial region. Coal-black spoil tips loom over tiny houses. They stop at a service station for a cigarette break. Aaron quietly groans as she gets out of the Ford. There's a bruise the size of a baseball where Pavlik's kick caught her in the small of her back when they fought.

Pavlik sees her pulling a face and points to his stiff neck to console her: the karate chop she delivered is also still making itself felt.

Montélimar marks the beginning of Provence. The landscape opens up, taking on softer shapes. The rapeseed is flowering, the low sun plays with the shadow of the car. Shortly before Avignon the traffic gets thicker. As they approach, Aaron can see the old Popes' Palace overlooking the city. She hitchhiked through here after finishing college. Baguette, melon and ham for three weeks, she's never eaten so well. She wishes she were eighteen again, when the world wasn't big enough for her dreams.

The holiday house that Butz and Fricke have rented on the Île de la Barthelasse is situated on the banks of the broad river, eight hundred metres from Makata's property. They couldn't get anything closer. From the garden they have a direct view across the Rhône, onto the remains of the Saint-Bénézet Bridge.

Sur le pont d'Avignon, l'on y danse, l'on y danse.

Soon they will be inviting Makata to a little dance.

If he comes.

Butz and Fricke have met with Adaja twice more. Makata's chauffeur also acts as butler, and there's a gardener and two chamber maids. They all live in town, only Adaja lives in the house. She says they rarely have guests. Sometimes men in suits come to talk to Makata. Frenchmen with bulging eyes and good manners; perhaps people from the secret service.

A side wing houses four bodyguards. Fricke followed two of them into town and checked them out. Good men, competent, know their stuff. They had only gone to drink a pastis, yet they sat down in a way that allowed them to cover the full hundred and eighty degree angle; backs to the wall, jackets half open. Both have buzz cuts and stomachs as flat as the Camargue.

French. Fricke reckons they're former Foreign Legionnaires.

From Adaja they know that Makata always arrives in a private jet, with another three bodyguards in tow. His chauffeur picks him up at the airport on his own.

Butz has been scouting for places on the island that might be suitable for the abduction. The first one is a small area of woodland which Makata has to travel through. A quiet little corner, secluded, dense conifer plantation, sparse traffic. Butz has a talent for this kind of thing. He can brood over a problem for hours, until he has taken absolutely everything into account.

The location's only weak point is a raised hide for huntsmen, situated on a clearing a hundred metres away. If anybody happened to be on watch, they might burst in on the action. A stranger with a loaded rifle signifies a risk.

Second option: a fruit orchard immediately after the woodland. The trees are in flower; the narrow road is hidden from view by cherry and peach blossom. But the risk of bystanders getting mixed up in the operation is even greater here.

The third variant would be to attack the house. Logistically this isn't a problem. Adaja knows the code for the alarm system. They would deal with the motion sensors on the wall the traditional way, putting them out of action with hard foam.

That leaves the bodyguards.

Seven men. Superbly trained. Better acquainted with the surroundings. Some might be patrolling the grounds, while others keep watch in the main building.

That's where the child is. The possibility of her getting caught up in a shoot-out horrifies them.

Pavlik chooses the woodland. They will check whether anyone is sitting in the hide shortly before the operation. If yes, one of them will neutralize the person.

A few days ago Chloé went to an opening event at the Musée Angladon; two bodyguards accompanied her. In the car park, Fricke took a closer look at the car. It is armoured, but with ceramic rather than steel, as he noted when he tapped the bodywork. The logo of the company that had modified the Bentley was engraved above the rear number plate: Barthez & Mercier. They know that the firm only produces armouring up to medium protection level 6 and specializes in particularly heavy limousines. The car already weighs two and a half tonnes ex factory; steel armour would put too much strain on the engine.

Class 6 means that the material will withstand 7.62 × 39 calibre ammunition from a distance of ten metres.

.308 Winchester steel core projectiles can pierce it.

According to Fricke, the tyres don't have an emergency run-flat system. If the tyres are flat, the Bentley can't move.

People are so prone to saving in the wrong places.

Fricke and Butz have timed the chauffeur on several occasions to see how long it takes him to cross the woodland. He likes to take it steady and invariably drives at fifty kilometres per hour.

They will lay a spike strip across the road to stop the car. The front windscreen of the Bentley is curved, which means it is a maximum of four centimetres thick. Pavlik, Fricke and Aaron will destabilize it with continuous fire from automatic rifles. This will allow Lutter and Butz, working from the sides, to bust the screen from its anchoring with sledgehammers. If they wanted, the bodyguards would meet a swift death.

But they will let them live.

The aim is to carry out a minimally invasive operation.

They will throw a sevoflurane cartridge into the car. The anaesthetic gas will fill the interior, taking effect within seconds.

By the time the other bodyguards arrive, they will have long disappeared with Makata.

That's the theory. Possible complications they have to consider:

The bodyguards get out and attack, resulting in a gunfight.

For some reason there are two cars this time, and the men in the escort vehicle make things difficult for them.

Because it's her birthday, Makata's daughter wants to go along to the airport to pick up her father.

And a hundred other things.

The next few days consist of mindless waiting. For much of the time they sit inside and listen in on what is going on at Makata's house. Butz has given Adaja a handful of bugs, which she has deposited in different rooms. She herself has a microphone on her skin, a transparent plaster above her collarbone. They can't communicate with her. Chloé demands that she wears her hair tied back. An earbud would attract attention, and a mobile might be discovered.

Chloé is on edge; on several occasions she shouts at the servants over some insignificant thing. One of the chamber maids is berated when she asks if she can take two days off to look after an aunt who is unwell. Chloé telephones a friend. She is fed up with Avignon, it's a 'cultureless dump in the middle of nowhere'. The months in Paris were the best. But they had to leave there 'because of that business', Chloé complains.

Have the French indicated to her husband that he should find somewhere less conspicuous to live?

Chloé's daughter Manon is allowed to do whatever she wants. She's a spoilt brat who has taken to poking about in the servants' rooms. At one point she is caught red-handed by Adaja. They hear Adaja sobbing; the child must have done something that has upset her. Manon runs out of the room giggling, Adaja continues to cry for several more minutes.

When Chloé gives her an order, she acknowledges this with a quiet 'Oui, Madame'. Her voice is brittle. That worries Aaron. Adaja has known for over two weeks what Makata has done to her parents and her brothers.

Her voice isn't just trembling with fear.

It is hate.

That worries Aaron even more.

Adaja's conversations with the other servants are held in whispers; everyone is nervous because the boss is coming. Chloé chases them around. The house has to be made spotless. The silver is cleaned, every glass is polished. Is there enough Cognac Napoléon? Has the humidor been filled with his cigars? Is there a bit of fluff on one of his suits?

Important questions.

In the grounds, a small circus company is setting up its tent. There is going to be a birthday performance for Manon and her parents. She doesn't have any friends that she could invite.

A deliveryman brings a parcel. Manon whines, but she isn't allowed to see inside it. Aaron knows that it contains a small ermine coat – dyed pink; Chloé spoke about it on the phone. One can do such amazingly tasteless things with money.

Aaron feels sick knowing that the woman will have a wonderful life even after her husband has been arrested and sentenced.

Finally he calls. He will be landing on the morning of his daughter's birthday, at eleven. That means the limousine will be 'in the box' at around half-past eleven. That's better than in the evening, when the light won't be any good.

Pavlik spends all day observing what is going on at the house. He has found himself a tree that is suitable for the purpose, four hundred metres from the property. Aaron accompanies him on one of his trips. She tips her head back and wonders how Pavlik is going to get up into the crown of the giant oak with his prosthetic. He climbs up first. At the top he grins. 'Normally I just jump up, but I didn't want you to get an inferiority complex.'

They look across to the property with monocular telescopes. The girl is roaming around the circus cages and teasing a white rabbit with a stick. The gardener is cleaning the pool. The bodyguards are hanging around, playing cards. Their jackets are made baggy by their weapons.

Revolvers. Unbeatable at short distance, useless for anything else. The men look unflappable.

Adaja is hanging up washing. Aaron zooms in on her. Every face tells of a life. In this one she sees one that never will be. A little slice of happiness in a village. A husband, children. Proud parents. Two grown-up brothers.

Chloé totters over to the circus tent in her high heels, waving about a piece of paper, probably new instructions. Adaja follows her with her eyes. Aaron sees the anger in them. A cold shiver runs down her spine.

The following day is Adaja's day off. She leaves the house early. Aaron follows her to the station and boards the train to Arles with her. Lavender fields snuggle into a blanket of morning mist. The sky looks as if it's been Photoshopped.

In Arles, Aaron bumps into Adaja on the platform, seemingly by accident, and apologizes profusely.

Adaja rushes through the historic centre. Dogs doze in the shade, souvenir traders are setting up their stalls. She goes into the amphitheatre. Aaron buys a ticket too and sits down on the other side of the arena. Adaja has no eyes for anything. She waits. After ten minutes, Jerôme arrives. They fall into each other's arms. For two hours they sit holding hands and talk. Adaja isn't wearing her microphone plaster, so Aaron can't hear what they are saying.

She takes her make-up mirror out of the bag and positions it in such a way that it reflects the sunlight into the woman's eyes. Adaja sees Aaron and recognizes her from the station. Adaja stands up and pulls Jerôme away with her. They scurry through the tourist crowds this way and that.

She turns round several times.

Aaron stays invisible.

When they sit down in a street café, Aaron browses in a second-hand bookshop and gives them another two hours.

Then she goes out onto the street and repeats the game with the mirror. Adaja stares at Aaron, then says something to Jerôme. They hug and Jerôme saunters off. Aaron sits down at the table and asks Adaja what she said to her brother. That she has a doctor's appointment, Adaja replies, and that they'll meet back here at midday.

It is hard to gain the trust of a woman whose soul has been battered. Aaron does everything right when she asks: 'What was Jerôme like as a child?'

Adaja wavers.

'This has nothing to do with my work. You don't need to tell me if you don't want.'

'He was magical. All he had to do was smile and the day would be beautiful. He often got up to mischief, but nobody could be angry with him. Also because he was the youngest, they always get away with things. He was a good pupil. Inquisitive and cheeky. He had a small shaggy dog, Chipie. I buried him next to our parents.'

The waiter comes. Aaron orders two coffees. They sit in the sun and both feel cold.

'And Louis?' she asks.

'His skin was as dark as molasses. The other kids called him "Mukish", that's a type of ghost. He idolized an American baseball player. Louis never saw him play, but he said that the man always pokes out his tongue. He liked that. Perhaps because he was very different himself. He was very serious and thought about things a lot. Louis was always very conscientious. I don't understand how it happened, with that radio part—'

The pain cuts off Adaja's voice.

After a while, she recovers. Aaron passes her a tissue. She lets the woman speak. She has to give Jerôme so much of what little strength she has and can never talk about herself.

'Chloé's daughter was in your room. You caught her doing something that made you cry. What did she do?'

'I only had the one picture of our family,' Adaja whispers. 'I found it half burnt in the rubble of our house. She tore it to pieces and laughed. You shouldn't think about a child like that, but I wish she had been in the village back then.'

They remain silent for ten minutes. When Aaron looks at her watch, it is a quarter to twelve; Jerôme will be back any minute. She looks at Adaja firmly. 'Makata will never enter that house again. We're going to take him when he's on his way from the airport. You no longer need to fear him. Justice will be done for your parents and your brothers.'

'Do you promise that?'

'Yes.'

Adaja kneads the tissue.

'Go away with Jerôme, as soon as it's done. But not before. That's important. Do you understand?'

She nods.

'Do you have any papers?'

She shakes her head. 'Makata always took care of that.'

'I will tell you a phone number now. You have to learn it off by heart and you must never write it down.'

Adaja repeats the number three times.

'Ring that number once you've left Avignon. Tell them who you are, that will be enough. They will ask you for passport photos and a postal address. You'll get a French passport and a social security number.'

Adaja is so grateful she finds no words.

Aaron leaves. After the next street corner she stops and peers back at the café. She sees that Adaja calls over the waiter and asks him to clear away the second coffee cup.

Well done.

It will stay our secret.

Jerôme is on time. Aaron watches them; two people who have nothing except a longing never to lose each other again. At three o'clock they say goodbye to each other with a heartfelt embrace. Adaja walks away towards the station, Jerôme disappears into the town centre bustle.

For Aaron and the others he is just a means to an end, an instrument they use to get Adaja to cooperate and prevent her from slipping away before Makata arrives. If she were to disappear overnight, Chloé would tell her husband. That could make him suspicious; menials without rights, such as Adaja, are open to attack from police and secret services. They present a risk.

Aaron decides to follow Jerôme without thinking much about it. It's as if she has known him for ever. He buys Gitanes Maïs from a street hawker. He nicks an apple as he passes a fruit stall.

He spends some minutes sitting on a bench, eating the apple. He looks around, he's learnt to be on his guard at all times. As his eyes dart about, there is an emptiness in his face that could swallow the sun.

Jerôme walks on. He's no longer just drifting, he seems to have an aim. But it isn't the station. His path takes him across the Trinquetaille Bridge, straight through the famous Van Gogh painting, onto the opposite bank of the Rhône.

The balconies of the tenement blocks are festooned with washing. A man, even more scrawny than Jerôme, loiters around between corrugated iron garages. He's scratching his lower arms. Aaron can see at a glance that he's a junkie. She cowers down behind a car.

Jerôme negotiates with the scrawny bloke. He pulls a sachet out of his jeans. He's lifted some smack from the Marseilles lab and is earning himself a little extra.

The scrawny man inspects the goods; Jerôme keeps an eye on him. With junkies who are on withdrawal and just pretend to have money, it can happen that they swallow the heroin.

Neither of them notices the two men who are strolling towards the garages behind their backs. They're wearing leather jackets, despite the warm weather. Aaron instantly knows: policemen. The junkie sees them first and runs away. Jerôme isn't fast enough. One of the men grabs him and throws him against the garage wall. The other lays into him with kicks. Jerôme curls up, tries to protect his head.

The two men don't let off. For them he is just a 'Bamboula', a dirty nigger dealer, and they are teaching him a lesson.

Aaron could keep out of it. They will be long gone with Makata by the time Adaja hears about Jerôme being arrested. But she thinks of how Jerôme had to throw his brother's body into the river, and of Chipie, his little dog.

The men don't hear Aaron's silent footsteps. Within three seconds, she is behind them. She stuns one of them with a stab into the throat meridian, then rams her index finger into the kyusho point on the other one's nape. They sink to the ground unconscious.

Jerôme struggles to his feet.

He stares at Aaron confused and fearful.

She says: 'Run and never come back to Arles.'

He begins to move, first hesitantly, then faster and faster, until he is running as if the devil was after him.

Aaron crouches down and pats down the men. Guns in holsters, handcuffs, police badges. She leaves the two lying there and disappears.

In the train to Avignon there's a man with a bandaged ear. He sees her look and laughs. 'My dog bit me. You won't believe this, but he's called Vincent.'

The evening before, they run through everything once more. Everyone knows what they need to do. They check the equipment, clean the guns, channel the adrenalin.

At ten, a phone rings in Makata's house.

Chloé answers it in the bedroom. She puts it on loudspeaker, perhaps she's busy varnishing her nails. 'Hello, chérie. Where are you? Already in France?'

'No, I'm still in Libya.'

Aaron hears Makata's voice for the first time. It is surprisingly pleasant. Confident and rounded.

'What time is the circus performance tomorrow?' he asks.

'At six.'

'We'll do it at three.'

'But why? Everything has been—'

'We have two guests coming for dinner at nine.'

'But that's when we were going to take Manon—' Chloé angrily begins.

He immediately interrupts her and adopts a harsh tone that won't tolerate dissent. 'There are men to whom you can't say there's something else that's more important. I may have owned a country once. One of these two owns the entire world. Send everyone away apart from the bodyguards and Adaja. She will cook and serve the food.'

Makata puts the phone down. The bug transmits a clanging sound: Chloé has thrown something against the wall.

Aaron and the others exchange mute glances.

One of these two owns the entire world.

They go out into the garden. A wedding couple is being photographed on the Saint-Bénézet Bridge. Flash lights and laughter bounce across the water. A tourist steamboat glides along the Rhône like a large, glittering dragon.

Pavlik voices it. They have to know who this man is. Kidnapping Makata will have to wait until he makes the return journey to the airport.

Whenever that is.

The others disappear back into the house. Aaron is alone with Butz. It is warm, the air is like treacle. She thinks of her father. Would he approve of what they are doing?

Butz puts his arm around her. Despite the twenty-nine years that separate him and Aaron's father, the two are friends. She doesn't know who saved whose life.

Butz mutters: 'Your old man wouldn't let himself in for this, not in a million years. But he isn't here. And he didn't look into Adaja Bilenge's eyes.'

Pavlik, Fricke and Lutter return with beers. They sit by the riverbank. Cypresses tower into the night sky like extinguished torches. Fricke cracks a few jokes, which ebb away into silence. One by one, they all hit the sack. Eventually only Aaron and Pavlik remain.

'Will you ring Lissek?' she asks.

'I already have.'

'What did he say?'

'Our doubts don't count, only our actions.'

Aaron tosses and turns in her bed for hours. She knows that it's the same for the others. At ten she is sitting in the oak tree with

Pavlik. They see the chauffeur driving away with the Bentley. Alone, just as Adaja said. After an hour and a half, he comes back.

Makata gets out. A colossus, he must weigh at least hundred and fifty kilos. His upper arms are so fat they almost burst the jacket.

The staff have lined up in front of the house. Manon runs towards her father. Laughing, he spins her round like a chain carousel. He pulls a giant stuffed gorilla out of the car. Manon can't hold it, the chauffeur takes it for her. Chloé plants pecks on her husband's cheeks.

Aaron only has eyes for Adaja.

Her face crumbles in slow motion.

When Makata walks past her with Chloé and the girl, she curtsies like the others.

But she stares at the ground.

'Do you see that?' Pavlik mutters.

'Yes. She thinks we've abandoned her.'

He agrees.

An hour later Adaja cycles into town. She buys veal fillets, lobster, asparagus, truffles. At the cheese counter, Aaron approaches her. 'Excuse me, you seem to know your way round here. Can you recommend this Brie?'

Adaja doesn't reply. When she leaves the shop, Aaron walks beside her. 'We had to change the plan. We're still going to take him. Just not today.'

'Oh, I understand,' Adaja blurts out. 'I was so stupid to trust you. Nobody will ever do anything to Makata.' She quickens her steps.

Aaron keeps up with her. 'Please, you must believe me—'

Adaja stops. 'I hope you choke on your lies!' She tears off the microphone plaster, throws it on the ground and runs off.

Aaron can't pursue her without attracting attention. She steadies her breath.

★

All day she sits in the tree with Pavlik. He has the rifle in his lap, with the silencer attached. Manon struts around wearing her new ermine coat in the lunchtime heat. The circus performance begins at three on the dot. Jolly music rings out from the tent for an hour. They can't hear any applause, six hands aren't loud enough. Then the artists disappear; they will take down the tent tomorrow. Adaja has baked the girl a cake, which she carries out onto the terrace. Manon blows out the candles, the staff have to clap. So many empty smiles. Regardless of what wish this child makes, they hope it will never come true. At six all the servants apart from Adaja leave the house.

Darkness descends.

Aaron and Pavlik put on night vision goggles with long-range optical eyepieces. The ones that Pavlik is wearing have an integrated camera. He will photograph the guests when they arrive.

Three bodyguards patrol the property. On the upper floor, the curtains in Makata's study are still open. Aaron and Pavlik see him working at his desk, smoking a cigar. They hear the clatter of pots and pans in the kitchen, and music coming from Manon's room. In the other earbud Aaron would hear the team, if they weren't all silent. Lutter, Fricke and Butz are sitting in the Mercedes a few kilometres away; they will follow Makata's guests on their journey back.

Half-past eight. Screaming. Manon is crying, she refuses to be placated by her mother. Her father gets up and goes downstairs.

Aaron has been staring at the house for hours. For a sniper like Pavlik that's no problem, but her eyes are stinging.

She removes the night vision goggles.

'Damn,' Pavlik hisses. He reaches for the rifle.

She puts the goggles back on.

Adaja is in Makata's room.

She opens a drawer, takes out a revolver.

Aaron's pulse accelerates to supersonic speed. She's never climbed out of a tree that fast. In her left ear she hears Pavlik, who is informing the others. 'Adaja wants to kill Makata. Without us she won't get out of there alive. Aaron is taking the goods entrance. Lutter and Fricke: east side. Butz, you take the main gate. The bodyguards have priority.'

'What about the alarm system?' Lutter asks.

'Bollocks to it.'

'Roger.'

Aaron is sprinting towards the property across an open field. She attaches the silencer to the Browning. Through her night vision goggles, the world is a flurry of green lights. It feels like she is battling her way through a jungle of fear with a machete.

In her right ear she hears the child whining. Makata is downstairs, quarrelling with Chloé. On the left, Pavlik announces: 'Four bodyguards in the grounds. Two at the front, one by the tent, one at the north wall. Three more are in the annexe.'

Aaron manages the four hundred metres in eighty seconds. It will take the others at least another two minutes to get here. Too long. She has to get inside the house before Makata goes back upstairs. When she reaches the goods entrance she chucks the night vision goggles away and pushes a refuse bin against the wall. She pulls herself up by the top. The razor wire cuts into her wrists and underarms, and slices open her jeans.

As she jumps down, the floodlights flash up. The alarm begins to blare.

'Aaron is in,' Pavlik says.

She rushes towards the house, sees the first bodyguard, to her right. Hundred metres. His revolver is enormous, but at this distance it's as useless as a catapult. Before Aaron can take aim at him, his head explodes.

Pavlik. 'Six left,' he informs the team.

'Where are the others?' she pants.

'All outside. I can't make them out. They're being clever and staying under the tr—'

In her earbud she hears the plop of his silencer.

'Five,' he corrects.

To her right a bodyguard bursts out of the undergrowth and runs towards Aaron. Seventy metres. She shoots him in the heart at full run and plays it safe with a bullet to his forehead.

'Four,' she reports.

'Lutter and Fricke are in,' says Butz.

Revolvers shout out, then silence. A suppressed groan.

'I've been hit,' Fricke forces out. 'Flesh wound.'

Lutter radios through: 'We've got two. One has disappeared to the south. He's yours, Butz. No trace of the other.'

Aaron runs to the front door. 'What's Adaja doing?'

'Still in the study. Staring out the window.'

'I'm on my way,' Lutter calls. 'You take Makata, I'll take care of the alarm system.'

Revolver shots by the gate. A yell.

'Six is neutralized,' Butz reports.

Where is number seven? drums through Aaron's head. *In the house?*

She pushes open the door. She can't see anyone in the entrance hall. Carefully, she advances a step. The blood rushing through her veins sounds like waves breaking on a shore.

The man has been waiting in the blind spot. He wants to do it silently, with the knife, so that he doesn't give his position away.

Aaron drops the Browning. She intercepts the thrust with a three hundred and sixty degree block and plants a palm on the bodyguard's chin. She shoves his arm down, grabs his wrist, applies her weight to it and rams her knee into his stomach, leaving him gasping for breath. Before he can even form a clear thought, she has got hold of the knife. She cuts deep into his thigh, severing the artery.

Out of the corner of her eye she sees Makata running up the stairs.

The bodyguard collapses. All the colour has drained from his face. Blood spouts from his leg like water from a fire hose. Aaron tears his Colt out of its holster, throws it into a corner and grabs the Browning.

Makata is upstairs. She sprints after him.

'Adaja is standing in the middle of the room and is aiming at the door,' Pavlik tells her. 'Damn, hurry up!'

In his gun sight Pavlik sees the door fly open. Makata marches towards Adaja, without fear, as if her hands were empty. A hundred and fifty kilos of pure self-assurance.

'She can't do it,' Pavlik murmurs.

He shoots Makata in the arm.

It doesn't stop the colossus.

Aaron leaps into the room. Makata grabs the revolver and spins round with Adaja. He holds the gun to her temple. Tears are running down her face.

Aaron aims exactly at the bridge of Makata's nose. 'You're not going to get out of here. Let the woman go.'

His sweaty forehead is pulsating. 'You won't get me alive,' he scoffs.

The alarm system is silent.

'I can't shoot him in the head, the window frame is covering him,' Pavlik mumbles. 'Get ready.'

Glass bursts. Makata staggers. Pavlik has sent a bullet into his other arm. He lets go of Adaja. Aaron dives into the room, performs a roll and kneels beside him. She grabs his revolver hand, pulls on it, wraps both legs around Makata's arm and brings him down.

He shoots into the floor.

Her master says: *The earth's energy flows into your body through the kyusho point in the soles of your feet. This is also true when you're in a house. If your feet aren't touching the floor, use your hand for it. The Yang meridian at the base of your cranial is your point of contact with the sky. You are a lightning conductor. The energy has to leave your body through your other foot or your other hand in the direction of your enemy.*

Aaron presses her right hand onto the carpet and rams her left fist into Makata's jaw angle with colossal force. He instantly loses consciousness.

She stands up. Adaja hasn't moved from the spot. Her eyes are like dead leaves.

Two shots ring out downstairs, revolver. A whispered reply, silencer. Then a scream. Chloé. Aaron runs from the room. When she's at the top step, she sees the motionless child. A red crater gapes in Manon's chest. Lutter is reeling, blood running down his temple. In the doorway lies the bodyguard he shot in the neck.

Wailing, Chloé falls to her knees beside her daughter. The bodyguard's revolver is lying on the floor, a metre away. Lutter collapses.

Chloé reaches for the gun and aims it at him.

Her make-up is smeared, her lipstick a pale pink like Jackie Kennedy's. She is wearing a flower in her hair. She tears her mouth open and shrieks something in an African language.

Aaron pulls the trigger. The bullet splits Chloé's head in two.

Butz and Fricke come storming in. Fricke runs over to Lutter. It's a graze wound. 'Clean,' Fricke reports to Pavlik.

'Butz, help me,' Aaron calls. She runs back to Makata. He is still unconscious. Adaja is sitting on a chair, her hands folded in her lap, as if she were waiting for a job interview. Aaron tears down a curtain cord. Butz takes Makata's shirt off, cuts it with his knife and applies makeshift bandages to the bullet wounds.

There's barely any blood, no ruptured arteries, the two bullets are embedded in the fat. They tie him up and gag him.

Aaron pulls Adaja to her feet and drags her down the stairs. In the entrance hall she takes her by the shoulders and says: 'You have to disappear immediately. Drive to Marseilles. Do you know where Jerôme lives?'

Adaja nods mechanically.

'Go away with him. Do it tonight.'

She nods again, staring at the three corpses.

'How much have you got on you?' Aaron asks the others.

They always carry cash on their body during an operation like this, to enable a quick exit. She pulls her jeans down to her knees and fishes two thousand Euros in large notes out of the sewn-in pocket. Fricke adds a thousand; Lutter has regained consciousness and is also digging out two thousand. Butz joins them, he's got three thousand.

Aaron places the money in Adaja's hand. 'What's the phone number I told you to ring?'

Adaja stammers the numbers.

'Good. Now go.'

Adaja stumbles out of the house.

The bodyguard whose leg artery Aaron ruptured is lying in a red lake. He is still conscious. She shoots him in the head.

Pavlik steps over the dead man in the doorway.

'I thought I'd dispatched him,' Fricke mutters. 'My fault.'

Pavlik looks at his watch. Quarter to nine. Makata's guests will soon be here. 'Butz, Fricke, clear away the bodies at the front of the house. Aaron, kill that bloody light in the grounds.'

Lutter is staring into space. 'Suddenly the girl comes running out of the room. The guy crawls through the door and fires at me. The girl ran straight into his follow-up shot. I got him too late.'

What if the police turn up? The alarm system has drowned out the revolver blasts, apart from the last two. But it was blaring out for four minutes.

There are no sirens.

Just silence.

Lutter stays in the house, the others take up position outside. When the car arrives, Lutter will open the gate so it can enter the grounds. They don't know whether the men will arrive with bodyguards.

It doesn't matter.

They're going ahead with it. They wait.

It turns nine.

Half-past.

Ten.

Nobody.

All of this happened for nothing.

They go upstairs to Makata. Aaron removes the gag from his mouth. 'You've been stood up. Who is this man you spoke of?'

She reads the question in his eyes.

'Your wife and daughter are alive. Nothing will happen to them if you cooperate with us.'

Makata is in pain. He groans.

Pavlik fixes him with his eyes. 'Is that your reply?'

Makata thinks.

Then he gives up. 'I don't know.'

Fricke gives a bitter laugh.

'I don't know his name. He called me, in a hotel in Tripoli. On a number that only six people have. He said: "If you want, you'll be the president of the Republic of Congo a month from now." I thought he was joking. He said: "There's a box outside your door." I opened it. Inside was the head of the president's most important advisor.'

'What did he want in return?' Aaron asks.

'That's what I was going to find out tonight.'

His voice is firm. He's telling the truth.

They look at each other mutely. They can't take Makata to the Federal Public Prosecutor now. Not anymore. Once they announce his arrest, the French will know who was in Avignon. They had factored that in. Only the plan hadn't included nine dead, seven of them French citizens. This kind of bloodbath would cost Lissek his job. And it would cost them theirs too.

But should they allow Makata to live?

Who will ever hold him to account?

His eyes are as cold as a spent cartridge case. His naked chest shows a tattoo, Jesus on the cross.

Pavlik is the first to draw his gun.

Then Aaron. Fricke. Lutter. Finally Butz.

30

Today

There is a small room next to Demirci's office, where she spends the night every now and then. With some missions, she finds herself constantly staring at the phone. In these situations she prefers to be here, rather than in her apartment on Potsdamer Platz. Pavlik has told her that Lissek sometimes camped out in this room for weeks. At first she was surprised; she had been under the impression that her predecessor was a bit of a cold fish. That was silly of course. If he had been, those forty men and women wouldn't have followed him through thick and thin.

She is lying on the narrow bed, staring at the ceiling. The traffic noise throbs away behind the window. Helmchen had stayed until ten. Demirci sent her home; it's enough if one of them drives herself crazy.

Two a.m., three hours until the jet takes off.

Draped over the chair are a pair of overalls, a waist belt, knife, balaclava, ballistic helmet, protective vest, thigh holster and tactical gloves. Guppy must have brought the stuff over.

She knows that Lissek used to accompany such missions dressed in combat gear, to demonstrate that he is one of the team.

She won't be using any of these things. Demirci will wear a business outfit. Her message will be: I know what you are capable of, and you know it too.

The special phone rings. She instantly grabs it. 'Yes?'

'It's me.'

Aaron.

'Where are you?'

'Atlas mountains, a small hotel. Pavlik has gone to lie down, he didn't get a wink of sleep last night. We're setting off in four hours.'

'Any new developments?'

Aaron's voice is flat. 'You know I was in Avignon eight years ago.'

Demirci's heart skips a beat.

'Of those that were there, only Pavlik, Fricke and me are still alive. Lutter died that same year in Santiago, and Butz five weeks ago.'

Aaron goes on to give an account of Layla's interrogation.

They talked about someone. Bas Makata. They wanted to meet with him. In Avignon.

She describes what happened in the Congo. She takes her time. She can still remember every detail.

What God would allow that?

Aaron tells her how it all turned into a nightmare. The Night of the Long Knives. Nine dead. The head of the presidential advisor in a box.

Demirci's voice is raw: 'You liquidated Makata.'

'We wanted to. But we couldn't do it.'

'Why?'

'Because we're police, not executioners.'

'What did you do?'

'We loaded him into the transporter, with the bodies of his wife and daughter. We buried the two bodies in the Camargue. Then we drove Makata to Marseilles. Butz and Fricke knew where Jerôme lived; the house was shared by lots of Africans. We chucked Makata inside the entrance, naked and tied up, and wrote on his belly: *I am Bas Makata, the butcher of Kinshasa.* We waited in the Ford. An hour later Adaja arrived. We left then. His body was never found, but a week later an arm was washed up on the beach of Bandol. It had been sliced off clean, as if cut with a machete.'

Demirci eventually finds her voice: 'Did you tell Lissek?'

'Yes.'

'And did he condone it?'

'As you will,' Aaron replies.

'What makes you think that?'

'Because you believe in justice and because you aren't a heartless arsehole.'

A long silence follows. Then Demirci asks: 'Why do you think Varga and Berg didn't go to Avignon?'

'They were probably there, an hour or even a day earlier. Their bodyguards may have been watching Makata's property and seen what was happening.' Aaron's voice is bitter. 'We were so close.'

A headache is hammering against Demirci's forehead.

'Where are we flying to tomorrow?' Aaron asks.

'You're taking Layla to the safe house in the Alps.'

'The Teufelsbach hill farm?'

'Yes. You'll continue to interrogate her there.'

'She needs to go to a hospital, she has cancer.'

Damn.

'Can the treatment be delayed?'

'I'm not a doctor,' says Aaron, 'but I doubt it. She's very ill.'

'We can't give her the same level of protection in a hospital. And we'll have to find a solution for the boy too.'

'It's never easy. Says so on the board in the corridor.'

'What do you think: does Layla know more?'

'She's worried about her son. It will be easier once we're in Germany.'

'Try to get some sleep too.'

Aaron doesn't reply. Nor does she hang up.

She knows something. But she isn't sure whether to trust me with it. It would mean losing her information advantage.

The silence at the other end continues.

Demirci says: 'I'm glad that you're back with us. I haven't even got round to—'

'There's something I'm puzzling over,' Aaron interrupts her. 'It's doing my head in.'

'Yes?'

Aaron tells her that Holm wanted to have the deposit box number forty-seven. She lists everything that could be a part of the puzzle: Alexander the Great, Georges Noël, Château Lafite, Beverly Wilshire, Robert Browning, Judith Traherne, Bach, Lubichowo, the Rosa Luxemburg quote.

'What quote is it?'

'Patience is a revolutionary virtue.'

'Which works by Bach?'

'The cello suites.'

'How do you spell Lubichowo?'

'I don't know.'

Demirci suddenly feels hot. 'What's the name of the painter that Holm mentioned? Noël?'

'Yes.'

'That's an anadrome.'

She hears Aaron's breath quicken.

'You know, a word that forms a different word when read backwards. Reverse Noël.'

Leon.

Aaron gathers her thoughts: 'Load Leon Keyes' file and check whether the number forty-seven figures in it.'

Demirci runs into her office. She logs on and opens the document. She enters '47' into the search field.

The writing blurs in front of her eyes. She lights a cigarette and smokes half of it to calm herself down.

Then she picks the receiver up again. 'Leon Keyes' firm was based in Friedrichstrasse. But it hadn't been there for long. He moved three months before you went to Rome. The previous address was Rosa-Luxemburg-Strasse 47.'

31

The red of the sunrise they are driving into burns itself onto Aaron's retina. For two hours, they've been lurching along winding roads that have been turned into mud slides by last night's rain. They're heading downhill now, perhaps you can already see the Sahara from here. On the rear seat, Layla and Luca are so quiet it's easy to forget they are there.

Pavlik sits mutely behind the wheel. Aaron let him sleep after her phone call with Demirci. Just before they set off she took him aside and told him.

Pavlik said: 'You've solved it. Would have pleased Holm.'

'I'll have it written on a wreath for his grave.'

'Finally.'

'What?'

'You've buried him.'

Ten things that Aaron didn't recognize:
   her father's illness
   the truth about Barcelona

the bullet in Helsinki
the hole in the ice on the pond
that friendship proves itself in adversity
what André wanted to tell her before he died
how great her mother's unhappiness was
what it means to be appointed to the Department
Vesper
that Leon Keyes is the Broker

I could give you the key to the enigma.

The answer was so easy.

Key – Keyes.

She played it through in her head a hundred times, until she understood.

The consulting firm in Berlin was just a cover. The perfect operational base for his business with death. He isn't the kind of man who hides away. He enjoyed his pasta with salsiccia at the Gendarmenmarkt, cruised through the Tiergarten district in his silver Porsche and had a subscription for the most expensive box at the Berlin State Opera.

At first she thought that he had made a mistake with the illegal money in the Caribbean.

Good.

If he's made one mistake, he'll probably make others too.

Then it dawned on her that it wasn't a mistake.

It was ingenious.

The illegal money was already a part of Keyes' plan. He made sure that the BKA came across it. Simultaneously, he established his relationship with Varga. Keyes deposited the bug in his Porsche himself, in order to create the impression that he needed protection in Rome.

Aaron was nothing more than a tin opener for him.

Getting the list of politicians from Varga's safe meant he

had half of Europe in his pocket. Corruption is the basis for everything.

Those were *his* men in the hotel. The well-aimed shot in his leg was just to create the impression that they were after him too. Their submachine guns contained blanks, Keyes was wearing a vest with blood capsules.

That's why they let her live: so that she could witness his death.

The cellar of the Gran Sasso was teeming with security when Pavlik arrived. He only saw what he thought was Keyes' body from a distance. When Aaron was being taken away in the ambulance, he and the team rushed to stop it on its way to the hospital. They got Aaron out and raced to the airport with her. Keyes was long gone by then.

Corrupt or fake policemen. Easy to arrange.

Just one thing still puzzled her in the end: if he was just after the contents of the safe, Keyes could have simply sent an army into Varga's house. Luring in the BKA was extremely risky.

Then she remembered what Holm had said: *He needs it as a stimulant, it's his drug.* And it was the perfect opportunity for Keyes to disappear into thin air, to settle down in a different city on a different continent, to change his persona once again.

That same night, he had Varga liquidated. Probably by his own bodyguards, everybody has his price. They got rid of the body, and Keyes bagged the Cranach as a bonus.

Jet fighters tear past above the car; the Moroccan king is flexing his muscles on the border with the despised Algeria. Aaron's pulse flies with them.

Back then in Avignon they saved Adaja.

It was right to do it.

And wrong.

If they hadn't, they would have caught Keyes.

Her father would still be alive.

Aaron can see herself standing on the terrace of the Gran Sasso as though it was yesterday. In the pool, children are shrieking and trying to splash the sun. The cross of St Peter's Basilica shimmers like a mirage. Keyes brushes a stubborn strand of hair off his forehead and she thinks he is going to kiss her.

Instead he asks: 'Would you die for me?'

Aaron was prepared to do that.

As with every other person whose life she had been entrusted with. She never asked herself whether the individual concerned was worth it. When you sign up at the Department, you also agree to the small print.

But when she fought her way through the hotel with Leon Keyes it was more than that. Because of that smile. That strand of hair. That hand between her legs.

That's why I can't bring myself to call him the Broker.

There haven't been many men in Aaron's life. She is thirty-six and has only had four relationships. She likes sex; everything else is complicated because she is complicated. The last person she slept with was Daniel, in the rehab clinic. He had a glaucoma and ten years left before he would go completely blind; he could still soak up the world. She envied him for it.

Night after night, they listed all the nostalgic images they had left.

He was a beautiful person, she didn't need eyes to see that. It was as if she had never slept with a man before. Afterwards they lay listening to the stillness. Daniel said: 'The longer we're blind, the more we will see.' Weeks later, they went their separate ways, he was moving to Canada to live with his brother. When they hugged she picked up a faint scent of tree resin.

Aaron thought of Keyes then.

Not for the first time.

One evening, years after Rome, she was fed up with cold ravioli from the tin and decided to have a civilized meal in the small Alsatian restaurant on Winterfeldplatz. Between escargots and coq au vin, she wondered what it would be like to sit there with him. She could picture him sitting opposite, with his effortless charm. *How was your day, darling? Oh, nothing special, I doctored some accounts – what about you? Same old here too. I was in a shoot-out, the usual stuff.* And they would have drunk red wine and water from crystal glasses with clinking ice cubes.

That's what sun visors are for.

Only they wouldn't have been talking about accounts. *How was your day, darling? Ah, tons of work. I planned the death of a few thousand people, and now I could murder a steak.*

He must have known that Jörg Aaron was her father. From Vesper. It didn't bother him. Whatever fate it was that had brought the two of them together, he could have spared her father, out of respect for what Aaron had done in Rome.

But for Keyes he was just some man.

Some life, some money.

Would you die for me?

Yes, she would.

But not the way he imagined it back then.

'Killing is simple,' her father had said. 'But it doesn't come easy.'

This time he is wrong.

Pavlik turns off right and stops.

She taps her watch. 'Thirteenth of February. Friday. Seven p.m., sixteen minutes, one second.'

Pavlik and Aaron get out, Layla stays in the car with Luca.

'Where are we?' she asks.

'On a hill, five kilometres from the airfield.' He opens the boot and takes out the spotting scope. It can magnify objects up to a hundred and sixty times. Pavlik secures it to the tripod. 'Small town, around thirty thousand inhabitants. Beyond it there's nothing but desert, the airfield is in the middle of nowhere. It's just a runway. No buildings. Nobody around— Shit.'

'What?'

'That strip is damn short. I'm not sure if it will be enough for the jet.'

'I'm sure Guppy has checked it out,' Aaron comments.

'You know him. He likes to see how far things can be pushed.'

'How do they carry out the customs formalities without a building?'

'No idea. Hang on. I can see something. Camel herders. They're resting a short distance away from the manoeuvring area.'

'What do they look like?'

'At this distance, like camel herders.' He calls up Inan Demirci and switches to speaker phone. 'Are you on time?' he asks.

'Yes. How are things at your end?'

'All quiet here. Nobody can get within five kilometres of the airfield without showing in my sight. But the resolution isn't great. It's possible that there are men dug in somewhere.'

'We'll take a look on the approach, we'll do a loop.'

'Did Guppy say anything about the landing strip?'

'That it's too short,' Demirci replies.

'Wonderful.'

'The pilot knows. It's a hundred metres shy of what he needs. He says it depends on what the adjoining ground consists of. He'll decide at the last moment. If it's sand, we'll abort the landing.'

'How reassuring.'

'If necessary we'll divert to Fès. That would mean a seven-hour car journey for you.'

'I'm weeping tears of joy.'

'I'll pass you on to Mr Fricke.'

'Hey, did you know today is Friday the thirteenth?' asks Fricke.

'Yes, and I saw a black cat,' Aaron retorts.

'What radio frequency are you on?' Fricke asks.

'Nine hundred and fifty megahertz.'

'We'll tune in to you when we've touched ground.'

'What direction are you landing from?' Pavlik asks.

'Hang on.' A few seconds later he's back: 'We can land from either direction.'

'There are some Bedouin camping out two hundred metres west of the manoeuvring area. Check them out from above. It would be best if the pilot turns the machine at the opposite end.'

'Roger.'

'Who else have you got on board?' Pavlik asks.

'Kemper, Rogge, Nickel and Flemming.'

'OK, speak soon.' Pavlik puts the mobile away. He doesn't say anything.

She knows why.

Flemming.

Not because he's too big, too heavy, has too many muscles.

He spoke out against Aaron in the weights room. He has a problem with her. Will he give his all for her? That's what is troubling Pavlik. And her too, ever since Fricke told her yesterday.

Sometimes size does matter.

Fricke is a pragmatist. He took Flemming down a peg at the time, but that was something else. He likes mass, likes working with a sledgehammer.

'I don't like this,' Pavlik says. 'We're too far away and as inconspicuous as deer in a clearing. Three kilometres further on there's a water tower. It's better there.'

He puts the scope away again. After a short drive they are bumping over stones at a walking pace. Soft branches brush against the roof of the car; Pavlik is hiding the BMW under palm trees.

He's about to open the door.

'Wait,' she says.

Aaron concentrates.

Helicopter. Coming closer.

Pavlik should be able to hear it too by now.

'I'll take a look,' he mutters.

He opens the boot and gets out the binoculars. The helicopter flies over their position with a roar. It grows quieter. Sounds like distant gunfire. Falls silent.

Pavlik returns. 'Military. They're just out to tickle the Algerians. I'm going to climb up the tower and enjoy the view.'

'Can I come too?' Luca asks. 'I'm really good at climbing.'

'I don't think he would want you to,' says Layla.

Aaron can hear that she is in pain. Layla has barely moved the whole journey.

'Sure, that's cool with me,' says Pavlik. 'I can always make use of a climber.'

'May I, Mama?'

'Are you sure he won't bother you?'

'Come, Luca, we'll see who can get to the top first.'

'Do you need some Palladone?' Aaron asks when the other two have got out.

'I've already taken two.'

She senses that Layla is drifting off and leaves her in peace.

Outside, the desert wind whirls sand grains into her face. She shivers in the morning chill. Another fighter jet comes thundering towards them. She imagines it swooping down from the Atlas, drawing a line in the sky and disappearing in the glimmer above the Sahara.

She longs to let her gaze lose itself in the endless expanse, the world nothing but a shimmer, a wink of the prophet.

She can hear Pavlik and Luca up on the tower. 'Why have you brought the gun with you?'

'Because when I look through the sight, I can see all the way to the airfield.'

'That's very far. Then why are we whispering?'

'So that nobody knows that we're here.'

'The nasty men?'

'Yes.'

'Nothing can happen. Jenny is with us.'

'True. I guess you like her?' Pavlik asks.

'Yes, I always have. Why does your leg look so funny?'

'Give it a tap.'

'What's that?'

'It's similar to metal. Only harder. It's called carbon.'

'Are you a cyborg?'

'I might be. How come you know what a cyborg is?'

'From a film. Mama mustn't know.'

'It will stay our secret. I promise.'

Aaron smiles. Pavlik is good with boys.

The phone vibrates. Only Pavlik, Demirci, Guppy, the liaison officer, Reimer and Aaron herself know the number.

She answers. 'Yes?'

'Hello.'

Lissek.

'How—?'

'From Guppy. Am I disturbing you?'

'No.'

The connection has a slight echo, which means he is using an encrypted phone just like hers. She can hear the wind blowing; Lissek must be on his boat.

'Are you OK?' he asks.

'Yes.'

He waits.

Aaron takes a deep breath and recounts what has occurred

over the last three days. When she says that Leon Keyes is the Broker, Lissek growls: 'That's the craziest story I've ever heard. And utterly plausible.'

'He made us look like school kids in Rome.'

'You always meet twice.'

'Indeed,' she agrees.

He knows what her undertone is hinting at, but he doesn't respond to it. 'I knew Olaf Berg,' he mutters.

Aaron pricks up her ears.

'Way back, when I was still at the BKA. We were both undercover agents. He was a few years younger than me, we got on together. He was good. He meticulously weighed up every risk like a slice of tenderloin. Wolf rated him highly. The way he brought down Carlos says it all. The Jackal had holed up in the Sudan, he enjoyed the president's protection. The country is strictly Islamic. Nobody wanted to know that Carlos was having whores flown in and hosting parties that would have put Nero to shame. Berg flew there at the behest of Wolf and managed to get himself onto the guest list. He took photos and leaked them to the Iranian ambassador in Khartoum. Sudan was dependent on Iran for military support. The mullahs sorted it out; the Sudanese president had no choice but to extradite Carlos to France. That was world class, how Berg handled it. It's still part of the BKA syllabus today.'

'Definitely, but without mentioning his name; they no longer want to know about him.'

'Do you know why?' Lissek asks.

Aaron thinks of Pavlik's last phone call with Demirci. She had only told him what Jansen's real name was and that he used to work for the BKA. She's sure Palmer wouldn't have come out with that of his own free will. But Demirci had been tight-lipped about it.

'No – you?' she replies.

'Must have been something that happened after my time at the BKA. I would never argue with Wolf over which one of us has more skeletons in the closet.'

Aaron laughs quietly.

'When is the jet landing?' Lissek wants to know.

The digital voice says: 'Thirteenth of February. Friday. Seven a.m., fifty minutes, nine seconds.'

'In ten minutes.'

'Who's on board?'

'Fricke, Kemper, Rogge, Nickel and Flemming,' she replies.

'Will they be going to the hill farm with you?'

'Probably.'

'Good choice. Especially Nickel. He can cook.'

'I'm not so sure about Flemming.'

'Did I ever make a bad personnel decision?'

Aaron doesn't reply.

Lissek says: 'I've never found the courage to ask you to forgive me for sending you and Kvist to Barcelona. I don't think about it every day. But sometimes. Then Conny gives me a hug.'

Aaron's silence continues.

'I'll give you some free advice. If you get close enough to the bastard, don't ask him why he had your father murdered or what kind of a person he is or some other moral shite. You wouldn't get an answer that's big enough to fill the giant hole in your heart. And you don't need to let him suffer to make yourself feel better. The man has nine lives. Make it simple and make it fast.'

He puts the phone down.

Aaron stands motionless for a moment. If she kicks the bucket here in this place, these will be fantastic last words from Lissek.

Make it simple and make it fast.

But Erfoud can't possibly be the end.

Because she is going to kill Leon Keyes.

She clicks her tongue, locates the water tower and feels her way towards it. After twenty-two steps she touches stone. She walks along it carefully, until her toes bump against the stone steps that wind up around the wall. She climbs up. The wind has settled to rest in the nowhere.

When she is at the top, Luca whispers: 'We're here.'

She walks towards the voice, and suddenly stops. She can see Luca's hand. He's waving. It's more than a notion, more than a shadow. Aaron can truly *see* the hand. It is almost transparent, as if it were made of glass.

She staggers closer.

There's Luca's face.

A dull black mop of curls, with two button eyes.

'Come on,' he says.

Her breath is in tangles.

'Luca, please go back down to your mother,' Pavlik mutters. He is talking away from Aaron, staring into the sight of the sniper rifle and doesn't notice what's going on with her.

'OK.' The boy runs towards Aaron.

But she doesn't see him any clearer. With every metre he becomes more blurred, until she only senses him, although he is standing right in front of her.

He reaches for her hand and whispers: 'I know that you can see me. But I won't tell anyone.'

Then he's gone.

Aaron lurches like driftwood in a rough sea.

Pavlik says: 'There's a dust cloud approaching from town. Four cars. They're heading towards the airfield. It's not the customs people.'

She hears a plane.

'Is that the jet?'

'Yes. They're on the approach.'

Aaron's legs go weak. She taps her foot against a large stone and sits down. The sun is in her face. She's staring straight at it. Yellow explodes in her iris. She closes her eyes, opens them again and looks over at Pavlik.

He is just a blur in the midst of a blinding whiteness.

'They're looping round. The cars are stopping by the landing strip. Police cars, or at least they're supposed to look like police cars. Eight men are getting out. Uniforms, submachine guns. — The plane is coming in to land. Damn, I hope the strip is long enough. —They're touching down. Too fast, far too fast. That's never going to work. Hundred metres – fifty – end of field. Jeez, pull that machine back up. —Son of a bitch.'

'What?' Aaron urges.

'He's actually managing to bring the jet to a halt.'

In her earbud, Fricke pipes up: 'Life is no picnic, but for now it continues.'

She composes herself. 'I've never been so glad to hear your filthy voice.'

'No thanks, done that already.'

'Meaning?'

'I'm talking to Nickel, he's handing out sick bags,' Fricke explains.

'What did it look like from above?' Pavlik asks.

'Seems they really are Bedouin. They've got a load of supplies and hose pipes with them, they've come from the desert. That leaves the eight guys.'

'I'll sort that out.' Demirci.

'Alone? Not a good idea,' Fricke objects.

'Mr Rogge and you will accompany me. Take off your kit. We're on Moroccan territory and we don't want to provoke them. A concealed gun is enough.'

'Sounds like death by carelessness.'

'Mr Fricke, this isn't a debating club.'

'Relax, Zebedee,' Pavlik chips in. 'I've got them in my sight. If they twitch, I'll send them a greeting.'

The engines of the jet wail, the pilot is turning the machine.

Demirci is back. 'Perhaps they really are policemen. Perhaps they're the Broker's men. Makes no difference to us. Either way, he's bought them. Mr Nickel, Mr Flemming, Mr Kemper: if Mr Pavlik shoots, that's a go for you.'

Pavlik switches his microphone off, so only Aaron can hear him. 'She's leaving the plane with Fricke and Rogge. The guys haven't moved an inch, they're still standing by the cars.'

The adrenalin is triggering a breathing reflex in Aaron. She instinctively takes in too much oxygen, which she isn't exhaling back out. She knows that her calcium level is rapidly falling right now and that this is causing her stress. Aaron slows her breathing to just four inhalations per minute and lowers her shoulders when she exhales. She can feel herself growing calmer.

Fricke announces: 'Rogge and I will take the four on the left. The others are yours.'

'Contact,' Pavlik says to Aaron.

Demirci's microphone conveys the conversation clear as a bell. She speaks in French. 'Good morning.'

'Good morning, Madame. What's the reason for your journey to the Kingdom of Morocco?'

The man sounds relaxed.

'A patient transport.'

'Who is the patient?'

'A Canadian citizen. She is accompanied by her young son and two medical attendants.'

'What are the names of these attendants?'

'Malin and Erik Jøndal, Norwegian nationals.'

'Where are they? I don't see them anywhere.'

'And I see that you're not from customs.'

'We want to inspect your passengers.'

'Why?'

'Because we have reason to believe that these persons are wanted by the police. If this turns out to be the case, we'll take them into custody.'

'You'll do no such thing,' Demirci replies stridently. 'And in any case, no customs formalities are required.'

He almost sounds amused. 'Is that so?'

'Yes. It would greatly displease your Interior Minister. I assume you know the voice of your employer?'

Aaron holds her breath.

'She's getting out her phone,' Pavlik whispers.

'Good morning, Minister. I'm standing here with eight of your officers. If you'll permit, I shall pass the phone over.'

The policeman talks in Arabic. He is interrupted after just a few words. There are a few seconds of silence. Then his tone suggests that he is standing at attention.

Demirci says: 'I think that's cleared that up. You will leave us alone now. Have a nice day.'

'You don't give me any orders.'

'Do I need to trouble the Minister again?'

The men deliberate in Arabic.

Car doors are slammed.

'Honestly,' Pavlik comments, 'that woman could beat Lissek in a pissing contest.'

'How long will it take you?' Demirci asks.

Pavlik switches his microphone back on. 'Five minutes.'

He walks over to Aaron and takes her by the arm. She feels her way down the stairs and gets in the car with him.

He drives off.

'Are we going to fly to Germany now?' Luca asks.

Aaron turns round to him and smiles. 'Yes.'

She feels Layla's shaky hand on her shoulder.

'Thank you.'

32

The last traces of adrenalin only drain away when they are up in the air. Aaron is sitting with Demirci and Pavlik in the separate cabin at the rear. At the front, Layla is being cared for by the doctor and the nurse. Fricke is distracting Luca.

As soon as they came aboard, he took him aside and said: 'What do you reckon, shall we see if we can go in the cockpit? Perhaps the pilot will even let you have a go on the control stick.'

Aaron wishes she could have seen Luca's face. 'Really?'

'Of course. Between you and me, mate, he looks pretty tired. We'd better go and check on him.'

It is things like this that make her so fond of Fricke.

He surreptitiously slipped her the epilepsy drug and murmured: 'Best not read the information leaflet.'

Demirci is a silhouette in the seat opposite. Her outlines dissolve at the edges like white smoke.

'How did you wangle that?' Pavlik asks.

'As you'll remember, the BKA helped the Moroccans eliminate an ISIS cell. Well, the terrorists had been planning an attack on the king. In Agadir, where he was inaugurating a school. The Royal Palace was very grateful to Wiesbaden.'

Pavlik is surprised. 'And Palmer shares that kind of information with you?'

'He phoned the Moroccan Interior Minister.'

'Do I need to start liking him?'

'Sometimes it's love at second sight.'

'Don't go doing anything foolish.'

'Not as long as you're keeping an eye on me.' Demirci turns to Aaron. 'I need to tell you something concerning your father.'

'Yes?' she immediately asks.

'On the outward flight I got a chance to read the dossier that the GSG 9 sent over on my request. It contains a list of the operations your father was involved in during the years leading up to his death.'

Aaron's palms feel sweaty.

'Holm left you a final message. Lubichowo. The village isn't in Russia, it's in Poland, south of Gdansk. The leader of an arms smuggling ring lived there. His villa was a fortress, guarded by a dozen men. The Federal Police found out about it. They tipped off their Polish colleagues, who in turn asked for strategic assistance. The decision was made to send the GSG 9.'

'Was my father among them?'

'Yes.'

'When exactly was that?'

'A month before you lost your sight.'

'Was anyone killed?'

'Four. The leader, his wife and two of his men.'

'Do you have any further information about this Pole?'

'No, the dossier only contains the key data. But his wife came from Ireland. Like Leon Keyes.'

'She could have been his lover,' Pavlik mutters.

Aaron shakes her head. 'Keyes wouldn't share a woman with another man. Perhaps she was his sister. Or a close friend. In any case, it was something personal.'

They lapse into silence.

Aaron had thought that the knowledge of why her father had to die would trigger something inside her.

No.

There's nothing that can make sense of his death.

Someone knocks on the cabin door. 'Yes, come in,' says Demirci.

A stranger's voice. 'She's dehydrated. We're giving her infusions and morphine, that's all we can do for the moment.'

'How advanced is the cancer?'

'I'm not a specialist.'

'Will we need an ambulance in Munich?' Demirci wants to know.

'She has to stay lying down.'

'We have an armoured transporter waiting. I would feel a lot happier if we could use that.'

'We could slide a stretcher into it.'

'Good.'

The doctor withdraws.

'Where are you taking her?' Aaron asks.

'There's a clinic in Murnau with an oncology department. We've already informed them.'

'Why not Munich? The Rechts der Isar Hospital.'

'That's an enormous institution in the middle of the city; it would be a nightmare to protect her there. From Murnau it's only thirty kilometres to the hill farm. If we're lucky the doctors will allow us to take her there. If not, a Special Enforcement Commando of the police will take care of the clinic. The kindest thing would be to leave the boy with his mother. But it would make everything much more difficult. The safe house is the best solution for the child and for you.'

'You want to incarcerate me?'

'I want to save your life. Don't tell me that you don't know the difference.'

'Aaron, she's right,' Pavlik placates her. 'Keyes can't get to you up there. Six men are enough for the hill farm.'

'Eight. Nieser, Peschel and Mertsch are in Munich. They will reinforce the team,' says Demirci.

'My arithmetic makes that nine, including me,' Pavlik corrects her.

'You can forget that. Please go to the front now and have your wound looked at properly. You're going to come to Berlin and have fourteen days off.'

'That's not necessary. I'm fit.'

'No, you're not. End of discussion.'

The temperature in the cabin suddenly drops to below freezing. Pavlik lays his hand on Aaron's. They both know that Demirci wants to separate them so that she can have better control over Aaron.

'Have you spoken to Lissek, Ms Aaron?'

'Why?'

'Let me guess what he said. *Don't give the bastard a chance? Wipe him out? Finish him off?* Have you asked yourself why? I'll help you out: because Lissek knows you. He thinks it would be pointless to try to dissuade you. You're unconditional in your determination, more so than anyone I've ever come across. That's what makes you unique. It's your greatest strength and your greatest weakness. I understand that you hate Keyes. Just to be clear: I'm not denying you your revenge on moral grounds. On the contrary. It would be your right, and even leaving aside the death of your father, this man deserves to die a thousand times over. But I won't allow you to destroy your life and Ulf Pavlik's on top. He's your friend. You owe him a lot. Do the right thing. I would be very disappointed in you if you didn't.'

Aaron has no doubt that Pavlik is prepared to quit, to sacrifice everything for her. But she pre-empts him. 'I wouldn't have wanted anyone else with me in Morocco. But now it's good. Go home. I'll interrogate Layla; if she knows more, she'll tell me. Keyes isn't going to give us the slip. Sometimes one has to be patient. One day I'll be sitting in a courtroom and hear the verdict. Death isn't always the worst punishment. I speak from experience.'

Silence.

Does Demirci believe me?

Nothing more is said.

33

They must be over France by now. Avignon might be right below them. The city of retribution, the city of fear, the city of failure. Aaron is so tired. She plunges into sleep as if into unconsciousness.

In the blackness she hears a gentle squeaking. When she opens her eyes she sees an empty cradle. It is hot. She is in a desert. The ground is rocking. Aaron lifts her head and senses an enormous face far above her. Suddenly she knows that she is tiny and is standing on the outstretched palm of the devil.

'Look,' the devil whispers.

She stares at the horizon. A man materializes out of nothing. He walks towards her, emerging from the glowing heat as if he was stepping out of a mirror.

It's Leon Keyes.

The devil lowers his hand and lets him join Aaron.

'What a beautiful boy,' says her father's killer.

She becomes aware that Luca is sleeping in the cradle. He is lightly covered by a child's drawing, a ship with three funnels. His freckles are made of gold dust.

Keyes gives a sad smile. 'I once glimpsed a life that I would never have. In Varga's garden, when you came up with that story about the sun visor and rested your head against my shoulder. You said: "That was the most romantic thing that any man has ever done for me." In that moment I imagined that we could be together. In a place where I was a different person and you were different too. I imagined us perhaps having a little boy like that. It was very tempting. When we stood in front of the Lucas Cranach, I immediately knew that I wanted the painting. But I wanted you no less. How often in these past ten years have you thought of *me*, of Leon Keyes, the man with the cool lips?'

'That's not your real name. Holm used it as a clue because he read in my diary that I knew you under that name.'

'Oh, names. I can call myself whatever I want, but I'm always the same.'

They step out of the paining and contemplate its perfect beauty.

'I looked at the copy in the Vatican,' he says. 'It was incredible to know where the original is hanging.'

'In a cellar or a bunker?' she scoffs. 'Who can you share it with? What a miserable life.'

'You're mistaken. I enjoy sharing things.'

The painting grows hazy. They are sitting in a garden, alone, drinking wine and mineral water from crystal glasses.

'Do you believe in destiny?' he asks. 'Of course you do. I don't. Yet it's curious that our paths have crossed here. Last year, Ilja Nikulin stole two billion dollars from me, and ten years from now you'll fly to Marrakech, to steal them from me again.'

'I don't care about the money. But how would someone as corrupt as you be able to understand that? Someone who has sent thousands of people to their death. For profit.'

'You would be surprised to know how well I sleep. Besides, I share Racine's view: "Without money honour is merely a disease."' He picks up her shoes. 'Varga and I didn't talk about shoes. You wore these just for me; you should never wear any others.'

The house flickers like a translucent hologram. Her gaze passes through it. Behind the Circus Maximus, the Palatine glows in the evening light as if coated in red Japanese lacquer.

'It must be very enjoyable for you to see in your dreams,' he says. 'What's it like when you wake up? Does it feel like you can hardly wait to go back to sleep again?'

'I'm particularly enjoying this one. Looking into your eyes once more, knowing what a miserable death you'll die. If it's any consolation, you'll be the richest man in the cemetery.'

A rainbow stretches out over the garden and ends on Aaron's shoulder. It is made up of countless dragonflies. She is startled and tries to chase them away. But they won't leave off.

Keyes sips on his wine, completely relaxed. 'Your father tagged you. I can find you anywhere.'

Aaron hears a rustling. Luca is sitting in the grass. He is making a paper hat, completely absorbed in his task.

'Didn't I choose a lovely name?' Keyes asks.

Fear takes hold of Aaron's every fibre.

'He's the spitting image of his father, apart from the black hair. Berg was incredibly proud of him, he was always showing me photos. It sometimes made me think of you and me.'

'Have you been to Marrakech?' she asks.

'Of course. I was there until yesterday, but you stood me up.'

'And before? Did you ever meet Layla?'

'No. Berg didn't want that. He was afraid to show her his world. Perhaps he was also afraid of me. She's a beautiful woman. I might have liked her.'

'Layla wouldn't have been unfaithful to him.'

Music is playing in the house.

'Something in your smile was so exciting.

'Something in my heart told me I must have you.'

Keyes runs a finger along the edge of the wine glass and produces a high singing tone. 'Berg was very efficient, utterly dedicated to his work. He was perhaps the only person I ever trusted. But if I had wanted to take Layla for myself, I would have wiped him out with my little finger.'

'Well, you did. With the ice pick, in the souks.'

'There's no such thing as limitless trust.'

Aaron lights a cigarette. She is sitting in the James Dean Porsche with Keyes and christens the ashtray.

He smiles nonchalantly. 'That was always missing.'

They are driving through the night. Keyes only has one hand on the wheel, as if he was just out for a jaunt. Someone has sprayed onto a wall: *Desire is a dark house, uninhabited from the beginning.*

He notices her staring at his Oxford signet ring. 'Pretty, isn't it? It isn't real.'

'How carefree you are,' she says. 'Yet when I kill you it will be quick as a flash.'

'Who are you trying to kid? You hate me so much that you'll want to make me suffer. How many lethal moves have you mastered? How cruelly could you let me die?'

'You can't even begin to imagine.'

'Didn't you vow to your master that you would only use those techniques for self-defence?'

'For you I'll break my oath.'

'Perhaps you're also toying with the idea of gouging my eyes out to blind me. Wouldn't that be a compelling punishment? You know all about everlasting darkness.'

'You talk in the same contrived manner as Holm did,' she says dismissively.

'Are you surprised? You haven't decided yet who you hate the most: the man who blinded you, or the one who had your father killed. It's *your* dream. I'm exactly what you make me.'

'And how much do you hate *me*?' she asks.

'It's not like that for me. On the contrary. The two billion did hurt back then. I had to start from scratch again. Varga's safe was my start-up capital. It could have gone wrong. It all depended on the right number combination. You were impressive. It was damned clever of you to use the dates of St Anthony. That's what I love about gambling: there's always at least one unknown. That was you. You got me back into business.'

They are driving across the Ponte Sant'Angelo, towards the castle. It is dark, Aaron can barely see it. She hears an operatic aria she doesn't know.

They're in the hotel, walking to the lift. Drums are beating. A fortune teller is laying cards in the lobby. She looks up and considers Aaron with a sad look.

In the lift, Keyes smells so strongly of pine resin that she feels sick. 'Don't you like me?' he asks. 'Do you know what Dalí did before his first date with Gala? He rubbed a mixture of lavender, fish glue and goat droppings into his armpits and stunk like a billy goat. Gala embraced him and said: "My darling boy, we will never be apart again."' His glacier-grey eyes are playing with her. 'You were so happy. Clutching the bag with the phone close to you. Angels were dancing in your eyes. I was almost sorry to have to take it from you.'

Will I get my life back?

Only now does she understand what he had meant by that.

He brushes a stubborn strand of hair off his forehead. 'When we kissed – that was wonderful, wasn't it? And yet it was a lie. Only when we're in pain do we show what we're truly made of.'

The lift door opens and they step out into the hotel corridor.

Two-Holster and Green-Jacket are frozen in motion. Droplets of spit float in front of their wide-open mouths, bullets sit motionless in mid-air. Keyes takes one of the projectiles between his fingers, then lets it drop.

He opens the door to the stairwell. Below she sees Dog-Collar and White-Brow, a still life of icy precision. Their bullets are rotating, dabbing glittery dots of light onto the walls. Aaron and Keyes walk through this cabinet of curiosities.

'How perfectly you acted out your terror,' she says.

'Thank you. Beside you, it was easy.'

She looks up. Two-Holster is poised by the banister. Muzzle flash protrudes from the barrel of his Ruger like cooled lava.

'One of the best,' says Keyes regretfully. 'Not as good as Vesper of course. And Vesper wasn't half as good as you. There's always someone who is faster, harder, better. Even for you.'

They're in the basement passageway. A foam-covered body lies on the ground. Sinatra sings. The splinters of the fire extinguisher buzz through Aaron.

Keyes opens the door to the underground car park and makes an inviting gesture.

She doesn't move.

'I'm not going to give you your money,' she says.

'Oh, but you will. Because you'll have to decide whether the little boy you like so much stays alive or has to die because of you.'

34

The snow is falling thick and sticky as candy floss from clouds that are slave to the wind.

It is the wind of mercilessness. The wind of deadly dares, born from bitterness and anger, grown mighty over the mountains of hate. A wind that knows no forgiveness.

At Munich airport two BMW 7 Series and an armoured Ford Transit park in front of the Gulfstream. Eight men have taken position. Layla's stretcher is loaded into the transporter; Fricke lifts Luca in too.

Demirci watches as Aaron and Pavlik hug each other. She can only guess what the two of them have been through in Morocco. They have cheated death together. She has never experienced a friendship like that.

Before Aaron climbs into the transporter she whispers something into Pavlik's ear. She probably wants to make it easier for him. Does he believe what she said in the plane?

Not for a second.

Just like Demirci.

She has instructed Kemper, Rogge and Mertsch to prevent Aaron from leaving the hill farm alone at all costs. Demirci chose the three carefully. They only joined the Department after Aaron lost her sight and aren't as close to her as those who know her from the old days.

Yet she still had to repeat the order, before the men silently nodded. Reluctance was written across their faces. It was as if she had asked them to betray Aaron. They barely know her beyond the stories that are told about her. But from the day you are appointed to the Department you are a part of the team. You don't need a degree to understand that.

Demirci has no illusions: if it comes to it, she's not sure how much weight her order will carry. She had thought about asking Pavlik to talk to the men, but it wasn't really an option. It would have undermined her authority, and she would have made herself look small in front of Pavlik.

Pride is often stupid. Losing it is worse.

Her mobile vibrates. The display reads 'Svoboda'.

Demirci moves away a few steps and answers. 'Yes.'

'Didn't we have an appointment?' sniffs the Senator of the Interior.

'Oh. I cancelled it yesterday afternoon. Weren't you informed?'

'I didn't have much notice,' he whines.

'I'm sorry. I can't speak for your secretary.'

'What was more important?'

'Something private. I'm at Hamburg airport.'

'I see, I see. Private.'

Demirci raises her voice a nuance. 'Mr Svoboda, it's not your place to comment on my private life. Nor do I comment on yours.'

'What are you trying to say?' he snaps.

You know what. Six months ago you stuck your father into a cheap care home. The tabloids had a field day with it.

Senator of the Interior foists off own father.

'We should leave it at that,' she replies icily.

He huffs. 'How are things looking in Islamabad?'

'No news.'

'You have five men there. Are you going to tell me that they've just been sat there picking their noses for the past week?'

'It isn't as agreeable and comfy out there as it is in our offices.'

'Come on now, there are indications that the liaison officer is selling internal information to the enemy. The source is reliable.' Svoboda's voice grows plump and smug. 'The Chancellor has personally enquired. Shall I tell her that unfortunately you have a private appointment?'

'Seeing as you mention this source: I still don't know who it is.'

'That's a matter of national security, the Chancellery has asked for it to be treated confidentially.'

'I'm at security level four. If there's another level above, it's news to me.'

'What do you think? How eagerly would Palmer push ahead with the investigation if it was about one of your men? I don't know on which occasion you stepped on his toes, but he certainly hasn't forgotten it.'

'I can separate the one from the other.'

'The liaison officer in Islamabad is a close confidante of his. Did you know that?' Svoboda asks slyly.

'Are you trying to suggest that the Commissioner of the BKA is in cahoots with the officer?'

'Islamabad is a big marketplace and trading this kind of information is extremely profitable.'

Demirci has to make an effort not to laugh. 'Palmer and I are in the same pay bracket. I don't think he's worried about old-age poverty.'

Svoboda ignores her tone. 'People are saying that his divorce cost him his much-loved holiday home in the Canaries – and quite a few other things besides.'

'That makes him a key suspect of course.'

'Ms Demirci, we're talking about espionage here, not driving without a licence. I would advise you to show significantly greater commitment. Your reluctance to sink your teeth into this opens you up to attack.'

'My teeth are just fine, thank you.'

'I don't appreciate being met with irony.'

'And I don't appreciate being met with veiled threats. I'm not a political official. I can't just be dismissed like the BKA Commissioner. I may have a duty to furnish you with information, but you're not my employer. That role is held by the Interior Ministers' Conference. Try there. See if you can get a majority to vote in favour of my dismissal. Until you do, leave me to do my work.'

She ends the call.

Was that wise?

No.

But it felt good.

Demirci is alone with Pavlik for the onward flight to Berlin. She works through some files, he skims through a magazine. At one point their eyes meet. Pavlik hides what he is thinking.

She closes the file. 'You must miss your family.'

He doesn't look up. 'Yes.'

'Are the twins still with their host family in England?'

'Yes.'

The article he is reading appears to be incredibly absorbing.

Demirci knows that silence can grow into a mountain too high to be conquered.

'Ms Aaron has told me what happened in Avignon.'

This time he does look at her.

'Would you have told me too?' she asks.

He hesitates before answering. 'Probably not.'

'Why?'

'If we had your full trust, you would never have doubted us. And if not, I'd see no point in telling you anyway.'

'What was I supposed to think?'

'That Makata was the butcher, not us.'

'You thought about killing him.'

'You accuse people on the basis of their thoughts?'

Demirci remains silent for some time. 'You're right. I'm sorry.'

'Already forgotten. We've known each other for three months. We screwed up at the beginning, then it went well, now we're having our first crisis. That's how all the best marriages start out.'

She smiles. 'So we won't be needing a divorce lawyer?'

'That depends.'

He is being serious. Her smile dies away.

'On what?' she asks.

Pavlik firmly returns her gaze. 'Sometimes I act as though I could just up and leave the Department one day. That isn't true. Because I have a family to look after? No. I could pocket a kiss-my-arse fee as a consultant somewhere. And it's not as though I'm old or tired. Well, OK, tired yes. But I'm still making headway. Earlier, when you said you were withdrawing me from the operation, all I thought about was what I'd lose if I refused. These lads mean a lot to me. I didn't want to rush into something that I would later regret. Now I've had time to think about it. It was a mistake to get back in the plane with you. I'm going to take the next flight back to Munich.'

'You want to chuck it all in?' she asks blankly.

'Erfoud was too easy. Keyes knew that was where we were heading, but he didn't really try to stop us. He's going to do it here, in Germany. And I'm going to be there. Throw me out, if you think it's what you need to do. I'll camp out by the hill farm. I'm a sniper. I can settle down in a snow pit for two weeks and feel perfectly at home.'

'Mr Pavlik, I have eight men in that house. It's more secure than the Bank of England.'

'That's exactly what Bas Makata will have claimed about his estate on the Île de la Barthelasse. I assume Aaron told you that Keyes and Berg didn't turn up because they had the property under surveillance.'

'And?'

'There's another explanation.'

That's what Demirci has been thinking since her phone call with Aaron. What she took with her as she sank into a restless slumber. And it was the first thing she thought of when the alarm clock jolted her awake again at four.

'The operation was betrayed,' she says.

'Yes.'

'Who knew about it?'

'Us five. Lissek. Helmchen. Guppy. The Public Prosecutor and Palmer.'

'Why did Lissek bring Palmer into the loop?'

'He had the BKA to thank for the Marseilles connection. He wanted to let Palmer have a share of the classified information; it helps with bridge building.'

'Surely Lissek looked into it when you came back from Avignon.'

'No. His mantra was: once a poison chest has been closed, you should never open it again. But he did ask Palmer whether he had confided in anyone.'

Demirci's mouth is dryer than the Sahara. 'And did he?'

'Just one person. He was a state secretary at the Federal Ministry of the Interior at the time.'

'Svoboda,' she whispers.

'Yes.'

The fasten seat belt signs are flashing, they're coming in to land.

'He knows every one of our safe houses,' says Pavlik. 'And

Keyes will have no trouble in finding out that we had a stopover in Munich.'

Demirci presses the button of the intercom that connects her with the pilot. 'There's been a change of plan: I'm getting out in Berlin, Mr Pavlik will be flying back to Munich with you.'

'Understood. But we need to refuel.'

'Make sure that happens quickly.'

'Roger.'

'Thank you,' says Pavlik.

She looks out the window. The jet is descending into the blanket of clouds. Somewhere below, there are snowy fields, dense forests and frozen rivers. Some things one knows without seeing them.

Demirci directs her gaze at Pavlik. 'What I said about revenge still stands.'

'I'll do my best.'

'But not because you think I'm right.'

'No. If this was about my wife or my kids or Aaron, I would do exactly the same, any time.'

'Then why are you helping me?'

'To take revenge means to dig two graves.'

No matter how hard she tries, Aaron can't block out that smell. Whenever she's in a hospital she thinks of Barcelona, of the three weeks that she lay there, the nights without mornings, a thousand strangers' lives, of Matteo Varga's son, who looked at her with sad eyes and disappeared through the wall. Now she is sitting next to a different little boy. His hand crawls into hers. For two hours they have been waiting for the results of Layla's examinations.

She hears a phone ring, male whispering, a giggle, a lift. She took the endothelin blocker a little while ago. When she was fleeing through the souks of Marrakech there was so much adrenalin in her that she could have powered a village with the energy coursing through her body. When she was running to Layla's villa in the Palmeraie, it was a small town. And what awaits her today?

An adrenalin overkill.

Her cortex will turn into a battleground, and without the drug it would end up littered with dead receptor cells.

But the drug is turning her thoughts to mush. She feels dizzy and hot, she has a headache. Her teeth are grinding and there's nothing she can do about it. She recognizes this from addicts.

As much as she tries, she can't remember the dream she had in the plane. She knows that it was about Keyes. And Luca. But it's as if the dream had been a sculpture made of ice, which has burst into a million shards under the blows of a hammer.

A paper hat is burning in the fire. Dalí is kneeling naked in front of Gala. Red high-heeled shoes on the Palatine Hill. Freckles like gold dust. A fortune teller is laying cards in Varga's garden, and on each one there is a dragonfly. On a wall, someone wrote: *Desire is a dark house, uninhabited from the beginning.* A Porsche speeds through the desert towards a rainbow.

Keyes knows where we are.

He is very close.

'Ms Aaron?'

She stands up.

The doctor offers her his arm. 'Please follow me.'

She crouches down. Luca's face is a faint mist, like vapour on a glass pane.

'I'll be right back, OK?'

'OK.'

Aaron is led into a room and sits down on the chair that the doctor places behind her.

He sits down opposite her. His silhouette oscillates like a large jellyfish. White tentacles grab at something. 'Unfortunately I don't have good news. The urea values are catastrophic. I don't see any possibility of the kidney functioning again.'

'But she has two.'

The tentacles bounce up and down; Aaron presumes he is making a regretful gesture. 'The area is so badly afflicted that neither an operation nor radiation will help.'

She feels numb. 'You mean she's going to die?'

'You can get a second opinion of course.'

'I'm asking for yours.'

'Apart from pain management there's nothing we can do for her.'

'How long?'

'It could happen very fast.'

'Does she know?'

'Yes.'

'How did she take it?'

'Quietly.'

'Can I talk to her?'

'Not at the moment. We've sedated her.'

The doctor leads her back to Luca. She feels for the bench and sits down next to him. She takes his hand, chokes on the words. Luca doesn't speak. After an eternity she manages to say: 'We will visit her tomorrow.'

Aaron feels him tremble and lays her arm around him.

Minutes pass this way.

Fricke comes over. 'Does she need to stay here?'

'Yes. Inform the police, two of the men will need to wait until they come. The others will drive up to the hill farm with us.'

He walks off.

'Fricke?'

'All ears.'

'I want you with us.'

'Ain't got anything better lined up.'

Luca is still silent. 'It's nice there,' she says. 'It's high up in the mountains. You can almost see as far as Italy.'

Silence.

Aaron stands up. 'Come now.'

'First I want to see my mama.'

'She's sleeping now.'

'But I have to say goodbye to her.'

For minutes she sits motionless while she waits.

Then she says in the direction of the men: 'I want to smoke a cigarette. Where's the nearest exit?'

'I'll come with you.'

Flemming.

'It's OK if you just tell me where it is.'

'We have orders not to leave you alone.'

She stands up and hooks her arm into his. Aaron has to lift her arm to do this. He's a giant, she can feel his mass. He separates the air like a ship's bow separates the water.

A door seal snaps open, then she's standing in the snow. She lights a cigarette and holds the pack out for Flemming.

'I've given up,' he says.

'No vices?'

'Coffee.'

'Well, you're a wild one.'

'So are you, according to what I've heard.'

'What do you have against me – apart from that I'm blind?'

'You had to link arms with me. Question answered.'

She directs her eyes at his. 'Have you always been an arrogant prick, or only since Afghanistan?'

'It's a natural talent of mine.'

'I bet you have lots of friends.'

'What for? I'm a solo entertainer.'

Her phone vibrates.

Probably Pavlik. He wants to know about Layla.

'Leave me alone a minute.'

'Orders. Remember?'

'There's a glass door behind us. You can keep an eye on me.'

She doesn't know this. She just guessed it. But she can tell he's baffled.

The phone vibrates again.

She hears Flemming go. The door seal snaps again.

Aaron pulls the phone out of her jeans.

'Yes?'

35

The voice reverberates in her head like a gunshot.

'Hello, darling,' says her father's killer.

Aaron is dumbstruck.

'You're wondering how it's possible that I have this number, even though I didn't write it onto a sun visor. Well, as Berg said in his first letter to Layla: I have ways and means. I'll make you a fair offer: you can ask me anything you like, you'll get a reply to each of your questions. And when you're finished I will ask you something.'

Her voice sounds like a wire brush on rusty metal. 'Why did you have my father killed?'

'Lubichowo.'

'Who was the woman who was shot dead by the GSG 9? Your sister?'

'Why does it always have to be family? Varga was the same.'

'Did you know her from Dublin?'

Keyes laughs. 'You don't seriously think that I'm from Dublin. I'm not even Irish. The town I come from wasn't the home of great poets, it doesn't have a glorious history. Growing up there meant growing up with coal dust, fatty food and wild dogs. At eighteen I was gone. Of those I left behind only one meant anything to me, a friend from my childhood days. He was the son of Polish immigrants. Later, he married his first love. He moved back to his parents' homeland with her and became successful in the weapons trade. From time to time we met up and talked about the old days. It was nice. When I found out what had happened in Lubichowo I didn't hesitate for a second. The news of your father's death concerned me less than a share price fluctuation of half a per cent.'

'If you were engulfed in flames, a metre away from me, I wouldn't lift a finger to help you.'

'That casts a shadow on our relationship.'

'I'd sooner throw myself at Kim Jong-un.'

'You and me. Did you never think about it? I did. And you're very ungrateful. In Rome, I let you live.'

'Only so I could testify that you'd been killed.'

'Not at all, for something like that I just bribe a few policemen,' he says with that slight rasp in his voice that she once found so sexy. 'I did it because our kiss meant something to me. Because I was touched by your courage. Because you would have died for me.'

'How did you establish contact with Varga?'

'The blonde chick, Varga's table decoration that evening, was a recent acquisition. Her predecessor had worked for me. She was an exceptionally capable woman. It was a breeze for her to make Varga drool at a party and give him a bit of pleasure for a time. While he saw her as a bimbo who thought Titian was some type of fashionista, she spied on him and found out that he was planning to enter the German gas trade. I suggested to him that I might be of use in that respect. He promised me two million and assumed I would be overjoyed.'

'Why didn't *she* open the safe for you?'

'She tried to. Varga caught her red-handed. If you'd seen her corpse, you'd have wondered whether it was male or female.'

'She didn't talk? Despite being tortured?'

'Nobody betrays me. She knew that it wouldn't save her, and that it would spell the death sentence for her brother and her parents.'

Aaron's heartbeat is nudging her thoughts along in slow motion. 'The bomb that killed Varga's son, that was you,' she whispers. 'What harm had that boy done you?'

'The night I died in Rome, Varga left for his country estate in Tuscany. The child was asleep in the car. The painting was in an escort vehicle; he couldn't bear to be parted from it. My men liquidated him and his bodyguards near Montepulciano. They let his son live. They said that he wasn't a danger, that he couldn't identify any of them. I pondered this for days. I allowed the boy to be taken to Varga's brother. But in the end a child is as dangerous as a man.'

'Did I overlook something back then? Could I have known that you're alive?'

'Oh yes. *Tosca*. I especially asked the chauffeur to make the detour so I could tell you about it. That was fun, although not without risk. Your cover story was helpful, as it said that you don't like operas. I correctly assumed that this was true. Otherwise you would have found out much sooner. Baron Scarpia wants Tosca to sleep with him. In return he promises Tosca that the execution of her lover Cavaradossi will only be feigned. She agrees. But Scarpia lied, Cavaradossi is shot. With us it was the other way round. The execution was staged, and the man for whom you were prepared to die is still alive. It was obvious really.'

'What did you want Bas Makata for?' she asks.

'Respect. You're fast.'

'What for?'

'He was exchangeable. There are many Makatas.'

'Were you in Avignon with Berg?'

'Did I stand you up there? Sorry. Mind you, I waited in vain in Marrakech. So we're even.'

'Were you there?' she asks again.

'No.'

'Why not?'

'I was advised against it.'

'By who?'

Keyes takes his time. 'A gentleman ought to keep his promises, but in this case I'll have to owe you the answer.'

'You wanted to ask me something too.'

'Yes. When do I get my money?'

'I'll pin the bank draft to your corpse.'

'What's the point of your revenge? You aren't Black Mamba and this isn't *Kill Bill*. Give me my billions and we'll leave it at that.'

'You're scared of me? That's wise,' she replies coldly. 'You sent ten killers into that hotel in Rome, ten into the souks, ten to Layla's villa. That's the kind of coward you are. But you'll come to realize that there aren't enough men in this world to protect you.'

'And how many are protecting *you*? A dozen? Two? Is that supposed to worry me? Believe me: I'm not as cowardly as you think. We'll face each other. We'll be a close as we were in the lift in Rome. You're of value to me, you have to transfer the money into an account of my choice. I can't afford to delegate that; two billion is too tempting.'

Keyes is silent for a long time.

Aaron hears him breathe as she glows in the snow.

He says: 'You know, darling, a forward transaction is nothing more than a bet on the value of an investment in the future. You accepted Holm's bequest. You were prepared to risk everything for the truth. You banked on winning. But now you're in the red. Sorry, in the end all positions must be closed.'

Keyes hangs up.

The phone falls from Aaron's numb hand and into the snow. She doesn't even notice. Her headache explodes. She doesn't hear the door opening.

Flemming says: 'We're going now.'

36

The armoured transporter, escorted by the two BMWs, makes its way along the rural road. Nickel is sitting in the back with Aaron and Luca. The boy hasn't said a word since he came back from seeing his mother. In a bend, he slides up against Aaron's arm. He stays, seeking closeness.

She is shaking and sweating. It's as though every thought is being pinned to the inside of her skull with a stapler. Everything around her is lurching.

'When someone is reborn – what's it like?' Luca whispers. 'Do they know who they were before?'

'I'll have to ask my papa,' she replies.

'How? Can you talk to him?'

Aaron claws her way from one word to the next.

'In my dreams, if I wish for it really hard.'

He thinks about this.

'What do you talk about?' he asks.

'I tell him that I love him.'

'Can he give you a kiss?'

'Yes, he does that very often. Even if I can't remember the dream anymore: I still feel his kiss when I wake up. Don't you sometimes have a tear on your cheek when you wake up in the morning?'

'Yes. Was that my papa?'

'Of course. And your mama can do that too.'

'She said that she will always be with me, even if I can't see her anymore. Is that the same, do you think?'

'That's exactly the same. When did she say that to you?'

'A little while ago, when she was so poorly.'

She squeezes Luca against her.

'But if she's reborn and she doesn't remember me and I don't know that it's her, then we won't recognize each other.'

'What about you and me? We met in our dreams and we didn't even know each other before,' Aaron whispers back. 'But we still found each other.'

He ponders. 'Who do you talk to when you're sad?'

'My very best friend.'

'What's her name?'

'Sandra.'

'You're my very best friend too.'

'Yes, I am.' Tears well up inside her.

'But sometimes not talking is nice too, isn't it?' he asks.

'Yes.'

What remains is Luca's silence. There is nothing she could say or do to console him. Her heartbeat is slowing down more and more. It feels to Aaron as though it takes hours to form each thought.

How confident Keyes was on the phone. How arrogant.

She didn't bother asking Fricke whether the number could be traced. Her father's killer would never make that kind of mistake.

The droning of the heavy transporter and the twelve-centimetre aramid armour could be reassuring. Not even a grenade or a mine would crack the vehicle. The rear door can only be opened from the inside. They have a separate ventilation system; even a gas attack would be futile.

Still, these things don't offer complete safety.

What if Keyes' men set up a roadblock? Their colleagues in the two BMWs would have to leave their cars and engage in a gunfight. If the enemy managed to eliminate them, Rogge in the driver's cab of the transporter would have no option but to look on while they smash the windscreen. There is a button in the passenger cabin that will paralyse the vehicle's electronics, so it can no longer be moved from the spot.

But that wouldn't really protect Aaron, Luca and Nickel.

It depends where the attack takes place.

The Teufelsbach hill farm lies on a high plateau that is scarred with crevasses. The nearest police station is in Mittenwald, an eternity away. They will soon be turning off the main road. The last stretch is a steep track through spruce forest. It would be ideal there. Aaron thinks about the thick snow falling from the sky, she can feel the transporter sliding on the icy wheel ruts. Even if Rogge sends off an emergency call before he is liquidated, it will be at least half an hour before any patrol cars can get here in these conditions. The local police would be no match for Keyes' men.

They could use welders to cut open the transporter, kill Nickel and disappear with Aaron and Luca. Even on top form, and sighted, she wouldn't have a chance against seven or eight men. And now? She'll be glad if she can even get out the van without help when they arrive.

But once they're at the hill farm Luca will be safe.

Aaron will escape once the drug has left her bloodstream. Tomorrow at the latest. Right in front of Keyes. She has to face him. She has been thinking about how she can disappear from the house ever since they left Munich. Demirci will have taken measures to prevent this.

She doesn't have control over Fricke, though. He will help Aaron.

Once she is in a room with Keyes, once she is facing him, she will find a way to kill him.

She knows her way around the hill farm. She spent two weeks there one summer, questioning an Iranian who had defected to the West with information on his country's nuclear programme. Aaron had enjoyed taking a cup of coffee out onto the terrace early in the mornings, to watch the mountains yawning out clouds. Dewdrops hung like bells from the branches of the firs. It was so quiet that she could hear the ravens hopping around in the grass; there are lots of ravens up there.

But when she thinks of the hill farm she sees herself knocking on the Iranian's door and remembers how he didn't open, and how his dangling feet cast a shadow on the sun-drenched parquet.

The farm sits on a six-hectare plot and is secured with a high electric fence. There's a retina scanner at the gate. The rear of the house sits directly above a rock face that falls away steeply. Twenty metres below is karst terrain on which only brambles grow. To reach it one has to abseil down with climbing gear.

Up until the sixties, farmers lived in the house. When the old couple died childless, the place stood empty for years. It was colonized by a nudist commune in the seventies, but they abandoned their project when the first hard winter struck. Next the German Alpine Association turned it into a self-catering lodge, but it remained unused for long spells. Eventually the brochure of a shrewd estate agent came into the hands of an Egyptian businessman. The Egyptian had the grandiose idea to open a hotel. After years of bitterly disappointing returns he gave up and the hill farm fell into disuse. In the mid-nineties, the Department snatched it up for a song.

Following the conversion, the house meets the highest security criteria. There are seven rooms. One serves as a common room, two as accommodation for the team, two are for 'guests' and one is for the interrogations.

The seventh is *under* the house.

Lissek had a shaft dug into the rock, twenty metres deep, with a four by four metre cavern at the bottom. The safe room. If the hill farm were to be attacked, the residents could barricade themselves in behind the thick steel door, or leave via a second exit at the foot of the rock face. That would give them a considerable headstart over the enemy. A kilometre further along, they'd be in the forest.

'What's the code for the safe room?' Aaron asks.

'Three-six-nine-two-four,' Nickel replies.

'Have they installed any new gimmicks in the last few years that I don't know about?'

'There's a new microwave.'

'I've heard you can cook.'

'Spaghetti, macaroni, fusilli and penne.'

'With sauce?'

'Am I Jamie Oliver?'

The transporter turns off. Last stretch.

'Hey, big lad,' says Nickel. 'If you're up for it, we can play a game of cards when we get there. But I have to warn you: the others are real charlatans, you have to watch them like a hawk.'

'What are charlatans?'

'They're not as bad as cheaters, but worse than tricksters.'

'OK. I know about cheating.'

Aaron counts the seconds until they are at the top.

Luca's hand is back in hers. 'Mama explained everything to me,' he whispers. 'I can go to a friend of hers, she lives in Italy. Or to one of my uncles.'

'And is that what you want to do?'

'The friend visited us once. She sounds like one of those saws you can make music on. She didn't talk to me. She was always painting her nails and doing fashion shows with Mama.'

'And the uncles?'

'I don't know. I've only seen them at Grandma's funeral. There was a funny smell in the house.'

Aaron feels such an overwhelming affection for Luca that she wants to say: "You can come and live with me, if your mama agrees to it."

But he beats her to it. 'I can't stay with you, because you still have to do something. And then you have to do something else. Don't be sad. I still like you.'

37

The gate opens. They drive into the garage. Nickel opens the transporter door and a gush of icy air flows towards Aaron.

'Flemming, take them into the house,' Fricke instructs. 'We'll take a look round the compound. Nickel, check the rock face. Rogge and Mertsch, western section. Kemper and I will take the east side.'

Luca takes Aaron's hand and leads her. She feels as if she is staggering over the planks of a ship in a force eight gale. She pictures the house, with its wood façade that hides the reinforced concrete; the shingle roof with the shooting slits for submachine guns; the balcony that conceals the arms depot underneath. Close by is the wayside shrine with the Madonna figure. Lissek decided to leave it standing. Aaron knows that a hundred metres ahead there is a small woodland at seven o'clock, and to the right of her is the rock face.

She sinks ankle-deep into the snow.

Her collarbone itches.

She stops. Listens.

'What's up?' asks Flemming.

She tries to figure it out. She can't quite put her finger on it. Then she knows: she can't hear any ravens.

Aaron whistles. Some branches rustle. A bird flies away.

One.

'Are there any tracks in the snow?'

'Only ours,' he says.

'What does the snow look like?'

'It's coming down heavy. If someone had been here half an hour ago, you wouldn't be able to see it now.'

For seconds Aaron's body remains motionless while the ship rides mountainous waves. Then she carries on walking.

She holds Luca's hand tight to reassure him, but it's as though he is reassuring her.

'Steps,' says Flemming.

Slippery stone. Aaron steps onto the veranda. The planks are so stiff that there's no give in them at all, unlike when she was here that summer. Five blips; Flemming is entering the access code. There's a buzzing as the electric motor opens the heavy door.

Aaron takes a step inside the hallway with Luca.

Two blips; Flemming is about to close the door.

'Wait,' she whispers.

No sound. But a smell, very faint.

Fresh gun oil.

Aaron senses a movement under the stairs to her right. She gives Luca a shove, shouts: 'Run!' and dives headlong towards the shadow, without asking herself how fast she is in this condition. She pulls the man down and twists her body as she falls. Shots ring out. When her opponent hits the floor she already has the Glock in her hand. Aaron shoots into the man's yell. The air around her is a whirl of flying bullets. She smells blood.

'Flemming!' she bellows.

He doesn't reply; acrid gun smoke stings her lungs.

Someone grabs her from behind.

Aaron drops the gun and makes herself light. The man heaves her up and lays his lower arm around her neck. Her hands shoot behind her head. She interlocks them on the nape of the man's neck and hangs herself onto him. Aaron swings her legs and yanks him forwards, causing him to somersault over her and crash onto his back. She stabs her finger into one eye, feels it burst, bounces into a crouching position and, using her knee, drops her full weight onto her opponent's larynx.

While he suffocates miserably, Aaron drifts to the earth's core in a stream of magma. It feels as if she is dissolving, burning up.

She's back on her feet. Inexplicably, she's back.

It is quiet in the hallway, but outside shots are slicing the air.

Suddenly she feels Luca's hand in hers.

Pure fear grips her.

Why didn't he run away?

'How many do you see?' she forces out.

He doesn't reply.

Many.

The light reaches her as though it was travelling through the aperture of a camera lens that is steadily decreasing in diameter. It turns into a tunnel, an ever tighter tube, and then it is pitch black. No, more than that; it's not even black. It is absolute nothingness.

She hears the thunder of weapons in the grounds.

Then a groan.

Suddenly there is a gun in her hand.

Flemming gasps out: 'Down.'

Investigation report, Teufelsbach hill farm. Statement Simon Rogge:

Mertsch and I were on the western flank. There were four there with SMGs. Mertsch was hit. I took cover behind a tree.

I eliminated two, the others pinned me down with non-stop fire. On the radio, Fricke was yelling: Four here! And Nickel: Three on my side! I could see the front of the house, the door was open. Flemming was kneeling, wounded. Aaron and the boy were standing behind him. Two men appeared. I shot, they dived for cover. I couldn't believe it when Flemming stood up. He shielded Aaron with his body and shoved his gun into her hand. I heard him on the radio: Down. Aaron disappeared with the boy. Flemming drew his knife and walked straight towards the two guys. They fired at least eight shots at him, but he just kept going. There were still three in the house. I shot one in the head, the two others dived for cover. The door closed. I couldn't do anything more. The tree was all I had.

She stumbles down the stairs with Luca. The shots grow quiet, are just a patter. Suddenly Aaron feels the adrenalin. It has fought against the drug and has won. That's why the light has vanished, her pulse is hammering like a machine gun and the world is racing through her veins.

But she is awake.

AWAKE.

Her bloodstream is one giant superconductor that is transporting the stress hormone unhindered into the tiniest cells. She has never been so thankful for it.

The steps end and she almost trips.

Aaron stops. She knows that beyond the landing the stairs twist to the right. Then it's a further thirty steps, ending directly outside the safe room.

There is a bitter taste of salt on her lips. 'Look round the corner very carefully,' she whispers. 'Tell me what you see.'

'Two men. Down by the door.'

They need me alive. But they don't care about Luca. Luca!

Aaron slides him behind her, takes a leap and showers bullets into the well until the bolt hammers into a void.

Her breath is thrumming in her ears. 'And now?'

Luca grabs her hand again. 'They are lying there.'

'Are they moving?'

'No.'

She throws the gun away.

On the last few steps she staggers.

'There's a box on the left, next to the door. Do you see it?'

'Yes.'

'Can you reach it?'

'I'm too small.'

She lifts him up. 'You have to press five numbers: three-six-nine.'

Aaron hears three blips.

'Two-four.'

The code is complete.

'Underneath there's a button. You have to push it.'

The door opens. Aaron crouches down and feels for the bodies. Her fingers close round a sticky pistol. She hears steps pounding the floor at the top of the shaft. Luca pulls her into the safe room. She lifts him up. 'Hit the button!'

The steps are coming closer. Moving at a snail's pace, the forty-centimetre-thick steel is inching its way back. Aaron leans against the door with all her weight to speed it up.

She knows it's pointless.

'Faster!' she hears a man bellow.

Please, please, please!

The door closes.

Sopping wet, she sinks to the floor, squeezes Luca against her and feels his heart throbbing through his thick jacket.

Investigation report, Teufelsbach hill farm. Statement Sven Kemper:

Fricke and me were on the east side. There were four of them there. SMGs with drum magazines. Three were clever. They flattened themselves down. We could only see them because the snow glowed as they fired. We threw ourselves into a ditch and returned the favour. The fourth one was built like a brick shithouse. And I bet if you'd looked inside, all you would have seen is shit. He thought it would be a great idea to dart to the house. He managed two metres. Fricke wanted to ring Murnau, to alert Peschel and Nieser. It didn't work; the arseholes had a jamming transmitter. Suddenly it's all quiet next to me. I look over at Fricke and think: oh shit.

Aaron hears a gentle scraping behind the steel door. It's driving her crazy that she doesn't know what's happening upstairs. Her heartbeat is firing thoughts through her head like missiles. How many men has Keyes got up there? Are the others managing to deal with them?

Are they even still alive?

Five of them she barely knows.

Kemper is an experienced, level-headed man with a voice you can trust. Pavlik said his wife died of cancer last year; he's still reeling from it.

Rogge was part of the commando that protected Aaron in early January. He's got a good sense of humour; if you can't have a laugh with someone, they're no use.

All she knows about Mertsch is that he likes cinnamon-flavoured sweets and counts among the best; otherwise Inan Demirci wouldn't have chosen him.

Nickel is the youngest, only twenty-eight. He lives alone and has a tomcat called Mister Miyagi. She will never forget that he spoke up for her in the weights room.

Fricke.

His jokey nature hides many things. Such as the fact that he and his wife took in his fifteen-year-old niece after his older sister died. And that he has been lonely since their divorce and only has one night stands, because no woman wants to share this kind of life. And that he is one of the most sensitive people she knows.

The night after Pavlik's motorbike accident, Aaron waited until Sandra finally fell asleep, then she went downstairs into the living room. Fricke was just sitting there. She had never shared such a long silence with him. When the first daylight smacked against the windows like a bucket load of dirty water, he said: 'I only made that comment about the leg so that Lissek would punch me, because I couldn't feel anything anymore. I still can't. Can you belt me one too?'

She took him in her arms, he was shaking.

Flemming.

A demolition ball with ears, Pavlik had called him. He has a life she knows nothing about, a history that's alien to her.

His gun in her hand.

'Down,' he had gasped. That's what a person sounds like when they're wounded. Wounded and alone against superior forces.

Wounded and without a chance.

Aaron runs her fingers over the pistol she took from the dead man. It's a Jericho, primarily used in the Near East and in special units in the Balkans.

She whispers to Luca: 'We may need to get out of here. Can you see the other door?'

'Yes,' he whispers back.

'It opens with the same numbers. Say them.'

'Three-six-nine-two—' He pauses to think.

'Four.'

'Three-six-nine-two-four,' he repeats.

She visualizes the room from memory. Bare steel walls,

chairs, fridge, shelves with emergency rations, bunks. 'Go and fetch something so that you can reach the box.'

Luca lets go of her and pulls a chair across the floor.

'OK?' she asks.

'Yes.'

'But only when I tell you to.'

She puts her ear against the door to listen.

In that same moment an indescribable pain detonates in her head. The world is sucked in by a screaming tornado, shredded, obliterated. Aaron doesn't know that she flies through the air, doesn't know that she screams, doesn't know that blood is flowing from her ears.

All she can hear is a whistling, so piercing, so shrill that she thinks her head will explode.

She smells nitro.

Semtex.

They have blasted the door.

Aaron feels Luca's hand. She becomes aware that he is trying to pull her up. Her lips are moving, asking him to leave her lying there. But Luca tugs at her, doesn't give up. Something is banging against her chest. At first she thinks it's her heart, then she realizes that it's the little fists of the boy.

Try at least.

Aaron manages to get onto her knees. She's panting as though she had conquered Everest without oxygen. The whistling is getting louder and louder; it's tearing out her insides, it's a weapon, a knife.

Luca's fists again.

Thinking is the hardest thing in the world.

Where are the men?

They haven't managed it yet. The door is still closed.

How long for?

She pushes herself up, finds Luca's shoulder, staggers along next to him. A wave pulses through her body, so powerful that she feels the shock all the way into her teeth, into the tips of her hair.

A second blast.

She realizes that she has fallen down again, that there's no ground under her feet, that her legs are just feebly kicking the air.

Luca's hand is gone.

'Luca? Luca?' she thinks she is shouting.

There he is again.

She is standing.

He pulls her with him. Sudden coldness batters her. Her legs give way. She falls into something wet.

Investigation report, Teufelsbach hill farm. Statement Simon Rogge:

The two changed their positions and fired at me continuously. I disappeared into the woods. I waited for them in a snow drift.

Aaron tries to make out which direction they are walking in. An icy blast of wind hits her; they must be heading north. She feels a pressure on her ears as if she were diving, forty metres down. Panicked, she swallows, but it doesn't help.

Luca leads her through deep snow, every step is an effort. Something scratches her face.

Brambles.

Yes, north.

The boy stops. He writes something into her hand.

What does it mean?

His finger writes it again.

It's an M.

Men.

Frantically she asks: 'Where?'

B, he writes.

Behind us.

He pulls Aaron onward. Faster. Fear corrodes her muscles and turns them into a soft gelatinous mass.

They knew they wouldn't be able to break through the safe room's armour. They just wanted to drive us out.

Aaron starts to slide. She grabs Luca, holds him tight. They slither through snow and ice in a wild whirl. Something sharp scrapes against her; it feels as though her arm is on fire. She desperately tries to cling onto something with her free hand, but only gets hold of sticky snow.

Aaron falls into nothingness with Luca. She's gripped by a terrible fear that she might have to let go of him and he'd be gone.

A thousand needles prick her skin. She opens her mouth, swallows water and knows that they are in the Teufelsbach river. She fights against the flow that wants to pull her down. The river is no deeper than a metre and a half. Aaron could stand up in it, but not Luca. The adrenalin keeps her alert, the pain paralyses her. Somehow, her feet find purchase. The icy stream reaches up to her chest. Luca wraps his arms around her neck.

He's alive!

Aaron wades towards the other side with him. The gravel slides from beneath her. She goes down, slips under water.

Suddenly she's lighter.

Luca! I've lost Luca!

Panic-stricken she dives back down. She frantically moves her hands about, searching for the boy.

She's got him.

She stands up with him, clutching the shivering bundle. Where is the other bank? Something slaps against her left arm.

That way, Luca is trying to tell her.

Last few steps.

She doesn't know how she manages it.

Then they're across.

Aaron falls into the snow and lets go of Luca.

She cries. The pain gives way to a dull, fluffy feeling. Her body has left her, her voice has left her, the world has left her. All that remains is fear and cold and eternal silence.

Then she feels the boy's hand again.

He's tugging at her, wants her to get up.

Images flicker. Luca is lying in a cradle under a glassy sky. He is sitting in Varga's garden, making a paper hat. He is waving at her from the tower, his face luminescent like a creature of the deep sea.

Something hits hard against her face.

It must be Luca's fist.

Aaron is back on her feet. The seconds before are missing.

They're going downhill. She realizes that the boy wants to lead her north, away from the river.

There's forest there. One can hide there.

Aaron doesn't want to go there.

She intimates to Luca that they need to veer round to the right, parallel to the river, which will lead them to the edge of the gorge, where it plummets into the Teufelsschlucht.

Investigation report, Teufelsbach hill farm. Statement Sven Kemper:

Fricke had been hit in the left shoulder. He was losing quite a lot of blood. It was clear to us that we had to take those three guys out pretty quick, otherwise that would be it for Fricke. But we couldn't get out of the damned ditch, we were under constant fire. Then I saw Fricke burrowing in the snow with his hand. I asked him: Are you looking for something? He dug out a stone as big as a fist. I thought to myself, he's losing the plot. He just said: The punchline is about to hit home, and threw the stone over to the guys in a high arc. They immediately jumped up and ran. They thought it was a hand grenade. It was like target shooting at the funfair.

Classic Fricke.

Pavlik is racing along the icy road, pushing the 911 Porsche he hired at Munich airport to its limit. It's snowing so heavily he can't even see fifty metres ahead. Nothing is as hard to control on a slippery road as a car with a rear-mounted engine and wide tyres. Pavlik doesn't touch the brake pedal, instead he controls the speed using only the accelerator and clutch. The car oversteers and skids across hairpin bends.

It's like dancing a waltz. Pavlik loves this way of driving.

But not now.

He assumes that Layla had to stay in hospital. Fricke is most likely in command. Pavlik knows which six he'll have chosen for Aaron and Luca. He would have picked the same. Apart from Flemming. One by one he has tried to contact them. None of them answered. Aaron didn't take his call either.

The seventh responds – Peschel.

He's their best personal protector. Totally dependable. It was right to leave him and Nieser with Layla until the police arrive and take over.

'Are you still in Murnau?' Pavlik asks.

'Yes. The Special Enforcement Commando is here. We're going to drive up to the hill farm now.'

'When did you last have contact with the others?'

'So, when they left. An hour ago.'

That means they should have got there fifteen minutes ago.

'Something the matter?' asks Peschel. 'Where are you?'

'By the Walchensee, I'll be up there soon.'

'So, I thought you were in Berlin?'

'Something is going on at the hill farm. Hurry up.'

He cuts the call. On the right he sees the access road. Pavlik spins onto it, accelerates and races up a track as slippery as an ice rink. If he took his foot off the accelerator he'd slide all the way back down into the valley. The Porsche swerves, but he only lets it drift a little, to avoid careering into one of the snow banks.

Pavlik is at the top.

Bratatat bratatat.

Submachine guns.

Investigation report, Teufelsbach hill farm. Statement Simon Rogge:

The two guys were careful, they didn't just run into the woods after me. They took it nice and steady and used every bit of cover. I let them come real close and treated them to two bullets in the face. I went to the rock face on the western boundary, where Nickel had last reported from. Three corpses, I don't know how he managed that. He was lying a few metres further on. I immediately knew that he wasn't going to make it. I laid his head in my lap. He was almost gone and just said: Think up some good last words for me.

The gate is closed. Pavlik jumps out of the car with his gun drawn. He sees Fricke and Kemper. Fricke is moving stiffly. Kemper spots him and points to the house.

Pavlik positions his eyes in front of the retina scanner. The gate opens. To the left, Rogge is sprinting across the field. They meet on the veranda, flattening themselves against the wall.

Fricke's cheeks are hollow, the hand he is pressing against

his shoulder is covered in blood. 'There were eleven outside,' he forces out.

Rogge whispers: 'I saw five in the house, but there must be more. I dispatched one. I don't know how many Flemming took with him.'

Tension grips Pavlik's insides. 'Where are Aaron and Luca?' he asks.

'I heard two explosions. The guys inside probably tried to blow open the safe room. So she and the boy must have been in there. Perhaps they still are.'

'Or they went out the back way,' says Kemper.

'Mertsch, Nickel?'

Rogge shakes his head.

'OK,' Pavlik whispers. 'We have to go in. Rogge will open the door. Fricke, sit down here.'

'I'm fit,' he protests.

'Fit for hospital. No discussion.'

The door can't be opened without the electric motor. Rogge flits over to the button next to the code scanner and presses it. The door opens in slow motion. Pavlik is first to leap into the hallway and checks in all directions.

Six dead. Two with their throats cut.

He kneels down next to Flemming, who still has the knife in his open hand. Five bullets are lodged in his protective vest. Three have hit his arms, two his legs, one has carved a gash into his left cheek, one has injured his neck, one has mangled his right collarbone.

But he's breathing.

'Rogge, fetch the transporter and take Flemming and Fricke to hospital. Kemper, you're coming down with me,' Pavlik orders.

They creep into the shaft. The light is on. There isn't a sound.

When they reach the landing he carefully peers round the corner.

Three men.

Plus two bodies on the floor.

The door of the safe room is hanging askew on its hinges.

Bullets strike the wall close to Pavlik's head. He moves back into cover and holds up three fingers. They run back up. It's clear to Pavlik why the men have taken up position there. They're assuming Aaron has fled from the safe room with Luca. Some of the men in the grounds have probably abseiled down the rock face to pursue her. The three in the shaft are there to block access through the house. To help Aaron, they have to dispose of them.

Quickly.

Rogge is pulling up outside with the transporter.

Pavlik runs out. 'Fetch the spare fuel cans.' He sprints back into the house, grabs one of the dead men's guns and ejects the contents of the magazine into his hand.

Kemper understands. He picks up another man's gun, and another.

They heap them together.

Forty-one cartridges.

Rogge heaves the two large petrol cans into the hall. Pavlik and Kemper creep down the stairs with them. Where the stairway twists round, they upend the canisters and let a hundred litres of petrol flow down the steps. Pavlik ignites it with his lighter and chucks the cartridges down the shaft. The three men are trapped, there's no escape.

After a minute the fireworks begin. When it's gone quiet and Pavlik peers down from his place of cover he sees another two bodies.

The third man is alive. He is crouching on the floor in the embryo position. One of his trouser legs has caught fire. Kemper shoots him in the head.

The flames lick the sides of their boots as they leap down the steps two at a time. They inhale petrol fumes and soot, hold their arms in front of their mouths. The door is still held in place by two bolts. Kemper taps in the code. It moves with a creak, then stops and won't go any further.

They squeeze through the gap. The back door is wide open. Pavlik sprints outside and yells: 'Aaron! Aaron!'

Nothing.

She struggles up the slope at Luca's side. Every breath feels like her last one. Luca stops. She can feel a pull in her legs. Aaron is blind and deaf, yet she's experiencing vertigo.

She knows where they are: by the ledge, where the ground drops away to the bottom of the gorge a hundred metres below.

The boy desperately tries to drag her away.

She doesn't budge. 'Take me right to the edge,' she says without hearing herself. 'Then run away. Promise me you'll do it.'

M, he scribbles into her hand.

'I know. Luca you have to trust me. If you're my friend, do as I tell you.'

M, he writes again.

'Please!' she begs.

Hesitantly, he takes four small steps with her. The pull in her legs gets stronger.

Aaron is close to the precipice. 'Run!'

He lets go of her hand.

She turns round so she is standing with her back to the gorge. The cold leaves her, giving way to a sensation of infinite calm. It feels as though time is racing, but her breathing is slow and steady. She thinks of Keyes ten years ago, leaning against his Porsche with a smile like a postcard from the South. *Something in your smile was so exciting, something in my heart told me*

I must have you. His lips, cool against her cheek. *Why is six afraid of seven? Because seven ate nine.* She remembers the dream again, sees herself with Keyes in Varga's garden, where dragonflies vie for a place on her shoulder, driving with him to the Ponte Sant'Angelo, walking with him towards the glittering castle. *We will face each other, we'll be as close as we were in the lift in Rome.* The bullets are slivers of light on their faces. *In the end one has to close all positions, darling.* Glacier-grey eyes grow black, blending into her night.

Only when we're in pain do we show what we're truly made of.

It's not possible that Aaron, standing on this treeless rock, a metre away from the gorge, can smell pine resin. And yet she does.

Ten things that Aaron knows without needing to see them:
   that Leon Keyes is standing directly in front of her

She throws herself at him, grabs hold of his jacket, unbalancing him. She braces her left foot against his pubic bone and tips backwards with him into the snow. She hurls her father's killer over her head and into the abyss, lets go, exhales and imagines his scream.

She is at one with the world and ready to die.

Investigation report, Teufelsbach hill farm. Statement Sven Kemper:

It was snowing so heavily that visibility was down to zero. I couldn't make out any tracks in the snow; but Pavlik could, being a sniper. We went down to the river. Aaron and the boy were pushed off course by the flow; we lost their trail. I wanted to carry on northwards, into the woods, but Pavlik was sure that Aaron was by the gorge. Then we saw Keyes and two men. They were standing five metres away from Aaron, they didn't notice us. Luca ran over to us. They paid no attention to him, their guns were trained on Aaron. Keyes walked towards her. He knew that she was blind. He thought that meant defenceless. He was totally relaxed, an incredibly arrogant arsehole. As far as he was concerned, it was all over. A metre away from her he stopped. A mistake he'd sorely regret if he could. As he flew into the gorge, Pavlik took out the two men with head shots. I'll never forget Keyes' scream.

Aaron stood up and smiled.

38

After she had reached the fifth Dan, her master told her a story.

During the time of the Hōjō dynasty, a farmer by the name of Denji lived in Shimōsa Province. He had a wife and two children and he worked hard. He managed to feed his small family with the toil of his hands, but he was unhappy.

Ever since he was a boy, Denji had dreamt of becoming a samurai. He never talked about it. He grew into a man and worked his field without complaining. But secretly he practised martial arts and imagined himself confronting powerful enemies. He was careful to make sure nobody saw him.

One day, when he was in the forest looking for a rod to make a new bow, he found a samurai who had been killed and robbed by highwaymen. They had taken his sword, but they hadn't touched his suit of armour.

Denji buried the samurai, put on his armour and left, without saying farewell to his wife and children. For months he wandered across the land. People greeted him reverentially, they gave him food and drink and a bed for the night.

He never even once had to draw his sword. It stayed in the sheath and nobody noticed that it was made of wood, for he had wrapped the grip with cloth. Denji didn't think about his former life and those that loved him. Everything he had ever dreamt of had come true.

One evening he stopped at an inn. As always, the finest foods were put in front of him and he delighted in the feast.

Just then, a samurai sat down beside him, glad to come across another man of the same station. Denji was alarmed, but he didn't let it show. They drank sake together, and because Denji was afraid of giving himself away, he invented increasingly heroic deeds in order to impress the samurai. When Denji was so drunk he was slurring his speech, he laughed loudly at a joke made by his drinking companion and patted him in the face.

He had never heard of Bushidō and didn't know that it was an insult to touch a samurai's face. The man reached for his sword. He gave Denji the choice to fight or to die straight away. So Denji had no option but to draw his wooden sword. The samurai smashed it with a single blow and sliced Denji's head off. His body was burnt, and nobody mourned for him.

Aaron is lying on something soft, probably a back seat. She perceives vibrations, they're probably driving. Someone is holding her hand, probably Luca.

She thinks of what her master said after he had finished the story: 'There may be something that you long for more than anything else in your life. You're entitled to desire it. But when you've been granted it, you have to be prepared to pay the price, no matter how high it is.'

The adrenalin has gone. Aaron's body is hurting, as if every bone in it is broken. Somebody lifts her up. Then she's lying on something hard. She feels as though she's moving. Perhaps it's just a dream.

A glowing spike burrows into her left ear.

Aaron screams a silent scream.

She feels a prick in the crook of her arm.

Images and words come and go. Keyes is outside the Grand Hyatt, holding open the car door for her and whispers: 'I wouldn't want anyone else by my side in Rome.' A flock of white birds changes direction like smoke in the wind as they stand by the Garibaldi monument. When she tucks in the covers around Varga's son she sees an open children's book. *Pinocchio*; it's the page on which the puppet and its father Geppetto find each other again in the belly of the whale. The police music corps plays the wrong tune at Vesper's funeral. In front of the ferry, Lissek and she have a farewell hug, and he says: 'No matter what you find, in the end you find yourself.'

For a brief time she believes she is awake. She feels the proximity of someone familiar. There is a whispering inside her. 'Our photos are waiting for you. That day on the beach in San Diego, when we had the ice-cream eating competition. In the garden, playing Cowboys and Indians with the twins. When you fell asleep with Marlowe in our hammock. The two of us with fat cigars on my fortieth. And a thousand others. I know we'll look at those photos together. And we'll take new ones. Funny ones and sad ones, because we also share the sad stuff.'

Aaron wants to touch Sandra, but she's forgotten where her body is. She's kneeling on the Djemaa el Fna. The drums are beating in her chest, she is the centre of the world. Palmer receives her at his villa and the alarm starts up because the scanner thinks the cane is a weapon. *You will have a child. But not with him. You will be happy. But not yet.* She squeezes Luca against her in the icy river and she doesn't know whether she is rescuing him or he is rescuing her.

Aaron wakes up, she is lying on something soft. No pain. It is dark, and deadly silent. Her back is lifted. Somebody takes her hand and lays it on something.

She feels small bumps.

Braille.

Aaron reads: *You are in Murnau hospital. I am blind and work here as a masseur. I've brought in my Braille typewriter. I will write down what Professor Beck is saying. He's going to talk to you now.*

She wants to ask: *Will I stay deaf?*

Her tongue won't obey her.

Paper is pushed under her fingers.

Your eardrums are undamaged. We've carried out an electrocochleography and a brainstem electric response audiometry. Your inner ear is registering sound, but your cortex isn't processing it. You were probably exposed to more than a hundred and fifty decibels and have suffered a major acoustic shock. We could be dealing with an interruption of your ossicular chain, a neural dysfunction of the acoustic nerve or a defect of the cilia. This would mean that there's a chance of regeneration. There are also possibilities that don't give reason for optimism, I'm afraid. I'm sorry that I don't have a different answer for you.

Aaron accepts it. She was prepared to pay the price. But if it is her fate to remain blind and deaf, she will kill herself. She has endured everything, but that would be too much. She isn't afraid of going. True hell would have been to know that Keyes is still alive.

Two words. So hard. 'What day?'

Time passes. More paper.

Sunday. We sedated you for forty-eight hours. You need rest. Any kind of excitement is bad. If you think too much, it will cause you stress. There's somebody here who wants to talk to you.

A small warm body presses against her.

Luca.

Aaron can't stop crying.

New paper.

I was with you lots of times. I'm sure you were dreaming about your papa. Ulf and me had a snowball fight. Snow is great. Perhaps I will like it in Germany after all.

Talking isn't possible.

I was scared in the water. But I was still brave. Like you.

All she can do is cry.

She barely manages to move the one finger for reading.

The professor says you have to sleep again now.

Something is being done on her arm.

The images come flooding back. She's in La Mamounia. As she drifts off stoned in Pavlik's arm, he mumbles, 'I'm going down the steepest black piste in the world.' When she is four, she starts going to ballet classes. Her mother is happy because it's something girly. But Aaron never danced for fun. During the evening meal at the hotel in the Atlas mountains she is so sensitive that she feels Layla shivering and asks Pavlik to fetch her a jumper. DiCaprio has a bullet in his chest and says to the woman he loves: 'I've never seen anything so wonderful.'

Aaron opens her eyes. It is light. As if the sun was shining through her closed eyelids.

It's quiet.

For a long time.

Her hand is placed on a sheet of paper.

Good morning, Ms Aaron. We want to do a test. If you would prefer to rest some more, please say so.

'No. Now.'

Because she can't hear anything, she isn't sure whether she's said it or perhaps only thought it.

'No. Now,' she repeats.

She is helped onto something. She runs her fingers over it. Armrests. Wheelchair. She is taken somewhere. The light grows dimmer. Then it disappears.

A darkened room.

Something is on Aaron's ears.

Headphones.

She reads: *This is called sound-threshold audiometry. We will play a succession of sounds in different frequencies to you. We will give you a button. As soon as you hear something, please press it. Is that all clear?*

'Yes.' Aaron grips the switch.

Waits.

Waits.

Waits.

She asks: 'Have you started yet?'

There!

A delicate bleep.

As quiet as a sparrow on a different continent.

She presses the button like crazy.

A calming hand is placed on her shoulder.

There is light again. She is taken back to her room. They put her in the bed. She's so agitated that she is sweating.

Finally: a new sheet of paper.

The sound that you heard was very loud. But I think you would be able to detect much lower frequencies too. The reason you didn't react until the tone was so loud is probably because, as a blind person, you had exceptional hearing before the acoustic shock. You are coming from an incredibly high level. Your acoustic cortex was used to processing the most subtle noises. That's why the temporary loss of this ability is so severe for you. To put it simply: if your hearing had previously been average, you would already be close to a hundred per cent by now. It's just a question of time. I think it's likely that this will level itself out over the next twenty-four hours.

'Shout at me. Please. I need that right now.'

Far, far away she hears a voice. 'Congratulations.'

★

Aaron is asleep again. She is standing on the bridge in Avignon and an incredible light floods into her eyes, the kind of light that pours through the leaded windows of a cathedral. It's another world, but on the island is the house with the floodlights. In her earbud she hears Adaja singing an African nursery rhyme while she cooks. When they throw Makata into their van he sees the bodies of his wife and daughter. His tears are as thick as oil. It is night in the Camargue. They dig two graves. Stars are fading in the sky. Suddenly Aaron realizes that she is being watched. She whirls round and sees the glowing eyes of a white horse. It stands there motionless, making her shudder. Then it trots away and becomes one with the darkness.

She wakes up. It is light.

Still or again?

She feels for the bedside table, opens the drawer, finds the cane and her watch. She taps on it.

The digital voice faintly whispers: 'Seventeenth of February. Tuesday. Nine a.m., zero minutes, zero seconds.'

Ten things that Aaron hears today:

the distant clatter of a dropped tray

a dull snap, a window being tilted

a murmuring helicopter

a whisper: 'Are you hungry?'

her own faint 'Yes.'

the rattling of the cutlery

the bleeping of the blood pressure cuff

Professor Beck's laugh, when she asks him for his stethoscope

her heart

the door that opens almost silently

★

She knows this hand. Aaron directs her eyes at Pavlik. His shape is blurred, as though he was standing behind frosted glass.

'Did everyone make it?' she asks.

'Mertsch and Nickel didn't.'

Nickel, who sheepishly mumbled: 'I'm not a big talker.' Nickel, who distracted Luca from his sorrows in the transporter.

Mertsch, whom she didn't know.

'And Flemming?'

'Eight bullets. But he's alive.'

'Is he hospitalized here?'

'One floor lower. He's responsive. I saw him smile for the first time.'

'I dreamt that Sandra was here.'

'She was at your bedside all of the first night. At ten in the morning her phone rang. Her father had wanted to connect a new cooker. High voltage electric shock. He's in hospital. Her mother is ill with the flu and can't visit him. Sandra had to go back. Pretty awful timing.'

'Never trust a retired electrician with your appliances.'

Pavlik laughs.

'Can you do that again, please? Laugh, I mean.'

He does.

Neither says anything for a moment.

'When we brought you here I didn't think I would ever be laughing with you again,' he says.

'You were at the hill farm?'

'Yes.'

'Did you see Keyes' body?'

'What was left of it.'

It turned out so right for strangers in the night.

'Demirci was here too, but in Berlin one meeting is chasing the next right now. You can imagine what's going on.'

Silence.

'She said something very nice about you,' he adds.

'Yes?'

'That you deserve to be happy again.'

No, she's not going to cry now.

'Where's Luca?'

'With one of the nurses. Layla hasn't regained consciousness. Her kidneys have collapsed. They've switched everything off, she's dying. I'm about to take him to her again. I can't let him go through this alone.'

It's night. Someone came to do a last check on her hours ago. She takes the cane out of the drawer. Her legs are obeying her again. Wrapped in a dressing gown she goes out into the corridor. She cherishes every sound. The rustling of newspapers in the nurses' room. A coffee machine. The clacking of the cane against the skirting board. The pat-pat of her naked feet. Snow being swept against a window.

For five years she was so busy mourning her lost sight that she didn't appreciate what she still had.

The cane knocks against metal. She looks for the lift button.

'Goodness, what are you doing here, Ms Aaron?'

She recognises the man's voice. He's one of the nurses here.

'I want to go to the floor below. Will you take me there?'

'You're barefoot.'

'I love hearing my feet.'

He laughs. 'Well then.'

They take the lift. At the door to the room he leaves her alone. Aaron walks in. She stops. She hears the quiet pinging of the heart monitor. She feels her way forwards, searches with her hand stretched out and finds a chair.

While she wonders where the bed is, he mutters: 'Eleven o'clock, two metres.' Flemming's voice sounds as though nothing that is yet to come could be any worse than what is behind him.

Aaron moves the chair closer and sits down.

She remembers him grouching: 'We'll see each other at the next funeral.' Hears him gasping: 'Down.' Pavlik has told her what Flemming did.

How can she thank him without sounding mawkish?

He helps her out. 'The guy whose face you blasted away would've got me. We're even.'

'Not in a hundred years.'

'Yeah, I've been told that you're stubborn.' Five heartbeats pass. 'What you did up there, how you saved the boy, the fact that you're sitting here now, I'll never understand it.'

'Perhaps I'm not really sitting here. Perhaps I'm just a ghost. And you're a ghost too. We should both be dead.'

'I *was* dead,' he says. 'They revived me. Forget the stuff about the light. My only thought was that I haven't handed in my tax return.'

She laughs quietly. 'What's your first name?'

'I thought you lot believe it's bad luck.'

'Time to drop the *you lot*.'

'Alexis.'

'Did your mother have a crush on Anthony Quinn?'

'She's Greek. Father's German.'

'What do you look like?'

'Next to you, like the Hunchback of Notre Dame. My mother said: "A fella only has to look a little less ugly than a chimpanzee."'

'Can I touch your face?' she asks.

'Half of it is bandages.'

'The other half will do.'

She stretches out her hand, gently follows the contours and feels grooves that are far too deep for a man who isn't yet forty.

Aaron sees pain, willpower, sincerity, humour.

She grins. 'You can touch mine too if you want.'
'Both arms in plaster.'
'I guess that's a fair excuse.'
Silence.
Ten heartbeats.
Flemming says: 'They had the code for the house. Who from?'
The million dollar question.
'But not the one for the safe room,' says Aaron.
'Thanks to Guppy. He was there last week for a routine inspection. You know him, nuts about fish. He changed the code and entered the lucky numbers for the Pisces star sign.'

39

It's not the first time Demirci is in the Chancellery. But it's the first time she has been in the bug-proof room on the fourth floor, where the government's crisis management team is normally in session. She can't remember how many meetings she has sat through over the past few days. It takes at least three hours' sleep, a strong stomach, a healthy resistance against smart-arses and a bumper box of aspirin.

While the secret service coordinator mauls the intelligence service chief with questions on how it was possible for Leon Keyes to fly under his radar, Demirci scans the other people sitting at the table. The Federal Minister of the Interior, the head of the Federal Office for the Protection of the Constitution and the commissioners of both the Military Counter-Intelligence Service and the BKA. Also the Chancellor.

And Svoboda.

She thinks of the two dead men, whose relatives she had to inform. With Jens Nickel it had been the parents; ordinary people who own a newspaper shop in Lichtenrade. They sat there mutely and held each other's hands. She told them that their son was liked by everyone, that he could always be relied on and that it happened quickly.

The kind of things you say when no words will do.

Christian Mertsch's wife is a teacher at a primary school in Schöneberg. She was fetched out of the classroom. The moment she saw Demirci, she knew. She collapsed like a marionette whose strings have been cut. Demirci sat down on the floor and put her arm around her. Children were standing in the open classroom door, looking on in silence.

She took over the Department two and a half months ago.

Six dead to date. At night she stands at gravesides.

Now she hears Svoboda.

'We prepared the attack with the necessary calm and were gradually tightening the noose around Leon Keyes' neck.' His voice grows pompous. 'To quote Clausewitz: "Strategy is the economy of force."'

Two of my men died because of you.

And I can't prove it.

Demirci gives a frosty smile. 'Mr Svoboda, perhaps you would like to tell the Chancellor what led us to Keyes in the first place.'

She sees that Palmer, who is sitting next to Svoboda, is having difficulty suppressing a grin. Svoboda's face changes colour. At a gathering like this you can't hesitate for more than two seconds before providing a reply. Otherwise everyone in the room knows that you don't have one. Some of the gentlemen are quietly amused.

The Chancellor expresses her displeasure by lifting an eyebrow. 'Ms Demirci, if you would, please.'

'We had been monitoring an account at a bank in Saudi Arabia for some time. We knew it had previously belonged to Ilja Nikulin, the Russian Mafia Godfather who died eleven years ago. The funds in the account allegedly stemmed from a criminal joint venture between Nikulin and the Broker.

Through a contact at the bank we learnt that a financial investor in London had shown interest in the account. I got in touch with BKA Commissioner Palmer. He consulted MI5. They came across a fund that was controlled by Leon Keyes. We suspected that the sole purpose of the fund was a financial bet on a planned terrorist attack. At the same time, two of my staff travelled to Morocco, where they tracked down the widow of Keyes' closest associate. She agreed to become a state witness. We brought her to Germany to a safe house. The house was attacked, which resulted in Keyes' death.'

'It appears the house wasn't so safe after all,' says the Federal Minister of the Interior. 'How did Keyes find out about it?'

Demirci fixes Svoboda with her gaze and lets exactly two seconds pass before she replies: 'That's what we're going to find out.'

'What about this witness?' the Chancellor asks.

'She's dead.'

'Then how are we going to prove that Keyes was the Broker?'

Palmer takes over. 'The London fund was dissolved on the day after Keyes' death. MI5 arrested the fund manager. The house search was very fruitful. In return for lenient sentencing the fund manager provided an extensive statement. Thirty arrests have been made so far. Keyes is a cover name of course, but he's been identified as the Broker beyond doubt.'

Demirci has acknowledged Palmer's role because it was unavoidable. He didn't reciprocate the compliment – it would have made Svoboda suspicious.

'We've managed to gain far-reaching insights into the structure and logistics of global terrorist financing. It will take months to analyse everything. But it's already clear that this is the biggest success of the past ten years.'

'Who was the terrorist attack going to be directed at?' the Chancellor asks.

'We don't know. According to the evidence to date, only Keyes could have told us that.'

'Then it's possible that it will still take place?'

'Yes.'

Silence spreads across the room.

The secret service coordinator clears his throat: 'How much money is in the account in Saudi Arabia?'

'Two billion dollars,' says Demirci.

'What will happen with it now?'

She is prepared for the question. 'An unknown person has transferred the entire sum to Marrakech. We don't have access to it. We lack the necessary validation that the money belonged to Nikulin. The truth is: we can't even prove that it stems from illegal activities. Not all dreams come true.'

The Chancellor shrugs her shoulders. 'Well, if I think of how much we sink into the Euro rescue fund—' She stands up. 'Thank you. Good day.'

For a moment, Demirci's eyes meet Svoboda's. To describe her gaze as cold would be like describing the weather at the South Pole as fresh.

'Superb work, Ms Demirci.' The Chancellor stretches out her hand to her, without paying Svoboda any further attention.

The three armoured limousines drive through Tiergarten district to the Department. On the right, Bellevue Palace glides past.

The flag should be at half mast, thinks Demirci. *But the only ones who will remember Nickel and Mertsch are their friends, their families and us.*

She taps a message into her mobile: *At Rogacki's on Wilmersdorfer Strasse in half an hour.*

The rustic gourmet bistro in Charlottenburg was Helmchen's suggestion. It's a Berlin institution, half the neighbourhood goes there for lunch. Nobody would expect to see Demirci at one of the bar tables.

In the underground car park of the Department she gets into her private car and drives to Wilmersdorfer Strasse. The air in Rogacki's is thick with steam. She queues up with a tray, chooses the fried fish with potato salad and finds a reasonably quiet bar table in a corner.

Palmer arrives ten minutes later.

'Can you recommend the fish?' he asks.

'Absolutely,' she replies with a full mouth.

When he elbows his way back to Demirci, she has already finished. He tucks in. A day like today stirs the appetite.

'That's quite a story you just told,' he says. 'One could be forgiven for thinking it all happened exactly like that.'

'Yes, I almost believed it myself.'

'The Chancellor has you on her radar now,' Palmer comments between mouthfuls. 'Who knows, perhaps you'll be offered my position.'

'No thanks. Once you've shagged Brad Pitt, you don't move back home to Papa.'

Palmer gets a fish bone caught in his throat and coughs hard. Demirci vigorously thumps him on the back. 'I just wanted to see your face,' she laughs.

Gradually he manages to get his breath back.

'I wouldn't worry too much about your job,' she adds. 'Keyes is your success too. And Islamabad has resolved itself.'

He looks at her surprised.

'My people checked out your liaison officer's apartment. They discovered a hidden stack of notes taken from memory, relating to telephone conversations he had with you. According to those notes, you tried to haggle with him over the division of profits.'

Palmer's eyes narrow. 'And you called that *resolved*?'

'I did some extensive research into your liaison officer's career path,' Demirci replies. 'He was with the FBI in Quantico for a year. While at the BKA, he served in all the important departments, from terrorism through to organized crime, most recently as head of division. For two years he was assigned to Interpol, where they wanted to hang on to him indefinitely. You sent him to Islamabad because it's currently one of the most important outposts. And somebody like that supposedly keeps such notes in a cupboard under the kitchen sink? Typed out on a computer and printed out? Without leaving any fingerprints?'

'What did your people do?' Palmer asks blankly.

'They left the apartment as tidy as it was when they arrived and burnt the bumf. I informed the Chancellery that we found no proof whatsoever of any wrongdoing by your man. The operation has been terminated.'

Palmer growls: 'Svoboda won't give up.'

'Of course not. But he won't try it via the liaison officer again.'

'I so enjoyed watching the colour change on his face.'

'Which colour do you mean? Red, green or white?' she asks.

'All of them, in that order. Still, it won't earn us much more than a little breathing time. He's going to reform his troops.'

'Of course. He studied Clausewitz, after all.'

'The bastard has got it coming.'

'Oh yes, he certainly does.'

Both are deep in thought for a while, then Palmer asks: 'Who do the two billion dollars belong to? You don't have to tell me, but if you do, I'll believe that you trust me just a little at least.'

A few tables along, Demirci sees a woman feeding gammon steak to her pug.

Palmer follows her gaze and says: 'I hope that isn't a metaphor.'

She looks into his open, honest face.

'Jenny Aaron. Holm gave her the money.'

He is silent for some time. 'Why?'

'That's something he took to his grave with him.'

'What's she going to do with it?'

'I haven't asked her yet.'

'You could use it to replenish your piggy bank.'

Now *she* is left speechless.

'Don't worry, I can keep as quiet as a pug.' Palmer lays down his cutlery. 'The fish was good, apart from the bones. But not as good as mine.'

'You cook?'

'For friends. Perhaps you'll visit me sometime. My house is only a few minutes' drive from the office. I'm sure you can find a reason to fly to Wiesbaden. How about tomorrow?'

'Patience is a revolutionary virtue.'

'The head of the Department is quoting Rosa Luxemburg?'

'One of my teenage heroines.'

Demirci leaves, knowing that Palmer is following her with his eyes. Amused, she smiles to herself.

40

Pavlik's car is standing in the car park at Tegel airport, where he left it two weeks ago. On the urban motorway brake lights form a long dim chain in the hazy twilight. When they left for Marrakech, everything had been covered with a hard shell of old snow. Now it has melted, winter is revealing its hoard of dirt and leaving it for spring to clear up. Drizzle mottles the windscreen, Berlin is a leaden grey. The city is so ugly in winter that it's hard to believe how beautiful it is in summer.

Pavlik was born here. He doesn't mind the cold. He can ignore it like an aching muscle. But he loves the sea, the taste of salt and the lightness of the South.

When he was young, he sometimes thought of looking for a job abroad, perhaps in Portugal. He never did anything about it. In his life, everything has always just happened; his experiences have taught him that things have a way of working themselves out. At twenty, you have big plans and see far ahead. Later you realize that for the most part it has turned out completely different to how you imagined.

How could he have known about Sandra at that age? About the Department, the camaraderie, the friends he has found? The dead he has mourned? What did he know about the happiness of having a family that you love? Being loved in return.

He exits the orbital at Breitenbachplatz and drives along the botanic gardens. The brave organ grinder is standing at the entrance. Pavlik gives him a note every now and then because he always stays at his post, even in the lousiest conditions.

Five minutes later Pavlik is in Lichterfelde.

He grew up in a side road just along from here; three kilometres from the house he now lives in.

And yet it's like living in a distant country.

Every day his father had piled up more debts. He would go out and come home without a smile. In the evenings he didn't talk. The successes and defeats of a little life were ignored. He was never proud of his sons. Or if he was, he couldn't show it. If his father taught him anything at all, then it was to do everything differently with his own children.

After another two kilometres Pavlik is home.

He walks to the door. It is opened before he unlocks it.

'This is Luca,' he says to Sandra.

She smiles.

Luca asks: 'Are you Jenny's very best friend?'

'Yes, I am.'

'In that case I will stay.'

The Real Enemy

B lack and white race past the train window as if the world was a barcode. Sometimes there's the notion of a mast. Perhaps only because Aaron is imagining it. In the stations, steep shadows plummet into each other like in a desaturated Lyonel Feininger painting. At one point, she believes she sees smoke.

She called Sandra before she left. Her friend had been sad because she couldn't be with her for this. They were sensible. It wouldn't work, Luca needs Sandra now.

That was a half-truth.

They both know: Aaron has to go to Professor Reimer on her own.

It's positional warfare, he had said in Sweden.

She's ready. So ready.

She will take this battle on like she has taken on every battle in which the stakes were high. Not even for a second does she permit herself to wonder what will happen if the therapy fails.

It's unthinkable.

She doesn't have a plan B.

Stralsund is the last stop before the island of Rügen. The carriage empties. Aaron perceives a white, flat surface outside; an unused billboard perhaps.

She remembers how she went into Layla's room in the hospital; how she touched the smooth, freshly fitted sheet and laid down on the bed. The bed in which Layla died.

She lay there quietly.

Aaron wished she had been able to say goodbye. To Amari with the sad voice and anxious breathing. To Amari who had longed so much for her little boy. To Amari, whose happiness was so brief. She died without seeing Luca once more, without knowing that he is with people who cherish him.

'Next stop: Binz. Final stop.'

On the platform she uses her cane to search for the tactile strip. She finds her way onto the forecourt. The journey from Munich took eleven hours, that's why it's dark. She was here with her parents for a weekend when she was a child. She remembers very little about it. The only images of Rügen she has in her head are from magazines. White villas strung along an endless beach promenade, expansive undulating fields, the Baltic Sea smooth as a mirror. That and Caspar David Friedrich's *Cape Arkona*.

She hears steps rushing past.

'Excuse me, where's the taxi rank?' she asks.

'Straight in front of you. But there aren't any there.'

Aaron puts down her suitcase, folds up the cane and tucks it away. After a few minutes she hears the rattle of a diesel. White dots emerge from the dark.

A car stops. 'Hello, young lady.'

The driver puts her suitcase in the boot while she feels her way to the door and sits down in the back.

He gets in. 'Where to?'

She gives him the address of the institute.

'I can wait there,' he says as they set off.

'What for?'

'You must be picking somebody up. It's for blind people, isn't it? Someone in your family?'

She smiles. He hasn't realized. She has deceived him, like so many others over the past five years. That's over now.

She will see, she will no longer deceive anyone.

Especially not herself.

She will SEE.

'No, I'm staying,' she says.

After a brief drive they arrive. Aaron gives the man a note. 'Keep the change.'

He gasps. 'That's a hundred.'

She opens the car door. 'I know. Believe me, it's the best deal of my life.'

In front of the house, she clicks her tongue several times. Four storeys, the echo tells her. There's a sign by the door. *ReVision Centre* is inscribed on it in Braille.

When she rings the bell, she hears a woman's voice. 'Five metres straight on, then left.'

The buzzer sounds. Aaron taps her cane along the floorboards. There's a faint aroma of joss sticks. She has enough energy inside her to supply a metropolis.

The woman says: 'Good evening, Ms Aaron. My husband is already expecting you – here.'

Aaron takes the offered elbow and is led into Reimer's office.

'Ms Aaron is here now.' The woman withdraws.

A nebulous figure moves towards her.

Reimer takes the hand she is stretching out to him. 'Hello.'

'Hello.'

He holds on to her hand for a long time.

Then he runs his fingers over her arms. It irritates her.

Reimer says: 'You've travelled a long way to get here and you've invested a lot of hope in me. But I can't take you on as a patient.'

A trap door opens beneath her.

'Why?' she gasps.

'Your hands are freezing cold. Your entire body is hard as stone. You want to go into this therapy like into a battle for life or death. I only have to look at you to know that you're not at peace with yourself. You haven't listened to a word I said. And you haven't moved an inch from where you were when I visited you in Sweden. You'd be wasting my time and I'd be wasting yours.'

A million words. And not a single one passes her lips.

He opens the door. 'Katja, could you call a taxi, please?'

It's the same driver as before. Twice he tries in vain to get a conversation going. One part of her is sitting in his car, drained of all hope, the other is still standing in Reimer's office, waiting for the moment she wakes up.

In the hotel, the receptionist says in honeyed tones: 'Let's see, ah, there you are. Three weeks, is that right?'

Aaron is about to reply that her plans have changed and she will be leaving early tomorrow morning. But then without thinking she asks: 'Can I extend my stay for a week?'

'I'll have to check – just a moment – yes, that's fine.'

The receptionist has recognized from the cane that Aaron is blind. After the formalities have been dealt with, she offers to take Aaron to her room.

'I'd like to get some fresh air first. Do you have a terrace?'

'Of course. But at this time of year—'

'Could you take me there?'

When she's alone, she clicks her tongue. Garden furniture. Her cane finds a chair. Aaron sits down onto wet metal.

The drizzle sprays an icy film onto her face. Large trees creak as they shake off the wind. She lights a cigarette. After two puffs Aaron throws it away.

True understanding must permeate your mind, Bushidō states. *For to know and to act are one and the same.*

For the first time ever, she has no aim. No mountain she has to climb. No enemy to overcome.

Nothing to prove. Nothing to do.

Consider an affliction as a friend, not an enemy.

She knows this wisdom.

But she's never really thought about it.

Ten things that Aaron could do in these four weeks:
try twenty-eight different varieties of tea
re-house homeless hermit crabs
listen to the paintings in a museum
go walking instead of running
count invisible sheep
decalcify the chalk cliffs
blow away the clouds
buy a Great Dane and call it Caspar David
let spring arrive
spend two billion dollars on nonsense

She doesn't count the days, doesn't touch her watch. After some time she has ticked off the first five points on the list. She drifts along like foam on the sea. Every morning she breakfasts in the dishevelled beach hut with its smell of carbolineum and ancient wood. She discovers an endless array of new words for the sounds made by the waves. The wind. The silence. How awake one is when one sleeps without tablets. Now and then she speaks to Sandra on the phone. And Luca. His voice has already learnt to squeak again. He loves his little sister and his new bike. Aaron could be racing along in an Intercity Express at two hundred and twenty kilometres per hour and would still be sitting in a slow train.

On an evening like childhood she sits on the pier, dangling her feet and imitating the fog horn of a distant steamship. Somebody sits down beside her.

'My wife saw you yesterday on the spa promenade. She said you were laughing at seagulls.'

She is silent.

She extends her hand towards Reimer.

He takes it in his.

Hers is warmer.

'That's excellent news, Ms Aaron.'

AFTERWORD

For the past three years, I have taken a close interest in the lives and abilities of the visually impaired. The most important aspect of this is the people, taking note and listening to them. I would like to thank the blind men and women who always have a sympathetic ear for my questions: Kerstin Müller-Klein, Erika and Roland Theiss, Thorsten Büchner, Christian Spremberg and Manuela Kürpick.

They are the pros, and they continually surprise me.

Two close friends have been a huge help with their ideas and their wise comments: Murmel Clausen and Hans-Joachim Neubauer.

It has been a privilege to have the support of Professor Bernhard Sabel. He is director of the Institute of Medical Psychology at Magdeburg University and a world-leading brain researcher in the field of sight recovery. Bernhard is a true pioneer and the alter ego of my fictional character Thomas Reimer. He has developed a ground-breaking therapy which he applies in his practice, the Savir Centre.

Will it work for Aaron? I wish I knew.

Most importantly, Bernhard and his wife Conny have become good friends. That's what counts in the end.

I have been fortunate in benefiting from the expert advice of the following people: Dr Peter Kleinert (what would I do without you?). Raimund Alber, neuropsychologist and a specialist in helping the blind overcome trauma. Klaus Kreuter. Jürgen Tech. Petra Albert. Willi Fundermann, former head of BKA 24-hour deployment. Jürgen Maurer, retired BKA Vice Commissioner.

Katrin Kroll has become indispensable to me. Trust is everything. I never want to have any other literary agent.

Thomas Halupczok has yet again proved how brilliant he is. At one point he supplied just a single short sentence, and it changed the entire book. Above all, I want to thank him for his patience regarding my foibles. What can I say? I have the world's best editor.

And: Katja Wolf, fantastic commitment, many thanks!

It was a blessing that Alexandra Stender and Kristina Kienast asked Erik Spiekermann to carry out the typographical composition and typesetting. *Everything is finished, it just has to be done.* I love working with maniacs! Thank you, Erik. What fun!

Pages could be filled by listing everyone at Suhrkamp who has contributed their time and dedication. To name but a few: Edith Baller, Felix Dahm, Dr Petra Hardt, Christoph Hassenzahl, Nora Mercurio and Laura Wagner. If you are reading this novel or another of my books in translation it is thanks to them. I would also like to thank my English translator Astrid Freuler, whose questions demonstrated her meticulous approach.

In the end, my wife. Although I should say: in the beginning and the end. Living with someone who is mad about their work isn't always easy. She does, and I love her for it. And for so much else.

★

Named in this novel are companies and institutions which don't exist in the real world. This applies to 'the Department', the banks in Riyadh and Marrakech, and the Mafia groups and criminal enterprises, apart from the Camorra and Cosa Nostra.

The paintings *The Temptation of St Anthony* by Lucas Cranach the Elder and *The Wrath of God* by Hieronymus Bosch are as much products of my imagination as Chagall's *The Dream Dancers*, which featured in the first novel of this trilogy, *In the Dark*. Thinking up paintings is a delight, as long as I don't have to paint them.

Equally fictitious are the BKA operation against the Jackal, the background to Rabin's murder, Varga's empire and Nikulin's stock market bet against Gazprom. The terrorist attacks referred to never took place in reality, with the exception of the attack on the World Trade Centre.

Bas Makata is also an invention. Sadly, this is no consolation. There are many Makatas.

The effects of the endothelin blocker are medically accurate. However, Endothelinac is an imaginary brand name.

The English version of the thirty-sixth surah of the Qur'an corresponds to the audio translation provided with the recitation by Mishary Rashid Alafasy.

The last two sentences of the pain meditation on page 118 stem from the *Hagakure*.

The two quotes that refer to Angelina Jolie and Brad Pitt are a variation of a pun by the German actor, writer and comedian Harald Schmidt.

'Every mistake finds somebody to make it' is a quotation from Tennessee Williams.

Books that have expanded my horizon:
  Wieder sehen by Bernhard Sabel
  Ein neues Sehen der Welt by Jaques Lusseyran
  Die geheimen Techniken im Karate by Helmut Kogel
  Die Kunst des Gedankenlesens by Henrik Fexeus
  Das Buch der fünf Ringe by Miyamoto Musashi
  Du wirst sterben by Suzuki Shōsan
  Bushidō – Die Seele Japans by Inazō Nitobe
  Train Your Mind, Change Your Brain by Sharon Begley